VENGEANCE

D0957865

VENGEANCE

Oscar Balderrama & Lauren Certo

TITAN BOOKS

Arrow: Vengeance
Print edition ISBN: 9781783294848
E-book edition ISBN: 9781783295517

Published by Titan Books
A division of Titan Publishing Group Ltd
144 Southwark St, London SE1 0UP

First edition: February 2016
10 9 8 7 6 5 4 3 2 1

ARROW: VENGEANCE is a work of fiction. Names, characters, places, and incidents either are the product of the author's imagination or are used fictitiously, and any resemblance to actual persons, living or dead, business establishments, events, or locales is entirely coincidental.

A CIP catalogue record for this title is available from the British Library.

Printed and bound in the United States.

VENGEANCE

1

DEATHSTROKE

1

THE PAST

"Another disappointment."

Slade Wilson tossed the prisoner aside, the body landing limp and heavy on the freighter's wet floor. Blood seeped like tears from the man's eyes.

The sign of a coward too weak to survive.

Even in the large cabin the freighter was cold and wet, much like what they had endured on the island of Lian Yu. The deck was treacherously slick, but Slade rose and stalked toward one of the many pirates serving as his makeshift crew. The men had originally served another—a doctor by the name of Anthony Ivo—but Slade had gained their loyalty by offering a better bargain.

Serve him or die.

Fear didn't often visit brutal men such as these, but they knew what Slade had become. Within just a few hours they had seen prisoner after prisoner die at his hand, and they were afraid.

"Dispose of him!" Slade demanded. "And bring me another."

Obediently the pirate dragged away the lifeless body at Slade's feet, replacing it with another soldier and forcing him to his knees. He then handed Slade a rolled-up canvas pouch. As Slade slowly unfurled the canvas, two of his newest captives, a man and a woman, looked on in horror. They had known the man Slade used to be, before the *mirakuru* had begun to twist his mind. That man had been good and just. Not like the monster standing before them now.

The woman—Sara Lance—had fallen silent. She and Oliver Queen had devised a plan to use an antidote on Slade. It had been produced by Dr. Ivo to reverse the effects of the mirakuru serum, but their plan had failed miserably and now, without the cure, Slade couldn't be stopped. He was too far gone.

The male captive, however, hardened by years of torture on Lian Yu, wasn't yet ready to give up. He still believed he could reach his friend.

"Come on, Slade," Oliver said evenly. "You don't have to do this."

Ignoring him, Slade pulled a glass syringe from the pouch, its green liquid incandescent in the freighter's shadows. This was it, the mirakuru, a serum thought to be lost since World War II. Those worthy enough to withstand its torture were rewarded with abilities beyond the imagination. Superhuman strength, heightened senses, an inherent ability for the body to heal itself. The Japanese called it their miracle, and Dr. Ivo had traveled halfway across the globe in search of it.

It was responsible for driving Slade Wilson to the brink of madness.

Finally he answered Oliver with cold, detached malice in his voice.

"Of course I do, kid," he said. "I'm advancing the cause of science." Slade readied the syringe and glared at the terrified prisoner at his feet.

"Please… no…" The man tried to crawl away, his voice rising until he was screaming for his life. *"For god's sake… No!"* But it was futile. Slade snatched hold of the man's arm and prepared to plunge the needle into his vein.

"Wait!" Oliver cried out. "No, Slade, no—wait!" When Slade hesitated, he continued. "I know you blame me for Shado's death." He evoked the only name that still held sway over the monster. The mention of her name stopped Slade short. He looked up at Oliver, as if seeing him for the first time, his words like light piercing through a fog.

"I blame myself," Oliver said.

"As he should." There was another voice in the darkness—a familiar one. A voice only Slade could hear. "It's his fault we aren't together." It was Shado, reaching out to him from beyond the grave. Though only a wraith, to Slade she was as real as flesh.

"You said once that we were brothers," Oliver said, "and right now I am begging you, brother to brother, just *listen* to me."

Slade wanted to listen. He remembered their friendship. Glimpses of a recent past, before the sorrow…

"Don't listen to him," Shado said. "All his words are lies!"

"I wouldn't be alive right now if it wasn't for you," Oliver said.

"I *would* be alive if it wasn't for him," Shado hissed.

"Think about Shado," Oliver said, the urgency increasing in his voice. "She cared for both of us. She wouldn't want this. She'd only want us to escape Lian Yu. She'd want the nightmare to end!"

Without dropping the syringe, Slade grabbed his head in agony. It was as if his sanity was being torn in two. Somewhere deep within him, in a place the mirakuru hadn't yet transformed, he knew that Shado was dead. He had felt her delicate form, limp and heavy in his arms, her blood still warm where she had taken a bullet to the head. He had buried her with his own hands—yet there she was, standing in front of him, lovely as the first day he laid eyes on her. His beloved.

Seeing her now seared his heart anew, his grief and sorrow fresh as the night it was born. The night Oliver betrayed her. The night Slade made his promise.

"He's right," Shado said. "This needs to end." Slade felt her close by his side, a siren's song whispered in his ear. "You need to kill him."

He stared at the syringe of mirakuru, finally giving in to its powers, without reserve. It was time to end his grief and suffering. To avenge his beloved. Turning away from Oliver, Slade withdrew a mask from his pocket, a terrifying visage of orange and black he liked to wear when killing became inevitable.

"Do it," Shado said eagerly.

He pulled on the mask and drew his gun. The pirate who had been holding Oliver released him, dropping him to his knees. Oliver stared up. He had seen this mask before. He knew what it signified, what was to come. Desperate, Sara struggled unsuccessfully to free herself from her captor's grip.

"Slade!" she cried. "No!"

Slade leveled his gun at Oliver's head, taking aim.

"Pull the trigger!" Shado urged.

Oliver begged for mercy, still trying to reach him.

"Slade!"

Slade unleashed a wail of rage and anger, the last bit of humanity within him succumbing to the mirakuru's power. He applied pressure to the trigger, ready to fire.

KA-BOOM.

Suddenly an explosion rocked the freighter, shock-waves from the impact throwing everyone to the deck. Slade kept his footing, but dropped the syringe. An ear-splitting screech filled the air as sheets of metal shredded like paper. A hole appeared in the wall of the cabin, and water rushed in through the breach. Quickly the weight of the ocean began to drag the vessel under, threatening to split it in two.

A torpedo, Slade knew instantly. *It has to be Anatoly…* Oliver had to have given him instructions.

The boat began to lurch as water cascaded through its interior, causing untold damage. Then it groaned and began to collapse in on itself. Support beams buckled overhead, sending metal debris raining down upon Slade and his captives. In the chaos, the crew scattered without purpose, and even Slade became disoriented.

Using the confusion as a distraction, Oliver pushed upward and elbowed his captor hard in the gut, tossing him to the floor, then darted over to where his quiver was floating in the shin-deep water. He grabbed an arrow and rushed the man who was holding Sara, stabbing him in the chest, the sharp arrowhead penetrating flesh and bone and piercing the man directly through the heart. As he dropped to the ground, the winded pirate recovered from the blow and was reaching for a machine gun. Oliver shoved Sara behind a cargo cage.

"Go go go *go!*"

The thug unleashed a fusillade of gunfire, sparks flying and bullets ricocheting off the metal cage. One stray struck a lamp hanging nearby, setting off a shower of sparks that ignited an electrical fire, adding to the growing mayhem. The pirate exhausted his ammunition, tossed the gun aside, and fled across the tilting deck.

Finally getting his bearings, Slade watched his minion flee.

Coward, he thought. Then he saw it. Floating in the water a few yards away—the mirakuru, the syringe still intact. The leather pouch was nearby. He staggered toward it, the lurching ship knocking him off balance with each step.

Oliver spotted it, too, and yelled to Sara.

"Get off this ship!"

"Not without you!" she shouted back, terror in her voice, but Oliver was already in motion. With the arrow still clutched in his hand as a weapon, he sprinted toward the syringe and, just in time, snatched it away from Slade's grasp, sliding to a stop in the water. He scooped up the pouch, as well.

No! Slade staggered as the ship lurched again, and reached out. "Give it to me," he demanded. "Give me the mirakuru!"

Without hesitation, Oliver threw the serum into the growing electrical fire, the vials exploding luminous green in the blaze.

"No!" Slade bellowed, his blood boiling with rage. He launched himself at Oliver, overwhelming him with a flurry of strikes, driving him backward, away from Sara. Oliver did his best to parry the onslaught, but Slade overpowered him, landing a vicious kick to his chest and sending him sprawling into the cell door. He hit the ground with a grunt of pain.

"Oliver!" Sara ran toward them, trying to intervene. Consumed with rage, Slade snatched her off the ground and threw her across the flooded deck, toward the breach in the hull. She reached out and screamed, just as she had done on the *Queen's Gambit* two years before.

"Ollie!"

"Sara!" Oliver could only watch as she was sucked out to sea, her face locked in a terrified scream. Yet he had no time to process what had just happened as Slade Wilson stalked toward him. He had just enough time to scramble to his feet.

"Poor Sara," Slade said, taunting him. Mocking him. "How many times are you going to watch her die?"

The words had their intended effect. Overcome with rage, Oliver charged, but Slade met him head on, the two clashing in the middle of the listing deck, water flooding in, fire blazing around them, metal groaning overhead. Though the freighter was going down fast, neither man cared. Each was out for blood.

Oliver landed the first punch, but the force of the impact nearly knocked him off his feet. Slade, however, was unfazed. He stood, staring back at Oliver through that horrible mask of orange and black, awaiting his next attack. He was eerily calm.

The adrenaline coursing through Oliver was no match for the mirakuru. Slade easily blocked a punch to his face, returning the blow with one of his own. The force of it stunned Oliver, causing him to drop his defenses for an instant. Slade took the opportunity to land a vicious flying knee to his adversary's chest, followed by a quick left hook to the jaw, battering him down into the knee-deep water. Nevertheless, Oliver managed to rally and struggled to his feet as Slade began to circle him, the incoming flood cascading from overhead.

"You can't kill me," he said as Oliver, still fighting to maintain his balance, reared back for another futile attack. Slade flicked him away, kicking his opponent's leg out from under him. Then he grabbed him by the throat, lifting him into the air with one arm. Oliver clawed at the hand, desperate, his fingers tearing at the orange and black mask. He ripped it away, but Slade only responded by tightening his grip.

The mask dropped to the watery floor.

Gasping for breath, Oliver punched him across the face, then hammered his arm with his fist—one blow after another—trying to loosen his hold. Slade absorbed the punishment unfazed, the blows serving only to enrage him. He choked Oliver and forced him to his knees, then, letting loose a primal scream, punched him to the ground. Oliver landed heavily, face first in the water, wide-eyed and nose-to-nose with Slade's mask.

The omen of death.

He tried to stand, but he was in too much pain. Slade circled, watching him struggle, savoring the moment. Then he reared back and kicked Oliver with all his mirakuru strength, sending him flying through the air so that he twisted in flight before landing with a heavy splash on the floor's wet metal once again. Still, Oliver would not quit. Slade waited, watching as Oliver willed himself up off the floor, gathering himself together for one last strike.

Prolonging the inevitable, Slade thought. *Do you expect mercy? You didn't show Shado any mercy when Ivo shot her. I am going to ruin you, Oliver Queen.* If torture was what the kid wanted, he would gladly oblige.

They both charged again, when suddenly the ship rolled. There was another explosion, set off by the electrical fire. The bow separated from the rest of the ship, finally snapping in two. Both men were thrown to the deck as the last of the support beams buckled, sending twisted metal falling from overhead. There was a searing white, then blackness.

Slade found himself on his back, crushed under the fallen debris, its weight pinning him to the floor. This section hadn't yet flooded. As his vision returned, he spotted Oliver. Luck on his side yet again, he had been thrown out of the path of the falling wreckage.

He watched as Oliver approached, arrow still in one hand and—in the other—a glass syringe, miraculously intact. Slade knew instantly what was inside. He strained against the weight of the beams, his fury growing.

"What are you gonna do, kid?" he growled. "Stick me with a cure? It doesn't matter. I'll keep my promise. I'll take away everything and everyone you love. Sara was only the first."

He knew where Oliver was vulnerable, his words stabbing like daggers.

"She was only the first!"

Oliver's hold on the cure loosened.

"Your sister… "

His grip on the arrow tightened.

"Laurel… "

And the killer in Oliver's eyes emerged.

"Your mother!"

The last thing Slade saw was Oliver rearing back, raising the arrow high overhead and driving it down toward his eye.

Then the world went black.

2

Slade Wilson had been left for dead before, on a submarine run aground deep within Lian Yu. Then, as now, he had felt the darkness surround him, warm and inviting, its silence a soothing balm to his pain. How easy it would be to simply let go and fade off into the infinite black.

But he would not give in.

Not with the mirakuru in his veins.

Not with Shado in his heart.

The first time Slade had fought death's embrace, he had done so to save his beloved. This time, he would do it to avenge her.

Oliver Queen will pay.

As the serum in his blood continued to work, repairing his broken bones, Slade felt his consciousness returning, the world coming back in pieces.

His body pinned by metal.

His mouth and lungs, filled with salt.

His right eye, racked with pain.

Slade awoke to find himself still trapped beneath the fallen beams. To his horror, he realized he was underwater, his lungs straining for oxygen, the cabin completely flooded. He could see a pocket of air trapped a tauntingly short distance above.

Then the debris on top of him began to shift. The water that threatened to drown him might also prove to be his salvation. Using his enhanced strength, he pushed against the mass of metal, straining, the water lending some of the rubble just enough buoyancy for him to free himself. With every push jolts of pain shot through his eye. He kicked up toward the pocket of air, emerging from the water, gasping for oxygen in large, greedy gulps.

One thought consumed him.

Where is Oliver? The rage within him returned. Reaching up, he grasped the arrow that still jutted from his eye, and snapped off the long shaft, leaving a short piece still embedded in his skull. There would be time enough for that later.

He dove back underwater, looking for any sign of the traitor. There were bodies scattered amid the twisted and burnt rubble, and some went floating weightlessly upward. Many were pirates. Others, prisoners he'd tortured.

Where is OLIVER?

The freighter lurched again, a loud groan pulsing through the water. From the sound of it, the ship was mere moments away from going completely under, at which point the momentum would drag him to the ocean floor. He had to go. If Oliver had survived, he would make his way to shore. To Lian Yu. Slade would find him there.

Returning to the air pocket and taking a deep breath, he swam out through the gash in the hull, the hole through which Sara had been sucked. Straining against the riptide created by the vessel as it began to sink, he kicked his way up to the surface, toward the dying night sky.

Dawn was breaking over the horizon, illuminating the carnage. Emerging from the water amid floating debris, he spied the island, the rocky shoreline a half-mile away, alone in the middle of the North China Sea. Rocky peaks jutted out toward the early morning sky, their shadows stretching like fingers over lush, vibrant terrain. To an outsider the island must have seemed like salvation. Its postcard façade gave no indication of the horrors lurking in its interior.

Slade took a breath, then began to swim powerfully, an animal on the hunt.

Slade exploded from the waves and onto the beach. He rose, chest heaving, his body covered with abrasions, his blood leaving traces on many of the gray, inhospitable rocks. He pushed the pain to the back of mind. Whatever wounds the mirakuru couldn't heal were rendered insignificant by his deep grief for Shado... and his hate for Oliver Queen.

He grabbed the stub of the arrow still protruding from his eye—Oliver's failed murder weapon—and ripped it free, the arrowhead taking flesh with it. Tossing it behind him, he began his trek toward the island's center.

"Oliver!" he bellowed as he cut through the Lian Yu foliage, a man possessed. He'd long given up any pretense of stealth. There was no place on the island that Slade wouldn't search. Not the airstrip, not the burnt-out fuselage, not Yao Fei's cave. Yet everywhere he searched, he found no trace of his prey. Not a scent, not a footprint... nothing.

Days passed, and soon there was nowhere left to search. *Did he perish with the ship?* The thought infuriated Slade, but he refused to believe it. *When he dies, I have to be the one who kills him.* As this thought spurred him on, he emerged into a clearing and slowed at what he saw. His final destination—Fyers' mercenary camp, or what remained of it after the Scylla rockets had burned it to the ground. Nature had begun her slow reclamation, long grasses and weeds overtaking machinery that had sat immobile for over a year.

Slade walked amongst the charred remains of tents, searching for any sign of his enemy, but all he found was death. Decomposed bodies were scattered about, their stench long since faded, swept away by time and the island breeze. Again, there was no sign of Oliver.

His frustration boiling over, Slade slammed his fist into the closest truck, the sound of the impact scattering skyward a flock of birds. The vehicle rocked back and forth from the impact as its door caved in, until finally it settled to silence. It was then he noticed another body in the grass, where the birds had been.

It was Bill Wintergreen, his one-time partner and betrayer, still outfitted in his black body armor, his face obscured by an orange-and-black mask that looked identical to the one that Slade had worn, a long knife still embedded in his eye—driven there by Slade's own hand, he recalled with wry irony.

The bastard betrayed me, and he deserved to die.

The sight of Wintergreen pierced through the rage that had swallowed his mind, reminding him why he had been sent to this godforsaken island to begin with. Slade had arrived as an operative for the Australian Secret Intelligence Service, sent there on a covert mission to extract Shado's father, Yao Fei, and learn what Edward Fyers was plotting. His plans had quickly unraveled, however, his partner betraying him and his hopes for a safe return slipping through his fingers.

With lucidity came a realization, clear and apparent.

Oliver Queen was no longer on the island.

No, his prey still lived—of that Slade was certain— but he would be found elsewhere. To do so, Slade would need the resources of A.S.I.S. to help track him down. It had been more than two years, however, since he'd set foot on Australian soil.

Perhaps it was time to return...

Before leaving Lian Yu, Slade paid a visit to Shado's grave to say goodbye. It was as he remembered. The pile of heavy stones, the piece of wood acting as a makeshift tombstone, her name carved in the bark. Seeing it was enough to rip his soul anew.

"Don't mourn for me," Shado said. Just like that, she was by his side again. His beloved. Standing lovely in the morning sun. "Find him," she said, moving closer, whispering in his ear. "Make him pay for his betrayal."

Then she took his face in her hands, looking deep into his eyes.

"*Avenge me.*"

Slade's hand curled into a fist, then began to shake as the rage within him grew. He wanted nothing more than to deliver Oliver's head on a stake. To make him suffer as he did.

"Do you promise me?" Shado asked.

"I promise," Slade said.

"And do you keep your promises?" She was so close now, Slade could feel her breath on his lips. He met her gaze, steel in his voice.

"I do."

* * *

He stood alone on the beach, taking in the island for what he hoped was the last time. That's when he saw it, caught on a rock, twirling in the receding waves. His mask, its orange and black visage unmistakable. He walked over and picked it up, examining it for damage. The bottom half was torn and charred, a sign of its journey from ship to shore. Not fit to be worn again.

Slade had a different use in mind.

He found a piece of driftwood, about four feet long and sturdy, round like a post. It would've been heavy for a normal man, but in Slade's hand the wood was light as a feather. He gripped it tight then drove it into the Lian Yu shore, through clay and rock, embedding it deep and secure just beyond the tidal line.

Taking a moment and looking at his mask, he remembered how he and Billy had worn them when they were proud of their jobs, in that life of the distant past. Then, in an echo of his own injury, Slade secured the mask to the post by driving an arrow through its right eye. A message for Oliver, should he ever return.

Revenge is coming.

Then Slade headed toward the water, the mirakuru rage again fueling his momentum, driving him forward into a full-on sprint, launching him head first into the oncoming waves. He knifed through them and began to swim, his arms and legs churning the sea behind him into a frothy white.

A monster at sea.

3

For nearly two weeks Slade swam south through the cold Northern Pacific, navigating its treacherous waters without thought of sustenance or rest. With the serum in his blood, he believed himself a force of nature, invulnerable and unstoppable, but the same mirakuru rage that fueled his journey also blinded him, overriding the tactical judgment he'd developed over his many years at A.S.I.S:

Never underestimate the enemy.

Especially when that foe is nature herself.

Thirty miles off the northern Philippine coast a typhoon was building, transforming the sky above and the water below into a hell, yet Slade paid no mind to the clouds growing dark and angry on the horizon. He pushed forward, his mind twisted into a deathly tunnel vision. His only concern was exacting his revenge.

The storm hadn't yet reached its apex, but even in

its infancy it tested the limits of his enhanced strength. He gritted his teeth, plowing his arms into the growing waves, legs kicking furiously, swimming twice as hard for half the distance. The winds, so calm just an hour earlier, rose to a deafening roar, whipping rain in horizontal sheets against Slade's face, making it difficult to breathe.

Still Slade swam forward, refusing to deviate from his path. His muscles strained as he was battered again and again by waves grown to the height of buildings. The ocean tossed him about like a rag doll, thrashing his body, stealing his strength until it finally dragged him under.

He was pulled down into the ocean's darkness, all sounds of the roaring storm muted to an eerie silence. He tried fighting against the pull, but exhausted as he was by the storm, he lacked the power to break free. The current slammed him into razor-sharp coral, and the edges of rock plunged deep into his flesh, cutting him to the bone. Blood bloomed red behind him as he kicked back up toward the surface, reaching it and grabbing a few gulps of air before being dragged under once again.

In an echo of Sisyphus, each time Slade fought his way back to the surface he was dragged under again by the relentless assault. His arms and legs burned, and he was no longer advancing through the storm. His rage was forgotten, and his determination to move forward was replaced by one simple goal—to survive.

His strength ebbing, he was driven toward another set of bony rocks. Too fatigued to avoid an impact, he crashed against them, his head smashing violently against an outcrop. His body went limp. As the mirakuru struggled to keep his systems functioning, Slade floated in and out of consciousness. Balanced as he was on the edge of life and death, the serum's hold on Slade's mind started to loosen.

Suddenly there was the vision of a boy in the darkness. Seven years old with auburn hair and a shy smile, his eyes the same color as Slade's. His son, Joe, the boy he had left behind, so many years ago. The boy he had vowed to see again. His first promise, and one he'd nearly forgotten.

His eyes snapped open again. Summoning strength back to his arms and legs, with renewed vigor and determination he shot back to the surface, and emerged to find the sky above him clear. The water was impossibly calm.

He had found the eye of the storm.

And a reason to live.

A fisherman emerged from a seaside shanty, the water choppy around its pier but, luckily, only that. The typhoon had stayed fifty miles from shore while exhausting itself into an overcast sky. He stared off into the gray clouds on the horizon, the patch over his eye a reminder of a time when he hadn't been so fortunate.

He checked the knot anchoring his modest fishing boat to the shore, giving it a good, hard tug. It held fast as the boat bobbed with the waves.

Suddenly there was a figure emerging from the water nearby, set dark against the rising sun, staggering up from the beach. His clothes were tattered, his skin bloodied and his eye was missing from its socket. The fisherman froze where he stood on the edge of the dock.

"Do you have a radio?" the newcomer said in a voice that sounded more like an animal's growl. When the fisherman didn't respond, he repeated the question in Tagalog.

"Mayroon ka ng isang radio?"

Still the fisherman didn't speak, but he pointed to his boat. Inside the vessel's tiny cabin was a radio.

Dragging himself into the cabin, Slade clicked the radio's power switch, the speaker coming to life with a burst of static. Recalling the frequency from memory, he adjusted the set and then hit the button to speak, this time in English.

"This is Wedgetail three-two-five, requesting evac. Repeat, Wedgetail three-two-five requesting evac. Over."

Nothing.

Then the radio screeched back in response.

"Wedgetail three-two-five acknowledged. Identification."

"This is agent One-Two-Seven-Juliet-Papa-Charlie."

Another pause.

"Repeat that one more time?" The voice on the other end sounded wary, disbelief evident in his tone.

"One-Two-Seven-Juliet-Papa-Charlie." He paused, then decided to ignore protocol. "It's Slade Wilson. Bring me home."

After a long moment the voice on the other end asked for his location. Finding the boat's global positioning system, Slade gave the coordinates. The brief conversation ended, and he exited the vessel. Stepping from boat to dock, he staggered, bracing himself by clutching the rickety railing. The damage inflicted by the storm had taken its toll. He was exhausted and in pain, his wounds still open and bloody, his arms and legs heavy with fatigue.

For the first time since being injected with the serum, he felt mortal.

The fisherman, who hadn't moved the entire time, stared with a mixture of awe and fear. He stepped toward the wounded man. As if making a sacrifice to the gods, he took off his eye patch, revealing a scarred white eye. He handed the patch to the creature risen from the sea.

Slade grimaced with a smile of sorts, silently accepting the gift. Placing the patch over the gaping hole in his face, he turned and stalked off toward his extraction point, ready to head back to Australia and A.S.I.S.

Back to his son, Joe.

4

The Australian Secret Intelligence Service maintained three regional offices located across Australia. Its tactical branch—headquarters for covert operatives like Slade Wilson—was located out west, just outside of Perth, in a nondescript gray brick building.

Hidden in plain sight, the outlying structure gave no sign of the activities that took place within its walls. Most of the city's residents believed that the men and women who came and went peddled in life insurance, office supplies, or some other business too irrelevant to note. So no one was looking when the military-grade helicopter flew past overhead, and circled to land on the rooftop. Those who happened to see it would assume they were mistaken.

As the chopper made its approach, Slade peered out the open door, his mind clear of the effects of the mirakuru. A small welcoming committee awaited his arrival on the A.S.I.S. rooftop. Though mostly medical personnel, one man stood out. He wore a dark blue suit, the impeccable tailoring accentuating the sharp angles of his physique. He wasn't massive by any means, but his presence was imposing nonetheless. His eyes, stern and discerning, were the byproduct of a decade's worth of calculations, reducing the cost of human lives to their core statistics.

This was Wade DeForge, regional head of A.S.I.S., the man who initially deployed Slade to Lian Yu. He was the first to greet Slade when the helicopter finally touched down.

"I should know never to doubt your penchant for survival," DeForge said. "You're a bloody cockroach."

"We recognize our own," Slade responded. Then, remembering agency decorum, he added, "*Sir.*"

"Well, I'm glad you're not dead." DeForge extended his hand, which Slade accepted. Then DeForge moved on to the question Slade had been expecting.

"Is Wintergreen still M.I.A.?"

DeForge was practiced in keeping emotions hidden, and to the assembled personnel on the rooftop, he had succeeded, coming off simply as a commander inquiring about the whereabouts of the other operative who had gone missing. Yet Slade had seen a flicker of vulnerability flash in his eyes. The dying embers of a hope not quite extinguished, despite the commander's common sense.

Billy Wintergreen was DeForge's half-brother. He had been the best man at DeForge's wedding, and the godfather to his son. He was family, and they were close—as close as Billy and Slade had been before Lian Yu turned him into a traitor. But Slade wasn't prepared to reveal that on the rooftop, it wasn't for public consumption. There would be time for it later.

"No," he said, and he was surprised to feel remorse.

DeForge nodded.

Suddenly, Slade staggered, his legs buckling beneath him. His eyes went wide with surprise. Even a day after the storm, the mirakuru had yet to regenerate his strength. The medical personnel moved to help him, but DeForge got there first, grabbing his elbow and helping him to his feet.

"Get some rest," DeForge said, "then meet me for the debrief. Say, eleven hundred hours?"

Slade nodded. As the medicos took charge DeForge spun on his heels and headed back into the catacombs of A.S.I.S. All business, revealing none of the questions for which he would demand answers. What had happened on Lian Yu? How did he manage to survive?

How did Billy die?

Slade had two hours to figure out just how much truth he was ready to reveal. But for now, one concern was upmost in his mind.

What had happened to the mirakuru?

The doctor peeled back Slade's eye patch, visibly blanching at the sight of the damage left behind by

Oliver Queen's arrow. Slade could see hints of it reflected in the physician's eyeglasses. What had been his right eye was now a gaping hole, its edges rough and ragged. The doctor voiced surprise that Slade was still alive after an injury of that magnitude. The arrow could have gone directly into his brain.

"Can you tell me how this happened?" he asked.

Slade stared the man down.

"Viciously," he said.

Shrugging, the doctor knew better than to press the issue. He quickly cleaned out the wound, dressed it with some gauze and supplied a clean eye patch before moving on to the lacerations inflicted by the coral and rocks. He removed the temporary bandages applied by the extraction team, revealing the wounds underneath. Though they had made some progress since the storm, the gashes were still open, the flesh angry and red.

Slade hid his surprise. He had been nearly invulnerable since he had been injected with the mirakuru. The serum had never failed to regenerate his flesh and replenish his strength. After so many miracles, why was it failing him now?

The doctor stitched up the wounds and dressed them. Then he reached for a syringe, preparing to draw blood. Eyeing the needle, Slade turned toward the doctor, raising his hand and stopping him short.

"Why?" Slade asked.

"Standard procedure," the doctor replied. "A blood panel, to make sure you're healthy, not carrying pathogens, diseases." There was a long silence as neither man spoke.

"Fine." Slade thrust his arm forward, offering it up for the test. "But if you find anything, you tell me first."

The doctor nodded and then plunged the needle into Slade's vein.

As the vial filled with red, Slade wondered—was the mirakuru still in his blood? Or had it somehow been lost at sea?

Slade walked down the sterile hallway toward DeForge's office, metal and glass gleaming in the halogen lighting. He fought to keep his gait steady, and felt the curious stares of agents in the bullpen—glances snuck at him from behind computer screens and intelligence reports. They knew only that Slade was a field operative recently returned from a classified mission, the details of which fell beyond their clearance levels.

He continued onward, passing the training facility where he had first honed his combat skills so long ago. A large window revealed the space within, the gym equipped with every training apparatus imaginable. All potential field operatives were trained and tested here, shaped into warriors of stealth, serving their country with honor in the shadows. He watched the newest recruits being put through their paces by instructors, some of whom Slade recognized as veteran agents.

One of them, a man named Digger Harkness, Slade

spotted immediately. The two had crossed paths before, during their rise up the A.S.I.S. ranks. Slade watched as Harkness, a flurry of motion, pulled two boomerangs from his bandolier. The weapons arced through the air, their dulled edges striking with unerring accuracy, disarming and subduing a pair of recruits, one even caroming off into a third opponent.

Not bad, Slade mused. *Slick, even. Maybe better than the last time.* He had always felt the boomerang to be a bit gimmicky as a weapon, but in Harkness's hand, it became a lethal object—when he let it. The man gave Slade a nod of recognition, then turned back to the recruits who were helping their fellows up off the floor.

Nearing DeForge's office, Slade saw a wall of framed pictures. The lead officials of A.S.I.S., arranged by rank, Wade DeForge's picture at the top. Slade knew the hierarchy well. He traced a line down and over, a few ranks below DeForge. A man's picture filled the space, but some years ago that hadn't been the case. The occupant had been a woman. Slade felt an unexpected twinge of nostalgia, something normally foreign to him.

It's got to be the weakness, he thought with a hint of panic. *Where the hell is the serum?* Then he quickly cast aside the pangs of a past long buried, and continued on down the hallway, mentally preparing himself for the debriefing. The boss was going to have questions— namely, what had happened to Billy Wintergreen? How could Slade tell DeForge the truth? That Billy had betrayed both him and his country?

How could he reveal that he had repaid that betrayal, with a knife through the eye?

Entering the office, Slade immediately noticed the small framed picture on the man's desk. It was a picture of DeForge with his arm around a woman. The photo that once had been displayed in the hallway outside.

"I was wondering where that had gone," Slade said, pointing as he sat. DeForge didn't care to hide it, and Slade could respect that.

"I'd forget what she looked like if wasn't for this," DeForge replied, though Slade knew better. He stood next to the window. "You know Adie, keeping everyone at arm's length." He casually took his seat across from Slade, opening a folder. "I should probably thank you for that."

Slade took it in stride. "You tell her I'm back?" he said.

"Yeah," DeForge said, with the slightest bit of reluctance. "She's expecting you. They both are." Slade acknowledged the information with a nod. Reunions would have to come later. He steeled himself, ready for what was certain to come next. But he knew what he was ready to reveal, and what to hold back.

He couldn't paint himself as a monster.

"How 'bout we get on with it then?"

"All right," DeForge said. "How about we start with where you've been for the past three years?" He leaned in. "What the *hell* went wrong out there?"

Slade began with the basics. He and Billy had been sent to Lian Yu to find and extricate Yao Fei, a soldier who had been confined to the island by the Chinese military, to cover up a massacre. When they arrived, however, there was a military presence on the island, and he and Billy were shot out of the sky by a tomahawk missile, the rear of the plane disintegrating in the ensuing explosion.

"I managed to set us down alive, though by the skin of our teeth," he said. "Billy and I were captured, and imprisoned."

"But not by the Chinese," DeForge noted.

"No," Slade said. "It was an army of mercenaries, led by a man named Edward Fyers."

DeForge's eyes flashed recognition.

"And then what happened?"

"Torture," Slade answered flatly. He explained how, for more than a year, he and Billy had been subjected to every manner of pain by Fyers and his men, in an attempt to get them to break and reveal for whom they worked. He offered enough detail to make a normal man cringe, and watched for the response. DeForge showed no emotion.

"How did you and Billy escape?" he asked.

Slade paused, considering how to proceed. The truth of the matter was that Billy had been turned, betraying Slade and his country to join Fyers' army of mercenaries. But revealing that information would lead to too many questions he didn't want to answer. So Slade lied.

"Me and Billy managed to escape, with the help of Yao Fei," he said. "We hid in the forest, and managed to avoid capture while gathering intel on Fyers and his men. They were good, but we were better."

"What were you able to find out?" DeForge pressed.

"Fyers was a hired gun," Slade said, "and whoever was paying had big plans—Fyers had orders to shoot down a commercial aircraft headed for China. Then he'd pin the blame on the Chinese government, grounding all air travel in and out of the country, and destabilizing their economy.

"But you already knew this, didn't you?" Slade added. He kept his own face unreadable.

DeForge smiled. "What tipped you off?"

"You sent us in dark, no extraction plan," Slade observed. "As soldiers, we knew not to ask questions, but that level of secrecy, I knew something was up."

The commander nodded. He revealed that, prior to sending Slade and Billy to Lian Yu, A.S.I.S. had been tracking a shadow organization based out of the United States. The Advanced Research Group United Support, otherwise known as A.R.G.U.S.

"Australian intelligence suggested that Yao Fei was a high interest target," DeForge admitted, "but we had underestimated the scope of the organization's plan."

"Would've been great knowing that going in," Slade said.

"You know the game," DeForge countered. "What you *don't* know can't be tortured out of you." A.S.I.S. had been keeping tabs on Edward Fyers, he revealed—as they did with most mercenary groups—and knew he had been mobilized, but they didn't know to where or by whom.

"This gives us more on A.R.G.U.S.," he said, "and for that you have my gratitude." He paused, and Slade knew what was coming next. "What happened to Billy?"

Slade gave what he hoped was a pained look, and took a deep breath.

"Billy, Yao Fei, and I figured out that Fyers had the only communications equipment on the island, and the only way to get to and from Lian Yu. So the only way *off* the island was through Fyers and his men. That meant we had to hit them where they would least expect it—at their camp.

"The confrontation went sideways fast." Substituting in Billy and Yao Fei for Oliver and Shado, he gave a detailed account of the battle that had actually occurred. The rocket launcher, intended for use against commercial flights, was turned on the camp itself. He recounted the ensuing explosion, the carnage and bloodshed. "I did my best to cover his ass, but when the smoke cleared, I was the only man left standing. Fyers and his men, Yao Fei and Billy—they were all dead."

With that he stopped, and waited.

DeForge sat silent for a moment, his expression unreadable.

"What about Billy's body?" he asked. "Did you bury him?"

Billy's corpse flashed in Slade's mind, the knife plunged deep into his former friend's skull. He stared DeForge in the eyes.

"No," he lied. "There was nothing left to bury. Only ash."

Looking down, the commander tried to bury his feelings, but Slade could tell the finality of it all weighed on him heavily. Lifting his head, he shook it slowly.

"You really are a goddamn cockroach."

Slade left DeForge's office, satisfied he had pulled it off and wouldn't be under suspicion. That out of the way, there was another, far more important matter to attend to. He had been waiting for three long years.

It was time to see his son again.

5

Slade pulled his Jeep up to the curb and parked near the house, just out of sight of the front porch. The home sat in relative seclusion, on about three acres lush with green shrubs and eucalyptus trees. A brown picket fence lined the property's perimeter. A well-kept dirt path lined with smooth stones marked the walkway from the street to the porch.

Stepping out and quietly shutting the door, he smoothed out the suit pants and coat he was wearing after a quick change back at A.S.I.S. Dark gray and impeccably tailored, the stylish attire was his one flourish, the extravagance he enjoyed after returning from a mission. It had started as his cover story—rich businessman, freshly returned from international travel—but he had come to see it as a reward for survival.

It was also the perfect cover for his many bandaged wounds. All save his eye, however, which was concealed beneath a jet-black patch. That, Slade couldn't hide. He just hoped the sight wouldn't prove too jarring for either Adeline or Joe.

He started toward the front door, still moving with a slight limp. The house was equal parts Craftsman and Farmhouse, an architectural mixture common to the surrounding area. The pitched roof was tiled in gray, set low over the exposed brick masonry of the walls. Two chunky support posts framed the entryway, in contrast with the delicate trelliswork that was covered in green vines.

When he and Adeline were first married they used to joke that the house reflected their relationship. Seemingly without design, yet in spite of that somehow working. Or maybe *because* of it—they were never quite sure. Whereas a house's underlying architecture was immutable, though, the same wasn't true for a union between man and wife.

When Slade had left for his mission, their divorce had been final for just a few months.

Back when they first met, he had fallen for Adie immediately, intoxicated by how effortlessly stunning she was. Not only was she a natural beauty, she was also a sincere, good-hearted person. Where Slade's attitude was hard, Adeline had softened him—but it hadn't lasted. Their love had grown strained, even after Joe was born. Slade had debated the divorce for months, finally filing, and then quickly signing the papers—making his assignment on Lian Yu the desperate escape he needed.

The sound of his footsteps on the wooden porch drew Adeline to the door. It was open, the screen door loosely latched. Olive-complexioned with hair falling in soft brown curls, she was as pretty as ever, beautiful in a way that didn't aim to draw attention. Sensibly dressed as always, she chose function over fashion, wearing jeans with a buttoned-up flannel shirt, well worn and comfortable. The only effect the years had inflicted was to give her soft features an edge. Slade imaged he was partly to blame for that. She'd been left to raise the boy by herself.

Adeline regarded Slade, her face awash with conflicting emotions. Relief that he was alive, anger that he had been gone so long. Concern for the injuries she could see and ones she knew he was hiding, and frustration that he put himself in the position to endure that sort of damage to begin with. She unfastened the latch and opened the door, eyeing Slade's patch and shaking her head.

"Wade called," she said. "Do I even want to ask?"

"Probably not," Slade said, entering the house. "Just a scratch, anyway."

"Yeah," Adie replied. "I'm sure it'll grow back. Good as new."

Slade gave a rueful smirk, thinking about the mirakuru.

"You'd be surprised."

"Well, it's an improvement on that ugly mug of yours."

"DAD!"

Joe came flying out from the back of the house, surprising Slade and jumping into him, arms bear-hugging his waist. He didn't flinch, though he found himself stunned by the embrace—the unconditional love. He'd spent the better part of three years building up his defenses, detaching himself from his emotions in order to survive. There had been no room for attachments, or so he'd thought before meeting Shado. She had cared for him, putting his well-being before her own, breaching his defenses over time.

It was rare that he allowed anyone past the walls surrounding his heart. It's why he hated Oliver with such burning passion. For taking Shado's love for granted. For taking her away from him. He wanted revenge, not only for Shado, but for himself. His despair was rooted in the belief that a love like Shado's would never touch him again.

Slade had come to accept that there would always be a part missing within him. It was the way of the soldier. It was why he didn't stay home. Why he chose to be a soldier, more than a husband or a father. He never loved anyone more than his job and his country, yet in that moment, his son's arms around him, squeezing him tight, he felt the cold in his heart fade, and love pulling him back. Beginning to fill the hole that Shado's death had created within him.

Joe finally let go, looking up at his father and seeing the eye patch for the first time.

"Whoa," the boy said in awe. "Did you get that fighting the bad guys?"

"Fighting bad guys?" Slade replied, surprised. "Who gave you that idea?"

"Mom. She said you're a hero, and that's why you've been gone for so long."

Slade looked over to Adie, who shrugged.

So much for the cover story.

"Then yes," Slade said. "It was one especially *bad* bad guy."

"Did you get him?"

"Not yet."

"Did he karate you?"

"Did he 'karate' me? Where're you learnin' this stuff, kid?"

"The TV."

"Hey, J," Adie said, changing the subject. "Why don't you show your dad that new football of yours?"

"Oh yeah!" He looked to his dad, excited. "I'm pretty good now. I think I can beat you."

"That right?" Slade mussed up his hair, a tumble of loose curls like his mom's. "Go get that ball and let's see."

Joe ran off to the back yard, and Adie moved closer.

"Look," she said with some difficulty. "I know every time you're sent out, you might not come back. Rules of the game, but I really thought we'd lost you this time. I'm glad to have you back... at home."

"It's like I've always told you, Adie," he answered

wearily, feeling an old argument bubbling up. "It takes a hell of a lot to kill me. You were always too afraid of me not coming home."

"And you were never afraid enough." Adie was measured in her response. "But I'm not bringing this up for me. It's for him. He's had three birthdays since you last saw him. How many more do you want to miss?"

Slade felt her words land. He had come back to Australia to find Oliver Queen and exact his revenge, but now, standing in the house he had once called a home, he was face to face with the beckoning of an old role. One of father and husband, come home to be with his family.

Was there room within him for both?

Joe came running back in with the ball.

"I was gonna say we could go see a game, but the season doesn't start until winter." He looked up at his dad. "You probably won't be here, huh?"

Slade looked down at his son, staring into the brown eyes they both shared.

He didn't have an answer.

6

The doctor carefully examined each wound again, checking the hold of his stitches and changing the dressings. Aside from the missing eye—nothing could be done about that—everything else was healing. It'd be a slow process, but he'd eventually be back to normal.

Yet Slade had grown accustomed to a different timetable. With the mirakuru in his system, he should've been mended five times over by now.

What was happening?

"The blood test, doc," he asked, keeping his tone soft. "See anything out of the ordinary?"

The doctor opened up a medical folder, scanning the data through glasses on the rim of his nose.

"Well, your cholesterol numbers would be the envy of most men at your age," he said, eyeing Slade over the spectacles. "Benefits of an island isolation diet, I suppose. Not for me, though." Slade resisted the attempt at levity, and just stared. He wanted numbers, not humor. The man gave a sigh, removing and pocketing his glasses, getting to the point. "Aside from the damage to your right eye, and a slightly elevated blood pressure, you're the picture of health."

"No... pathogens?" Slade pressed. "No viruses?"

"If there were, Mr. Wilson," the doctor said, "you'd be the first to know." With that he exited, having delivered what he no doubt considered good news. And it would have been for most of the patients coming through his office, but for Slade Wilson, the results were confounding.

How could the mirakuru simply disappear?

"I'm not trying to rush you back into action," DeForge said without breaking stride. "Nevertheless, our A.R.G.U.S. intel, as limited as it might be, indicates that the organization is mobile somewhere in China, likely Hong Kong. They're ramping up to something big." He paused before pushing through the Advanced Tech door, turning to face Slade. "You're my best man. I'd love to have your ears to the ground."

DeForge wasn't trying to sweet-talk him— Slade *was* the best operative he had—but he could sense an ulterior motive behind the words. He'd known DeForge long enough to understand that no compliment was without its motive. Maybe it was about Adie. Life was simpler for everyone involved when Slade was away.

"Doc says you'll get back to full strength… when?" DeForge asked.

"Two months, give or take."

"Good. That should give Tech enough time to apply the finishing touches to the new field uniform." He led Slade into one of the many engineering bays. There, behind glass, held aloft by a wire mannequin, was an updated version of the field uniform Slade had worn when he arrived on Lian Yu. It was black, made to blend in with the shadows, and featured a special weave of promethium in its fibers, a nearly indestructible metal composite that was as light as it was durable. Bandoliers crisscrossed the chest with pockets holding any number of hidden weapons and devices. There were clips of ammo for the two high-caliber pistols holstered on each hip, ready to unleash hell.

The greatest difference was in the design and functionality of its balaclava. Though its trademark orange and black color scheme was still present, gone was the pliable rubber and fabric mask Slade and Wintergreen had worn on the island—the very one which Slade had left for Oliver on the Lian Yu shore. Replacing it was a helmet, forged completely of promethium, the metal smooth and glinting under the lights overhead. Bulletproof and impervious, the mask was terrifying in its simplicity.

Finally, running in parallel with the bandoliers across the chest, two straps crossed at the uniform's back, each holding a sheath for Slade's weapon of choice—twin twenty-seven-inch tactical machetes. He preferred the razor-sharp metal's quiet efficiency over the louder, and—in his opinion—less refined killing instruments contained in the lab, and unlike Digger's boomerangs, there were no gimmicks involved with his swords. Each just offered a silent, effortless death stroke, which Slade had delivered to enemies far too numerous to count.

He reached out and touched the uniform's cold metal, running his hand along it. DeForge certainly knew how to appeal to Slade's inner soldier. The body armor was, indeed, impressive.

"Nice, isn't it?" DeForge said. "Tough son of a bitch like you, I figure you'll be giving this a test drive in a couple weeks, if not sooner."

"About that—" Slade said, "—if it's fine by you, I'd like to stay grounded here for the time being." He could see a brief flicker of disappointment cross DeForge's face.

"Slade Wilson, desk jockey?" DeForge said. "It's hard to imagine."

He was trying to push buttons.

Not gonna work, he thought. Out loud he said, "I just got home. I'd like to spend some time with my son." Slade eyed DeForge. "After Lian Yu, I think I've earned that right."

DeForge eyed his soldier, sizing him up.

"Tired of dodging bullets?"

"For now, at least."

DeForge nodded, giving in.

"Any idea what you'd want to do?"

Slade pretended to consider the question.

"Help train the newbies, when I'm able," he said. "But I'd also like to help with intelligence. It might pay to have someone with my field experience processing data as you track A.R.G.U.S. I might see something a 'desk jockey' might miss."

"Very well," DeForge said, shaking his head. "I'll get you set up with Matt in Analytics." The commander started to head out of the equipment bay. "Slade Wilson behind a desk," he said, shaking his head again. "Hell really must be freezing over." He disappeared down the hall, leaving Slade behind with the prototype.

Slade took in the uniform, lost in thought. DeForge was right. The idea of not taking a mission was jarring, even to him. He was born to wear armor like the prototype that stood before him. Those suits were designed to fit men like him—men who lived to serve their country through whatever means necessary.

One day, he might find himself back out there again, but for now, staying behind was part of his plan. He needed access to A.S.I.S.'s surveillance capabilities. Under the guise of helping fight the good fight against A.R.G.U.S., Slade would use the technology to find out if Oliver Queen was still alive.

7

The Analytics Department, like the rest of A.S.I.S., was unspectacular to the layman's eye. Cubicles were arranged in an open office design, like those of a tech startup or a video game studio, with computer monitors aglow at every desk. The bullpen was quiet, each of its members focused on the task at hand— gathering and processing surveillance data acquired through means oftentimes falling outside the purview of the law. If the law even knew the organization existed in the first place.

"It'll probably be easiest to think of the system like it's another weapon."

Matt Nakauchi, one of the department technicians, led Slade to an open desk. Wearing a gray button-up shirt open at the collar and relaxed pants, he was by all outward measure a normal, average guy. The only glimpse of his underlying quirkiness came out while discussing the capabilities of the A.S.I.S. technology.

Then he spoke a mile a minute.

"It's probably more effective, too, at least in my opinion," Nakauchi added. "Quieter than a gun, more precise than a knife, but *way* less blood."

"You've never seen *me* use a sword," Slade responded with a smirk.

"But that's my point. What we do, no one sees." Nakauchi grabbed the mouse and started clicking. "While you normally take the enemy head on, we attack where he least expects it—in his moments of what we laughingly refer to as 'privacy.' Or 'her' moments," he added. "I don't discriminate."

Slade watched with mild bemusement as the tech opened up a program. Aerial images of Australia popped up on screen, most likely from drones, or spy satellites in orbit overhead.

"This is our latest weapon of mass data deconstruction—the Super Intelligent Image Recognition Algorithm," he continued proudly. "Or as I call it, SIIRA, pronounced like the California wine. Makes it classy."

"I won't be calling it that," Slade said.

"You will after I show you what it does." Nakauchi gave him a cocky grin as he pulled up another screen showing a seemingly endless list of files and data. "Imagine trying to find someone in all this nonsense, right? A total needle-in-a-haystack type deal. Unless, of course, you have a tool that will sift through all the hay for you." He punched a few keys and brought up a picture of Slade—one taken well before Lian Yu.

Maybe even before Joe. Both eyes intact. Slade stared back at himself, trying to remember the time when he was still whole.

"This is from your dossier," Nakauchi explained. "I use it not to point out your whole missing eye thing—apologies, by the way, because that sucks—but to illustrate its vast capabilities. If you were within the scope of a camera, it'll find you, adjusting for age, hair, scars, whatever. Watch." Slade leaned in as the tech ran a search. A few seconds later, security camera footage showed him buying groceries at a neighborhood mart. "Marmite, eh? I don't think I've ever actually seen someone buy a jar. It always just exists, you know?"

"I had a craving," Slade said. "What else can it do?"

"The Marmite or the computer?" Nakauchi asked, and when he didn't get a reply, he continued. "Do you remember what you were doing, say, ten years ago?"

"Waiting for my son to be born."

A couple of keystrokes later, and footage appeared on the screen—of a much younger Slade, pacing in the hospital waiting room.

"Scary good, right?" Nakauchi said.

Slade stared at the screen, wheels turning.

"How accurate is it?" he asked.

"It's still in beta, so there are some kinks, but I'd say it's accurate to roughly eighty-five percent. Definitely good enough to point that sharp sword of yours in the right direction."

Slade nodded. *Good enough indeed.*

* * *

"Is that the best you got?"

Digger Harkness stood over Slade Wilson, who lay on his back. The two had been sparring for the last thirty minutes. Harkness, who was trying to stay sharp between missions, had issued a friendly challenge. Hand-to-hand combat, first to five takedowns wins. The younger operative was eager to test himself against the legend.

Slade, for his part, gladly obliged. A month on from his injuries, he was itching to exert himself and test how well he had recovered. That his ego had been challenged only added fuel to the fire. He'd figured he would teach Harkness a lesson.

Instead, he was down four-to-one.

Frustrated, he slapped the mat and got to his feet. His chest was heaving as sweat broke across his brow. It felt like he was standing in quicksand. His agility and strength had yet to return. Harkness regarded him with a sly, cocky smile.

"Need a moment?"

Slade grunted in response, readying himself.

Harkness shrugged, and engaged.

It happened quickly. Slade parried, blocking an onslaught of punches and kicks, keeping pace initially, but then fading with fatigue against the younger man's relentless attack. Finally, Slade, his technique grown sloppy, threw a desperate punch that Harkness countered easily, using Slade's momentum to toss him to the mat one final time.

Check and mate.

The younger man extended a hand to help him up. With a dispirited sigh, Slade accepted. He didn't like losing, but he wasn't about to be a bad sport. Harkness slapped him on the back.

"Good match," he said, trying to sound genuine.

Slade laughed in self-disgust. "Hardly."

"You're just rusty." Harkness tossed him a bottle of water. "It takes time for the skill to come back around."

"Rematch when it does?"

"Sure," Harkness said, "but next time, we use our weapons." Slade nodded, watching him snatch up his bandolier of boomerangs and head off toward the locker room. The man was skilled, no question, but Slade believed himself to be the superior fighter. He had been overwhelmed, not by skill, but by fatigue—his strength and agility not yet fully restored from his arduous ocean swim.

Slade headed off to the showers, the sparring session confirming the results of the blood test a month ago. He was beginning to accept that the mirakuru was gone.

Using the SIIRA system, Slade located and tracked the Queen family and their associates. Oliver's mother, Moira, sister, Thea, and best friend, Tommy Merlyn, even his former girlfriend, Laurel Lance, the girl whose picture Oliver had kept in his wallet all those years on the island.

He spent his time carefully assembling details, a voyeur from thousands of miles away. If Oliver Queen was alive these people would know, and they would lead Slade to his revenge.

He grew to despise them. Just another opulent family, living in the rarified air of luxury and decadence few would ever know. He watched as Thea and Tommy coasted on the riches of their parents, and wondered if Oliver's upbringing had been the same. Slade pulled up old news reports about Oliver's party days, saw him wander the halls of Queen Consolidated, screwing around with starlet after starlet. Unmotivated and soft. How in the world had a spoiled, pampered brat like that managed to find the depth of character needed to survive an island like Lian Yu.

How had he become a cold-blooded killer?

The thought that this man had felled him infuriated Slade to no end. He figured someone else had to feel the same way—if not about Oliver himself, then about the privileged family who spawned him. So he began searching for people who might be enemies of the Queens.

The enemy of my enemy is my friend. Or at least a prospective ally.

He decided to begin his investigation with Queen Consolidated. He looked for patterns in legal action taken against the company, in attempted acquisitions of its subsidiaries, and in the behaviors of its competitors. It was during this avenue of inquiry that he came across a young female executive at Stellmoor International, a rival company. The executive's name was Isabel Rochev, and she had been at Stellmoor for years, working her way up through the ranks. Rochev had made a career out of snatching up Queen Consolidated's weaker satellite divisions, like a bird circling its prey.

She would dismember the companies for profitable parts before unceremoniously discarding the carcasses. The losses ultimately made no difference to the Queen Consolidated bottom line, the fact of which was hammered home in the company's press materials. These were subsidiaries of little consequence, which made Rochev's actions more obvious—clearly this woman had an agenda beyond simple business.

Slade knew what hate looked like.

Yet hate wasn't enough to find Oliver Queen.

Four months into his research, however, and to his own surprise, Slade's disgust with the Queen family began to evolve when he realized how broken they were as people. Though they put on a brave face in public, behind closed doors—in their most private spaces—the Queens were a family fractured by grief. It had been more than three years since the sinking of the *Queen's Gambit*, where Oliver and his father Robert had disappeared and were presumed dead. Yet the family's sorrow remained as raw as the day it happened. He watched as Moira lost herself in work and in the arms of Walter Steele, a high-ranking executive at Queen Consolidated, while her daughter, Thea, tried to drown her sadness in an ocean of prescription drugs.

The ripple effects were present in the Lance household as well. Laurel's father, Detective Quentin Lance, spiraled down a rabbit hole all of his own: of alcoholism.

Though he tried to stay vigilant in his search, as the days passed by he actually found his hatred *waning*. To his surprise Slade found himself filling with regret.

Regret for himself.

Why am I wasting so much time on this wretched family, in chasing a ghost? he wondered. For all intents and purposes, Oliver Queen was dead. Meanwhile, he had his own family waiting for him at home, so close and so very much alive.

Slade decided to go home early for a change.

Home. A place Slade hadn't known for such a long time. Though reluctantly at first, Adeline still allowed him to return to the house. The smell of dinner wafted out to greet Slade as he walked up the path, and he could make out details in the scent—carrots and onions caramelizing in a pot, the fat of stew meat browning in butter, aromatics of black pepper and thyme. The savory fragrance marking the beginnings of a stick-to-your-bones stew. After his time on Lian Yu, the once unexceptional meal had become a cherished luxury.

Joe sat cross-legged on the floor of the den, doing homework. Adie heard him come in and poked her head out from the kitchen.

"Got tired of invading people's privacy?" she asked.

"Decided I'd rather have some of my own," Slade replied.

"You know better, but it's good for you to hold onto your illusions," she said. "Now you can help Joe with his homework."

Slade slung his coat over a chair and sat down next to his son. He felt himself sink into the carpet, the boy's warm form nestled against him. Joe looked up at him and smiled, then put his head back down toward the task at hand. He was scratching out a small essay in pencil, his writing the expected haphazard scrawl of a ten-year-old. Slade recognized his own handwriting in a few of the vowels.

"What are you working on?" he asked.

"A book report," Joe answered. "We're reading a ghost story book, and Ms. Cho wants to know if we thought it was scary, but if we didn't think it was scary, then we have to write about what we think is *really* scary."

"Sounds tactical." Slade grinned. Knowing an enemy's fear meant possessing the means to control him. Why wouldn't the same hold true for school children?

"What does tactical mean?" Joe looked up at him.

"That your teacher's a smart lady," Slade said. "So, was the book scary?"

"Not really." Joe shrugged. "It did have spiders in it, but I see those every day, and really big spiders don't exist."

"I don't know, mate. I've seen some pretty big spiders."

"How big?"

"The size of your face." Slade used his hand and fingers to mimic a spider's crawl. "And they would leap at you, like this!" He grabbed Joe's head lovingly, causing the boy to squeal in laughter.

"So if it's not spiders, what are you afraid of? Dragons? Vampires?"

Joe shook his head. "Mom says they're all fake, and you can't be afraid of stuff that's fake."

"All right, tough guy," Slade said. "What's something you're scared of that's not fake?"

Joe paused, considering. Then he shrugged again, matter-of-fact.

"I guess I was scared I wasn't going to see you again," he replied, "but I don't think that counts."

Slade was stunned. Fighting off the emotion swelling within him, he mussed Joe's hair.

"I think that counts just fine."

* * *

Slade found Adie over the stove, stirring the pot of stew. She waved him over, dipping the spoon into the pot.

"Here," she said, offering the spoon to him. "Taste this."

"You were wasting your time at A.S.I.S.," Slade commented, licking the spoon dry. "Because you're a goddamn good chef."

"Please." Adie took the spoon, rinsing it in the sink before putting it back in the pot. "You were stranded on an island eating twigs and dirt the past three years. I could serve you a leather shoe and you'd love it."

"Depends on the leather." Adie mimed some fake laughter and went over to the cutting board to slice up lettuce for a salad.

"How did the homework go?"

"Fine. Joe writes like I do, which isn't ideal."

"You mean gibberish?"

"No," Slade said, stealing the spoon back from the pot. "Like he's writing in the midst of a seizure. Must mean he's smart."

Adie playfully grabbed the spoon back. "And that, my friend, would come from me."

"No argument here," Slade agreed. He paused for a second, looking at the stew simmering on the stove. "Joe said he was afraid that I wasn't coming back."

"We both were," Adie said. Like it had been with Joe, her tone was matter-of-fact. She continued chopping up lettuce greens. "Does that surprise you?"

"Not really." Slade dipped a finger into the stew

for another taste. "But hearing it, coming from him. I never really thought about it before."

"Is that why you're home early tonight?"

"What do you mean?" Slade eyed his ex-wife, caught off-guard by the question.

"I know you, Slade," she said, still chopping. "You're not pulling these hours trying to find A.R.G.U.S. agents. You're after something else."

Slade grabbed a kitchen towel from the handle of the oven, wiping his hand. He peered closely at her.

"You sound like you've been thinking about this for some time," he said. "Where's it come from?"

"We've been divorced more years than we've been married, Slade," she said. "I lost the right to question you a long time ago, but I will say this…" She scooped the salad greens into a bowl and wiped her hands dry on her apron. Then she turned toward her ex-husband, meeting his gaze. "Whatever happened to you out there, whoever was responsible for that eye—leave it there. Leave it behind. Forget that island."

Before he could respond she kissed him on the cheek, then exited, taking the salad out to the dining room table. Left behind in the kitchen, Slade inhaled the smell of the stew, felt its warmth in his belly, spreading up and outward to his limbs. Then he heard his boy laughing in the next room and walked over to the doorway, looking in. He saw his ex-wife tickle his son, trying to get him to help set the table.

Moving over to a chair in the den, he let his

weight sink deeply into the soft cushions. He gazed out through the window, taking in the last of the day's light, the sun setting fast on the horizon, stars emerging from overhead. He closed his eyes, breathing in deeply, the smell of dinner in the air and his son's laughter in his ears.

For the first time in longer than Slade could remember, he felt happy.

The Japanese had developed the mirakuru while under duress, the atrocities of World War II bearing down upon them. Desperate to level the playing field, they kept the serum's existence secret, hiding the laboratory in a submarine deep in the North Pacific. Safely hidden, they rushed the drug directly into clinical trials, testing the serum on their soldiers before research could be adequately conducted.

The results were immediate and terrifying. Many of the soldiers died instantly, their organs ruined by the serum's effects. The select few who survived, however, emerged with strength and agility far in excess of normal men.

In that respect, the mirakuru was a success.

However, with those abilities came an unintended consequence. The soldiers' minds became twisted, slowly overtaken by a vicious rage that sent them rampaging through whatever and whoever had the misfortune of standing in their path. These superhumans could not be controlled. So the Japanese abruptly ended the trials before further research could be conducted, deeming the situation too high risk to continue.

Dr. Anthony Ivo, the scientist who had traced the serum back to that submarine run aground on Lian Yu, had managed to counter the serum's destructive effects while studying its regenerative properties aboard the freighter. He developed an antidote based on a simple observation—the serum could be exhausted. With every feat of strength and injury healed, the concentration of the mirakuru thinned within a subject's blood, lessening its effects. In a sense, the drug could "run out."

Yet if any trace of the serum managed to remain, it would replicate itself. As time went on, it would regain its strength and its grip on the host.

All the mirakuru needed was time.

☒

Slade squared off against Digger Harkness in the
A.S.I.S. training room, holding his tactical machete
at the ready. Harkness gripped his dual metal
boomerangs. Unlike their first session months before,
he looked harried, his chest rising and falling, sucking
wind. Slade, meanwhile, was the picture of calm, the
only outward indication of exertion the sweat beading
near his temples. The hair there had started to gray.

With a nod, each to the other, the men rushed forward,
clashing at the room's center. Harkness was a swirl of
motion, spinning his body with arms outstretched. The
arc of the boomerang blades struck high and low in
the same movement. Slade parried the attack with his
machete, deflecting each blow with quick protective
thrusts up and down, finely carving the air.

Abruptly Harkness switched tactics, sending one of
his blades airborne toward Slade's head, causing him
to duck. As the blade arced back around, Digger used

the momentary distraction to charge, slashing at his opponent. Slade blocked the strike, but then Digger spun, caught the second blade as it returned, and swiped him across the arm, drawing blood.

The wound did little to stop Slade, however, serving instead to anger him. He charged with a battery of thrusts and swipes, driving his opponent backward. He threw the machete, surprising Harkness, embedding it in the wall just wide of his head and diverting his attention. Then he landed a kick to Harkness's chest, following it with a low roundhouse sweep to his legs, knocking them out from under him.

Harkness landed on the sparring mat with a loud thump, his boomerangs clattering to the floor in either direction. Slade grabbed his blade from the wall and pressed its edge against the man's neck. Harkness put his hands up, conceding the point and the match.

"I'd say you've recovered," Harkness grunted. "Fully."

Slade helped Harkness to his feet. "One more round?"

"And suffer another defeat to the 'Silver Fox'?" Harkness replied wryly. "No thanks, mate—I've had my fill of humiliation today."

"Don't feel too bad… mate." Slade slapped him on the back. "I owed you one."

"I guess what they say is true," Harkness said. "What goes around, comes around." He grinned at the thought, and as the men headed off toward the showers, he changed the subject. "So when's your next deployment?"

Slade shook his head. "Not looking for one."

Harkness gave Slade a curious look. "A man of your skill, I figured you'd be itching to get back in the game."

"Trying something different," Slade said. "New priorities."

"Then I wish you luck, my friend." Harkness regarded the man, meeting his eye, drawing from an experience unspoken. "Warriors like us, it's not easy leaving that part behind." Slade nodded, knowing all too well the depths of that truth—but he had made his peace. Adie was right. For the better part of a year, there had been no sign of Oliver Queen. For Joe's sake, maybe it was time to consider the Starling City playboy dead and buried.

"Sorry about your arm, by the way," Harkness said. "Though it doesn't look as bad as I thought."

Slade glanced at his wound, surprised to see that the cut, so bloody mere moments ago, had already begun to heal.

Slade sat at his desk, his search for Oliver put aside, when a new batch of intelligence arrived from the agency's ongoing surveillance activities in Hong Kong. A man had been stabbed, murdered in an alleyway just off of one of the busiest urban streets. According to the Chinese authorities, the crime was a common one, an unfortunate act of violence perpetrated against foreigners by local area gangs. They had declared the victim a John Doe.

A.S.I.S. Intel, however, had identified the man as Adam Castwidth, a well-known handler of mercenaries with suspected ties to Edward Fyers, the mastermind of the carnage on Lian Yu.

The incident had A.R.G.U.S. written all over it, and Slade was tasked with reviewing the emerging surveillance. The importance of the task, however, did nothing to assuage the tedium. He did his best to stave off boredom as he analyzed the hundreds of photographs and security camera videos taken near the crime scene. An endless procession of faces streamed across his computer screen, the SIIRA program crosschecking each designated person against the internal database. A haystack being deconstructed one straw at a time, in search of a needle.

He broadened SIIRA's processing parameters, asking the program to isolate every face of unknown origin in the crowd. It was a long shot—despite widespread paranoia, most people weren't worth cataloging in a database. Nevertheless, the technique had proven successful a few times before.

One image caught Slade's eye. It had been taken just a few moments before an innocent bystander had discovered the body. The majority of the crowd was being drawn toward the commotion. However, one man—Caucasian, medium-length brown hair—was clearly moving against the tide. The man's face was mostly obscured by shadow, his face turned to the side, the motion of his walking blurring the features.

As recognition began to dawn, Slade felt the hair rise on his arms and his heart rate quicken. His vision tunneled and the sounds of the bullpen dropped away. Though the man was little more than an obscured blur, his identity was unmistakable. It was the face of the man who had betrayed him, and left him for dead.

Oliver Queen?

Slade isolated the picture, then had SIIRA run a search based on a computer simulation of how Oliver would appear today. The program reported a fifty percent possible match. It would have been a coin-flip for most, but it was confirmation enough for Slade.

His hand began to tremble slightly, and the familiar sensation startled him. Oliver's picture was beginning to set off the mirakuru rage that had remained dormant for so long. His mind began to spin backward. In his mind's eye, Slade relived the moment he arrived on Lian Yu with Billy—their band of brothers stronger than ever. Another flash of when Shado joined Slade and Oliver in the fuselage. Slade and Shado, sparring together vigorously, and as their training continued, falling for her for every moment she challenged him.

Finally he saw Oliver, drenched as he hovered over Slade with an arrow, before driving it into his head.

The crunch of plastic snapped him back to the present. He looked down and opened his hand. The computer mouse fell from it in pieces, crushed.

* * *

"Harkness is already in Hong Kong, infiltrating A.R.G.U.S."

"Then pull him back," Slade demanded.

"I'm afraid I can't do that," DeForge replied.

"*Why not*?" Slade's voice boomed in the office. Then the room fell into a tense silence. Slade stood over DeForge at his desk, fists clenched. The commander calmly stared him down.

"You gonna sit, or you gonna punch me?" he said. "Either way, make up your damned mind."

The confrontation shook Slade from his rage. He sat down, his weight balanced on the chair's edge. Neither man broke eye contact.

"Full disclosure?" DeForge said. "It hasn't been easy for me, seeing you back in their lives. But I put my feelings aside because I know how much you mean to Joe… and Adie." The commander broke eye contact at the mention of her name, a reluctant concession. "So like *hell* I'm gonna stand idly by and let you leave them again. Not to search for some bloody rich kid from Starling City."

It was Slade's turn to let his composure slip.

"Yeah, Slade—I've been keeping tabs on your work. All those late nights you've been putting in? Adie was worried." He let that land. "Why the obsession with Oliver Queen?"

Slade was caught unawares. Oliver was supposed to

be his private crusade. Now that DeForge knew, what was his next move? No sense keeping secrets now, but there was no need to tell the whole truth, either.

"Because," Slade said carefully, "he's the one who killed your brother."

DeForge scowled, and scanned Slade's face.

"If that's true, then why didn't you disclose it in your debrief?"

"No one would've believed me," Slade lied. "I needed proof he was still alive, and now I have it." He held out the photo of the man leaving the Hong Kong alleyway. DeForge looked at it, shaking his head.

"This is little more than a blur."

"*No*," Slade said, his voice a growl. "That's him. SIIRA confirms it."

"That program is far from infallible," DeForge argued. "Despite what Mr. Nakauchi might have you believe."

"How can you not want justice?" Slade demanded. "*He killed your brother!*"

"Even if that were true," DeForge replied, his composure back in place. "There's no justice to be gotten from the corpse of the wrong man." He opened a folder on his desk, and slid a sheet of paper over to Slade. "We intercepted this email, earlier this month. It's a report sent by one Tommy Merlyn to Laurel Lance. They're names I believe you'll recognize."

Slade started reading. Merlyn had traveled to Hong Kong in search of Oliver, after his email portal had been accessed in a local Internet café, but the entire incident had been a ruse designed by kidnappers to lure him there and hold him for ransom. If it hadn't been for the local police, Merlyn would have still been in their clutches, maybe even dead.

Oliver is dead, the report said, giving supporting data. *It's time to move on.*

Slade slumped under the weight of the revelation.

He had been so sure.

DeForge broke the silence. "When you asked to be kept out of the field, I honored that request, despite my misgivings," he said. "Do the same. Be with your family. Stop chasing ghosts."

Slade nodded and exited the office in a daze. As he walked down the hallway, the glow of the halogen lights harsh overhead, his footsteps echoing, he tried to clear his mind. For the briefest moment, the possibility of Oliver had reignited his hate. He was shocked at how quickly it had overwhelmed him.

Thinking of Adie and Joe, he tried to smother his rage.

Like Tommy Merlyn, he knew it was time to move on.

9

It had been nearly two years since he had returned home, yet with the passage of time came new purpose.

The new A.S.I.S. recruits, a mixture of ten men and women, were lined up against the wall of the training room. All were young and eager to impress. Future killers in the making.

Slade walked the line, evaluating them.

Amateurs.

The hair at his temples had grown grayer as the seasons had changed from winter to spring to summer. His tremors had increased, as well, and he felt one emerging in his right hand, flexing it away with a clench of the fist. Then he grabbed a set of training batons from the weapons rack.

"Does anyone know what these are?"

One of the more cocksure recruits, a man named Ian, stepped forward. He was baby-faced but handsome, his close-cropped hair colored sandy blonde. He was the spitting image of Oliver Queen. Slade did a double take, shaking it off.

"Eskrima fighting sticks," Ian said. "From the Philippines."

"You sound like a man who's held them before," Slade replied.

"I'm a black belt. So yeah, I'd say I have."

Mocking the kid's boast, Slade raised his eyebrows. "Impressive." Then he turned to the class. "Most 'masters' wouldn't declare themselves as such, unless they were seeking a challenge." His eyes fell back on Ian. "That true?"

Ian stepped forward, not backing down. He nodded toward Slade's eye patch.

"Aren't you a little handicapped, old man?"

"Disabled *and* old," Slade said. "Guess you have no excuse if you lose. Grab your weapons."

As Ian moved to the weapons rack, Slade fought off another tremor in his hand. Again he flexed it away, and walked to the mat's center, preparing for the sparring session. When he turned to face Ian, however, he found himself face to face with Oliver Queen.

It's not possible, Slade told himself. He closed his eyes, shaking off the hallucination.

When he opened them again, Ian's face had returned.

Ian stared at him, bemused. "You alright?"

"I'll be asking the same of you soon," Slade said. "*Go*."

With a nod, Ian launched himself at Slade. He showed proficiency, but in a way that suggested that he had never fought beyond the boundaries of a ring. Not at all practical. Drawing from his field experience, Slade easily parried the man's attack, then surprised him with a deke to the head, followed by a quick strike to his plant leg, flipping the young agent on his back.

"You fight like you're at the gym, kid." Slade's use of "kid" slipped out, catching him unawares. It had been Slade's nickname for Oliver back on Lian Yu, during their sparring sessions together as friends. Before the betrayal. The reverie momentarily distracted Slade, allowing Ian to flip back onto his feet and land a strike to Slade's head—a glancing blow but enough to disorient him.

A stilted fighter but hardly stupid, the young recruit took advantage of Slade's lapse in concentration, launching a variety of strikes both by stick and kick, driving him backward. Slade parried, but Ian was getting into his stride and finding his mark more often than not.

Slade's vision blurred, until all he could see was Oliver Queen, attacking him. The hallucination faded in and out with each blow like radio static caught between stations, and rage kicked in. The rush of mirakuru-driven adrenaline cleared his vision, allowing him to strike back.

He did so brutally, without mercy.

Blow after blow landed with force until, powered by the serum, he gathered in for one final strike. He reared his hand back and, in one fluid act of fury, drove his stick down through Ian's own, shattering it. The strike continued onto the man's leg, breaking the bone with a sickening snap. Ian reacted with a loud howl, jolting Slade out of his rage. He looked up.

The recruits were staring at him in horror.

Wade DeForge, passing in the hallway outside, was drawn to the commotion and entered the training hall. He locked eyes with Slade.

"What the hell is going on?"

Slade surveyed the scene, taking in Ian on the ground, writhing in pain, and the class, all riveted in place in various stages of shock. He dropped his fighting sticks onto the mat and made his way out toward the door of the training room, eyeballing DeForge as he passed.

"He asked for a fight," Slade muttered. "So I gave it to him."

"Hey," Joe said, tapping Slade's arm with the back of his hand, a few days after his fight. "You know that guy or something?"

The contact snapped Slade from his thoughts. He was staring at a pudgy-faced man at the end of the cereal aisle, who regarded him with a quizzical look before moving off. Just moments before, Slade had seen Oliver Queen standing there. He had tracked him across the crowded grocery store, following him to aisle four's multi-colored array of boxed processed grains.

His mind wandered frequently now, lost in visions

of Oliver standing in a nearby crowd, or in line at the bank, or browsing cereal in the breakfast aisle.

He chose to ignore Joe's question, instead grabbing a neon-colored box of sugar-laden children's cereal from the shelf. He showed it to his son, who was nearly three inches taller now, and edging into adolescence.

"You still eat this crap?" Slade asked.

"Nah," Joe answered, grabbing another box off the shelf—an equally egregious choice. "I eat *this* crap."

"*Much* more nutritious."

"Okay, *Mom*."

"I'll show you." Slade grabbed his son and mussed up his hair. "Ready for some footy?"

"Only if you're ready to get your butt kicked."

"We'll see about that."

As Joe headed off toward the registers, Slade glanced back toward the end of the aisle, the space between reality and fantasy beginning to blur.

The wind stretched white clouds into streaks across the blue sky, like waves across an ocean overhead. Joe kicked the ball high into the air so that it tumbled end over end until it landed in Slade's outstretched arms.

He yelled to his son across the field. "You knocked that one out of the park!"

"Practice makes perfect, right!"

The "park" was nothing more than an empty patch of field, surrounded by overgrown brush, somewhat secluded from the main road. Perfect for a quick practice session of Aussie rules football.

"Still remember how to kick it?" Joe taunted, smiling widely.

"Funny." Slade reared back and kicked the ball, his restored mirakuru strength sending it high over Joe's head and deep into the overgrown brush.

"Damn, Dad," Joe said.

"Sorry, mate. Guess I'm rusty." Slade jogged over to his son. "I'll get it."

"It's gonna take both of us." Joe started off into the tall brush.

"Keep on your toes," Slade warned. "This is adder country."

"*I know.*" Joe disappeared into the brush. Slade didn't have to see his son to know he was rolling his eyes in exasperation. The thought made him smile. Following him in, he headed northwest to Joe's northeast.

"See it yet?"

"Nope. It's pretty deep in here."

As Joe continued off, Slade heard rustling in front of him. Not easterly enough to be Joe. The movement stopped abruptly, as if whatever had been making it had been caught. Slade paused, straining to hear over the rushing wind. Then, through the vertical stalks of brown and green, about ten yards off, Slade saw him.

Oliver Queen, as real as flesh.

The young playboy flashed him an evil smile, and headed off through the brush in the direction of Joe.

"No!" Panicked, Slade started plowing his way through the thick growth, vegetation ripping from the ground. "*Oliver... no!*" He paused, breathing heavily, listening for movement.

Suddenly, there was rustling behind him. He quickly turned, on the offensive, and grabbed for Oliver's throat. What his hands found instead was the neck of his son, wide-eyed and terrified. Joe dropped the football to the ground.

Slade released Joe's neck.

He slowly backed away from his son, feeling his hand jerk.

"What the *hell*, Dad—why did you do *that*?" Joe rubbed his neck. "Who's Oliver?"

Slade opened his mouth, trying to answer, not sure of the words, when he heard more rustling in the undergrowth behind Joe. He grabbed his son, putting himself in front of the boy. He expected to see Oliver, but what he saw emerging instead was a snake. Its bands of brown and black and gray belly identified it immediately as an adder.

The snake hissed at Slade, then it lunged, its venomous teeth ready to strike. Acting on instinct, Slade dodged the strike and snatched the snake by its neck. Then he grabbed the animal's tail and ripped the body in two, blood running warm down his forearms. He dropped the ripped corpse to the dirt, where it landed with a thud, and looked into his son's eyes.

There was confusion, mixed with fear.

"He was going to hurt you," Slade said.

"I know."

"Then why are you looking at me like that?"

"Don't you get it?" Joe said, his voice hoarse. Again he rubbed his neck. "Shit, Dad, that could've been *me*." Joe spun away from his father and headed off through the brush, back to the field. Looking down, Slade saw his son's football, forgotten in the dirt.

It was covered in blood.

"Earth to Wilson." Matt Nakauchi waved his hand in front of Slade's face. "You hear anything I just said?"

Slade was sitting at his desk, absentmindedly leafing through intelligence photos sent by Harkness from the ground in Hong Kong. His mind was pulled in two directions—between thoughts of Oliver Queen as ever, and then of how close he had come to breaking his son's neck. His delusional hallucinations were growing more frequent as the weeks progressed.

He hadn't noticed Nakauchi talking to him at all.

"What do you need?" Slade asked.

"Guggino's up my ass about that hard pull on the recon from Tel Aviv. You mind heading down to archives and finding it?" Nakauchi regarded Slade, saw the haggard look on his face, mistaking it for fatigue. "The dark might do you some good, man."

Slade nodded, then headed off toward the elevators.

The archives were located in the basement, a sprawling yet claustrophobic space due to its low ceilings, crowded shelves, and sparse light. Slade didn't mind, however, finding the dark confines comforting.

While searching for the reconnaissance files, Slade stumbled across a box of archived intelligence on Lian Yu—all of the info A.S.I.S. had gathered on the island before the mission. Curiosity getting the better of him, he opened the lid and rifled through the contents, the majority of which he had been given prior to deployment.

Lying among the documents on Yao Fei, Slade found a thumb drive. It was labeled with a name that knocked the breath from his lungs.

Shado.

Back at his desk, Slade hurriedly popped the drive into his computer, revealing its contents—a series of movie files, all predating his deployment to Lian Yu. He clicked on one, opening the video large on his screen.

Emotions welled up as he saw his beloved again for the first time since the island. The videos were of a younger Shado at college, smiling and carefree, and just as beautiful as he remembered. Seeing her move and hearing her voice, it was as if she were alive. Slade reached out, forgetting for a second that she was only a picture on a screen, a minute fraction of a life suspended in time.

His reverie was broken by a familiar voice, filled with derision.

"I thought you loved me."

He looked up to find Shado standing next to him, returning for the first time since he had left the island. She sneered at him, pointing to a picture on his desk. It was of Adie and Joe.

"You lied."

Slade felt his hand jerk. He closed his eyes, simultaneously telling himself she wasn't real, while desperately craving the opposite.

"I thought you made me a *promise*."

"Oliver Queen is dead," Slade protested, desperation in his voice, trying to make her understand. "He's dead!"

"Did *you* kill him?"

"No." He reached out. "Please…"

Shado backed away, just beyond his reach.

"Then you broke your promise."

Slade watched as she disappeared before his eyes. He grabbed his head, the agony overwhelming.

"No, don't leave, wait…" He closed his eyes, fighting off the pain. When he opened them, he found Nakauchi staring at him in shock.

"Who are you talking to, man?"

Slade didn't answer. He peered around the room, trying to see where she'd gone. Then he quickly realized where he was. At work. Surrounded by prying eyes. Suddenly filled with an overwhelming urge to be anywhere other than A.S.I.S., he moved past Nakauchi and ran into the hallway, right smack into Wade DeForge.

"We need to talk," the commander said.

"Not now." Slade tried pushing past DeForge, but the way was blocked.

"That's not a request, Slade."

"Get out of my way," Slade gritted. His rage boiling over, he shoved DeForge back, throwing him into the wall. Nearby agents reacted, moving to pursue, when the commander threw up a hand, holding them off. Slade tore down the hallway and out of the building, the mirakuru nearing its crescendo.

One last domino to fall.

10

He sat alone in the den, the television blaring in competition with the cacophony inside his head, the mirakuru fueling a rage that had no outlet. He was chasing ghosts again, his mind fixated on thoughts of Shado and his failure to bring Oliver Queen to justice.

She was right, he thought. *I broke my promise.* It was as if the past few years hadn't happened.

Dark thoughts began to form, about Joe and Adie, competing with his rational thought. What right did he have to a happy life? How could he love another? This life was a sham—an expression of his failure to avenge Shado.

No, that was wrong. Why couldn't he love them too?

Slade tried to distract himself by flipping through channels on the television. He scrolled through, sounds of sports and explosions and infomercials blasting in quick succession, until he finally stopped, landing on the local news. A reporter stood in front of a screen, indicating that a storm was on its way, coming in from the east.

Joe entered the den, football under his arm, and approached Slade cautiously.

"Dad?" he said. "Want to kick the footy around before dinner?"

"Don't you listen?" Slade responded, his eyes vacant, fixed on the screen. "There's a storm."

"Come on, we haven't played in—"

"I said NO," Slade snapped at his son, the outburst driving him backward. Joe looked at his father, confused and emotional, close to tears. The confrontation drew Adie from the kitchen, where she was preparing another stew.

"Joe, can you give me a second with your dad?"

Joe nodded and slunk off toward his room, his shoulders slumped. Once he was out of earshot, Adie spun on Slade.

"What the *hell* is going on with you?"

Slade resumed flipping through stations, not answering.

"Goddammit, Slade," she snapped, stepping between him and the television. "I'm trying to talk to you."

He looked up at her, his eye cold and distant.

"Then talk."

Adie bristled at the detachment in his voice.

"I should have known," she said. "I honestly thought it would've changed you, almost dying like that, but you're still the same guy. I thought you could be here for us, but it couldn't last. I was an idiot to think that it might."

Slade kept flipping through the stations, his finger pressing the button with no aim other than to sustain the clattering din, the only protection against the building chaos in his brain. Frustrated, Adie slapped the remote out of his hand. The TV stopped on a sitcom, its laugh track weirdly out of place.

"You want back out there, fine," she pressed, "but stop torturing us with promises you can't keep."

"Promises?" Slade said, the mention of the word focusing his ire. "You have *no idea* what promises are." His rage building, Slade rose out of his chair and began to stalk toward her, the laugh track from the television continuing to blare. "What it's like to fail someone you love."

"I thought that was *us*," Adie said, her words raw.

"You never loved me," he said. "Not like she did."

"Like who?"

"Shado Fei, most likely." But it wasn't Slade's voice.

They turned to find Wade DeForge pushing through the open front door, flanked by two A.S.I.S. agents. More could be seen through the windows, taking tactical positions around the house. All were kitted out in their field gear, SIG Sauers loaded but holstered, knives sharp but still sheathed.

"We found her buried alongside her father on Lian Yu," DeForge said. There was intensity under his usual calm. Anger. "Yet oddly, there was no such grave for my brother."

"What's going on, Wade?" Adie demanded, growing wary.

DeForge slowly circled Slade, positioning himself between the two. The agents followed suit, positioning themselves either side of Slade, at the ready should anything occur. The television continued to chatter noisily in the background.

"I'm revealing him for the liar he is," DeForge replied, his eyes never leaving Slade. "You were so fixated on Oliver Queen, there had to be a reason—something you weren't saying. My curiosity got the best of me, and I wondered if he had been on that island. So I sent a team back to investigate—to find you some proof of his death. Initially my goal was to ease your mind." DeForge's jaw clenched, rare emotion welling up. "Instead, they discovered Billy's corpse. Lying exposed in a field. With *your* knife through his eye—DNA evidence proved that easily enough."

"No," Adie said. "This has to be a mistake. Why would he kill Billy?" She turned to Slade, both angry and pleading. "Tell him he's wrong, dammit!"

Slade didn't respond.

The sitcom's laugh track suddenly cut out, preempted by a special report. Breaking news out of Starling City. A graphic flashed across the screen.

Lost Billionaire Found.

Then the anchor began to speak.

"Oliver Queen is alive," he said. "The Starling City resident was found by fishermen in the North China sea just five days ago, yet fully five years after he went missing, and was presumed dead…" Photos of Oliver flashed on the television, as the reporter continued. "News of his recovery sent ripples through the markets, including the Australian Securities Exchange, which closed notably higher." The noise in his head subsided, his rage finding a singular, deadly focus.

Finally, he knew. *Oliver is alive.*

And it's time to make him pay.

Slade turned to walk out the door, but was cut off by two of the agents.

"You treacherous bastard," DeForge said. "Do you have *nothing* to say?"

Slade turned back toward his commander, staring him down.

"Oliver Queen betrayed me," Slade growled. "And for that, he will suffer. *Just like your brother…*"

"Oh God…" Adie said.

"…And I will put down anyone—*anyone*—who stands in my way."

DeForge drew his weapon, the other agents following suit.

"This is your only goddamn warning. Come with us peacefully, or I will shoot you down in your own house."

"Don't test me," Slade said.

"Would everyone just stand down!" said Adie. "Slade, don't do this!"

"This is your last chance," DeForge replied, but Slade

turned his back on his commander and started toward the door. DeForge gave the nod to his men and they advanced, preparing to subdue him. The agent nearest Slade grabbed for his wrist to restrain him. Slade spun, taking the agent's arm and snapping it over his shoulder. As the man howled in agony, Slade unsheathed the agent's own knife and stabbed him through the heart.

Gunfire erupted as four agents who had been waiting outside burst through the windows. Slade ripped the knife from the dead agent, re-arming himself, and pushed the body in front of him as a temporary shield from the close-range fire. Seeing an opening, he threw the knife into the head of the second flanking agent, his body hitting the floor with a sickening thud next to Adie's feet.

DeForge advanced, keeping between Slade and Adie. He pulled the trigger, firing round after round, driving Slade into the den toward one half of the group of breaching agents. The others followed him in from behind, but their quarry moved too fast for a hit, rolling for cover behind his armchair. Then, using his extraordinary strength, he grabbed a wooden credenza and threw it into two of the officers. One managed to avoid the impact, but the other was battered into the wall, his skull crushed.

Slade continued to move, racing around the perimeter, drawing gunfire before purposely flipping into the room's center. He paused for the briefest of moments, allowing the men to take aim, then he leapt out of their sights. The resulting fire took out one of the agents, leaving holes in the wall behind him. Through to the foyer, DeForge managed to hit the deck, still firing, but a stray bullet caught Adie.

She gasped, but didn't cry out.

"No!" DeForge stopped shooting as she slid to the floor, her body obstructed by a bookcase. He moved closer to her, crouching all the way, but it was too late. The bullet had struck her temple, killing her instantly.

Oblivious to what had occurred, Slade rushed the remaining men, engaging them in close quarters hand-to-hand. He broke one agent's leg with a vicious downward kick and smashed his face in with an elbow, killing him instantly. The last agent, attacking from behind, was able to find purchase with his knife in Slade's upper back, but the blow did nothing to abate the deadly assault. Slade simply pulled the man off and threw him through the wall toward Joe's bedroom.

Then he turned his attention to Wade DeForge. The commander gave a guttural roar and rushed forward, guns blazing. Slade ducked well enough to avoid a headshot, taking bullets to the shoulder and upper arm. Undeterred, he used one arm to grab DeForge by the neck, while using the other to bend the man's gun hand slowly backward toward his own body. Then he squeezed the trigger finger, sending four bullets through DeForge's chest and stomach.

Shock flashed through DeForge's eyes. Then, they rolled back in his head.

Slade dropped the commander, watching his body hit the wooden floor with a sickening thud. When he looked up, he saw Joe standing not five feet behind him, by his mother's body. She lay partially propped against the bookcase.

A pool of blood was beginning to bloom on the boy's chest. The bullets had passed clean through DeForge's body, striking Joe directly in the heart. He tried to mouth something before falling to the ground in a heap.

The sight staggered Slade, breaking through his rage. He took a step toward his dead son and ex-wife, eyes welling. *What have I done?* Slade fell to his knees, lifted his son's form, and found himself on the edge of hysterics, regret and rage bursting forth, Joe and Adie's blood on his hands.

"This is *his* fault."

Suddenly he stopped, and looked up to find Shado standing over him.

"He's to blame," she hissed, "for all of this." She pointed to the television, the news report still playing amidst the carnage. Footage of Oliver Queen filled the screen.

Slade dropped his son's body and stood up, the rage overtaking him once again.

"Find him," Shado said. "Make him pay."

She caressed his face.

"Avenge me."

Slade nodded, dead focus in his eyes.

"He will have allies."

"Then so will you," Shado answered.

Slade nodded, a plan beginning to take shape.

"This time, I will wait."

"Yes…"

"When he least expects it, I will strike…"

"*Yes…*"

"…and I will make him suffer."

2

ROCHEV

1

THE PRESENT

Dark, melancholy clouds blanketed the morning sky in Starling City. The rain had been falling consistently and showed no signs of letting up, enveloping the skyline of the beautiful city in gray and rendering it nearly invisible.

From her corner office window at Stellmoor International, Isabel Rochev watched through golden-brown eyes as pedestrians ran for cover. Her long brunette hair was lightly curled and flowed perfectly over her shoulders. Her face was stern and expressionless. She wore thick black stockings to complement a maroon pencil skirt, which hugged her slender figure in all the right ways. She completed her outfit out with a soft cream silk blouse, which was buttoned up to the collar and left enough room to show off a small, understated necklace.

Dark chocolate wooden bookcases lined the walls, stacked with books and magazines. The walls were covered in art that she had collected over the years—Isabel took great pride in her collection of original pieces. An abstract painting was propped against one of the walls, the canvas splattered with deep tones of red and a charcoal gray. Her newest acquisition, its colors appeared to vibrate. On the opposite wall was a framed sketch of Starling City that Isabel had bought while at a local art fair many years ago, when she had first arrived in the area. The tall buildings lent themselves to an elegant rendering.

Turning, she moved to her glass desk. No personal effects interrupted her workspace. As a young girl, Isabel had dreamed of a life where she would have a thriving career that she had built on her own, and that at the end of the day she would go home to have a family by her side. She had believed she could have it all—it wasn't a question of how, but of when.

Today all she needed was a computer and her favorite ballpoint pen, feeling most at ease when she was working. She perched her reading glasses on her nose and returned to her keyboard, typing furiously. Abruptly the glass door to her office swung open as her assistant, Theodore Decklin, entered with a latte and a notepad in hand.

"Good morning, Miss Rochev," Decklin said as he placed the latte next to Isabel's computer. "I was hoping we could go over today's agenda."

Isabel continued to work without acknowledging him, so he leafed nervously through the pages in his notepad and continued.

"Today you have a meeting with the board at 10:30, followed by a business lunch with Mr. Wu—anywhere in particular I should make a reservation?" he asked.

Isabel removed her glasses. "It is 10:15, and I am not done with the proposal for the meeting about which you so *kindly* reminded me," Isabel said tersely. "So I suggest you leave me to do my work." Without another word, Decklin turned on his heel and left her office. Isabel rolled her eyes, put her glasses back on, and returned to business. Her fingers typed with precision as she fell into a rhythm. A slight smile played across her face as she read through her report.

Suddenly a loud and vocal commotion erupted outside of her office. She glanced toward the door, then returned to her keyboard.

The exchange continued, and became louder.

I'm not paying them to talk, Isabel fumed, and she rose from her desk, grabbing her files and stepping briskly toward the office door. She pulled it open, and discovered that most of her staff were huddled together, staring at the television monitor. BREAKING NEWS flashed upon the screen.

"Oliver Queen is alive," the newscaster announced.

The blood drained from Isabel's face, and she felt a moment of dizziness. The Stellmoor employees buzzed with questions.

"What does this mean?"

"Where was he?"

"Is he coming back to the city?"

But she didn't hear any of their inane chatter. Tears started to burn in her eyes—tears that she hadn't allowed herself for years. The files fell freely from her grasp, hitting the floor with a clatter.

She felt the rate of her breathing start to pick up rapidly, as her employees began to turn in her direction. Several looked shocked at the emotion that was evident in her expression. Some looked away, as if afraid of what it might mean.

2

SIX YEARS EARLIER

Isabel hopped off the subway and alighted in Starling City. Her hair was pulled back into a loose bun and she wore thick-framed glasses. Patent leather flats accompanied a tweed knee-length dress that was a little too tight for her full figure. She looked a little frumpy, and slightly unsure of herself. A business student and time-poor, she quickly checked her watch and picked up the pace as she reached the sidewalk.

I'm going to be late…

She wove her way gingerly through the pedestrians, trying to appear invisible as she passed them. When she finally reached her destination, the headquarters of the mega-corporation Queen Consolidated, Isabel smiled as she entered the building.

"Good morning, Bobby!" She greeted the security guard as she swiped her QC badge to enter.

"And hello to you, Miss Rochev," Bobby replied. "You look happy for a Monday."

"Not much to complain about when you intern at the number one company in the city," Isabel said, grinning now as she headed for the elevator.

A few minutes later Isabel arrived at her cubicle, placed her bag down, and logged into her computer. She walked over to her cubicle neighbor, Marcus, to see his head down, buried into his arms on his desk—asleep.

Isabel giggled.

"I guess I don't need to ask you how wild your weekend was."

Sitting up with a jolt, Marcus looked groggily at her.

"Ergh," he responded. "I hate Mondays. I have all this work due to Mr. Klein by the afternoon staff meeting. I'm not nearly finished, and this hangover won't quit."

"Okay, well, I'm happy to help you if you need it," Isabel said.

Marcus smiled weakly. "You love work way too much for an intern, my friend."

Later in the afternoon, Isabel and her friend Becca caught up while en route to a meeting. They chattered down the hall, carrying their notes with them.

"So tell me about your weekend," Isabel said. "Anything fun and noteworthy happen?"

"Nothing out of the ordinary. I partied way too hard at Spark."

"What's Spark?"

"It's a club! Geez, Isabel, you *have* to come next time—the boys are so cute there, and they'll buy you endless shots." Isabel smiled shyly at this revelation. It sounded pretty far out of her comfort zone. "Then I don't really remember how," Becca continued, "but I ended up at Big Belly Burger, and I woke up yesterday with this massive hangover." She frowned, remembering the pain, then brightened. "But next time—you are coming!"

"Yeah, well… maybe," Isabel said doubtfully. "I'm not much of a drinker." This warranted an eye roll from her friend.

"So what did *you* do this weekend?" Becca asked.

"I pretty much just worked on my reports that were due to Mr. Klein. I wanted to get a head start on things. Then I went for a jog—"

"Seriously," Becca interrupted, "you *need* to come out with me—you need a life. It can't be all about business school and this internship."

Isabel turned without stopping. "I don't see anything wrong with getting my work done," she protested. "Plus isn't now the time where we *should* be all work and no play—"

WHAM!

She ran right into someone as she turned the corner into the hall. Her files and notes flew up into the air and landed, scattered, on the ground. Recovering her balance, she bent rapidly to pick them up.

Becca burst into giggles.

"I am so sorry! I am so sorry, I wasn't paying attention," Isabel babbled as she looked up to see who she had hit. It was none other than the CEO of Queen Consolidated, Robert Queen. Isabel felt her heart start to race and her stomach drop to the floor. Then, to her surprise, a loud, contagious laugh escaped her victim's mouth as he bent down to help Isabel pick up her work.

"It's my fault really," he protested. "I was too distracted by such a young woman saying that her life should be all work and no play, Miss..." Mr. Queen said as he handed Isabel her files.

"Rochev," Isabel managed to croak out. "Isabel Rochev."

Ohmigod, he's talking to me.

"Isabel. What a beautiful name. What department do you work in that keeps you from living your life in such a way?"

"I'm just an intern, Mr. Queen," she replied meekly.

"Intern? All the more reason to be out there enjoying yourself—you only live once, you know?" he said with a wink.

"Yes..."

"What is it that you want to do, Miss Isabel Rochev?" Mr. Queen asked.

"She wants to take your job," Becca blurted out.

"Well... not exactly," Isabel said, glaring daggers at her friend. *I can't believe she said that!*

"My job!" he responded, and he smiled. "I like that.

Hopefully someday," he added without taking his eyes off her. "A word of advice, though, since you're going to be taking over for me one day—business is supposed to be interesting, and fun. If you concentrate too much on the tedium, you'll miss out on all the good." Mr. Queen gave Isabel another wink, then adjusted his tie.

His confidence was almost intoxicating.

"I hope to be seeing more of you, Miss Rochev," Mr. Queen said, placing a hand on Isabel's shoulder as he moved past her to continue down the hall. She and Becca turned slowly to watch—his swagger undeniably attractive—as Isabel touched her warm cheeks, which were flushed with embarrassment. She took a breath, feeling completely the fool. To her surprise, however, she also felt intrigued, and wanted more of whatever it was that she had just had.

A few days later, Isabel was in her cubicle working diligently on a complicated report after business hours. She was startled when her intern advisor, Mr. Klein, suddenly appeared, peering down at her, giving her a strange look.

"Working late again?" he said. "Isabel, I can't tell you how impressed I am with your work. The presentation you did with your team went above and beyond the call of duty." Humbled, she thanked him profusely and expressed her gratitude for all his support and guidance. But she could tell there was something else on his mind.

"You've made an impression on me," he said, "and, it would appear, you've also made an impression on Mr. Queen. He'd like to speak with you directly… in his office."

Isabel gulped hard. "Mr. Queen?" she said. "Why does he want to talk to me?"

Mr. Klein smiled. "Don't worry, Isabel, your future here at Queen Consolidated will be bright and long, of that I'm sure. There's no reason you should be intimidated." With that Mr. Klein went on his way, leaving Isabel in a panic-stricken daze.

What did he mean by that? she wondered.

She got up abruptly, reached into her desk drawer, and pulled out some perfume and gum. After a few puffs of perfume, and shoving gum into her mouth, Isabel headed for the elevator. During the ride up, she fretted about what might be waiting for her at the top. Emerging from the elevator, she saw Robert Queen standing next to the large glass doors. He was dressed in an impeccable suit.

"Miss Rochev, please come in!" He beamed as Isabel entered his office, outfitted with a lot of dark, expensive-looking furniture. She sat down nervously in a leather club chair, scanning her surroundings, admiring the artwork on the walls and the array of books displayed on high shelves. There was a framed photo on the side table next to her—it was a photo of the Queen family. Everyone who worked at Queen Consolidated recognized the golden ones. Robert and his wife, Moira, were smiling while Oliver and Thea made faces into the camera.

Isabel smiled. Suddenly her eyes went wide as she realized she still was chewing her gum.

He'll think I'm an idiot—a stupid little girl.

As Queen turned to step behind his desk, she pulled it out of her mouth. Glancing around, she couldn't find a wastebasket, so she slipped her hand under the edge of the chair and stuck the gum there.

"Your daughter is adorable, Mr. Queen," she said nervously, motioning to the photo.

"Oh, don't let her cuteness fool you," Mr. Queen said. "She's a handful, that one—but so smart and beautiful. I love her for keeping me on my toes." He smiled proudly as he offered Isabel a glass of Scotch from a nearby sideboard. She set the glass on the table, hoping he wouldn't notice.

"Most girls tend to do that to their fathers," she said, and she laughed in spite of herself. He smiled in agreement.

"My son, Oliver, he was easy as a child," he said. "We'd play catch, or I'd take him to a game and he would be the happiest kid in the world. Now, Thea, on the other hand, she loves to challenge me in ways I never thought possible, always asking for the moon, and I always try to give it to her." Mr. Queen was glowing with pride as he spoke. That made Isabel smile.

Abruptly he grabbed his glass of Scotch and raised it.

"Cheers," he said. "To challenges and new possibilities."

"Oh… I probably shouldn't," she replied, eyeing her glass and trying not to sound too meek. "I'm not much of a drinker."

"Nonsense, this is the 'mixing work and play' part of the job, Miss Rochev," Mr. Queen said, giving her a wink as he took a sip from his drink and sat down on the couch opposite her. "Still, you're probably wondering why you're here. I can assure you, it's nothing to be alarmed about.

"As you know," he continued, "being CEO of this great company comes with great responsibility, and I take pride in knowing what everyone is doing within these walls. I asked Mr. Klein how the presentations were going, and he immediately singled you out among our fine crop of interns this year." Isabel was thrilled to hear this, but tried her best to hide her growing excitement.

"And as much as I hate to admit it, I am not getting any younger," Mr. Queen continued. "I won't be around forever and even though my son, Oliver, will someday take over the company, Queen Consolidated will only survive with good, strong-willed people on the board helping him, supporting him. We're only as good as our best employees." He reached for his Scotch and took another sip. Then he peered at her intently.

"I'd like to become your mentor, Miss Rochev. You

show great promise, are a true asset to the company, and I want to make sure you get the chance to shine."

What... how...

Isabel sat very still, unable to speak. She wasn't exactly sure what she could say that wouldn't sound completely unprofessional—and then it would be over. She ran her fingers through her hair, thinking carefully about how to thank him.

"Mr. Queen, I don't even know what to say," she replied slowly. "Working here has been a dream of mine for so long. I love coming to the office every day, and I am so flattered that you see potential in me. I'd be honored if you became my mentor." She paused, trying to maintain her composure. She then picked up her drink and extended it toward him.

"To new challenges and endless possibilities," Isabel said as the two clinked their glasses together.

3

Monday morning, and Isabel arrived at her cubicle, as usual. She walked with confidence and purpose, dressed in a sleek black pencil skirt with a pink long-sleeved shirt on top. She had traded in her patent leather flats for a refined black stiletto. Her hair had a light curl to it, and her heavy glasses were nowhere to be seen.

"Oh… you look fancy, who are you trying to impress?" Becca inquired.

Isabel smiled, knowing she looked good. "No one."

"Perhaps… Mr. Queen?" Becca suggested.

"Becca, he's my boss!" she protested. "Actually, I'm going to try to make the intern mixer tonight, if I can get everything done in time."

"Finally!" Becca squealed. "We get you out of this cubicle and into the world with us! I'm so excited!"

For more weeks than she could count, Robert had been Isabel's mentor, meeting with her regularly, showing her the ropes. She had already learned so much–things she would never find in a book or back in a classroom. She felt as if she mattered in some way to the company, and, more importantly, to some*one* in the company. Robert had real life experience—at building an empire, and making a name for himself.

That was what she wanted, and to get it she had to continue making changes. One of them was to practice the art of socializing.

The end of the day arrived, and the two women prepared to leave. They were interrupted when Mr. Klein popped over to tell Isabel that Mr. Queen wanted to see her. She managed to hide her excitement at the prospect of another late night spent with Robert, talking endlessly about business, and even life in general.

Her friend shot her a look.

"Next time, Becca, I swear," Isabel said as she grabbed her belongings and headed for the elevator to the top floor.

Takeout Chinese food was spread out on the coffee table, mixed with work papers. Isabel sat on the floor eating with chopsticks while Robert sat on the couch across from her. She laughed, despite the fact that her mouth was filled with lo mein.

"I can't believe you were arrested in college!" she said. "That's insane."

"Oh, yes, I was young and dumb as most teenagers tend to be—it's probably where Oliver, gets it from," Mr. Queen said as he stuffed a dumpling into his mouth. He looked at his watch. "It's past nine o'clock, please don't let me keep you if you have weekend plans."

"I'm right where I want to be," Isabel said as she scooped noodles into her mouth.

Robert grinned, looking pleased with Isabel's response.

"So, what about you?" he asked. "What crazy stories do you have from your childhood?"

Isabel put down her chopsticks and took a long sip of water, clearly not wanting to give away too much information.

"C'mon, Isabel," he prompted. "I've been your mentor for four months now. This is the third Friday in a row we've sat and chatted over cheap takeout, I think I have earned the right to know a little bit more about you. Where are you from? What are your parents like? They must be proud of their daughter." He moved from the couch to join Isabel on the floor.

"As cliché as it sounds, my parents were simple people," she replied reluctantly. "I was born in a small town in Russia where they were also born. My father, whose name was Viktor, made some poor business choices while we lived there. He became indebted to the Bratva, the Russian mob, and, well…" She stopped for a moment, before continuing. "When I was nine years old, they ended up taking both my parents' lives." Isabel looked away, and tears slowly welled up in her brown eyes. "So I was shipped off to the States as an orphan. I don't remember much—I feel like I've blocked a lot of those terrible memories from my mind.

"From that time on, I spent my childhood going from facility to facility, until finally I landed in a foster home. The couple that raised me are lovely people, but I never felt a very strong connection to them, which is why I think I'm sometimes unemotional about things... except for right now," Isabel said, wiping away her tears and feeling as if she could die from embarrassment.

Robert reached for her hand. She tried to hide her reaction, but then, in that instant, it didn't feel all that surprising. In fact, it felt right and—above all—comforting to her. She smiled at the gesture, wiping her eyes again.

"You are a strong... and special young woman, Isabel," Robert said. "I am in awe of you." Isabel felt her heart leap at the compliment, and did her best to brush it aside.

"So I just poured my heart and soul into school," she continued. "My parents—the real ones—always told me they wanted my life to be different from theirs. I made a promise to them, and to myself, that one day I would make something of myself. That one day people would know my name, and it would *mean* something..."

"That is very admirable, Isabel," Robert interjected. "However, as I've said to you before, don't forget that there is more to life than work." He paused, then continued, "Work is wonderful, and gives you a purpose, but don't let that be the only purpose you have for yourself. Don't be afraid to take a chance, every now and again."

Isabel looked into his eyes as she felt his thumb softly stroke her hand, and realized her mouth had gone dry and she wasn't physically able to speak.

"I know what it's like to come from nothing," he said. "I remember coming to Starling, and not knowing what to do with myself. I had so many doors slammed in my face. But you and I share a lot of the same qualities, it seems. One of them being perseverance.

"Many people assume that this name, this empire, the money is all something I've had my whole life, but the truth of the matter is, I married into the money, the connections—and the good and bad that come with that. I know what it's like to struggle—to want and see something for yourself that some days just seems so unobtainable. Yet I'm living proof that it *is* obtainable."

Isabel smiled, appreciating Robert's willingness to share.

"It's given me such joy to watch you grow these past few months, and there isn't a shadow of a doubt that good fortune will come to you." He winked. "And that people will know your name."

Isabel beamed at his words. She slowly let go of his hand and leaned into him, grabbing the fortune cookie from the table behind him.

"For now, I'll have to settle on a fortune cookie,"

she said as she unwrapped the cookie from its plastic. Robert grabbed a cookie for himself. Isabel carefully cracked open hers, popping half of it into her mouth as she unraveled the fortune.

"The greatest risk is not taking one," she quoted, looking coquettishly at him.

"A voyage will fill your life with untold mysteries," Robert read enigmatically, looking at Isabel.

The two sat in silence for a moment, breathing each other in. Isabel reminded herself of her position—that she was an intern, and Robert was her mentor—but her heart yearned for him. She wanted to find out all there was to know about him, but she stopped herself—realizing her feelings were growing into something beyond the professional. He was the reason she got out of bed in the morning. He was the reason she had changed her wardrobe, and he was the reason she had pep in her step.

Suddenly, flooded with emotions she didn't know how to process, Isabel reached for her bag, thanked Robert abruptly for a good time, and left his office.

4

Isabel stood in the gathering gloom on the cold doorstep of the Queen mansion, wrapped up in fear.

She had been curious for quite some time about Robert's home—how he lived, how lavish his home really was. Standing there nervous in her slate-gray business suit, in her feeble attempt to keep this uncharacteristic personal setting professional, she finally found the courage and knocked on the door. Robert answered in jeans and a polo shirt, a casual look Isabel wasn't used to seeing.

"Isabel, so happy you could stop by," he said, giving her a hug. "Please come in and be warm."

As she entered she couldn't help but gasp at its beauty and scope. Isabel's entire apartment could have fit into the foyer, with its wide-open space and art scattered on the walls. An array of American landscapes surrounded her. A large golden chandelier hung from the ceiling, looking impressively expensive. Robert led her into the living room, where they were met by plush white furniture and a black grand piano in the corner. The gas fireplace was lit with a roaring flame.

"This house is incredible," she finally said.

"Thank you, although I can't take credit for much," Robert replied. "My wife hired decorators, and an old college friend of mine did the overall design."

Isabel carefully sat on a pristine white sofa and put her briefcase on her lap. She opened it up, pulled out several folders, and placed them on the glass coffee table.

"Here are the files you requested," Isabel stammered, trying to keep composure as Robert took a seat next to her. *Why didn't I sit in a chair?* she chided herself.

"Thank you, but I have to be honest," Robert said with a note of reluctance, "I called for them as an excuse to see you." He stopped, and seemed to gather his thoughts. "I can't stop thinking about you," he confessed. "I had to see you."

Isabel blushed at his honesty. It had been several days since their encounter in the office, and despite the effort she had put into maintaining a purely professional attitude, she was afraid and excited by what this meant. Her head asked so many questions, but her heart was fluttering with emotion.

"Is your... family at home?" she stuttered.

"Moira and Thea are having a mother-daughter weekend in the city, and Oliver is out for the night with his friend, Tommy. He won't be returning till much later, if at all." He smiled, then placed his arm along the back of the couch. After a moment, he spoke again. "I know you probably think this is wrong of me. I know, I am married… but there's just something about you, Isabel."

His words hung there in the air, and she was unsure what to do.

Finally her emotions overcame her, pushing rational thought to the back of her mind. Like a spectator hovering outside of her own body, she felt herself lean closer to him on the couch, and he did the same. The two hovered with their lips close—timid and eager at the same time. Finally, Robert pressed his lips to hers, as Isabel felt the kiss for which she had been longing.

He put his hands on her face, and Isabel melted, putting her arms around his neck, taking his advice and letting go of herself, feeling his heart beating against hers. Her heart, ready for whatever was to come as Robert lifted his hands off her face and moved them down to unbutton her blouse.

They lay on the Persian carpet, wrapped naked in blankets by the fire. Isabel nestled herself into Robert's chest and was taken aback by how natural it felt. She realized how strong her feelings were.

"I don't want this to end," she said, searching his eyes.

Robert kissed her forehead. "Nor do I."

Just then, a car sped into the driveway. Robert rose quickly, going to the window. She followed, and saw

Oliver stumble out of a car, clearly drunk. Robert rolled his eyes at his son's childish actions, and Isabel hurriedly started to gather her belongings.

"What should I do?" she asked.

"Don't worry," he replied. "Oliver won't remember anything in the morning, regardless of what he sees. And you can leave out the east wing of the house— there's a side door."

Despite his calm, Isabel quickly dressed, then scurried over to the door, kissing Robert on the lips. She slipped out into the night and peeked her head around the corner to see Oliver and his friend shouting in the driveway.

"I wanted to go home with her," Oliver shouted.

"One little problem, buddy," his companion replied. "What would you do tomorrow morning when you woke up and it wasn't Laurel. It would be Sara—her sister, and there'd be hell to pay."

"That's easy," Oliver said, slurring the words slightly. "After I'm done with Sara, I'll just sneak into Laurel's room and act like nothing happened. I'm smooth like that, Tommy." He stumbled toward the door.

"Oh, yeah, real smooth," Tommy said as the two entered the mansion. Isabel waited for the door to shut, and then ran to her car. She jammed the key into the ignition, started the engine, and drove into the night, her heart racing.

Never again, she promised herself—but she knew she was lying.

5

A trail of clothes led to Isabel's bedroom, and right up to her bed. She and Robert lay tangled together in the sheets. They smiled at each other, happy and content. She rolled toward him, nestling herself in his arms as she liked to do after lovemaking.

"I love you," Isabel said, and even after all the weeks, she was surprised at how naturally it came out.

"I love you, too," Robert said, kissing her on the forehead.

"I wish we could stay here forever," she murmured. "Forget about everything else in the world, and just be."

"Why don't we?" he asked. She just laughed at him, reaching for her robe and getting out of bed. "I'm serious, Isabel," Robert said, sitting up in the bed. "I have been doing some thinking, and I think it's time I left Moira."

She turned to him.

"Excuse me?"

Robert got out of bed and together they moved

to the kitchen. He went over to the coffeemaker and turned it on, familiar with the way it worked.

"Yes, I think it's about time I left Moira," he repeated. "We're terribly unhappy together, and I can't stand being away from you. When I'm with my kids or Moira… I'm only thinking of you." He handed her a cup of coffee.

"I can't believe this," Isabel breathed. "This is amazing," she added, and then she frowned. "But what about the children? What about your reputation?"

"It won't be easy by any means," he acknowledged. "I'm still a father, and I want to be there for my kids, have custody of them—which I'm sure Moira will fight. Still, you and I could have a fresh start together. I've been dying to retire. You can take over, and then *you* can bring home the bacon."

"I… I don't know what to say," Isabel said. "You've taught me so much, but I'm nowhere near ready."

Robert went to her, grabbed both of her hands, and placed them on his chest.

"It would happen gradually," he said. "You'd take part in more and more of the day-to-day processes, slowly but surely, so no one becomes alarmed. Even after I step down, I'll work with you behind the scenes. The most important thing will be trust." He peered into her eyes. "There is no one I trust more than you."

"Not even Oliver?" Isabel said. "And what about Walter?" she asked. Walter Steele was Robert's CEO and closest friend.

"Oliver is young and foolish, and wasn't born a

leader," Robert said ruefully. "Walter will be taken care of—I owe him that much—and you, Isabel Rochev, were born to lead. You will be my future. I promise."

Overwhelmed by his words, she kissed him passionately as he pulled off her robe.

Isabel and Becca sat in a booth in an upscale bar near Morton Square. Isabel took a sip of her wine as her friend scanned the room.

"Oh! He's cute!" Becca said as she motioned toward a guy at the bar. "He's in a suit, too, which means he probably has a job."

Isabel glanced over at the guy, and shrugged.

"What, you don't think he's cute?" Becca asked.

"Look at his left hand," Isabel said, smiling and taking another sip of her wine. "He's married."

Becca slammed her fist on the table.

"Seriously! All the good ones are either married or gay, I swear."

"Don't I know it," Isabel said under her breath.

"Care to elaborate on that, missy?" Becca said.

Isabel shrugged her shoulders and took another sip, evading the topic.

"Well, take some advice from someone who… knows someone who knows," Becca said. "Don't get mixed up with married men. No matter what they say, they never leave their wives." She summoned the waitress over for another round.

* * *

THUD. THUD. THUD.

Isabel opened the door to her apartment, and was shocked to find Robert on her stoop—with suitcases.

"What are you doing here?" she asked. It was winter, and the hall was cold.

"Isabel, we've been together for almost a year now," he said, "and it's all become clear to me. I want to start a new life together, leave this one behind, start over somewhere new where no one knows us."

Suddenly she realized he wasn't there to move in, and found herself skeptical about this sudden urge to leave town.

"What about your children," she said, "and being a father to them? What about the company, and all of those wonderful challenges you said I... we could take on?" In response he stepped through the door and grabbed her tightly round the waist, brushed a lock of her hair out of her face.

"One day when my children are older and in love... they'll understand why I'm doing this," he said. "For now, let's just go, and leave it all behind."

Is this for real? Isabel thought to herself. For as long as she could remember she'd wanted Robert to say these words to her, yet now that the moment appeared to have arrived, she didn't know what to say. She wasn't even sure how she felt.

What about the work I've done? she thought furiously,

turning away. *What about the company you promised me? What about my career?* Questions flooded her mind, but she turned back and saw the love in his eyes. In that moment, she realized that was the only answer she needed.

"Give me twenty minutes to pack my bags."

At the airport, Isabel was thrilled at the sight of Robert's private jet on the runway. She was wearing a long coat that billowed in the wind. Robert put on his sunglasses, ready for his escape to begin.

"I've never been to Fiji before!" Isabel said.

"Get used to it, my love." He swung his arm around her shoulders, kissing the top of her head. "We can go anywhere and everywhere you want to go, from here on out." Her head spun at the possibility of becoming a jetsetter, a far cry from the lost orphan she'd always felt she was, deep in her heart. As they strolled onto the tarmac their luggage was loaded onto the plane, and as they took their seats they were handed two glasses of champagne. Isabel extended hers instantly.

"A toast—to a day that I have been waiting for my whole life," she said. "You have made me something that I never thought I could be—happy. I owe you so much, and I cannot wait to start this journey with you." Tears appeared at the corners of her eyes as they embraced and clinked their champagne glasses together. Isabel took a long sip, then sat back, smiling in anticipation of their future life together.

Robert's phone buzzed. He reached deep into his pocket, and when he pulled it out, he saw a text from Moira.

Please call me—it's Thea.

Worried, he quickly dialed the number.

"What's happened?" Robert asked.

"Thea was practicing jumps on her horse, Apollo." Moira sounded terrible. "Somehow she lost control and was thrown. She's broken her arm in two places, and one of them is bad. I'm at Starling General, and she's asking for you. Where are you?"

Torn, Robert looked at Isabel, who was finishing her champagne and giving him a puzzled look.

"I'll be there," Robert said, and he ended the call.

"Everything okay?" Isabel asked.

He didn't know what to say as reality struck home. It dawned on him that as much as he wanted to start a new life with Isabel, it wasn't that easy. If it wasn't Thea, then it would be Oliver, or even Moira. Try as he might, he could never escape Starling City. His business, his name—everything that came with his position would follow him.

Thea's accident drove home a hard truth—one he couldn't avoid. Robert knew that a life with Isabel would mean a life where his kids looked at him differently. Or perhaps he wouldn't see them at all. Oliver and Thea would know he was capable of lying to them, shattering all that was once good in their relationship. They would look at him as a cheater, and the thought of losing his children scared Robert to his core.

Oliver and Thea were his life even if that meant a life with Moira.

"I have to go, Isabel," he said finally.

"Go? But our plane is about to leave!" She stared at him as he threw his bag over his shoulder.

"It's Thea…" Robert began. "She broke her arm falling off her horse, she's in the hospital, scared, she needs me. I have to go to her."

"Kids break bones all the time," Isabel protested.

"Isabel, I can't—not today. Tomorrow we'll go, my darling. I promise." He touched her face. As tears welled up in her eyes, Robert turned and started to walk toward the cabin door.

"Robert… please! You said you loved me," she cried out. He turned back.

"Isabel, try to understand, I'm a father. I have to be there for my children. They are everything to me." He went silent, and then added, "Tomorrow will be here before you know it."

Isabel wanted to believe him, but she knew Becca was right. A married man would never leave his family. She had been delusional in thinking she could change him.

"But you told me yourself that Thea isn't yours," she said, rising from her seat. "It was Moira who betrayed you. How can you go running back to someone who doesn't love you like I do?"

Robert went stiff at the mention of Thea's paternity, and in that moment she knew she had lost him. Years ago, Moira had slept with Malcolm Merlyn. For the longest time Robert had blamed himself—he'd told Isabel as much—but he had finally let go of that guilt.

Or so it had seemed.

"Thea is mine, Isabel," he said. "She may not have my blood running through her veins, but I've been there since the day she was born. I'm sorry, my love, but after work tomorrow we're off to Fiji, I promise."

She walked over to him, held his face in her hands, and looked into his eyes.

"I'm sorry," she said. "I know you need to do this. Tomorrow after work."

6

The next day Isabel got off the subway and walked, blinking, into the sunlight. She put on her sunglasses and turned toward the office, her high heels clicking on the pavement as she rolled her suitcase beside her.

"Good morning, Bobby," she said as she pulled out her badge.

"Morning, Miss Rochev," he replied. She swiped her badge, but there was a loud, obnoxious *beep* and the screen flashed DENIED.

That's weird, she thought, and she tried it again. Bobby stepped off of his stool and came over.

"Sometimes the magnetic strip gets worn out, Miss Rochev," he said as he took the badge from her hand. "Let me have a look." He examined the badge, rubbing the magnetic strip to remove any debris, but couldn't find any damage. So he walked to a nearby phone and placed a call that she couldn't hear.

Then he returned.

"Can you just let me up, please, Bobby?" she said, keeping her voice steady. "Mr. Queen is expecting me."

"Actually, Miss Rochev, I need you to stay right here for the moment," he replied, and the tone of his voice had changed.

"Is anything wrong?"

"Just stay put for the moment, Miss Rochev," Bobby said as he returned to his security post and began checking in other employees. Her worry grew stronger as more employees passed her. Suddenly Walter Steele emerged from an elevator car and crossed the lobby. Isabel felt a sense of relief seeing him, and she smiled at him.

"Miss Rochev," Walter said, his expression unreadable.

"Good morning, Walter," she answered. "How are you doing? Is Robert in yet?"

"I'm sorry to be the one to tell you, Miss Rochev, but Queen Consolidated no longer requires your... assistance. Your position has been eliminated."

Isabel felt her heart sink to the floor.

"What do you mean, eliminated?"

"If you would be so kind as to leave the premises as soon as possible, I would appreciate it," Walter said firmly. "We will forward your personal belongings to your home address."

Isabel's confusion crystallized into anger, and before she knew it, she was engulfed with rage.

"He put you up to this, didn't he?" she demanded,

her voice rising. "Robert Queen can't even be man enough to do it to my face," she shouted. Walter reached for her arm, shifting into the role of comforting friend.

"Please, Isabel, just go quietly."

Suddenly she felt something inside her snap. Her face grew hot as emotions flooded her brain. Tears that she would normally hold back flowed down her face. She saw vividly all the mistakes she had been making. She was angry with herself for putting her trust in Robert, and she knew for certain he had only made his empty promises to string her along.

Her heart was breaking… and her career was over before it ever began. Her dream of becoming someone people remembered—that was gone. Her name would only be remembered for the illicit love affair she had had with her boss.

"You tell Robert I'm not going anywhere," she cried out. "He can't hide like a coward behind the company. You tell him if he wants me gone, he will have to do it himself."

Walter let go of Isabel's arm, and turned to make his way back to the elevator, signaling for security as he went.

"You tell him that one day he will be sorry he ever did this," she continued. "I can promise you that—he'll regret it! He will learn how it feels to lose everything!"

Bobby approached Isabel, a pained look on his face, and told her that it was time for her to leave—but she refused to move.

"Call Robert Queen," she demanded loudly. "Get him on the phone, tell him that I'm not going anywhere!" Bobby pleaded again for her to go.

"Please, Miss Rochev, you need to leave or I'll have to physically remove you from the building, and I really don't want to do that."

"I don't care!" she shouted. "I don't care what you say! Everyone needs to know that Robert Queen is a *liar!*" Crowds of employees began to gather, watching her unravel completely. Two additional security guards approached her to try to soothe her, but there was no comforting her, so they moved in more forcefully, each gripping an arm.

"He'll be sorry he did this to me!" she cried. "Tell him that he had better watch his back!" She threw her arms around, trying to escape their grasp. "He can't do this to me! He can't do this to me! *He promised me!*" she cried as the guards dragged her toward the door.

"This isn't how it was supposed to be!" she shouted out as the guards finally removed her from Queen Consolidated. When they released her, Isabel looked around, noticing the many eyes staring at her. She took a few steps back, looking up to the top of the building, knowing that Robert was probably watching her from his window.

He will be sorry about this, Isabel thought furiously to herself as she finally walked away from the building. She promised herself, however, that she would return to Queen Consolidated one day.

7

A few days after the scene at Queen Consolidated, Isabel was driving recklessly through the streets of Starling City. She pressed her foot to the floor, catching a glimpse of herself in her rearview mirror.

Her eyes were bloodshot and beady, her once flawless complexion pale and ghostly. She didn't recognize who that girl was in the mirror, and wondered how things had got this bad. She wondered when Robert had managed to take hold of her life like this. She felt foolish for letting him have this power over her, only to realize that it was one of the reasons she had been drawn to him in the first place. She cursed his name repeatedly as she swerved down the street.

"You think you can just make a fool out of me, and that I will just disappear," she muttered out loud to herself. "Well, you have another think coming. You think you can just fire me and ruin my life—well, I can ruin your life, too."

She made a hard right in her tiny car, and the open gates to the Queen mansion came into view. Isabel stopped the car just before the gates and took a minute. Inexplicably, she suddenly felt a little sad for him.

A sorry excuse for a man, and an utter coward, Isabel thought to herself. Only a weak, insecure person would do the things that Robert had done. She recalled the times they had talked about having children of their own… together. The thought sent a shiver down her spine as she saw now what a terrible father Robert was if he was capable of such lies.

She put her foot on the gas and drove through the gates.

Pulling up to the door, she got out of the car, her body shaking in a combination of fear and anger. She remembered the first time Robert had invited her to the house, the first time they had slept together. Isabel smiled a little, thinking about how she had felt about Robert in that moment, and her heart broke a little more thinking about where she was now.

As she reached the front door, she quickly snapped back to reality.

KNOCK. KNOCK. KNOCK.

Isabel tried to compose herself as she heard footsteps approach the door. It opened, and Moira Queen stood there.

"Isabel Rochev," she said. "I need to speak with Robert."

"I know who you are, Miss Rochev," Moira said

flatly. "Robert isn't here—he's taken our children out fishing on his boat for the weekend."

Isabel remained silent. Her plan to talk to Robert, to deliver the speech she'd composed in her head, was out the window. And though she couldn't say why, she hadn't been expecting Moira to even be in the picture.

"I know why you are here, Miss Rochev," Moira said, "and I feel sorry for you. That a woman can sleep with a married man is one of the most disgusting things I can imagine."

The words cut Isabel deep—she was surprised that Moira knew about the affair. Even more so when she remembered that Moira had been a cheater as well.

Does she hate herself as much as she does me?

"You didn't think I knew, did you?" Moira continued. "You're nothing but a fling to that man. A name on a list. You're just one of many other silly girls before you who were foolish enough to think that a man like Robert would trade in the life he has now… for you."

Suddenly Isabel felt a strange calm come over her. She finally felt able to shut off her emotions like a faucet, and no longer felt like crying. In fact, she decided then and there that she would never cry again—for Robert Queen, or for anybody. She was done feeling self-pity.

"Now, do yourself a favor and get off my property before I call the police," Moira snapped as she went to close the door in Isabel's face.

"Or what?" Isabel said. "You see, Moira, we both involved ourselves with a foolish man—a man who told me many, many secrets about his life. Your life. So it would be in your best interest to watch your back. Be careful, because you never know when I might decide to have a chat with the press about the precious Queen family, perhaps sell your secrets to the highest bidder… especially when it comes to little Thea," Isabel said coldly. "How wonderful it is that she's healing so quickly."

The door stopped, and Moira peered out again. Her eyes were wide with fear.

⧓

Classical jazz was playing softly in the background of a dark establishment. Patrons sat in leather-lined booths that lined the walls, speaking in low voices. Cherry hardwood shone throughout the establishment. While the majority of the people enjoyed a happy hour cocktail with coworkers as they exchanged stories about their days, Isabel was sitting alone on a tall stool at the bar.

Just a year after the debacle with Robert, Isabel was the picture of crispness and style. She was dressed in a dark red business suit. Her hair was long and poker straight. One black stiletto tapped on the bar's ledge. A handsome bartender placed a martini in front of her, two olives, and she smiled at him devilishly as he threw her a wink and returned to work.

The local news played on the television above the bar.

"And in business news, Ramsford International—a

subsidiary of Queen Consolidated—has been bought out by Unidac Industries," news anchor Bethany Snow reported. "The takeover was engineered by Isabel Rochev, and this makes it the third subsidiary Queen Consolidated has lost to Rochev in the past six months."

A small smile crept across Isabel's face as she took a sip of her martini.

Exiting her sleek black Mercedes Benz, she grabbed her black leather briefcase and marched into her office at Unidac Industries. She walked with her head held high, steadfast and confident. Her subordinates lowered their gazes when she approached, and Isabel long since ceased to greet people with a smile. She remained focused on the task at hand, and had no time for chitchat or pleasantries.

As she arrived at her corner office her executive assistant, Theodore Decklin, greeted her with her morning latte and the rundown of her schedule for the day.

"First thing today, Miss Rochev, is the board meeting at 9 a.m.," Decklin informed her. Without saying a word Isabel handed him her coat and briefcase, grabbed her latte and files, and headed for the conference room. When she got there, the other nine members of the board were already in place. She took her seat at the long table, and while the other board members chattered away, Isabel kept her thoughts to herself as she sipped her latte and reviewed her papers. Suddenly, the glass door swung wide open, and Malcolm Merlyn entered.

Malcolm Merlyn, CEO of Merlyn Global.

Thea Queen's father.

Confidence radiated off of him in waves as he stood in front of the group. Dressed impeccably, he looked down at the people in the room almost as if they were bugs that begged to be squashed. All conversation ceased.

"Apologies for my tardiness this morning," he said, and he smiled. "There's nothing like a first impression."

There was a smattering of laughter, and all eyes were on him.

"I know we all have a lot to do, a lot on our plates, so I will keep this brief. It is with great pleasure that I stand before you to announce the partnership between Unidac and Merlyn Global. For those of us at Merlyn Global, it was a no-brainer when it came to choosing companies with which we want to work." To Isabel's surprise, he turned to look directly at her. "Much of the reason stems from the tireless work led by Miss Isabel Rochev, who we've watched with great interest as she scooped up one after another of Queen Consolidated's subsidiaries."

The board applauded politely, and Malcolm continued.

"Nobody believes in this city more than I do. I was born here—Starling City is my home—and as most of you know, when my wife Rebecca was alive our family shared the common goal of making Starling City a better place. A better place for our children to grow up, for the community to work together, offering job opportunities for everyone. And even though my wife may not be here to witness it, this is still a goal toward which I intend to work, and tirelessly.

"This partnership will bring two great companies together, and it will help to make Starling City stronger," Malcolm continued. "Thank you for your hard work, and your support."

The board members stood and applauded Malcolm's speech. Isabel rose to her feet with them. Malcolm made a circuit around the rectangular table, shaking the hands of each board member. When he reached Isabel, he gripped her hand tightly.

"I look forward to working with you, Miss Rochev," he said, looking her straight in the eye.

The following morning, Isabel entered her office to find Malcolm Merlyn sitting at her desk. She was taken aback by his boldness, and she was intrigued.

"Mr. Merlyn," she said calmly. "To what do I owe the pleasure?"

Malcolm smiled his devil smile and rose from her chair.

"I think the better question is how can I help *you*, Miss Rochev," he said enigmatically. "Shall we sit and discuss?"

They moved to the side of the room and sat on the couch. Isabel sat stiffly, and folded her arms defensively over her lap.

"Miss Rochev, as a smart businesswoman, you shouldn't be surprised to know that I'm thorough when it comes to business. I don't just jump at an opportunity simply because it's there. I do my research, especially on the people who created the opportunity in the first place. In this case—that would mean you," he said. "I feel it only fair to tell you that I'm a very close family friend to the Queen family."

Isabel shifted in her seat. To this day, the mere mention of them caused her spine to tighten. Yet she had learned to keep her composure when the subject came up.

"What's more," he continued, "I know about your past… relationship with them." The tension increased, and she decided to get to the point before it became painful.

"Mr. Merlyn, what are you getting at?" she asked, keeping a tight rein on her tone.

"Well, as I said yesterday, I believe in this great city of Starling. However, you and I both know that it has been suffering for a great deal of time. The slums known as the Glades, for example, are tragic for many reasons, as I know firsthand. My wife's life was taken there." He paused for effect, then continued, "However, I'm confident that with the joining of our companies, this is the chance for Starling City to turn over a new leaf. This is only the beginning."

Isabel stared blankly at him.

"I can't do this alone, though," he continued. "I need all of the power players in Starling City to be on board... including you, Miss Rochev. You *especially* are essential to my plans."

"And why is that?" Isabel asked. "What are you proposing?"

"I'm proposing what you have wished for the last two years—something you fervently desire," he said. "To remove Robert Queen from the picture, permanently."

That took her by surprise, and she let her façade slip. Her eyebrows furrowed, and she cocked her head to the side.

"With your help," he continued, "we can make this happen."

The sky was black, and not even the moon could be seen. Isabel sat at her desk with her glasses on, typing on her computer, her office only lit by the glow of the screen. Another late night, but she hardly noticed. Finally she commanded the power and respect she had craved her entire life, and this time no one was going to take it away from her.

She took a breath and stopped typing.

Isabel went to her cabinet and pulled out a bottle of Scotch. It was the same brand that Robert used to share with her in his office, so long ago. She poured herself a hearty drink and touched her lips to the glass as her phone rang.

"It's done," a voice said. "It should make the news tomorrow…"

"Thank you for your help."

Click.

She put the phone down slowly, not exactly sure how to feel. Although she was now firmly committed to Malcolm Merlyn's plan, she was still a little stunned. To her surprise, she was unable to catch her breath for a minute, so returned to the cabinet and retrieved her Scotch, taking a hard swig, letting it burn on the way down.

Then she returned slowly to her desk.

As she sat, a single tear traced its way down her cheek.

9

THE PRESENT

"Here, Miss Rochev," a young intern said. "Miss Rochev?"

Isabel's eyes were still locked on the television. Her mouth remained slightly open, her breathing fast as the shock overtook her body.

"Miss Rochev," the intern said again, tapping Isabel on the shoulder.

Her mind was awhirl with the events that had led to the *Gambit* going under water, taking with it Oliver and his father. Snapping out of it, she looked at the puzzled intern as he proceeded to pick up the files she had dropped.

"Thank you," Isabel said absently, and she scanned the room. "People should get back to work." Wthout another word, she slowly stepped back into her office, her mind racing a million miles a minute.

Oliver Queen is alive.

How is this possible?

Five years ago, Isabel thought that with the help of Malcolm Merlyn, she had finally put the debacle of the Queen family to rest at last. Yet there it was—proof that Oliver still lived. Had it all been a ruse on Merlyn's part?

Is Robert alive, as well?

Isabel went to her desk and pulled out a key to unlock the bottom drawer. There she pulled out a metal box, opening it slowly—even timidly—and pulling out a picture.

Her and Robert. She hardly recognized herself. The photo had been taken on Robert's boat, and Isabel wore a bikini, her suntanned skin glistening. Robert was kissing her on her forehead, and she was smiling. Looking at the picture, she remembered what it was like to be happy, even if it was just a fleeting moment. Another smile flitted across her lips.

Are you alive?

Are you still out there, too?

Suppressing the smile, she locked the photo away again.

Seven o'clock, and she shut down her computer, checking her desk again to make sure the drawer was locked. Pulling her trench coat from the hook on the back of her door, she headed for the elevator.

The parking structure was nearly empty, and the only sound that could be heard was the clicking of her heels. It was this way every night, yet as she approached her Mercedes, a strange feeling swept over her. She stopped in her tracks, peering over her shoulder cautiously to see if anyone else was around.

Stillness.

Shaking her head, she let out a sigh of relief as she spotted her car just a row away. Approaching the driver's-side door, she reached into her bag for the keys. Looking up, she saw her reflection in the window… and froze.

There was a man, standing behind her. He wore a black suit jacket, and an eye patch.

"He's dead, Miss Rochev."

His raspy voice echoed against the concrete walls, spurring her to motion. She spun around, dropping her keys in the process.

"Who are you?" she demanded, her hand back into the purse. "What do you want?" Finding her pepper spray, she pointed it at the intruder—yet he didn't flinch.

"Even if I had both my eyes, Miss Rochev, that wouldn't have much effect on me." Raising his hands, he held them palm out, both empty. "Please, Miss Rochev, I'm just here to talk."

"You chose a strange time and place for that," she said without lowering the pepper spray. "Who are you?"

"My name is Slade Wilson," he said. "I'm here to tell you that you don't need to worry—he's dead."

"I don't know what you're talking about."

"Robert Queen is dead," Slade said.

At the sound of his name, she felt light-headed, and finally lowered the pepper spray. She studied the newcomer, dressed in a sharp black suit, his hair sprinkled with salt and pepper around the ears. The patch fit snugly against his right eye.

"I... I don't understand," she said.

"Oliver Queen has returned," Wilson said. "Starling City's golden boy has returned after all these years. You've been wondering if Oliver's return would mean there's still hope for his father, but I can assure you that Robert is gone."

"Why are you telling me this?" she demanded, her composure returning. "What do you want?"

"I'm telling you this because I know what it's like to lose someone you love. Someone you care about so deeply it runs through your veins, is enrooted deep within, and suffering a loss of such magnitude weighs on your soul for the rest of your life." As he spoke she felt her cheeks grow warm, the tears forming in her eyes, and was afraid to blink for fear they would fall onto her face.

"I know that type of loss, Miss Rochev," he continued, and if he noticed her emotions, he didn't let on. "I'm here to help you."

"I don't need any help," she snapped.

"You may not see it now, but you and I share a common interest—one that has weighed on us for too long." He paused, and a glint showed in his eye. "One that needs to be destroyed."

What the hell is he talking about? Fear gave way to

anger. "What could we possibly have in common?" she demanded.

"Our hate for the Queen family."

Suddenly the dizziness returned, and all the emotions she'd held in check began to boil over. She remembered the lies and broken promises, the times he'd abandoned her for those children—Thea's spelling bee and dance recital, rushing to Oliver's side to bail him out. Indignities she'd endured, only to have Moira dismiss her as if she was nothing but a street rat.

"The Queen family is poison to this city," Wilson continued, as if he could read her mind. "They infect anyone and everyone around them. They believe their money lets them weasel out of any situation. Above all, they are liars, and murderers. Oliver not only took my eye—he stole away someone I can never get back, and I'm going to do everything in my power to make sure he gets exactly what he deserves.

"I know what Robert did to you, and yet somehow the Queen family remains unscathed. But the time has come for them to feel the pain they've inflicted on us."

Every muscle in Isabel's body tightened at Wilson's words. Robert set out to destroy her, to leave a once promising career shattered at her feet, and now Oliver was back, a spoiled brat poised to become CEO of Queen Consolidated—the position that was once promised to her.

The thought made her sick.

"How do we make this happen?" she asked.

10

Isabel met Slade in a rundown abandoned warehouse in Central City. It was constructed entirely out of cement; the walls, the floor—all were solid and soundproof, despite the decay. Dressed for business in her favorite gray pantsuit, she entered the building not knowing what to expect, knowing full well that if she screamed there wasn't anyone who would hear her.

Suddenly she began to sweat, panic rising at the fact that she had trusted a complete stranger.

"Welcome to day one, Miss Rochev," Slade said, appearing from a side door. He had ditched his business suit in favor of combat attire. His black leather boots squeaked against the concrete, his muscles bulged out of his black tank top. "I'm eager to start the training," he added. "You, however, aren't properly dressed for this."

"Excuse me?" Isabel said. "I was under the assumption that we were going to discuss the way in which we would destroy the Queen family. You said nothing about any 'training.'"

"The plan for their destruction has already been set in motion, and is not up for discussion," he growled. "Right now, you need to change into these." He handed Isabel a set of workout clothes.

Thrown off guard by the tone with which Slade addressed her, she nevertheless took the bundle. Ducking behind a concrete retaining wall, she slipped out of her suit. Moments later she appeared wearing a black spandex outfit with an orange tank top.

"Now what?" Isabel asked irritably.

"Now we fight," Slade said, handing Isabel a bamboo stick with which to spar. She furrowed her brow.

"Mr. Wilson, I'm a businesswoman—not a ninja," she said evenly, looking at the stick as if it might bite her. "All I want is what was once promised to me, and to see the look on Moira Queen's face when I get it. So, if you expect me to hit you with a bamboo stick, you need to tell me how it will enable me to take control of Queen Consolidated."

Without answering Slade grabbed another bamboo stick, staring at it. The look on his face went grim, and spoke of an anger that threatened to burst forth.

"Oliver Queen has returned to his beloved Starling City a changed man," he said, his voice low but clear. "Long ago, I made a promise to him that I would take everything and everyone away from him. In order for the plan to work, I need to be able to inflict physical pain on him, as well—and you need to be able to do the same." He struck a defensive pose, and waited.

Isabel took a deep breath, taking in what Slade had just told her. She glanced down at her stick, raised it suddenly, and charged Slade. He blocked her assault with his stick, and she swung again, this time finding only empty air. Again and again she swung, and each time he countered her until a rage began to grow in her, as well. With each frustrated assault, it flared stronger and stronger.

"Anger is good," he said. "Now let's *really* begin."

Alone in the warehouse, Isabel grabbed one of two long swords that lay nearby. The blade glistened in the harsh strip lighting of the warehouse. She touched the tip, pricking her finger just hard enough for it to break the skin, and watched a tiny bead of blood trickle down her finger. She wiped it away, numb to any pain, then scooped up the second sword. Her hands trembled ever so slightly as she thrust them outward.

"What do you think you're doing?" Slade barked, appearing without warning, making her jump and drop one of the swords to the ground. "You're not ready—you'll lose a finger, or worse."

Furious with herself, she snatched it up again.

"It's been three months," she protested, "and I'm done fighting with sticks. If you don't think I'm ready, then prove it!"

Slade eyed her for a moment, then removed his suit

jacket and slowly undid his tie. He went to a long case and unlocked it. Inside were his own swords.

"Very well, then," he said, taking out the swords and showing them off, the blades flashing. "Let's see what you've got."

Isabel dropped into a fighting stance, her muscles taut. She stood strong and straight, and weeks of training had resulted in perfect muscle definition. She was filled with hate and rage, which she embraced enthusiastically. Her life was focused on one thing, and one thing alone.

Revenge on the Queen family.

Pushing the air out of her lungs, she lunged forward and swung her sword. Slade deflected it, but she could tell from his expression that she had surprised him. He lashed out in return, and she danced aside, pressing her own attack. With each swing she focused on his lessons, applying every trick he had taught her. Her confidence mounted, even as she was covered in a sheen of sweat.

She moved close and swung the blade in her left hand. Slade dodged and used his right-hand sword to nick her arm. With a cry she pulled back and glanced down at the gash. Though it was superficial, there was blood flowing down her bicep.

Slade ignored Isabel's cry and raised his sword again, bringing it into play. Isabel quickly parried it, wielding her sword hard against his. Suddenly he spun around and kneed Isabel in the stomach, sending her tumbling to the ground. He paused as she gathered herself and stood, dropping again into a defensive stance.

Trying to ignore the pain, she launched a flurry of strikes she hoped would overwhelm him, but the wound was too distracting, and he easily maintained the upper hand. Fatigue left her arms feeling heavier by the minute, slowing her down until Slade found an opening. He knocked one of the swords out of her hand, and as she glanced in the direction of its flight, he kicked his leg out, dropping her to the floor.

She landed face first on the concrete with a loud *crack*. She lay there lifelessly for a moment while Slade hovered over her. Finally she moved her hands under her body and lifted herself up, blood trickling from her lip and nose. Isabel staggered to her feet and raised her hands up to surrender.

"Please, don't," she grunted. "I can't… I'm sorry."

"Let this be a lesson," he said disdainfully. "I'll be the one to say when you're ready." With that he moved to the case and placed his swords inside. Then he walked silently to the door, leaving her standing there in a pool of her own blood.

Isabel drove her Mercedes down a long, never-ending road. The windows of the car were down, and her long brown hair blew in the wind, whipping around her head. Spotting the warehouse in the distance, she let out a deep breath as she pressed her foot harder onto the gas.

Entering the dimly lit building, she pulled off her

sunglasses. Isabel wore a black patent leather flat on her left foot and a medical boot on the other. She limped across the cement floor, looking around, but Slade was nowhere to be found. Moving to a side door, she opened it and peeked down a long corridor. She heard talking and headed in that direction.

The fluorescent lighting was harsh, so she replaced the glasses and started down the hallway. The sound grew closer until it became apparent where it was coming from, and Isabel put her ear to a door. Twisting the doorknob, she pushed in to find Slade sitting behind a dilapidated desk, wearing a stylish three-piece suit. He didn't move, and his eyes were fixed on the television in front of him.

"The Starling City vigilante was at it again last night, taking down Martin Somers," a news anchor announced. "The commissioner of police continues to ask all citizens to come forward with any information about the vigilante, and strongly recommends that if you encounter him in person, do not engage."

"Do not engage, indeed," Slade said, turning his chair around. "To what do I owe the pleasure, Miss Rochev?"

"I'll keep this short, Mr. Wilson," Isabel said, removing her sunglasses to reveal two black eyes. "I'm out."

"What do you mean, out?" he asked calmly.

"You almost killed me!" she snapped. "I fractured two ribs and my left foot. I'm lucky that I still have all my teeth. I may hate the Queens just as much as you, but I cannot do this. *We* can't do this."

"Is that so?"

"Your plan needs more people," she asserted. "I'm only one person and yes, I firmly believe I can take Queen Consolidated on the business side, but you need someone else—someone who can back you up on the street. Someone like the vigilante."

Slade smirked at her.

"The vigilante *is* Oliver Queen."

Isabel's eyes widened as the pieces of the puzzle began to fit together. All the things Slade had told her suddenly started falling into place.

"You said Oliver had a new journey..."

"And indeed he does," Slade continued. "His crusade is to right the wrongs of his father, and clean up the city—one millionaire at a time."

Isabel scoffed at the mention of Oliver's father.

"Regardless of whether Oliver wants to spend his nights in green tights, I need help. *We* need help. Even more so if he *is* this vigilante. We need to take the city from him by force."

"You make a valid point," Slade said, much to her surprise, "but you're wrong about the nature of the help we need. I can handle the streets, and the vigilante—of that I'm certain. No, the city needs to *turn* on the Queens, to reject all they represent—and to make that happen, we need someone on the inside."

He smiled—something he didn't often do.

Isabel shuddered in spite of herself.

3

BLOOD

1

The streets of the Glades were run-down and filled with trash and dirt. Graffiti was scrawled along every bridge and billboard. A crowd of homeless people huddled around a trashcan fire to keep warm, for the night was bitterly cold. Police sirens sounded in the distance—most likely racing to a crime scene of the sort that made the Glades infamous. Such was the neighborhood's legacy.

Crime and filth.

Nestled on Stark Road between two abandoned businesses sat Zandia Orphanage. An unusual commotion could be heard from the streets. Cheering and laughter grew louder by the moment, in stark contrast to the building's surroundings. Inside, a group of neighborhood residents sipped on cheap champagne and munched on crudités.

Sebastian Blood loosened his tie before he reached for two plastic cups.

"Thank you for coming, Dr. Vaca," he said, handing the doctor his drink. Sebastian's chocolate-brown hair was slicked back as he showed off his smile.

"Of course, Sebastian," Vaca said. "Becoming the new Alderman for the Glades certainly warrants a celebration."

"Well, I couldn't have done it without tireless support—it's meant a great deal to me," Blood said, clinking his glass with the doctor's. He took a sip of his drink, letting the bubbles tickle his throat.

"It's the least I can do, Sebastian. After all, you've been in my corner many times, a genuine friend to the Rebecca Merlyn Clinic. I look forward to your work as alderman, and have high hopes that you'll bring new awareness to the clinic... and more importantly, to the Glades." Dr. Vaca peered over Sebastian's shoulder, and waved his arm to indicate a pair of newcomers. "You remember the Gomez family, don't you? They were at your rally three weeks ago."

Sebastian extended his hand. "Hello again, Mr. and Mrs. Gomez, thank you so much for coming to our little soirée."

Although cheerful, Richard and Amelia Gomez looked tired, as well. Amelia's makeup was thick under her eyes to hide the dark circles that lurked there.

"We just both wanted to personally thank you for all the attention you've brought to the clinic during your campaign, Mr. Blood," she said. "When our son Bobby was diagnosed with cancer, we didn't know what to do. There was no way our insurance company would help us, yet the thought of our boy not getting treatment because we couldn't afford it, well, it was... heartbreaking."

"And how is he doing?" Blood asked.

"He's in remission," Richard Gomez replied, and he beamed. "That wouldn't be the case if it wasn't for the clinic and Dr. Vaca."

"I'm so glad to hear it," Sebastian said sincerely. "I hope now as Alderman of the Glades I can continue to help families just like yours. If I have my way, the Merlyn Clinic will thrive for years to come."

Suddenly he jumped a bit as he felt a strong hand gripping his shoulder from behind. Sebastian turned to see his longtime friend, Cyrus Gold, standing there.

"Congratulations, old friend," Cyrus said, throwing his arms around Sebastian. "I couldn't be more proud of you."

"Thank you, Cyrus," Blood said, embracing his friend tightly. To the others he said, "Please allow me to introduce one of my dearest friends, pastor Cyrus Gold of the orphanage's sister church."

"It is a pleasure to meet you all," Cyrus said, "and what a joyous occasion, celebrating our new leader, Alderman Blood." He vigorously shook hands with each person in the group.

"What parish do you belong to?" Mrs. Gomez inquired.

"I am with St. Pancras parish," Cyrus said. "St.

Pancras is the patron saint of children, martyred as a teenager because he refused to sacrifice his faith. A true conviction for what he believed in—it only seemed fitting to name our parish after him. My mentor, Father Trigon, sadly passed away a few months ago. He believed that no child should suffer or be forgotten, and that's what led us to partner with Zandia Orphanage."

"It must be so rewarding for you to see all the children of the Glades find a place to call home," Mr. Gomez said, but it was Sebastian who replied.

"It's a beautiful thing that Cyrus and Father Trigon have done for these young men and women," he said. "Without them, they would have been lost, roaming the streets, getting into who knows what sorts of trouble—but here, they have someone to care for them, and make sure they are safe. I have to say that I'm in awe of what Zandia has done for the children of the Glades."

He raised his cup to Cyrus and, smiling, toasted his longtime friend.

2

FIFTEEN YEARS AGO

Father Trigon sat in his office in Zandia Orphanage, his glasses perched on the edge of his nose while he pored over paperwork. His hair was black with a few white ones starting to sprout around his ears, and his eyes were tired from too many hours spent with exhausting children. He rubbed his forehead, and looked up when there was a knock at the door.

Cyrus Gold entered his office.

"Sorry to disturb you, Father," the gangly teenager said meekly.

"Not at all, my child, please come in," Father Trigon said as Cyrus skittishly took a seat across from him. "What can I do for you?"

Cyrus paused for a second, and avoided making eye contact. Father Trigon saw the struggle on the young man's face, and reached his hand across the table, grasping him reassuringly.

"You can tell me anything, my boy," he said. "You are in a safe place."

"I found a boy last night," Cyrus blurted out. "He was out wandering the streets alone. He looked lost so I asked him where his home was, but he didn't answer me. I could tell he'd been crying, and his face was bleeding as if he had been in a fight, but still he wouldn't speak. I couldn't leave him alone there—who knows what could have happened to him if he was left in the Glades.

"So… I snuck him in last night," Cyrus confessed.

Father Trigon removed his glasses. "I see. Where is the boy now?"

"He's sitting outside your office," Cyrus said.

"And have you been able to get the boy's name?"

"No," Cyrus admitted. "I don't know what his name is, or where he came from, or if he has a home. He still hasn't spoken." Cyrus choked back tears.

"My son, you did a good deed, even though rules were broken," Father Trigon said. "Your intentions and your heart remain in the right place. Why don't you bring in your new friend, and we can all have a chat."

Cyrus rose from his chair and slipped out through the door. The priest could hear him speaking, and finally he entered with a very scared, frail little boy. He was very small, and skinny—looked as if he hadn't eaten a hearty meal in weeks. He had a few bloody scratches on his right cheek and a bump on his forehead. His clothes were worn and too small. Cyrus guided him into a chair, and sat next to him.

Father Trigon smiled at the boy.

"Hello, my name is Roger Trigon—what's yours?"

The boy did not answer.

"You don't have to be afraid, my child. Here at Zandia you are free from danger, and in a place of love and worship. No one is here to hurt you." The boy remained silent. Father looked to Cyrus for a moment, and then tried again.

"Do you know where your mom and dad are? They must be worried about you." The boy furrowed his eyebrows at the mention of his parents. Father Trigon realized he might be getting somewhere and continued, "Did you run away from your parents? Parents may not always be easy to get along with, but parents are God's teachers to show their children the righteous way."

"Not *my* parents," the boy croaked out.

"What do you mean, my son?" Father Trigon leaned closer. "Tell me what happened."

"No one is around, ever," the child said, and he began to cry. "There is always darkness wherever I go. I'm always so afraid. I lie awake listening to the footsteps getting closer to my bedroom door—afraid of what my father may do to me when he comes home drunk and upset. Even when I do sleep I hear the footsteps still… getting closer to me.

"But they aren't my father's," he continued. "It's the man in black—the one with a skull for a face. His teeth are jagged and sharp and just when he gets close enough I always wake up. I cry out, but my mother doesn't come to comfort me. I'm alone."

Cyrus and Father Trigon listened intently.

"How did you end up on the streets?" the priest asked.

"I woke up to tell my parents again about the man in black, but my father beat me, saying I shouldn't make up stories. My mother was too busy to care about anything, especially me." The boy cried, wiping his snot and tears on his sleeve. "Please, don't make me go back! I can't go back there!" he shouted as he started to cry harder.

Father Trigon rose from his seat as his heart broke for the pain this child had endured. He wrapped his arms around the boy, holding the back of his head tightly to his chest. The frail body shook as he wept, the sobs going deeper and deeper.

"You are safe here, my son," the priest said, "and I will never make you leave, I promise. Soon, you'll stop being afraid, or haunted by your dreams. I will see to that." He released his grasp on the boy and bent down to face him, wiping the tears away from his puffy red eyes, still wide with fear.

"What is your name, my boy?" Father Trigon asked.

"Sebastian," the boy said. "Sebastian Blood."

The outside of the house was worn, the paneling covered with gray chipped paint. Trees and bushes had become overgrown in the yard, while mildew and moss covered the foundation. Young Sebastian Blood walked slowly up his gravel driveway, returning home late at night after a week away. He arrived at his front door, frozen in fear, not knowing what beating lay ahead of him.

He entered to find his mother passed out cold on the couch with the television still on, blaring an infomercial. There were old takeout containers scattered on the coffee table next to a stash of pills and empty beer bottles.

Sebastian continued down the hall to find his father bending over in the door to the fridge. His gun sat on the kitchen table next to an empty beer bottle. Sebastian kept his eye on it, knowing that his father was probably wasted, and afraid of what he might do.

Suddenly, his father noticed him.

"Where have you been, you little punk?"

Sebastian remained silent.

"I asked you a question, you little shit," his father said, his voice getting louder. "Where have you *been*?" When Sebastian turned to walk away, the man reached for his gun with a speed belying his condition, and pressed it to Sebastian's head.

Sebastian closed his eyes tightly, feeling the cold metal on the back of his skull. Still he remained silent, sweating in anticipation, waiting for the bullet to pierce his brain.

WHAM!

The back door swung open as two dark figures kicked through it and entered the house. The newcomers were both dressed in black, head to toe. One of them wore a mask of the devil. It looked like bone, obscuring the face so only the eyes could be seen, and the horns that crowned it were long and twisted.

The other figure had the face of an acolyte—all white, but with black, dead eyes. The devil and the acolyte pulled Sebastian's father away, hitting him behind his knees and sending him to the ground. They grabbed his head and banged it repeatedly against the kitchen table until blood started to pour from his mouth and nose. With each impact Sebastian cringed.

Sebastian's mother, Maya, ran into the room and screamed at the sight of the violence. Her eyes sat deep in the sockets of her gaunt face, while her black shoulder-length hair was in disarray. She begged for the devil and the acolyte to stop, and they let Sebastian's father go. The pudgy form crumpled to the floor, barely conscious, blood mixing with sweat and other stains on his dirty white T-shirt.

"Sebastian, call the police," he mumbled, spitting out blood, but Sebastian stood frozen, unable to move. He found himself almost glad to see his father in such pain—the very pain he handed out to his son, all too often—and the thought made him ashamed.

The devil and acolyte turned their attention to Maya, and Sebastian's emotions shifted to fear. The acolyte twisted her arm behind her back.

"Let go of me!" she screamed. "Sebastian, help me!"

The devil began to cackle. The mask muffled his voice.

"What irony! You beg for help from a son who has received no help from his parents. God himself said there is nothing like the love of a mother and father, yet here you are, having shown this boy neither love nor compassion."

The acolyte went over to Sebastian's father and picked him up off the floor. His face was swollen and already bruising. He tried to fight off his attacker, but he was too weak to put up a struggle, and quickly fell back onto the tiles. The devil picked up the pistol, opened it, and saw the bullets loaded inside.

"Please! Don't kill us!" Maya screamed. "Don't kill my son! He's just a boy!"

The devil moved to Sebastian and knelt down before him. He offered him the gun.

"Are you worthy of delivering retribution?" he said. "Thou shall not let one deceive them with empty words, for the wrath of God comes upon the sinners of disobedience and negligence." He raised the weapon to Sebastian, whose eyes widened. He looked at the man dressed as the devil, and wondered whether he should listen to him.

This was his opportunity to get revenge—revenge for the times that his father had ignored him and pushed him aside like a dirty old shoe. For the beatings he had endured, and those given to his mother, as well.

He reached his hand out, his fingertips touching the barrel of the gun, then he grasped it with purpose.

"Sebastian, don't listen to them!" Maya screamed. "We love you! We've always loved you. Your father and I will be better. We *will* get better, I *promise*."

Sebastian turned to his father, expecting… *wanting* him to beg for his life, as well.

"You don't have it in you to kill anyone, you little bastard," he sneered through ruined teeth. "You're not strong enough—you're a weak little boy."

Sebastian lifted the pistol, shut his eyes, and pulled the trigger, shooting his father in his abdomen twice. He was knocked back, and when he looked a sea of red blood flowed out of the gunshot wounds, quickly soaking through his father's shirt as his eyes rolled back in his head.

His mother was shrieking incoherently, and when Sebastian turned the gun toward her, she begged him to spare her, the words tumbling out between gasping sobs.

"Please, Sebastian, I love you!"

Sebastian's fury burned deep into his soul, and he felt more alive than he ever had before. He steadied himself to pull the trigger, when without warning the devil stepped in front of the pistol. He slowly placed his hands on the weapon, guiding it to the table and removing Sebastian's hands from it.

"Spare her, boy," he said. "As a mother, the giver of life, the greatest torture is hers to bear—knowing that death is too easy an option for her to escape what she has done, and how she has treated a gift from God."

Sebastian stared at her with nothing but true hatred. The devil put his arm around the boy and led him out the door into the black night.

The devil and the acolyte took Sebastian to an abandoned factory in the Glades. He felt the fire running through his veins, still on a high from the feeling of revenge. There was no sense of remorse or regret for what he had done; in fact, he felt at peace with his choice.

They led him down into the basement of the decrepit building. It was cold and wet and smelled like mothballs, and he was taken aback when he saw a group of boys and men sitting in makeshift pews. The devil offered Sebastian a seat in one of the pews. Confused, unsure of what was happening, Sebastian sat down as the devil stepped to the front of the congregation.

"Tonight is a joyous night," he announced. "Tonight is the night that we celebrate maintaining a strong, protected united front." The group clapped and cheered in their seats. Sebastian slowly put his hands together, wondering if he had made a mistake.

"We have a guest of honor tonight," the acolyte announced. "My friends, please meet Sebastian Blood."

Sebastian felt every set of eyes turn to him as he sank a little lower in his pew. His adrenaline rush now diminished, he began to grow frightened at the situation he'd got himself into, and he felt himself start to sweat.

"Sebastian, meet Brother Langford," the devil said, and a man rose and went to the front of the room to join him. The devil placed his hands on Brother Langford's shoulders. "Brother Langford is here to help guide you on this new journey. And meet Brother Daily," he said as a teenager rose from his seat, and moved to the front of the room. He linked arms with Brother Langford, and next, the devil introduced Brother Clinton Hogue, another young teenager. Brother Hogue linked arms with Brother Daily.

"Brother Daily and Brother Hogue were much like you, Sebastian. They were young boys, underappreciated and forgotten by the world... until they found us. Together we join forces. Together no one will ever be forgotten." As he spoke the devil and the acolyte linked arms with the rest of the group, then they finally removed their masks.

It was Father Trigon and Cyrus Gold.

He had suspected as much, but it still shocked him.

"Sebastian, you are part of the brotherhood now. We live to protect our brothers of the city. We started this group to protect the young and the orphans of Zandia." He waved his hand around to indicate everyone in the room. "You will no longer be alone. Each life that has and will be taken for this cause is a sacrifice for the greater good." Father Trigon reached for a bag and pulled something out as he motioned for Sebastian to come join them at the front.

The boy stood and approached the rest of the group. Father Trigon presented Sebastian with a skull mask, the one from his dream—the teeth long and jagged, just as Sebastian had described. Horns ran down the jaw line and curled upward like tusks.

"From here on out, Brother Blood, the terror you once felt will no longer haunt your dreams. Here on out—you shall not live in fear, but live in the power that your mask possesses, and strive to keep the brotherhood alive, helping those who need it most."

Sebastian looked down at the mask, no longer doubting, and no longer feeling the fear he once did. He knew that Father Trigon was right. He knew that his parents deserved what they got, and that this brotherhood was where he belonged. This was his new family, the only family he would need. Sebastian reached out, taking the mask. He took a deep breath and placed it over his face.

Father Trigon beamed with pride.

"Welcome home, Brother Blood."

3

A few weeks later Father Trigon and Sebastian walked the streets of the Glades together. Father Trigon's clerical collar was snug around his neck. He buttoned up his jacket and put a winter hat on Sebastian as they continued on their way. The two arrived at Saint Walker's mental institution. Father Trigon opened the door to the hospital and was greeted by one of the nurses.

"Hello, Father Trigon!"

"Good afternoon, Wendy, how are you doing?" Father Trigon asked. "How's your family?"

"Everyone is doing very well, and thank you for asking," Nurse Wendy replied warmly. "Who did you bring with you today?" she asked, peering over the counter.

Sebastian snuck out from behind the priest, smiling innocently to the woman.

"Wendy, this is Sebastian Blood," Father Trigon said.

"Sebastian, it's a pleasure to meet you," Wendy said

with a kind smile. Then she set a clipboard on the counter. "If you both don't mind signing in for your visit…"

"Of course not," Father Trigon said, scribbling his John Hancock on the notepad.

"Are you here to see anyone in particular today?" she asked.

"A new patient, Sebastian's aunt, Maya Resik," the priest said with a devilish smile.

Maya sat wearing a white hospital gown, looking out her barred window. Her eyes were red and swollen, her hands cuffed together and resting in her lap. She heard the clicking of the door and turned her head in fear of who it might be. Relief rushed over her as she saw her son enter.

"*Sebastian!*" she exclaimed with joy, but the boy did not go to her. The priest stood next to him, gripping his arm tightly. "Sebastian, *mi amour*! Come to your mother!" she begged, but the boy didn't budge.

"You are not his mother, Maya," the priest said with a firm voice.

"Yes I am, Father," she protested. "Sebastian, come to me!"

The father gripped Sebastian's arm tighter, his skin turning white from the grasp.

"A mother protects her child and keeps him from harm," he said, a hint of anger in his voice. "A mother teaches her son to live in the Lord's ways. You have done none of this. You have failed this child. You are no mother, Maya, especially not to this boy."

She let out a cry, tears streaming down her face. "I am so sorry, my son. I am so sorry. I *have* been a terrible mother—but I've changed. I want to be better for you."

Sebastian looked up to the priest, and then to his mother. He was numb to his mother's words—they no longer had any real effect on him. He felt that he was now part of a real family. One that showed him love, and what it meant to be passionate about something. It was an unbreakable bond.

"Thou shall not let one deceive them with empty words," Sebastian said.

"For the wrath of God comes upon the sinners of disobedience and negligence," Father Trigon said.

Maya's eyes grew wide, putting two and two together. "You are the devil! It was you that night! You are the reason my husband is dead. You did this to my son!" she shouted, and she lashed out, becoming increasingly hysterical. She accused Father Trigon of stealing her son, making him believe his lies, and abducting her poor Sebastian. Then she screamed at the top of her lungs for help, until an orderly—a young woman—finally entered.

"Maya, calm down!" the orderly said gently.

"He is the devil, he is the devil! HE'S TAKING MY SON!" she shouted, and she strained against the cuffs that held her hands. Finally the orderly reached into her pocket for a syringe. She grabbed Maya's arm, holding it as steady as she could, then jabbed the needle into it, sedating her. The shock caused Maya to stop shouting, and as the sedative took effect, the orderly stroked her hair.

"The father is not the devil," she said soothingly. "He is a man of God, and that boy over there is your nephew, not your son. You're confused, Maya." When Maya was completely calm, the orderly helped her to stand and guided her to the bed. She tucked her in.

"My son…" Maya said weakly. "He is with the devil."

Father Trigon went to the bed and hovered over her. Maya's eyes were glassy and bloodshot, and he placed his hand on Maya's forehead. Maya stiffened in fear, knowing what Father Trigon was capable of doing.

"Peace be with you," he said, then he turned and guided Sebastian out of the room, leaving Maya to cry for her son.

"Sebastian, I told you I would protect you," he said as they walked toward the exit. "Brother Langford and I—as well as all the other brothers—work as a team. The halls of Saint Walker are filled with men and women who have failed their city first by failing their own flesh and blood. Many of them, like you, have been given the chance to make life better for others, so that some day—after I am gone—you will continue to protect the vulnerable people who abuse and disgrace their home."

Sebastian looked up to the father, a feeling of awe

shuddering through him at the new journey that had been set forth for him. One which would last for the rest of his life.

4

THE PRESENT

In stark contrast to the celebration held at Zandia Orphanage, a fete was held at the Queen Mansion to welcome all of those who had been elected to the office of alderman. Many of the city's elite were in attendance, including Mayor Altman and the event's hosts, Walter Steele and Moira Queen.

Must be nice to be rich, Sebastian thought to himself as he grabbed a glass of champagne off a passing tray. He admired the elegant crystal that contained a very expensive Dom Pérignon. Overall, however, he was unimpressed by all the glitz and glamour—the forced laughter, the hobnobbing, the cronyism. Yet he knew that, as the alderman of the Glades, he would be expected to participate, knew that if he wanted to save his city he needed to play the game.

Sebastian saw Moira and Walter in the distance,

elegantly dressed and brilliantly poised, smiling while they talked to their guests. He took a sip of his champagne, placed his glass down, and approached the pair as they finished their conversation. Walter walked away, but Moira remained.

"Excuse me, Mrs. Queen," he said, tapping her shoulder. She turned and gave him a warm smile as he extended his hand to her. "Sebastian Blood, Alderman for the Glades."

"Mr. Blood, what a pleasure to meet you," she said, shaking his hand. "Congratulations on your win—you must be very excited."

"I am excited, and very eager to get to work," he replied.

Walter returned with a glass of champagne for his wife, and placed it in her hand.

"Walter, I'd like you to meet Mr. Sebastian Blood," she said. "He is the alderman for the Glades," she added as the two men shook hands.

"A pleasure, Mr. Blood," Walter said.

"Thank you so much for having me in your home—it is quite exquisite," Sebastian said, glancing at the art on the walls.

"Thank you," Moira said, following his gaze. Then she turned back to him. "Where are you from originally, Mr. Blood?"

"The Glades, actually, born and raised," he said, and was amused to see their curious expressions. "It's true that most of the people who come from the Glades end up on the streets. I guess I'm just one of the lucky ones that had a great upbringing."

"Well, you have your work cut out for you, Mr. Blood," Walter observed. "What are your plans to help the district, since it holds such a close place in your heart?"

"I have a five-year plan which I really think will breathe new life into the city," Sebastian replied.

"Many men have come here before you, Mr. Blood, and have said the same thing. Unfortunately, the Glades remain what they are—a wasted part of the city," Moira said. Sebastian stiffened at her words, but he knew the power the Queens wielded, and getting them on board would be essential if he was to succeed.

"You couldn't be more right, Mrs. Queen," he said smoothly. "However, my successors do not know the Glades like I do. I plan to begin by arranging funding for the Zandia Orphanage, as well as expanding the Merlyn Clinic. With those as success stories, we'll be off to a good start."

"Zandia does great work with the children there," Moira agreed.

"I know that from personal experience, as my parents died when I was a young boy and I spent most of my time at Zandia. As far as the Merlyn Clinic goes, I think it's important for the people of the Glades to receive excellent healthcare, so they can get themselves cleaned up and off the street." He paused, then added, "Correct me if I'm wrong, but aren't you close with Mr. Merlyn and his son?"

A strange expression flitted across Moira Queen's face, but it was rapidly replaced by a warm smile.

"Oh, yes, our sons were very good friends," she said, "much like Malcolm was with my late husband and me."

"I'm glad to hear it, and I appreciate you taking the time to let me prattle on about my plan," Sebastian said, giving his best charm. "I hope that perhaps the three of us will be able to sit down and discuss it in greater depth."

Moira was about to reply when a young man stepped up and touched her on the shoulder. She leaned away and the fellow whispered something to her in a low voice. She went stiff, then turned back to Walter, her face drained of color.

"Moira, everything alright?" he asked.

"It's Oliver… he's… he's alive." She quickly placed her drink down and moved toward the door, with Walter following quickly behind her.

Sebastian remained, forgotten entirely.

5

A ripple of excitement shuddered through Sebastian as he arrived at Starling City Hall for his first day on the job. As he and his fellow politicos made their way to the conference chamber and exchanged courteous pleasantries, it seemed to him as if the air crackled with possibilities.

Each made his or her way to a pre-assigned seat, and Councilman Charles Hirsh took his position at the head of the table.

"Good afternoon, ladies and gentlemen," Hirsh said loudly enough to be heard over the din, which quieted. "Thank you for coming today." He placed his briefcase in front of him and opened it. He pulled out the morning newspaper. Even at a distance, the headline could be read.

"I'M ALIVE!" It accompanied a photo of an outdated photo of Oliver Queen, standing next to his father, Robert.

"Nothing like a little excitement to start out the day, eh?" Hirsh commented. "Leave it to the Queen family to keep the city on its toes." A slight ripple of laughter ran through the chamber.

"The question remains, however," Councilman Steve Petros noted, "is Robert Queen still out there?"

"I hope not," another member added, though Sebastian couldn't see who it was.

"I disagree," another said. "His foresight and influence led to a great many positive things for Starling City." This led to a number of individual discussions throughout the chamber, and the murmured din returned. Eager to begin, Sebastian found himself impatient with his fellow aldermen.

"Councilman Hirsh," he said sharply. "Might we get started with the day's proceedings? I have a proposal for the Glades which I would like to present to the group." His words caused a momentary lull, and Hirsh shot him a look.

"We'll begin shortly, Mr. Blood," the councilman said. "Just hold tight." He turned his head to take in the entire group, and asked, "Where do we think Oliver Queen has been all this time, and what was he doing?"

"Well, it doesn't sound as if he was on Gilligan's Island," a voice said. Petros again.

"Judging from the reports, he doesn't seem to be very forthcoming with details," another observed—a woman.

"I was with the Queens when they received the news," Sebastian interjected. All attention turned in his direction, and he felt his face grow warm. "We were discussing the plans for the city, and for the Glades," he added.

"Please elaborate, Mr. Blood," Hirsh said, a touch of condescension in his voice. "What was it the Queens said to you at that moment?"

"I had told them about my five-year plan for the Glades," Sebastian said, yielding a few snickers. He suppressed a frown. "We agreed that our goal was to get the people of this great city off the streets, and into good homes and jobs." Picking up steam, he spoke clearly. "Walter and Moira seemed very interested in restoring the city, and helping to fund the efforts that would be needed."

He stopped, and for a long moment no one spoke.

"Mr. Blood," Charles Hirsh said, "if you are going to survive here as an alderman, it will be in your best interest to understand that rich people make a lot of promises. However, I wish you the best of luck pinning them down on anything tangible." With that he pulled out his agenda, motioned for the council to do the same, and began the meeting. Mortified, Sebastian sat back in his chair. Deep down, he knew Hirsh was right. The rich weren't the answer to the city's ills.

They were the problem.

*   *   *

The day was warm and bright, but Sebastian's mood wasn't as he walked briskly to the Merlyn Clinic in the Glades. It was his lunch break. His thoughts were bleak as he mulled over how little he had accomplished in the first month as an alderman. Try as he might, he remained marginalized and unheard.

The brisk walk helped to clear the cobwebs, however, and he reminded himself of why he had chosen this path. He told himself there were bound to be bumps in the road—that these things took time. By the time he arrived at the clinic, he'd decided that he wouldn't let himself be pushed aside.

Approaching Dr. Vaca's office, he found the door ajar. Peering inside, he found the doctor surrounded by a mountain of paperwork. He knocked quietly.

"Hi there, Dr. Vaca," he said as cheerfully as he could manage. "Just checking in to see how things are going."

Dr. Vaca removed his glasses and wiped his tired eyes. "Sebastian, hello, my friend! Please come in." He rose from his chair and held out his hand. "How are things going for you as our new alderman?"

"Life is quite… satisfactory," Sebastian replied. "I can't complain." He glanced around at the cluttered surroundings. "What about you? How are things going here at the clinic?" The doctor didn't answer at first, and his brow furrowed slightly.

"I will be honest with you, Sebastian, not good. Not good at all. I struggle every day to keep this clinic above water, and every day becomes a bigger challenge."

The doctor lowered his voice. "There are times when I despair." He paused for a second, leaning back in his chair. His eyes were red, and his complexion was pale. "You remember the Gomez family from your celebration party? Well, their son just experienced a relapse."

"That's terrible," Sebastian said, a hollowness appearing in the pit of his stomach.

"The clinic is suffering, and I don't think we have enough resources to care for him. I feel terrible, but I just don't have the means." He stared at the forms on his desk. "We need to expand the clinic, add new features, and we need the funding to do so. I'm trying everything I can think of." He looked up, and a flicker of hope appeared on his face. "What about you? Have you made any progress in your plans?"

Sebastian felt as if his heart was breaking.

"I'm sorry, Dr. Vaca, but no. I haven't made much progress this last month." He tried to put on his most optimistic face. "Still, I have high hopes that things will turn around, and soon."

"I wish I could say I believe you, Sebastian," the doctor said, the flicker gone, "but I know how these things run. We are mired in the legal red tape of the city. The truth is, they just don't care about us anymore, and it's getting harder to care myself, being here days on end, seeing how we continue to suffer.

"People just don't believe in the Glades."

"I'm sorry, doctor, but I don't know what to say." Sebastian rose, shook the doctor's hand, and left.

There has to be a way, he thought bleakly as he began the trek back to his office. Suddenly a scruffy young man stepped in front of him, forcing him to stop, and shoved a flyer in his face.

"Hey, man—check it out."

Sebastian jumped as the kid startled him from his trance. He took the flyer and looked at it.

OPENING SOON
VERDANT
Drinks and Dancing
No Cover

Another new club was opening there in the Glades—owned and operated by none other than Oliver Queen. There was a photo—of Queen, of beautiful people, *rich* people, laughing and partying.

Laughing and partying, while Bobby Gomez is dying.

Sebastian stared down at the flyer in disgust, crumpling it in his hand and pitching it into a trashcan before continuing on his way.

Sebastian paced back and forth at the security booth, wiping his sweaty palms on the sides of his pants, trying to stay focused as Bobby, the security guard, waited for the signal to let him into Queen Consolidated.

"I have an appointment with Mrs. Queen and Mr. Steele—they should be expecting me," he said again, and Bobby just nodded with a smile. Sebastian checked his watch. *I'm here on time*, he fumed. *They run the largest corporation in the city—why can't they keep a simple appointment?*

He jumped as the phone rang. Bobby picked it up, put it down without a word, and motioned him forward.

"You're good to go, young fella," he said, and he escorted Sebastian to the elevator.

On the ride up to Walter's office, Sebastian took a few deep breaths to gather himself for his meeting. The others on the council saw his as a lost cause, but he had to try. The elevator dinged as Sebastian arrived at the top floor and Walter Steele's office. The elevator open, Sebastian straightened his tie, and walked through the glass doors.

Steele's assistant introduced herself as Anna, and offered Sebastian a seat. He sat only for a moment, however, as Moira appeared.

"Hello, Mr. Blood," she said with a smile. "Thank you for waiting."

"Mrs. Queen, thank you for taking the time to meet with me," Sebastian said, shaking her hand.

"Yes, well, unfortunately, Walter and I will need to reschedule. Something has come up," she said apologetically. "I don't know if you heard, but my son recently has returned…"

"Yes, I may have heard something about it," Sebastian replied. *I was there, you know—not that you would remember.* "My congratulations."

"Well, then, you can understand how much my family has going on right now," Moira said, swinging a handbag over her shoulder. "Please give Anna a call, perhaps next week or the week after. She'll try to find an opening in the next month or so." She turned away from him, indicating that the conversation had ended, and made her way toward the elevator.

Something in Sebastian snapped.

His body stiffened as he felt every muscle tighten up. He clenched his fists tightly, nails digging into his palms, and the pain centered him. He reached his breaking point.

"Of course I understand," he said sharply. "It must be exhausting, going to all of the fancy events and club openings, especially where your son is involved."

Moira turned on her heels.

"Excuse me, Mr. Blood?"

"I'm just saying, why waste time on the bigger problems in the city when your son is opening a club in the Glades. Other problems such as the Merlyn Clinic turning away sick patients, *dying* patients, due to the lack of funding."

Moira Queen looked as if she was ready to squash Sebastian like a bug.

"If you're so worried about the clinic, Mr. Blood," she said flatly, "perhaps you should speak with the person whose family started it. I'm sure Malcolm Merlyn would be eager to hear of your concerns." At that moment the elevator doors opened, and Moira stepped inside.

"Have a good day, Mr. Blood," she said as the doors closed on Sebastian, yet again.

His face hot with anger, Sebastian stormed into the mayor's office. Mayor Altman sat behind his desk, signing papers and using his shoulder to hold a phone to his ear. At the sight of his visitor, he made a quick excuse and hung up the phone.

"Alderman Blood," the mayor said, rising from his chair. "You seem agitated."

Sebastian started to speak, then stopped himself and ran his fingers through his hair, his frustration boiling over. He stood at Altman's desk, breathing heavily, then sat down on the chair, putting his head between his legs.

"Alderman Blood?" Mayor Altman repeated.

Looking up, Sebastian hoped the despair didn't show on his face.

"Mayor Altman, I need your help." He took a deep breath. "People are homeless, starving, *dying*—people I serve, who look to me to help—and no one cares." He told the mayor of his visit to the clinic, of his meeting with Moira Queen. When he was done, Altman frowned.

"Alderman Blood, as much as I sympathize, there are other issues you should be focusing your time on— issues that are more important to the city as a whole. I know your heart rests with the Glades, but you need to face reality—the Glades are a lost cause. They were before you arrived, and they will be after you're gone. There are other parts of the city that are struggling, as well, sections we have a better chance of saving. We can't go tilting at windmills, just because one boy is dying."

Sebastian felt as if he'd been punched in the gut.

Anger and despair rendered him speechless, yet he clung to a single, basic truth. He knew that if he had given up hope as a child, he wouldn't have been here today. If Father Trigon had given up on the timid little boy in his office, he wouldn't have survived to fight for his city, his district. He remembered going to see his mother, how dead inside he'd felt when he looked at her. Sebastian looked at Mayor Altman now, and felt just as empty.

Then the emptiness filled with rage.

"Mayor Altman, if the Glades are such a lost cause, then tell me how Oliver Queen got the permits, the tax credits, needed to open a new club." He paused and stared. "How is it a nightclub is a priority, while a medical clinic is allowed to crumble? Where are our priorities when a wealthy brat is given a free ride, just because of his name?"

Mayor Altman sat stiffly and adjusted his tie.

"Alderman Blood, what are you saying?"

"I'm just wondering, what could cause you, cause the council, to support a major new startup in a dying neighborhood? And what would cause Queen to take such a risk? Will he pay taxes? Will the Glades benefit in any way?" Leaning closer, he asked, "Or will that money go elsewhere? Will it line the pockets of other people—people who don't need it just to survive?"

The mayor rose slowly, and Sebastian did the same.

"I'm… not certain what you're saying, Alderman Blood, but I don't like the sound of it," Mayor Altman said, his voice growing louder. "Perhaps I haven't made myself clear. The Glades are a hellhole. The district has the lowest voter turnout in the city. The votes that got you elected, Mr. Blood, wouldn't have even landed you on the ballot anywhere else in the city. No one cares about that place—not even the people who live in it.

"So I suggest you get out of my office, and find something productive to occupy your time."

As he stalked out of City Hall, Sebastian's cell phone rang. He pulled it out of his jacket pocket and found an incoming call from Dr. Vaca. His stomach sank to his feet, and he braced himself.

"Hello, Dr. Vaca," he said. "How are you doing?"

"Hello, Sebastian," the older man said. "I am sorry to bother you—I know you are a busy man—but I just admitted Mr. and Mrs. Gomez into the clinic, and I thought you should be aware."

"What happened?" Sebastian said. "Are they okay?"

"They are okay, yes, but their home was broken

into last night, while they were sleeping. The intruders didn't inflict too much damage, so they only suffered minor scrapes and bruises. However, they lost many belongings, and are quite shaken up. I was hoping maybe you could stop by the clinic to say hello, try to lift their spirits."

He stopped in the street, allowing the news to sink in.

"Of course I will, doctor," he said, keeping his voice even. "I'll stop in as soon as I can." But inside, he was anything but calm. *What is happening to my city?* he thought, his mind in chaos.

The Glades were indeed a hellhole, but innocent people lived there. The mayor was wrong—people *did* care. *He* cared, and it was time to do something about it. If the system wouldn't help, then he would need to act outside of the system.

Anger turned to resolve, and Sebastian continued down the street, heading for the clinic.

6

In the basement of St. Pancras parish, Sebastian placed the skull mask upon his head, taking a moment to gather himself. It made him feel strangely *alive*, gave him confidence and reminded him of the purpose of the brotherhood that gathered before him. Cyrus Gold and Clinton Hogue sat before him, as did Brother Michael Daily, who wore the uniform of the city police department. They had answered his call, as had so many others.

"My brothers," he began, "we have not met since the passing of our leader, mentor, and dear friend, Father Trigon. As we all know, Father Trigon believed in the good of the people who live here in the Glades, and because of him the halls of St. Walker's are filled with the guilty." Murmurs of agreement filled the hall. "But I am here to tell you, my brothers, that our work is not done.

"Despite his efforts, the city is falling apart. Just

last night, good people were maliciously attacked, their home invaded a short distance from here. Yet the officials of Starling City turn their backs, and call the Glades a hopeless hellhole."

At that, a deep scowl appeared on Brother Michael Daily's face, and angry muttering filled the room. Sebastian held up his hand for silence.

"The residents of the Glades should not be living in fear. They should not be reduced to political silence. My brothers, we need to unite and speak up, or nothing will change. Our brotherhood must give them their voice back, and prove to them that they are not abandoned. The time is now, brothers."

He lifted his hands, and the brotherhood rose from their chairs. They began to clap, and Sebastian felt the thrill of empowerment. Yet there was no time to waste. They had to act. Their mission needed to begin as soon as possible.

A few nights later, the brotherhood gathered again, and the sense of anticipation was electric. They waited largely in silence, the occasional murmur breaking the quiet, only to die down again.

The door opened and Brother Daily entered. He and two other brothers dragged a pair of thugs down the hard wooden stairs to the basement of the church. Brother Cyrus Gold stood at the front of the room, wearing his mask and patiently waiting as they were pushed to the concrete floor and surrounded.

"What the hell is this?" one of the thugs demanded. "What're you gonna do to us, priest? Preach to us? Make us see the light?" The other thug snickered at that.

"No," Brother Cyrus said as the lights in the basement went out. "The dark."

The thugs began to panic and cried out, looking around frantically in the gloom. Then a single bright light snapped back on, and they came face to face with Brother Blood.

"I am here to show you what fear *really* looks like," Brother Blood said as the thugs found themselves gripped by many hands, hauled to their feet, and bound to chairs. The prisoners struggled to escape, cursing and rocking the chairs from side to side. Their efforts became panicky as the gleam of several knives appeared in the darkness.

"Cease your struggling, and shut up," Brother Blood said. "It won't do you any good." Then he looked around. "Begin, brothers," he instructed, as the brothers pressed their blades into use. They sliced their prisoners, just enough to cause pain and make them bleed. They dragged the knives across arms, stomachs, and legs as the thugs screamed in pain.

When they were done, the brothers used the knives to cut the prisoners loose.

"Spread the word," Brother Blood said as the hands gripped them again. "Let it be known that the Glades are off limits to criminals. This is no longer a playground for scum like you. Tell your friends that they can join their neighbors to make the Glades stronger, or they will face the devil."

Then he drew his own knife and ran it over the thugs' palms, slicing them open and watching the red blood drip onto the basement floor.

Weeks later, Sebastian sat in his office, his frustrated anger a thing of the past. He was pleased at the progress that had been made. Civic groups had begun to clean up the Glades, and new businesses had begun to open. As they showed signs of prosperity, others began to invest, and a sense of community pride had begun to flourish. They still had a long way to go, but it was a beginning.

There was a knock on his office door.

"Sebastian, are you ready for lunch?" Cyrus Gold asked as he entered.

Sebastian looked up from his desk.

"Yes, in just a moment, Cyrus." He motioned for his friend to enter. "Come sit down, I have wonderful news." Cyrus took a seat on the couch, and Sebastian swiveled in his desk chair to face him. Excitement was clear in his expression.

"Good news, you say?" Cyrus replied. "Even after all we've done, the strides we've made, City Hall continues to act as if we don't exist. What more can we expect of them?"

"It's what we've been waiting for," Sebastian said. "They've finally begun to see the light. Expansion plans have been approved for the clinic."

"That's amazing," Cyrus said. He stood and hugged his longtime friend. "Congratulations, brother."

"I couldn't have done it without your support—and the support of everyone in the brotherhood. The last couple of months have been a whirlwind. The night watch program is thriving, crime is down by thirty-five percent, and it finally feels as if we're starting to make a difference."

"Father Trigon would be proud," Cyrus told him.

"I hope so." Sebastian bowed his head, remembering the man who started it all. "I hope he knows how grateful I am, for all that he did for me."

"I'm sure he knows." Cyrus placed a hand on Sebastian's shoulder. "It's wonderful what you are doing—thanks to you, the sky's the limit, Sebastian."

"Indeed it is," Sebastian agreed.

7

In the common room of the Zandia Orphanage, a small group of people attended a fundraiser for the Rebecca Merlyn Clinic. Spirits were high—Dr. Vaca beamed as he discussed the plans, while Richard and Amelia Gomez introduced their son Bobby to the donors. Though exhausted by the rigors of his treatment, he grinned broadly at the attention he received. Sebastian played his part, and socialized with his supporters.

When he finally left the festivities, Sebastian was on a high. The Glades finally were beginning to thrive, and as discouraged as he had been a few months earlier, Sebastian knew he had put into motion what was needed to fulfill his plans and dreams, regardless of any opposition from the city political machine.

Arriving at his modest apartment, he flipped a light switch and glanced ruefully at the bare white walls and sparse furniture. A small worn loveseat sat in his living room next to a side table. The sole occupant of the table was a houseplant that had long ago given up the ghost. The television stood near a fireplace that Sebastian had never used.

His bed, unmade, was in the center of the second-floor bedroom. A dresser was pushed off to the side near the closet, where an open door revealed a row of suits, pristine and crisp in a wide variety of colors. The suits weren't his concern, however, as he approached the room—there was a figure sitting on his bed in the gloom, the only light coming from the street. Whoever it was, he didn't move a muscle as Sebastian crept slowly forward, reaching for a knife he kept in a pocket.

"I'm not here to hurt you, Mr. Blood," the intruder said as he rose calmly, straightening his suit jacket. Even in the semi-darkness Sebastian could see that the man was dressed impeccably, his body language confident and his limbs muscular.

He wore an eye patch, a black smudge in the semi-darkness.

"My name is Slade Wilson," the man said, extending his hand.

Sebastian didn't reach for it.

"What do you want?"

"I… we… have a business proposition for you," the man said as a woman stepped into the room behind Sebastian. "Mr. Blood, please meet Miss Isabel Rochev," Slade added as the newcomer made her way to stand next to him.

"I ask you again," Sebastian growled, "what do you

want? One more time and I call the police."

"Oh, I don't think you want to do that," Wilson said, holding up Sebastian's skull mask. Sebastian's eyes widened, and his hand shot out to grab it, but he found his wrist held in an iron grip far more powerful than the intruder's size would have suggested. When the grip relaxed, Sebastian stepped back.

"You've been working hard, Mr. Blood, trying to turn this city around," Wilson said, "and while they might appreciate the results you've achieved, not everyone would be thrilled with your approach to the problems.' He held up the mask again.

"But I know a little something about wearing a mask, and while it can be a valuable tool when used right, it will only get you so far. I—" He gestured toward the woman. "—we would like you offer you our assistance in what you are doing for your city. In fact, we would like to offer you the city itself."

What the hell is he talking about? Sebastian wondered. He frowned, but kept quiet.

"We've been doing our homework," Wilson continued, "and it's clear you'll do anything you can to save Starling City, or you wouldn't go running around late at night with your… brothers. We can offer you something more powerful—an army with which to take control, make the city yours, and position you as mayor."

"Mayor?" Sebastian responded with skepticism clear in his voice, and the woman—Rochev—scoffed.

"I told you, he isn't ready," she said.

"Now, Miss Rochev, Mr. Blood's actions speak for him, and his love for his city runs deep within him. Deeper than most, in fact…" He turned to face Sebastian again. "…which is why you will accept my offer."

"I don't know who you think you are, Mr. Wilson, stalking me, breaking into my apartment, but I've already begun to turn this city around without your help, and I will continue to do so." He pointed to the mask. "That proves nothing, and I will not be threatened in my own home, nor swayed by some bogus proposition."

Wilson smirked, and despite himself Sebastian found it disconcerting.

"I assure you my offer is valid," Wilson said. "And we have no intention of threatening you. I believe you will see the value of having a different set of allies, and change your mind. For the time when you do…" Slade handed Sebastian his card. "Let's go, Miss Rochev." He stepped past Sebastian and out of the room, followed closely by his companion, and they were gone.

Sebastian rounded the corner at a brisk pace, approaching the clinic for an afternoon meeting with Dr. Vaca, when he came to an abrupt halt. The entrance was boarded up. Long two-by-fours were nailed to the doors, and no one was around to be seen. Shaking off his initial confusion, he reached for his phone.

Vaca picked up on the first ring.

"Doctor, I'm down at the clinic," Sebastian said. "What's going on?"

"It all happened so quickly, I haven't had the time to call you," the doctor said, his voice panicky. "Malcolm Merlyn shut down the clinic this morning, before we could open. His support has been pulled."

Sebastian felt his face grow warm.

"I'll call you back." He cut the connection and stood there, staring. In one quick moment so much of his work—the clinic that represented the progress he had been making—had been snatched away. Anger turned to steely resolve. He turned on his heel, walking even more briskly than before.

"I don't care if he is in the middle of something," Sebastian said, the volume of his voice rising in Malcolm Merlyn's office. As the assistant disappeared into the room behind him, Sebastian paced the outer office.

She returned, and moments later Sebastian stood before Merlyn himself, sweating and seething with anger. Despite that fact, Merlyn casually leaned back in his desk chair, and his expression revealed that he was unimpressed with Sebastian's entrance.

"That was quite a racket you made coming to see me, Mr. Blood," he said, gesturing to a guest chair. "Please take a seat—you must need to recover after such a performance."

"Thank you, but I would rather stand," Sebastian

said firmly. "We don't need to bother with the niceties, Mr. Merlyn. Why did you close the clinic?"

"Ah, that." Merlyn rose to his feet. "Mr. Blood, I should have closed that clinic down *years* ago," he continued. "It was my wife's project, and it should have been shuttered when the people of the Glades murdered her."

"Do you have any idea how many people rely on that clinic?" Sebastian said. "You can't just—"

"Save your energy," Malcolm said, raising his hand to halt the conversation. "I've heard about your crusade—everyone has. 'Alderman Blood is here to save the Glades,'" he said with a condescending sneer. "But you won't, Mr. Blood. The Glades are already dead, and the people who live there will get what's coming to them. So I strongly urge you to do yourself a favor, and find a new cause to support—something that people will actually care about. Because despite your juvenile delusions, no one will ever care about the Glades.

"The clinic is shut down for good," Malcolm concluded. "Now if you would be so kind as to leave my office a little more quietly than you entered, I too have more important matters to address." With that he reached for the phone.

A short time later Sebastian arrived at City Hall and saw light coming from under the door of Mayor Altman's office. Taking a deep breath and squaring his shoulders, he knocked lightly.

"Come in," Mayor Altman called.

Sebastian entered to find him filing paperwork and watching the local news, with anchor Bethany Snow on the screen. The sound was low. Sebastian caught a glimpse of himself in the window, and realized how disheveled he was. His hair was unkempt and messy, his dress shirt half tucked in and his tie hanging loosely around his neck.

Not a good look, he mused.

"Sebastian, what happened?" Mayor Altman asked with concern.

"I've come for some advice, Mr. Mayor. I realize that the last time I did this, I let my emotions get the best of me, and ask that you forgive me," Sebastian said.

"I appreciate that, thank you," the mayor said. "So what has happened that has left you looking like... this?" he added.

"Malcolm Merlyn closed the Glades clinic today," Sebastian replied.

"I know," Altman said. "I heard." Sebastian thought he sounded disheartened, as well.

"Mr. Mayor, the community depends on the clinic—for so many people it's their only alternative. They wouldn't know what else to do, where else to go." He paused, then continued. "Perhaps if we work together, show a united front, we can come up with an alternative. It might even be to our advantage," he offered tentatively. "Provide us with some political capital."

The mayor sat back for a second, rubbing his forehead with his fingertips, when suddenly a banner headline on the television announced breaking news. Both men turned their heads, and Mayor Altman reached for the remote, turning up the volume.

"We now go live to the Queen Mansion," Snow said in a voice-over, "where we've been told Moira Queen has called a press conference." The image on the screen was of an empty podium, and while they watched Moira Queen stepped into view, wearing a red dress suit. The look on her face was startling—a combination of fear and anguish—as she took a deep breath and began to speak.

"God forgive me," she said, her voice breaking. "I have failed this city. I have been complicit with an undertaking for one horrible purpose… to destroy the Glades and everyone in it." As a startled murmur broke out in the pressroom, Queen continued, struggling for control, revealing that she feared for her own life and the lives of her family. Yet she couldn't stand by and remain silent. The conspiracy, she said, had been the brainchild of one man.

Malcolm Merlyn.

As she spoke, Sebastian felt a strange vibration, and his eyes went wide. Bethany Snow reappeared on the screen and announced that they were cutting to a live feed from the streets of the Glades. When the image changed to show a street view, however, it was as if the camera operator couldn't control his device. The picture rocked violently, making it difficult to focus on what was occurring.

It looks like an earthquake, he thought. *But that's impossible... unless...*

Crowds flooded the streets, which were cracking and shifting as the vibrations appeared to increase. Pieces fell from the buildings, striking people down at random, leaving bodies crushed and bleeding. Here and there fires could be seen, sending angry flames and clouds of smoke into the night air. The current of bodies grew as chaos reigned, and people trampled one another to escape.

Sebastian glanced at the mayor, whose face had gone white. Without a word, the young alderman bolted from the room.

Out in the street traffic was at a standstill, so Sebastian ran, determined to reach the Glades. The closer he got, the stronger the vibrations became, threatening to throw him to the ground. When he reached the perimeter of his neighborhood, all he found was chaos as far as the eye could see.

What has Merlyn done? he wondered incredulously. *How could he accomplish so much destruction?*

Another quake, and he was thrown to the ground, landing hard on his palms. He looked up and saw the building above him start to crumble to the ground. Scrambling to his feet, ignoring the stinging pain in his hands, he spotted a teenage boy about to be buried by the falling rubble. Moving as fast as he could, he grabbed the kid around the waist and dragged him to one side just as the bricks and mortar struck the ground and scattered in all directions.

Making sure the teen wasn't hurt, Sebastian started running again. He passed the clinic and was horrified to see gaping holes in the walls. All of the windows were shattered. A portion of the fire escape had broken loose and was lying in a twisted tangle of metal on the ground. Pausing only for a moment, he started toward Zandia Orphanage. As he did, fear gripped his heart, telling him what he was going to find.

Finally he turned the corner…

Thank god.

It was still standing.

"Sebastian! Brother!" Cyrus called out, waving his arms above his head.

"Cyrus," Sebastian yelled, running over. "Are you okay?"

"I'm fine," Cyrus replied, and he pointed. "The children are in the basement of the church, and we're watching over them. The walls are solid—they should be safe from this insanity."

"Have you heard from Dr. Vaca?" Sebastian asked. "I went to the clinic, and it's all but leveled."

"I don't know, I can't reach anyone," Cyrus said. Then his voice turned angry. "The Queen family is behind this madness, they admitted it on the news."

"I know, I saw Mrs. Queen's confession," Sebastian said. "It's Merlyn—somehow he's responsible for this. I don't know how, but he's engineered an earthquake, and it's confined to the Glades. The wealthy have been playing us all along, and we're nothing but fodder for their ambitions. Our lives mean nothing to them, and it's time for us to do something about it." As if to punctuate his point, the ground shook again.

"Brother, it is time for retribution," Cyrus replied.

It's past time, and I finally know what to do, Sebastian mused with a cold fury. "It's time for the one percent to feel as we have, Cyrus," he agreed. "It's time for a war to come, and for a new leader to guide us into safety." He peered into the distance. The place he had worked so hard to save, to pull from the ashes, was being destroyed, brick by brick. Innocents were dying, and Sebastian knew now that what he had been doing could never have been enough.

"This ends now."

He pulled out his cell phone and Slade Wilson's business card. Then he punched in Slade's number.

"I'm in," he said. "Give me my city—give me my army."

4

REVENGE

1

Night fell over the Glades, the moon full in a cloudless sky. Moonlight cascaded upon the neighborhood in ghost-like fingers, the eerie bands of luminescence threading themselves between the broken buildings, reflecting off glass and metal, then dissolving in alleys dark and menacing.

The area had been decimated by the earthquake. They called it the Undertaking—the unnatural event engineered by Merlyn and his confederates—and it had left an abyss of hopelessness and despair in its wake. Shortly after this devastation, Merlyn disappeared from Starling City. So did Oliver Queen, taking with him the vigilante who was his alter ego.

Now Slade drove through the neighborhood, the headlights from his Aventador cutting a swath through the darkness. He had been driving most of the day, digging deep, visiting locations personal to Oliver—his family's mansion and sprawling estate,

Queen Consolidated, even the graves of Sara Lance and Tommy Merlyn.

Finding nothing of value, he next targeted Queen's closest allies, locating the apartments of John Diggle, Felicity Smoak, and Laurel Lance. Each was a dead end, yet he continued to explore, experiencing every inch he could of Starling City. This was the home Oliver loved, to which he had returned, and which he desperately sought to save. Slade was determined to know it intimately—so that when he crushed it to dust, he would know and revel in the depths of Oliver's despair.

As Slade drove through the Glades, it made all the sense in the world that this forsaken place had been the domain of the vigilante. He had seen the killer Oliver had become, and knew the blackness at his core. That was the *true* Oliver Queen. It was natural that he would gravitate toward the area most overcome by the dark. Yet after Tommy Merlyn's funeral, he had vanished without a trace.

Retreating like a coward, Slade thought. *Abandoning his city.*

He took a turn, his headlights illuminating graffiti on walls still standing among the destruction. He smirked as he read what it said. BLOOD FOR MAYOR. In the vacuum created by the vigilante's departure, his new acquaintance, Mr. Blood, had stepped in, anointing himself as Starling City's would-be savior.

Slade slowed as he neared the nightclub Verdant, the last stop on his tour through the city. To the unobservant eye, Oliver's decision to convert his family's old steel factory had seemed to make perfect sense. A rich playboy became an entrepreneur, catering to other rich ne'er-do-wells. The club was the plaything of a dilettante with nothing better to do.

Slade knew better.

The building was centrally located, tactically ideal for a certain hooded vigilante and his exploits. Blueprints of the property confirmed Slade's suspicions, revealing an unaccounted sublevel beneath the club, easily missed below the dancing feet of Starling's youthful elite. Oliver had hidden his operation in plain sight, using his reputation as an all-night party boy to cover his *other* nocturnal excursions.

Clever… thought Slade, a malicious smirk crossing his face. *But not clever enough.* Revving his engine, he peeled out and headed back toward downtown.

He stepped off the elevator, his dark suit gleaming under the warm lights of the hallway. A swath of dark red carpeting led him past thick octagonal columns on either side, and toward a lacquered oak desk at the suite's center. Heavy and substantial, the piece was the focal point of the overtly masculine space, its dark cedar echoed in the surrounding décor. The windows behind it were obscured by floor-to-ceiling curtains, and there was a small bar off to the side. The overall effect was one of power and intimidation.

Slade smoothed the lapel on his tailored suit.

He found Isabel waiting for him, seated at one of two leather chairs opposite the desk. She had found the suite in an office building on the edge of downtown Starling City, easily secured in the post-Undertaking recession. Like Slade, she was dressed sharply and ready to get to work.

"As you requested," she said. "Paid for with an account at Starling National, established under your name. It was an odd request, though, considering your desire for stealth."

"Crumbs meant to draw out the rats," Slade said, settling in behind the large desk.

"In that case, why not open the curtains and enjoy the very expensive view?"

"Because, Ms. Rochev," he said, with matter-of-fact confidence, "when next I gaze upon the skyline, it will be from the penthouse of *your* Queen Consolidated, while the city burns."

A rare smile crossed Isabel's face. She had worked with many a successful CEO, but none had Slade's level of foresight and cunning. She relished the thought of dismantling the company Robert Queen had spent his life building.

"What of Mr. Blood?" Slade asked. "Have you found anything else?"

Isabel shook her head. "If he has secrets beyond the brotherhood, they're well hidden." She handed him a dossier.

"For his sake," Slade said, "let's hope they stay buried."

"He'll have questions," she said. "What do you plan on telling him?"

Slade opened the folder, staring at Blood's life, laid out in text.

"I will tell him exactly what he wants to hear."

Sebastian strode in and was immediately taken aback by the suite's opulence. Seeing the expensive clothes worn by Wilson and Rochev, he was reminded of the Starling City elite—the ones who had destroyed the Glades and left its residents to suffer. Reminding himself that he *needed* these people, he tried to shake off the thought.

For the most part, he succeeded.

"Welcome, Mr. Blood," Wilson said, standing to extend his hand. "You remember Ms. Rochev?"

"Of course." Blood nodded to Isabel, standing at the small bar.

"Can I interest you in a drink?" she asked.

"I'm okay, thank you," Blood said.

"We insist," Wilson said. "To mark the occasion." He nodded, Isabel poured two fingers of Scotch, and handed Blood the glass. He took it reluctantly.

"A toast," Wilson said, raising his own glass. "To changing Starling City for the better."

Blood took a sip of the golden liquor, recognizing it as the same eighteen-year-old Macallan he kept under his desk for special occasions. He didn't think this was a coincidence. Slade noticed his reticence.

"You seem on edge," he said. "Is something the matter?"

Blood took a moment, debating internally what to say. Resolved, he went on the offensive.

"That is a very nice suit you're wearing… and all this?" Blood said, gesturing to the surrounding suite. "Impressive. But if I'm being honest, it all reeks of the very wealth I'm trying to expel from this city."

Wilson nodded. "I assure you, our intentions are aligned."

Blood set his glass of Scotch on the massive desk, where it landed with a thud.

"You know the Scotch I drink, the brotherhood I lead, the mask I wear," he said pointedly. "Yet I know nothing about either of you. So excuse me for being a little wary of our arrangement."

"Then allow us to put your mind at ease," Wilson said. "What would you like to know?"

"What's in it for you?" Blood asked. "What do you gain by making me mayor?"

"Revenge." Wilson smiled, and his voice was tinged with malice. The answer caught Blood by surprise. "The people who betrayed your city wronged me… wronged *us*, as well. Together, we will make them pay for those transgressions."

"How?"

Wilson nodded to Rochev, who pulled a briefcase out from beside her chair. She opened it, revealing five vials of incandescent green liquid.

"That is mirakuru," Wilson explained. "This serum grants power beyond measure. With it, you can build an army of the worthy, strong enough to bring Starling City to its knees. Then the fat cats won't be able to hide from reality—they will finally know the plight of the Glades."

The screams from the Undertaking were still fresh in Blood's mind. As he thought about the lives lost in the earthquake, and people left behind to suffer, his reservations began to recede. Wilson was right. Blood *did* want revenge.

"And when the city cries out for its savior," Wilson continued, "you will answer, reshaping the city as you see fit."

"What about the vigilante?" Blood asked, taking the case from Rochev. "I doubt he'll stand idly by as an army overtakes his city."

"That supposes that he's not too preoccupied," Wilson said, lacing his fingers together and placing them on the desk, "being hunted as Starling City's public enemy number one."

"Have you heard of the Copycat Hoods, Mr. Blood?" Rochev asked. She handed him a copy of Starling City's newspaper, *The Star*. On the front page was a headline. "THE VIGILANTE GANG STRIKES AGAIN." The article detailed the murder of a local businessman with ties to the Merlyn Global Group, the sixth such death since the Undertaking. The group of men responsible were masked, dressed like the vigilante, and assumed to be acting on his behalf.

"Of course," Blood said, glancing at the paper. "I know of them through the brotherhood." He put the paper down on his lap. "But you already know this, don't you?"

"We would like you to make contact with these men," Rochev said, pushing ahead. "Point them toward a new target."

"Who?"

"Mayor Altman."

Sebastian couldn't conceal his shock.

"You want me to orchestrate an assassination?"

"No," Wilson said. "A cleansing."

"Our hope," Rochev added, "is that the mayor's death will be blamed on the vigilante himself, making his capture a priority for the Starling City Police Department and district attorney's office. Their preoccupation with each other should give you ample space to test the serum, and build your army."

"While also creating a vacancy at City Hall." Blood marveled at their ruthless cunning. "And given the circumstances, everyone will be too afraid to fill it."

"Except for you, Mr. Blood," Wilson said, his hand stroking his beard.

"Promises like these don't come without a price," Sebastian said. "What's yours? What will I owe you?"

"Your loyalty and discretion," Wilson said, his voice like gravel, "and an expectation of excellence. I do not tolerate mistakes."

"Then we're good partners," Sebastian replied, deciding to meet the challenge head on. "Because I don't make them." He stood and shook hands with both Wilson and Rochev.

"One final word, Mr. Blood." Wilson stared at him. "Should your activities put you in the path of the vigilante, do not engage him. Do you understand?"

Sebastian nodded, then turned and walked the long hallway toward the elevator doors—noting as he did the carpet underfoot, the color reminiscent of of blood.

"Robert gave me my first taste of Scotch. 'A man's drink,' he said. I thought it meant he viewed me as an equal." Isabel took a long sip, feeling the alcohol's pleasurable warmth travel from her mouth down through her throat to her chest.

"All just part of the seduction," Slade said, eying Blood's glass on his desk.

She nodded, then asked something that had been on her mind since their meeting with Blood.

"Our mayor-to-be hates everything the Queens represent," she observed. "Why not tell him that Oliver is the vigilante?"

"We need his ambition and unwitting servitude," Slade said. "Not his questions. The less he knows, the better."

"Yet you trusted me with that knowledge."

"Of course," he said. "Mr. Blood is merely a puppet.

Your role is far more important."

"I didn't realize you valued corporate takeovers so highly."

"I do when they strike at the very heart of my enemy."

The two shared a smile. They both understood the importance of Queen Consolidated. Isabel, however, had known this long before Slade Wilson had entered her life. Revenge would only be hers when she had dismantled their precious company, piece by piece.

"When do you want me to start?" she asked.

"Tomorrow."

Isabel let slip the briefest hint of surprise.

"You doubt yourself?" he said.

"Never," she said. "But it *is* soon. The company is weak, but it's not yet fully vulnerable. There are still variables I can't control."

"There's only one thing I care about," Slade said, "and that is drawing Oliver Queen back to Starling City."

"How can you be sure it'll work?"

"The company is his family's legacy," he responded. "It's as important to him as his city. He will not allow either to be taken from him without a fight."

"Well, that legacy is about to end," Isabel said.

"I have no doubt," he replied, then he rose up from the desk, preparing to leave.

"Where will you be in the meantime?"

He paused, smoothing out his jacket lapel once more. Then he met her eye, his face without expression.

"Purgatory."

2

Hidden behind dense foliage, Slade crouched in silent wait, beads of sweat dripping from his forehead to his neck, then to his chest. His black shirt and tactical pants were soaked. Though it was fall, the heat of summer still had yet to relinquish its hold on Lian Yu. He had almost forgotten about the island's unrelenting heat. He had hated it for the entirety of his stay but now, so many years removed, he found the oppressive humidity oddly comforting.

Perhaps that was the reason, out of all the places in the world he could have chosen, Oliver had taken refuge here. Lian Yu may have been hell, but it was a hell they both understood. That he and Oliver had willingly returned to the prison they had so desperately tried to escape was irony not lost on Slade.

Suddenly, Stockholm syndrome made a hell of a lot of sense.

He rose up from his crouch, slowly moving forward,

straining to distinguish signs of movement among the sounds of the forest. Oliver would take shelter in the place he knew best. Slade had started his hunt at the burnt-out fuselage, had been tracking Oliver for nearly an hour, following his trail through the dense foliage, a predator stalking his prey.

Nature and time had covered the structure in dense green vines, all but obscuring it from view, but the camouflage had done nothing to obscure Slade's memory. This was where he and Oliver had first met. Slade had easily gotten the drop on the inexperienced rich kid, holding a blade to his throat, ready to slit it.

If only I had, he thought.

Slade stopped suddenly, hearing movement on the ridge below him. He took cover behind a tree, looking down through the foliage. Then he spotted him, about sixty yards away. Oliver Queen. Slade gasped at the sight of him. He was shirtless, glistening with perspiration, his chest and back riddled with tattoos and scars, memories of pain expressed in flesh. He held his bow out in front, arrow nocked and at the ready, eyes trained on the brush ahead of him.

This was the first time Slade had laid eyes on Oliver in the flesh since their confrontation on the freighter, when Oliver had plunged the arrow through his eye, leaving him for dead. Reacting viscerally, Slade grasped the hilt of his tactical knife, thoughts of ambush and murder passing through his mind. It would only take a few seconds, the edge of the blade ripping through

Oliver's neck, laying it open, remedying Slade's hesitation from their first encounter.

Then he shook off his bloodlust, relaxing his grip.

Too easy, he thought. *He has to suffer*.

Hearing a noise above the island's wild din, Slade retreated a few steps back from the ridge. Cutting through the chorus of bird chirps and rustling leaves was the sound of an aircraft. Small, with twin propeller engines, the plane was making an approach, flickering in and out of view behind cloud cover. Oliver spotted it, as well, looking up in time to see a dark speck drop from the plane's body. As it hurtled toward the island, growing in size, it was clear that the mass was in fact two people, one tethered in front of the other.

Seconds later, an olive-green parachute opened, slowing the couple's descent, course set for the Lian Yu shore. Oliver immediately abandoned his hunt for game and took off, feet pounding dirt in pursuit of the approaching visitors.

Slade, however, stayed put.

They had arrived, right on schedule.

He took cover in the brush just beyond the fuselage, and watched as Oliver led John Diggle and Felicity Smoak—his two trusted allies—inside the hull. As expected, the two had made their trek from Starling City to deliver the news that Isabel Rochev's company, Stellmoor International, was attempting a hostile takeover of Queen Consolidated.

It had taken them weeks to track down Oliver, during which time Slade had followed their every move. Using his mirakuru-enhanced senses, he eavesdropped as the two attempted to persuade Oliver to return from his self-imposed exile.

Yet despite their pleading, Oliver said no. He told them he had failed his city. He had been unable to prevent Malcolm Merlyn's Undertaking from devastating the Glades. More than that, he believed he was responsible for Tommy Merlyn's death, and was further racked with guilt. He had arrived at the conclusion that the city—the people in his life—were worse off now than before he had donned the hood.

He refused to put it back on again.

He wouldn't come back.

However, Diggle and Smoak knew what Slade also knew—that to convince Oliver to return to Starling City, they would have to appeal to him not as the vigilante, but as head of the Queen family. They told him about Queen Consolidated, that it had become vulnerable after the earthquake and his mother's incarceration. It was in danger of being acquired by Stellmoor International. If Oliver did not intercede, thirty thousand employees would be out on the street.

Hearing this, Oliver finally relented, and agreed to return home. Everything continued to unfold just as Slade had anticipated. Oliver's weakness would always be his family.

A short time later Slade watched from the trees as Oliver, Diggle, and Smoak boarded the plane and took off, disappearing through the clouds, headed back toward Starling City. He pulled out a satellite phone from his munitions pouch and keyed in the number for Isabel, who answered immediately.

"Is it time?" she said.

"He'll be there by morning," he said. "Are you prepared?"

"I'm insulted you have to ask."

"Good."

"Are you headed back now?"

"After some unfinished business," he said. "I'll be in touch."

Slade hung up then ventured deeper into the Lian Yu forest, course set on a familiar path.

It had been nearly four years since Slade had visited Shado's grave. Time, however, had done nothing to buffer him from the pain its sight evoked. If anything, it made it worse, reminding him of how long his promise of revenge had remained unfulfilled. He felt the familiar rage boil inside of him, his hand beginning to tremble.

"Be still, my love."

He turned to see Shado by his side. She caressed his face, calming him.

"Don't lose sight of your plan," she said.

Slade flexed his hand, regaining control. He looked deep into her eyes.

"Years ago, I made you a promise," he said. "I will not fail you."

"Will Oliver Queen suffer?" she asked.

Slade nodded. "Soon, suffering will be all he knows."

Before leaving the gravesite, Slade noticed that the makeshift cemetery had a new inhabitant. A burial plot marked with the name Taiana, fashioned in the same primitive style as those for Robert Queen, Yao Fei, and his beloved. Though new in comparison to the others, the displaced dirt around it had long since settled, indicating that the grave was not fresh.

Slade gazed upon the mound of rocks, thinking the woman lying beneath fortunate. As someone Oliver truly cared for, Taiana was better off dead and buried than suffer the reckoning that was to come.

Slade emerged from the trees and stepped onto the rocky beach. He watched the waves crashing on the shore, remembering his leap into the sea. How shortsighted he had been, thinking he could best Mother Nature. It wasn't a mistake he planned on repeating.

He spotted the mask, still staked where he had left it, about twenty-five yards from the cresting waves. His orange and black balaclava, arrow through the eye, the reminder he had left for Oliver. He yanked the arrow out and pulled the mask free, holding it out in front of him, taking in its terrifying visage. Though the years of exposure to the elements had battered it, and left its bottom half tattered like flayed flesh, Slade felt the mask still had one last purpose. When he next left the balaclava for Oliver to find, it wouldn't just be as a reminder of his betrayal. This time, the mask would be a harbinger, foreshadowing the death of Oliver Queen and everyone for whom he cared.

He pocketed the mask and stalked across the rocky shore, back to the boat he had hidden off the coast. Once on board, he set course for Starling City.

3

A group of staffers passed out pamphlets in front of what remained of Cyrus Gold's badly damaged church, while Sebastian Blood, trying his best to draw attention to the neighborhood's plight, was interviewed by the local news. He was promoting a blood drive in support of the local hospital, Glades Memorial. Their blood banks had been in low supply ever since the earthquake. A throng of the neighborhood's downtrodden began to gather, drawn to the activity.

Officer Daily kept an eye on the crowd.

"The message from City Hall is clear," Sebastian said to the reporter. "No one cares about the Glades. We're on our own. Only by banding together as a community, by helping our brothers and sisters, can we hope to rebuild this neighborhood. This blood drive is the start."

"Restoring the hospital's blood bank is a noble cause, but what good is it if it's leaking through a sieve?" the reporter asked. "Crime in the Glades is up over seventy-five percent, murder up twenty. Can a blood drive really hope to counteract that sort of demand?"

"Like I said, Inez, this is only the first step. A reminder that we possess the strength to find our own salvation."

"What about the vigilante? There are many in this community who still remain optimistic that he'll return."

That struck a nerve within Sebastian, yet he did his best to stifle his reaction.

"The criminal element fled to the Glades to *escape* that murderer," he asserted. "Rest assured, the vigilante is no savior."

"But you might be, Alderman Blood?" The reporter gave him a wry smile. "Is that your claim?"

"My aim is only to give a voice to the voiceless," he said, refusing to rise to the challenge. "The Glades will rise again, and with it, this city."

With that, the interview ended. As the news crew packed up their equipment and the throng dispersed, Sebastian saw a man linger. He was in his twenties, an artist type with close-cropped hair. He had the look of a loner. Sebastian walked over to investigate.

"You really think you can make a difference?" the man said.

"These streets are my home," Sebastian answered. "I won't rest until they're safe. What's your name, son?"

"Max," he said. "Max Stanton."

"Well, Max," said Sebastian, handing him a pamphlet, "whenever you're ready to help make this neighborhood a better place, please join us. We'll be conducting these every three weeks. Come on by."

Stanton took the leaflet without a word, and disappeared down the street. Sebastian watched him, then he glanced over to Officer Daily, who nodded, indicating it was time. Sebastian shook hands with the few stragglers, said goodbye to his staffers, and then drove off, headed toward another church. This one was still intact, positioned underground, in the darkness beneath the city.

The man's scream reverberated throughout the chamber and out into the forgotten sewers beyond, the piercing sound of agony sending rats scurrying for cover. Then his struggle gave way to a quiet death, his body's contortions ceasing, the echoes of his wail fading off into silence.

Deep underneath the Glades, the members of the Church of Blood—Officer Daily, Cyrus Gold, Dr. Langford, Clinton Hogue, and Dr. Vasak, also known as "the Technician"—looked on as Brother Blood, his skull mask terrifying in the shadows, removed the syringe of mirakuru from the man's arm. Blood nodded to Dr. Langford, who moved to check the victim's pulse. The doctor hesitated momentarily, the sight of the blood flowing from the man's eyes giving him pause, before he continued, feeling for the pulse at his neck.

Langford shook his head.

Blood removed his skull mask and regarded the body. Then he turned to his brotherhood and saw various levels of shock reflected on each face. He wasn't surprised. When Wilson tasked him with testing the mirakuru, he had mentioned only that many of the test subjects would die. In no way were they prepared to witness the torture it inflicted.

He looked to Cyrus Gold, his trusted ally and confidant, and knew at a glance that the man had something on his mind. He was too respectful, however, to speak out of turn.

"Brother Cyrus?"

"You said this 'miracle' would save our city," Cyrus said, "but do these men deserve to endure such agony? Is this truly necessary?"

Blood looked to the rest of the men, inviting them to voice any misgivings. Dr. Langford met his gaze.

"We've killed before in the name of the brotherhood," the doctor said, "but the guilt of those men was clear. Here, I'm not so sure."

"I apprehended this man after an attempted smash and grab at Pearl Liquor," Officer Daily offered. "He's definitely no innocent—but did he deserve to go out like that? I don't know."

The rest of the men nodded and muttered, indicating that they agreed. Blood nodded in return.

"Does your belief in our purpose waiver?" he asked. There was no sense of challenge in his voice. The men shook their heads no. "And in me, as your leader?" Again, there was no dissension. "I agree that what we've witnessed is horrific. Inhuman, even—and I'd be lying if I said I wasn't shaken—but there's one thought that keeps me certain that what we're doing, however gruesome, is necessary." He walked over to a bulletin board. Dozens of photos were tacked there—the faces of all the men and women lost during the Undertaking. Five hundred and three victims in total.

"The memory of the five-oh-three," he continued. "To avenge their loss. To take this city back and fix it in their honor." He approached each man, looking them in the eye, seeking to communicate the confidence that was building within him. "These men are being sacrificed for the greater good, to protect those who cannot protect themselves."

The echo of Father Trigon's purpose further emboldened the men.

"Together," he said, "we will save this city."

Blood went on to explain his plan. While the aim of the blood drive was indeed to help restore the hospital's supply, there was an ulterior motive behind the altruism. By offering incentives to draw a larger pool of donors, he could also use the program to select his test subjects for the mirakuru. Under the guise of offering free mental health exams, Dr. Langford would catalogue each prospective sacrifice, while Officer

Daily, through his resources at SCPD, would perform background checks.

They would isolate the scum of the Glades, ensuring that the men sacrificed for the greater good wouldn't be missed.

"Turn on the television, Brother Blood." Sebastian was sitting alone in his office when Officer Daily entered.

Blood did so, and was greeted by the grave face of Channel 52 News anchor Bethany Snow. She brushed her blonde hair out of the way.

"Breaking news out of City Hall," she said. "Mayor Altman is dead, shot and killed tonight at the hands of four hooded men with suspected ties to the vigilante…"

Blood took a sip of his Scotch.

"Thank you, Brother Daily."

"I'm afraid I have bad news, as well." Daily handed him a report. "The medical supplies from FEMA— the ones headed for Glades Memorial? They've been hijacked en route. We don't know by whom."

Sitting bolt upright, Blood flipped open his laptop and began scanning the key news sites, but there was nothing. As he watched, however, news about Altman's assassination began to share space with news of Oliver Queen. He had re-entered the public eye for the first time since the earthquake, and the sight of the playboy sickened Blood. There were people dying in his city—people who needed medical supplies—

yet the "journalists" saw fit to cover the exploits of a spoiled rich kid.

Like Slade, Blood viewed Queen as a coward. He had fled the city, instead of accepting responsibility for the horror his mother's involvement had wrought upon the Glades. Not that Blood was surprised. All of the Starling City elite were cowards in his book. Heartless. Turning a blind eye to the plight of those they deemed beneath them.

Soon, the rich would no longer be able to ignore them.

Outside of Starling City, in an abandoned industrial complex shrouded in shadow, the hijacked FEMA medical supply truck pulled to an abrupt stop, a black SUV following close behind. There were two holes in the truck's windshield, the marks of kill shots aligned to the heads of passenger and driver. Whoever the hijackers were, they were ruthless.

Slade Wilson stepped out from the shadows. He was dressed in his A.S.I.S. prototype armor, his face obscured by the metal helmet, colored orange and black. He held a briefcase by his side, and his weapons were holstered.

The truck's new driver, a severe-looking Chinese man with ornate tattoos down his arms, climbed down from the cabin and retreated to the SUV behind him. Slade recognized the tattoos as Triad, the same criminal element he had tracked in Hong Kong.

A woman exited the SUV. Dressed in form-fitting black, she was beautiful. Her namesake white hair fell in long, soft curls down her back, vibrant in the moonlight. She approached Slade.

"Did you have any trouble?" he asked.

"None," China White replied. "Disappointingly uneventful."

Slade handed her the briefcase. "Payment for future deliveries, with enough extra to hire added protection. I've included a dossier on a man codenamed Bronze Tiger. I believe you know his work."

"A job like this is hardly worthy of a man of his skill. He thrives on prey not easy to kill."

"With every shipment you hijack, Glades Memorial edges closer to being shut down. I expect this to draw out the vigilante, putting you in direct conflict."

"Good." An intensity filled China White's eyes, one born of hate. "I owe him pain."

"That's my hope."

She climbed into her SUV and drove away into the night. Once they were gone, Slade removed a pack of explosives from his bandolier. He affixed them to the cargo of the truck, set the timer and walked away.

The explosion was bright against his silhouette.

4

Isabel strode through the doors of Queen Consolidated, wearing a deep red skirt suit, flanked by two members of her Stellmoor International acquisition team. The last time she had stepped foot in the building was over a decade ago, when Walter Steele had cast her aside unceremoniously, like so much trash, and Bobby and his security detail had forcibly removed her.

She didn't expect to see Steele—he had cut ties with the company after his divorce from Moira. Bobby, however, was where she had last seen him, checking identification at the front desk, the years having done little more than add gray to his hair and pounds to his gut.

"Can I help you?" he asked.

"That depends, Bobby," she answered. "Are you going to ask me to 'stay put' again?"

Bobby furrowed his brow, eyes squinting.

"Do I know you?"

"I told you the Queens would regret what they did to me," she said. "Today I make good on that promise."

Recognition began to dawn as Isabel and her team began to push past the security turnstile.

"Isabel! You're Stellmoor International?"

"While you still have a job, Bobby, tell Mr. Queen that Ms. Rochev is on her way up." She headed off toward the elevators, the click of her heels echoing in the hall.

As Isabel walked into the penthouse suite, memories came flooding back to her. Talking into the early morning with Robert, their bodies intertwined, plans made for a future he had lacked the spine to keep. He had always told her he liked her in red. She figured it was appropriate that she wore the color today, to mark the moment she began her takeover of his beloved company. She continued on toward the office that used to belong to Robert Queen, but was now occupied by his son.

Felicity Smoak intercepted her in the waiting area. Isabel looked the blonde woman up and down, taking in her blue form-fitting dress, leg exposed from lower thigh down. She wore glasses, as if the prop could somehow lend her legitimacy. Another hot-to-trot "assistant."

Like father, like son, she thought.

How could this woman be responsible for the vigilante's tech?

"Ms. Rochev? Hi, I'm Felicity Smoak, I'm with

Oliver—not *with* with, *just* his assistant… not that there's anything wrong with the secretarial arts but—" She paused, then said, "Can I interest you all in a bagel? We have some delicious schmeer."

"My only interest is in talking to Oliver Queen," Isabel said. "Where is he?"

"He's running just a wee bit late. You know, traffic. If you'll follow me to the conference room, I'm sure he won't be much longer. And like I said, bagels!"

Isabel paused before she and her team followed Felicity down the hall, taking one last look at Robert's old office. Soon, she would claim it as her own.

Normally, Isabel would have found Oliver's tardiness surprising. Robert was always incredibly punctual. Then again, she knew his son was no businessman.

Finally he arrived, flanked by his African-American bodyguard, John Diggle, and Smoak. She hadn't seen him since he had been a drunken teenager. Now he was older, she was struck by the echo of Robert's features in his face and build, tiny time capsules locked away in his DNA.

Rising up from the table, Isabel extended her hand, introducing herself to Robert Queen's progeny.

"Isabel Rochev."

"Oliver Queen," he said as he shook her hand. "Sorry I'm late."

The feel of his touch on her skin sent her backward

to her first encounter with Robert, meeting him in the hallway by happenstance. She shook off the memory. She wouldn't allow nostalgia to derail her plan. She steeled herself, falling back on the one trait that allowed her to survive—her ruthlessness.

"Late for this meeting," she said, "or a career in business?"

"I didn't realize hostile takeovers were filled with so much hostility."

"Not at all. I'm actually in quite a good mood."

She and Queen both took their seats at the table, ready to get to work. Felicity joined them, taking the seat across from Isabel.

"Really," Queen continued, challenging her. "So destroying companies agrees with you?"

"Winning agrees with me." Isabel stared him down across the table, confidently pushing his buttons.

"You haven't won yet."

Isabel paused, fighting off a smile. The son was as naïve as he was handsome.

"Since you majored in dropping out of college, let me put this in terms that are easy for you to understand." She saw that her insult had landed, and continued with matter-of-fact detachment, "You control forty-five percent of Queen Consolidated stock. I control forty-five percent, leaving ten percent outstanding—but, in two days the board will release the final ten percent."

"And I'll buy it before you do."

"With what money?" she said, struck by his utter

cluelessness. "I doubt your trust fund is that large, and no angel investor will go near the company that built the machine that destroyed half the city."

Queen opened his mouth to respond, but said nothing.

"Companies rise and fall, Mr. Queen," she said before he could find his tongue. "Your company has fallen."

Abruptly a commotion erupted outside the office, and cut through the room's silence. Without warning, the Copycat Hoods—the men hired by Sebastian Blood—burst through the conference room doors, semi-automatic rifles and shotguns locked and loaded. Queen stood up, muscles tensing on instinct.

"Oliver Queen!" one of Hoods said through a voice modulator. "You've failed this city."

Though Isabel knew who these men were, the interruption was unexpected. This wasn't part of the plan. She kept her eyes focused on Queen, wondering if she was about to see the vigilante emerge. He surveyed the scene, then locked eyes with Smoak. He seemed to be fighting the impulse to engage, the struggle slowing him to stagnancy, freezing him.

One of the Hoods pumped his shotgun, ready to fire, but in one swift movement Diggle removed his Glock and beat him to the trigger.

"Get down!" he said, laying down cover fire. Isabel, her instincts honed by her training with Slade, saw the conflict coming and retreated under the desk a split second before Queen and Smoak. As bullets passed overhead, she met Queen's eye, surprised to find him so slow to react.

This was the feared vigilante?

A deer caught in headlights?

Diggle's bullets found purchase in the Hood's Kevlar vest, sending him sprawling backward. The other two returned fire with their rifles, shattering glass and shredding Smoak's precious bagels. Though Diggle was doing his best to fend them off, their firepower was overwhelming.

"Fall back!" he yelled to Queen, snapping him out of his indecision. "Oliver, go! Go, go, go, go!"

Queen grabbed Isabel, ushering her through the room's rear exit before turning back toward the conflict. Safely behind cover, she watched as bullets shattered the glass door. Then Queen emerged with Felicity in tow, bullets nipping at their heels. He ran toward the exterior window, grabbed a chain from the blinds and crashed through the glass, escaping the gunfire.

Isabel heard the gunmen turn and run off, their prey having escaped, the SCPD likely on the way. Then she brushed fragments of glass off of her dress and surveyed the damage to the building. The first broken pieces of a company she planned to dismantle in forty-eight short hours. When it came time to kill the business Robert Queen had spent his life building, she would not share Oliver's reluctance to take action.

* * *

Two days later, Isabel was seated in the Queen Consolidated conference room again, and there was no longer any sign of the carnage that had occurred. She wore her black dress, feeling the color appropriate for the occasion. This was a funeral for Robert Queen's company.

Oliver Queen stared pensively out the window, his back turned to her. She knew what he had been through the past two days. The Copycat Hoods, after failing to kill Oliver, decided to go after a more vulnerable target—his sister, Thea. They had kidnapped her, and to rescue her Queen had been forced to resume his activities as the vigilante. Yet despite the direct threat to the life of his kin, he had still refused to kill, choosing instead to deliver the Hoods unharmed to the authorities.

If he lacked his killer instinct as the vigilante, how could he ever hope to harness it now, in the moment he needed it most? Without it, he had no hope of defeating her, and saving his father's company.

It's like shooting fish in a barrel, she thought, and despite her impending victory, she found it somehow hollow. Unsatisfying. *Enough of that*, she told herself. It was time to deliver the finishing blow.

"You can't win this," she announced. "I now own fifty percent of the stock. By tomorrow, I'll have what I need control your company. Any attempt to fight me will lead to litigation and leave you penniless. And trust me, poverty isn't as glamorous as Charles Dickens made it look."

Finally, Queen turned and approached her.

"What if I found someone to invest new equity capital?"

"A white knight?" she said. "With all due respect, your last name is now associated with mass murder. Even you don't have that good a friend."

"You're right," Oliver responded. Then he gave her the subtlest of smirks. "I have family."

Isabel heard the conference room doors open behind her. She turned, and was shocked to see Walter Steele enter, followed by Felicity Smoak. The sight of him sent her back in time to the moment when she learned that her internship with Queen Consolidated—and her relationship with Robert—was over. The sensation was enough to send her reeling.

She rose slowly from her chair.

"Mr. Steele," she said, trying to regain her composure. He nodded to her, clearly recognizing her as the young girl he had cast aside many years ago. "It was my understanding that you had resigned as CEO."

"I did," he acknowledged. "I'm now Chief Financial Officer of Starling National Bank." He walked past her, joining Oliver at the head of the table. "And my institution has committed rescue financing to Mr. Queen. We bought up the remaining shares of Queen Consolidated when they were released this morning."

"Now I know I majored in dropping out," Queen said, driving the dagger home, "but I'm pretty sure that makes us partners going forward. So I guess we will be seeing a lot of each other."

Despite the turn of events, Isabel felt herself struck by the young man's demeanor—so different than it had been before. Again, she was reminded of his father. Perhaps she had dismissed her enemy too quickly. She wouldn't make that mistake again.

"You aren't at all what people say about you," she said.

"Most people fail to see the real me."

She regarded him, swallowing her anger. He may have won the battle, but she would not relinquish the war. The company would be hers. Then she gave the exit signal to her team from Stellmoor, and exited the room.

Back at Slade's penthouse office, all the anger Isabel had kept bottled up in the conference room came pouring out. She paced as Slade, calmly sitting behind his desk, allowed her to vent.

"I don't lose," she said. "Do you know why? Because I control all the variables. I *told* you the company wasn't yet fully vulnerable. You forced me to attack too soon."

"I promised you the company," Slade replied. "The timeframe was open for interpretation."

"I was supposed to take Queen Consolidated from Oliver Queen, not partner with him."

"Yes, but now you're in position to hurt him far more than a simple takeover could."

The comment piqued Isabel's curiosity. Calming slightly, she took a seat.

"How do you mean?" she asked.

"A blow delivered in stealth cuts more deeply than one foreseen and defended. You now have a unique opportunity to work alongside our enemy, earning his trust and learning his weaknesses."

"His trust?" she said. "I just tried to take his company. The man hates me."

"Give it time. I expect Oliver's nighttime activities and familial responsibilities to stress him beyond measure. When they do, hate will be a luxury he cannot afford. He will have no choice but to rely on you." He leaned forward and peered at her. "Let him."

"Fine." Isabel nodded, acquiescing to the new plan. Then she asked a question that had been bothering her since the attack by the Copycat Hoods. "Speaking of Oliver's nighttime activities, I thought you said the vigilante was a killer? I've seen nothing so far to suggest that."

"It appears he's trying another way," Slade observed. "Guilt over the death of the Merlyn boy, no doubt—but rest assured, Ms. Rochev, there is indeed a killer inside of Oliver, and I aim to bring it out."

5

The crowd of protesters outside Glades Memorial had grown to nearly forty. The men and women from the neighborhood were angry, fed up with being ignored by the city in the aftermath of the earthquake. They held signs, hoping to make their voices known.

SAVE THE GLADES!

REMEMBER THE 503!

BLOOD FOR MAYOR!

Sebastian Blood stood near the throng, conducting an interview with a group of local news reporters. He had organized the protest to raise awareness about the theft of the hospital's medical supplies. More such incidents had occurred, and as of yet the SCPD had done little to stymie the thieves. A young man named

Roy Harper had intervened in one such incident, and had been arrested for his efforts.

The thefts continued. Without the supplies, the hospital was dangerously close to shutting down.

The protest yielded the added benefit of getting Sebastian publicity in advance of his mayoral campaign. Though he hadn't officially announced his intention to run for office—it was still too soon after Altman's death—establishing himself as a leader would smooth the way for a full-blown campaign. Especially if his protest led to official action by the police.

"This city is failing on all counts," he said to the reporter, his anger simmering. "We cannot stand by while the doctors on the other side of those doors are working with the bare minimum of resources, simply because the police department sees us as a lost cause. Meanwhile, thieves are seeking to make a quick buck off the misery of the Glades."

In the midst of his impassioned speech, he looked up and, to his surprise, found Starling City's most famous spoiled brat watching from the back of the crowd. Oliver Queen was a long, long way from his pampered confines. Already running hot from his speech, Sebastian decided to single out the rich kid and give him a proper Glades welcome.

"Oliver Queen, isn't it?" he said, turning the attention of the protesters and reporters. Queen looked caught, feeling the eyes of the crowd and lights of the cameras on him.

"Alderman," he said.

"What brings you to Glades Memorial, Mr. Queen? I assume someone of your means can afford the best medical treatment money can buy. And I can assure you, you're not going to find that here."

"And that's wrong, Alderman Blood," Queen responded. "The people of the Glades have suffered too much not to have access to basic medical services."

Sebastian felt his anger grow. The audacity of this man, born of privilege, speaking as if he knew the plight of the Glades. He bore down on Queen, striding over and bringing the crowd with him.

"Well, that's very compassionate of you to say," he said, "although I wonder where your family's concern for its fellow citizens was when they ordered the construction of the earthquake machine that killed 503 people."

The mention of the Undertaking and its victims began to incite the crowd. They grew louder, their anger palpable. They began to chant.

"Five-Oh-Three! Five-Oh-Three!"

"Ladies and gentlemen, ladies and gentlemen, please!" Sebastian made a halfhearted attempt to calm the crowd. Though Diggle, sensing trouble, was trying to lead his boss away, for some reason Queen hung back for a moment. He moved closer to Sebastian, as if he had something to say.

"I will be doing everything in my power to atone for my family's culpability in this tragedy," he said, and he sounded earnest. Yet Sebastian wouldn't be swayed.

"I'm sure the people of the Glades will sleep better knowing that..." he replied, his intensity building, "...if they still had a place to sleep. If their homes hadn't crumbled around them. If their stores and their businesses hadn't been condemned." His words enraged the crowd. They shouted at Oliver as he fled back to the car, Diggle leading the way.

"You did this to us!"

"Go back to your mansion, rich boy!"

Caught up in the moment, Sebastian joined them.

"Spare us your mercy visits, Queen!" He watched as the crowd followed Queen and Diggle to their car, surrounding it as they quickly entered. "You've done enough to this city already!"

As Queen's car started up and made its way through the throng, one of the protesters took the end of his placard and smashed it through the passenger-side window. The sound of the glass shattering brought Sebastian back to reality. Violence wasn't his intention.

He would have to be more careful once his mayoral candidacy was official—yet as far as the car window went, he felt little remorse. It was a reminder of the plight his Glades brethren faced daily. One that wouldn't be easy to fix.

Just a few days later, Sebastian paced the anteroom outside Oliver Queen's office at Queen Consolidated.

The last time he had waited outside this door, the office had belonged to Walter Steele. He had been so nervous, waiting for his big meeting with Walter and Moira Queen. He had also been so naïve, thinking people like them could ever really care about the Glades. All the neighborhood was to them was a prop upon which to hang fake empathy, their promises to improve the area nothing more than bluster.

Finally, through the glass, he saw Queen approach, his assistant at his heels. Queen had requested the meeting, voicing the intent to make amends after the incident outside Glades Memorial. The request had piqued Sebastian's curiosity. After being publically ridiculed, most in Queen's position would have placed as much space between them as possible. He wondered what the Queen heir had to say.

"Alderman," Queen said, holding the door open for him to pass through. "Thank you for coming." He extended his hand.

"Mr. Queen." Sebastian ignored the gesture, instead walking past him into the office, to the floor-to-ceiling windows and the panoramic view of Starling City. "This is some view," he commented. "How small the rest of us must look from up here." He waited until the blonde assistant had left, then turned to face his host, with no intention of making the encounter easy.

"I was surprised when you said you wanted to meet," he said.

"Not as surprised as I was when you turned a

frenzied mob on me," Queen replied as he took a seat on his couch, gesturing for Sebastian to sit.

"Oh, that shouldn't have been too surprising." Sebastian settled into the chair across from him. "My constituents hold a lot of anger toward your family."

"They have a right to," Queen admitted. "My mother was involved in something... unspeakable. But I'm my own man, and I'm not your enemy."

"You're not a friend—to me, or the people of the Glades."

"I am hoping to prove otherwise." Queen began to pull out his checkbook.

"Mr. Queen," Sebastian said quickly, becoming annoyed. He leaned forward in his chair. "Not every problem can be solved by money. Real change will never happen until your elitist friends realize that it's morally unacceptable to allow thousands of their fellow citizens to live right down the street, but in a third world."

"Then let's show them," Queen responded without hesitation. Sebastian sat back, surprised. "I'll host a benefit. Invite some of my 'elitist friends,' and then you and I can help them see what needs to be done."

"People seeing you," Sebastian said, leaning back on the couch, contemplating the possibilities. "Seeing you stand up, the CEO of Queen Consolidated, taking responsibility and being this cause's public face. That *would* make a difference." His brow furrowed as he tried to grasp the concept.

Queen stood, buttoning his suit jacket.

"Then let's make a difference." Again, he extended his hand.

Sebastian regarded the man who stood before him. Was this merely a publicity stunt, a way to get back into the city's good graces? Regardless, having the Queen name backing his cause couldn't hurt. In fact, it could be quite beneficial for his impending mayoral campaign.

Swayed, he stood and took Queen's hand in his.

"Listen. I am truly sorry for what happened outside that hospital," he said. "Sometimes my emotions get the better of me."

Queen nodded, accepting the gesture.

Sebastian exited the office and began to head back to the Glades. He thought that the rich kid seemed sincere. A year ago, Sebastian might have even given him the benefit of the doubt, but he knew about the promises made by the rich. They were fragile and easily broken. Why would Queen's promises be any different from those made by his mother?

No, I won't be fooled, he thought.

Sebastian Blood snatched a glass of champagne from a passing waiter's service tray and took an eager sip. He looked around at the men and women gathered for the Glades Memorial benefit—all members of the Starling City elite, their day-to-day existence so far removed from the plight of the Glades. Dressed in clothes costing a week's worth of medical supplies, they engaged each other in breezy small talk, fake laughing, and glad-handing the night away while waiting for Oliver Queen to show his face.

Just as when he was elected alderman, Sebastian felt out of place. He hated playing into the dog and pony show, though he knew it was a necessary evil. Yet until Slade Wilson came through on his promise, until the army had been built and the mayorship given to him, he would have to grit this out. He walked through the transformed Queen Consolidated space, shaking hands and introducing himself, his smile the fakest of them all.

Until he saw Laurel Lance wandering around the space, stunning in her sleek black dress. He knew of her through his work with the city. She was an up-and-coming member of the district attorney's office, having joined after her non-profit law firm was lost during the Undertaking. He had seen her picture before, but in person, her beauty was breathtaking. He felt a genuine smile forming, the dumbfounded expression of a boy seeing something he might like to play with, if lucky enough to be given permission. The champagne giving him courage enough, he called after her as she passed by.

"You look like a woman who's looking for someone."

She turned and he smiled at her, turning on the charm. She regarded him for a moment, then continued walking, scanning the crowd. Sebastian followed.

"A friend of mine," she said. "He's throwing this benefit."

"Ah, Oliver Queen." He fell into step as she slowed.

"I didn't realize you were friends."

"Very old friends." She stopped finally, squaring him up, her manner turning somewhat cold. "So you can imagine how I feel about you putting him in the crosshairs of public opinion, Alderman."

"For what it's worth, I've apologized to Mister… Oliver… for my rhetorical excesses. In fact, it's that détente which brings us all here tonight."

She relaxed a bit, and a look of surprise flitted across her features.

"So where is Oliver?" she said.

"That's exactly the question I'm asking myself."

"He's been known to arrive late to events before. I'm sure he's on his way."

"Well, at least I'm in good company while we wait." He smiled at her again, raising his glass to toast. Lance paused momentarily before finally giving in to a smile, clinking his glass. It seemed to him as if a spark passed between them.

Looking out over the city, Sebastian could see the part of the Glades leveled by the earthquake. Though Laurel Lance's presence had distracted him momentarily, whatever attraction was at play was extinguished by that sobering image. He glanced at his watch, calculating that Queen was over an hour late and counting. Clearly, the man shared his mother's propensity for failing to make good on his word.

Decision made, Blood began to move toward the podium, Lance at his heels.

"It doesn't seem Mr. Queen is going to honor us with his presence this evening," he said to her.

"So where are you going?"

"To address his guests." He turned to face her. "It's time they realize what kind of man their host is."

"You're just going to crucify him in the media again?" she said, anger appearing in her tone.

"Crucifixion has such a bad reputation," Sebastian said earnestly. "But the Romans used it to punish people who acted against the public good."

Lance tried to convince him to stop, but Sebastian ignored her and stepped to the podium.

"Ladies and gentlemen?" he said, tapping the microphone, grabbing the crowd's attention. They stopped their conversations and clapped politely in response. "Thank you, but you should hold your applause for Oliver Queen. This evening's event was his brainchild. As such, you could be forgiven for wondering why Mr. Queen isn't with us tonight."

He looked out on all the wealthy he so despised. Then he left the podium, rounding to the middle of the room, unbuttoning his restrictive suit jacket. He spoke to them as he had the protesters outside Glades Memorial, cameras flashing from the gathered media.

"And the answer, I'm afraid, is painfully apparent. He doesn't care. I told Mr. Queen that this city's problems cannot be solved with his money, and that he needed to stand up and be counted as someone who cares. So where is he now? I don't know where Oliver Queen is. All I know is that he isn't *here*. This city is dying. And it needs someone to stand up and breathe new hope into it. Tonight, it is painfully obvious that that person is not Oliver Queen."

The speech was met with stunned silence. Sebastian regarded Lance with a look, feeling a momentary twinge of regret, then made his way through the crowd, glad that he had painted Oliver Queen in his true light—as a liar, a man of big talk but little action.

If anyone was going to save the Glades, it would be Sebastian Blood.

"Oliver Queen finds himself in the hot seat once more, at least in the eyes of City Alderman Sebastian Blood."

In their penthouse office on the outskirts of downtown, Slade Wilson and Isabel Rochev watched a news report on the failed Glades Memorial benefit. Blood had continued to eviscerate Oliver in the press, stopping outside the venue to give an interview to Channel 52. A chyron across the bottom of the screen read, *BLOOD TRUMPS QUEEN*.

"Oliver Queen's failure to show up at his own benefit shouldn't surprise anyone," Sebastian said to the reporter. "He's no different than the rest of the Starling City elite, who have failed to show up when it comes to ending the suffering of those left devastated in the Glades." He then looked directly into the camera, speaking to the city with a mayoral air. "Oliver Queen is not a friend to the people of this city."

Isabel smiled. The cost of transforming Queen Consolidated into a venue worthy of a black-tie benefit wasn't beneficial to her company's bottom line. She had resisted when Slade asked her to allow it to happen.

Now she understood.

"This is why, isn't it?"

"He does look quite mayoral, doesn't he?" Slade responded. "It seems that Mr. Blood's political influence grows, as well."

Then BREAKING NEWS crossed the screen. The anchor, Bethany Snow, read from a report as China White's picture appeared in the upper left corner of the screen.

"After a prolonged pursuit, police have arrested Chien Na Wei, a high-ranking member of the local Chinese Triad, which was responsible for the recent hijackings of pharmaceuticals bound for Glades Memorial. Representatives praised the efforts of the SCPD in saving the hospital from being shut down..."

Slade leaned back in his chair, mulling the news. China White was a trained assassin, one who would choose death over incarceration. He had expected Oliver to oblige, needed to release the killer within him to stop her. Apparently, the kid honestly believed he could save his city without taking a life. The problem with choosing a more honorable path, however, was that it was far more difficult than quickly slitting an enemy's throat.

Isabel regarded him with a smirk.

"Capture is odd behavior, coming from a killer."

"Oliver's trying to make amends for past bloodshed, by refusing to shed more," Slade responded. "Forcing him to break that vow is just another way I can make him suffer."

"What about Ms. White? Can we trust her not to talk?"

"All she'll say is that a man in a mask gave her money and asked her to steal," Slade said. "The more important point tonight is that the SCPD received credit for the arrest—not the vigilante."

"Judging from what my sources in the D.A.'s office have said, Laurel Lance is responsible for that. She's apparently made it her mission to bring the vigilante to justice."

"His former lover, unknowingly leading the crusade against him," Slade noted, relishing the thought. "Oh, the irony."

"Doubly so, actually. She was also seen flirting a bit with our mayor-to-be."

"That could prove beneficial."

Isabel nodded. "What now?" she asked.

"Time to turn up the heat on our CEO." Slade leaned forward in his chair. "Oliver will likely want to redouble his efforts to rehabilitate his image. This time, if he tries to use his family's business as a prop, stop him."

6

Isabel grabbed a drink at the bar, taking in the sight of the gathered business emissaries as they ate and drank Queen Consolidated funds. She had arranged the fundraising event at Queen Mansion ostensibly to raise investment money for the company. In reality, she was applying pressure on Oliver, stretching him thin between his duties as CEO and vigilante.

She sipped her vodka soda, wondering what new excuse her business partner would come up with tonight when he finally showed. Reading between the lines of his assistant Felicity's feeble explanations, she assumed he was out chasing down leads on the latest epidemic to befall the Glades. A local ganglord had been flooding the neighborhood with military-grade assault weapons, transforming the streets into a war zone. She didn't understand why Queen—and Sebastian Blood too, for that matter—could be so obsessed with that downtrodden neighborhood. If it were up to her, she'd just as soon let the neighborhood perish. Malcolm Merlyn had been right. Much better to simply level it and rebuild anew.

She spotted Blood across the room, glad-handing his way through the crowd. She had to give the man credit. For as much as he despised these people, he did know how to fake a smile with the best of them. No wonder he was a politician. She watched as he made his way closer to Laurel Lance, sneaking glances in her direction even while shaking hands with the mogul from Gregio Inc. It seemed the reports were true; their mayor-to-be was indeed smitten with the A.D.A. Judging from the glances he received in return, the feeling was mutual.

"He's here." Isabel looked up to see Felicity approaching, Oliver entering behind her. He looked a bit haggard, though he did a good job of hiding it.

"Sorry I'm late," he said.

"This party is to attract investors for your failing company," Isabel said without preamble. She enjoyed twisting the knife, making him feel guilty for his absence. "Being fashionably late might do well for the club circuit, but it doesn't inspire confidence in Wall Street… is that blood on your face?"

She had spotted some splatter on his cheek, pointing it out to make him squirm, while doing her best to hide her enjoyment. Felicity jumped into action, fumbling her way through more flimsy excuses.

"Don't worry, it's not *his* blood," she said, before

realizing her error. "I mean, of course it's his blood. Why would he have someone else's blood on his face? Who taught you to shave, mister?" And then she pulled him away, extracting him from the situation before any additional damage could be done, and disappeared into the crowd.

Isabel took a sip of her drink, relishing how badly they were floundering. She had barely begun to turn up the pressure.

Sebastian nodded politely, half-listening to the businessman's argument for deregulation while he eyed Laurel across the room. Fortunately Mr. Young's cell phone started ringing, and he excused himself to answer. Never had Sebastian been so grateful for such a rude gesture. It allowed him an escape, yet when he looked up, Laurel had disappeared. As he started to move through the party in search of her, he heard a voice behind him.

"You look like a man who's looking for someone."

He turned to see her standing there, a nearly empty champagne glass in her hand. She was, as usual, stunning, her sleek black dress exposing the soft curve of her shoulder. He grinned, remembering his line from the Glades benefit.

"I would say I'm looking for a friend, but after the way I attacked him on TV, I doubt very much that Mr. Queen considers me one."

"Sounds like we're in the same boat." Laurel finished her drink then swapped her empty glass for a full one. "I'm sure you've heard that I'm second chairing his mother's murder trial?"

Blood nodded, grabbing a drink and raising it.

"To us, the Queen family pariahs."

Laurel clinked his glass, enjoying the gallows humor. As gorgeous as she was, Sebastian saw weariness beneath the beauty. In addition to seeking the death penalty for Moira Queen, she herself had recently been the victim of a heinous crime. He softened, deciding to carefully broach the subject.

"I also heard about your run-in with that serial killer, the Dollmaker," he said. "You're lucky he didn't add you to his list of victims. I was going to ask if you were okay, but I figure you're pretty tired of that question by now."

"You have no idea."

"It's pretty obvious you're doing just fine."

"All thanks to the vigilante, believe it or not." She took a long sip of her drink.

"I'm inclined to say not, what with you leading the task force against him."

"Trust me, I've been wondering about his motives," she replied. "It would have been easy for him to let me die, thus removing a thorn in his side." Her brow wrinkled at the thought.

"Some of my constituents have begun to view the vigilante as a savior of sorts." Sebastian said it as if it left a bad taste in his mouth.

"Well, he may have rescued me," she said, "but he's no savior. He's just a man hiding behind a mask, and he deserves to be brought to justice."

"I certainly hope so," he said, picturing his own mask. "Speaking of justice, mind if we talk a little shop?"

"Not at all."

"Are you guys any closer to figuring out how that fellow they call the Mayor is smuggling his guns into the Glades? My district is a war zone right now."

"We're trying, but as you know, it's a bit like the Wild West out there."

Sebastian was about to respond when he saw Oliver Queen walk past, in conversation with his blonde assistant. He overheard a piece of their conversation.

"Not this time," Oliver said. "Tonight it was guns."

"What a coincidence," Sebastian said, raising his voice and interjecting himself into their conversation. "We were just talking about guns." He found it amusing, the idea of Queen discussing firearms. A rich kid, discussing issues at a remove from the reality. As if he had ever faced the barrel of a gun.

As if he had ever pointed one, with the intent to kill.

"Hey, Oliver," Laurel said, and he thought he saw a flash of embarrassment cross her face. He instantly sensed the tension between them.

"Hello, Laurel," Queen replied quickly.

"What's your interest in guns, Mr. Queen?" Sebastian asked.

"Never touch them myself."

What a surprise, Sebastian mused. "The gun violence in the Glades has reached epidemic proportions," he said aloud.

"Which is why the D.A.'s office has committed to ending gun violence," Laurel said.

"Well, I'm sure the police are doing whatever they can," Queen said dryly, "to catch whoever's bringing the weapons into the city."

Sebastian traded a look with Laurel, who looked away out of embarrassment.

"Did I say something funny?" Oliver asked.

"They know who's been arming the gangs, Oliver," Laurel said. "The Mayor."

"I thought the Hood copycats killed the mayor."

"Not the actual mayor," Sebastian said derisively. "A local ganglord who calls himself the Mayor. Thinks he's the man to save our city."

"But that position has already been filled, hasn't it?" Laurel said, goading him a bit. Sebastian laughed, enjoying the implication.

His reputation was growing.

"This Mayor has only one goal—" he told Oliver, "—to create chaos, so he can rule the Glades with the barrel of a gun."

He watched Queen processing the weight of this revelation.

"How about we change the subject?" Sebastian said, letting him off the hook. "Mr. Queen looks bored.

I imagine the only gun violence he sees is when he's skeet-shooting off his yacht."

Queen smiled at the jab, and Sebastian looked upon the man with a mixture of contempt and pity. It seemed as if the rich playboy genuinely cared for his city, and it was unfortunate that his affluence kept him removed so far from reality. Though he would try, Oliver Queen would never understand the city's problems.

Not like Sebastian.

The following day, Oliver surprised Sebastian by calling him and asking to meet at Queen Consolidated that afternoon. All he said was that he wanted to continue their conversation from the night before. Sebastian agreed.

Thus he was waiting in the conference room when Isabel Rochev entered, closing the door behind her.

"Ms. Rochev," Sebastian said with faux formality. "So pleased to finally make your acquaintance."

"Do you know why Mr. Queen is meeting with you today?" she asked.

"I'd guess it's to make another attempt at appeasing his guilty conscience," he replied. "Though I do find it odd that Oliver Queen, of all people, is offering me help with the Glades, while you and Mr. Wilson sit idly by in your penthouse."

Isabel bristled slightly. "There are larger issues in play. You know that. So you would do best to be patient—and watch your tongue."

"That sounds like a threat."

"If it is, it does not come from me." Isabel let that land, and Sebastian chewed on the implication. Then she changed the subject. "What's the status of the mirakuru testing?"

"Things have been... difficult, since the Mayor turned the Glades into a war zone. Like I said, some help would be nice."

"Then perhaps you'll get it from Laurel Lance. I saw you two looking quite comfortable together last night."

"You're spying on me now?"

"Slade would like you to pursue that relationship."

"Why?"

"It can't hurt having the ear of an A.D.A. More importantly, getting closer to her will hurt the vigilante."

Sebastian darkened. "And why should I care about him?"

"Because, Mr. Blood, right now—even as Starling City's public enemy number one—the vigilante's influence is still greater than yours."

He seethed silently for a moment, and was about to respond when through the glass he saw Oliver Queen finally arrive. He pushed his way through the closed door.

"Mr. Blood. I see you've met Miss Rochev. She's my—"

"Superior," she said.

"Partner," Queen said.

"On paper."

"Is that why you asked me to come down here, Mr. Queen?" Sebastian asked. "To mediate your job title?"

"You and I have gotten off on the wrong foot... repeatedly," Queen began.

"That seems to be your metahuman power," Sebastian commented with a laugh.

Letting that slide, Queen continued. "I was inspired by what you said the other night, about gun violence in the Glades," he recalled. "And I had an idea that might help."

"Really? Another party at your stately manor?"

"No," Queen said. "I want to sponsor a 'cash for guns' event. I give you the money, and you get your constituents to lay down their arms. Everybody wins."

"Especially you," Sebastian suggested. "Trying to repair your family's tainted name by ridding the Glades of guns."

"You just get the money, Mr. Blood. I don't want my family's name involved."

"Mr. Queen," Isabel said, "may I have a word with you?" She shot Sebastian a look, indicating that it was time to end his meeting.

"Let me think it over," Sebastian said, then he stood and exited.

Once they had the room to themselves, Isabel moved to shut Oliver down.

"We are not sponsoring that event," she said.

"Yes, I know," he said. "I am."

"With what money? Your investment party cost QC fifty grand, and no one invested a dime. I will not continue to authorize corporate funds, just so you can keep pretending that you are the CEO."

"Fine," Oliver said. "I'll pay for it myself."

Isabel laughed. "Maybe you haven't noticed, but your personal trust fund isn't exactly what it used to be, and this company isn't either. As much as I would love to make this city safer, my first obligation is to Queen Consolidated. And yours is, too."

She turned and exited the conference room, leaving Oliver to ponder his predicament. He had no idea that this was only the beginning.

Sebastian agreed to the "Cash For Guns" event, but only on the condition that Queen stay out of the spotlight. This function was to be about the Glades and only the Glades. To his surprise, Queen followed through and agreed to the conditions they'd established.

For Sebastian, it was a chance to show his constituents that true leadership took place in daylight, not under a hood in the middle of the night. Tents were set up in a central Glades location, on the cracked concrete of an abandoned lot beneath the freeway overpass. Buyers were instructed to offer top dollar in exchange for the guns, no questions asked.

Foot traffic was brisk and steady from the opening moment, Queen's money providing incentive enough for residents to give up their arms in the name of creating a safe community. Police stood watch at the perimeter, squad cars positioned nearby.

As Sebastian made his way through the assembled crowd, shaking hands and exchanging pleasantries, he spotted Oliver Queen's sister, Thea, standing with the young man who had attempted to stop one of the thefts from Glades Memorial. Moments later, and much to his surprise, he saw Oliver Queen himself on the event's fringe, taking in the proceedings rather pensively. He was dressed down, and attempting to blend in with the crowd.

So his habit of breaking promises continues, Sebastian mused, frowning. *At least he's consistent.* He approached the playboy, snapping him out of his thoughtful stare. "You don't show up when you say you will, and when you promise not to, here you are."

"Is it going well?" Queen asked.

"Last check, we've taken in over two hundred guns in only three hours." The good news did nothing to change Queen's expression. "Try not to look so happy about it."

"I've got a lot on my mind, Alderman."

Sebastian could sense that he was genuinely troubled. Buoyed by the success of the event so far and feeling charitable, he offered a sympathetic ear.

"After all, my job *is* to help people with their problems."

Queen turned to face him. He hesitated for a moment.

"Two people that are very important to me are having a tough time. Sisters, actually, and neither one of them is making it very easy for me to help them."

"Sooner or later, we all go through a crucible," Sebastian suggested. "I'm guessing yours was that island." Queen nodded, and he continued. "Most believe there are two types of people who go into a crucible—the ones who grow stronger from the experience, and the ones who die. But there's a third type. The ones who learn to love the fire. They choose to stay in their crucible because it's easier to embrace the pain when it's all you know."

Queen didn't reply, but Sebastian saw that his words had resonated. Despite their different upbringings, the look in his eye indicated he understood pain the same way Sebastian did. Perhaps there was a depth within the playboy he had overlooked.

"That's why I'm on the clock," he explained. "To help this city before the people get used to living like this."

"Living isn't for the weak," Queen offered. "An old friend of mine once told me that."

"That's a wise friend."

The two men regarded each other with newfound respect, when the screech of tires broke the moment. It was followed by the sound of automatic gunfire, sending the crowd of people into screaming panic. Sebastian and Oliver watched as the ganglord the

Mayor arrived atop an armored pickup truck, flanked by men armed with assault rifles pointed up into the air. As people scattered, the truck crashed through wooden police barricades, smashing them to pieces. Then it squealed to a stop at the lot's center.

The police drew their guns, pointing them at the gang leader, but the Mayor simply stared them down, unfazed. As the officers struggled with what to do next, he addressed the crowd.

"Listen up, people," he shouted. "This is your mayor speaking. Now I don't recall this here event being sanctioned. What happens in the Glades only happens if I allow it."

Incensed, Sebastian walked out from behind cover.

"You're not the leader of this community!" He summoned every bit of his mayoral presence, realizing this was the moment he had been waiting for—the opportunity to confront the man who had the audacity to take his title. "You don't speak for these people!"

"And neither do you. Not anymore." The Mayor pointed two fingers at Sebastian, a gesture for his men to open fire. In doing so he marked the Alderman for death.

But Sebastian wasn't ready to die. His ego and rage had blinded him to the fact that he had exposed himself, making him an easy target. Now he was staring down the barrels of two semi-automatic rifles.

The gang members opened fire.

At the same time, Oliver dove, managing to pull

him to safety behind a police cruiser. Pandemonium erupted as the officers opened fire, exchanging bullets with the gang. Having made his statement, the Mayor ordered the men to retreat. The truck screeched away, leaving chaos in its wake.

Sebastian watched in shock as Oliver took off to check on the crowd. The man he had always assumed would be his enemy had just saved his life.

The next day, Sebastian was on his way to Queen Consolidated when Officer Daily called him with an update. The night before, the Mayor, now identified as Xavier Reed, had been apprehended by the SCPD—or so the official story claimed. As with China White and the hospital supply thefts, many gave credit to the vigilante. Citizens of the Glades, in particular, were worshipping him like a hero, going so far as to give him a name.

The Arrow.

Sebastian had fumed over the news. It seemed as if the vigilante's influence was growing lockstep with his own. Perhaps Isabel Rochev was right. "The Arrow" was a problem that needed to be addressed. Yet that would be a concern for another day.

The Mayor needed to pay for the chaos he had inflicted upon the Glades. It was time to show him what fear looked like.

"Reed's arraignment will be this afternoon," Daily

said. "He'll be most vulnerable after the proceedings, during his transfer back to lockup."

"And you're sure this can be done quietly?"

"He'll just be another inmate, fallen through the cracks. Trust me, Brother Blood, no one's going to miss this scum. He'll be yours to do with as you please."

"Good," Blood replied, a thrill passing through him at the prospect. "We'll see if Mr. Reed possesses strength enough to survive."

"There's another development you should be aware of," Daily continued. "I pulled over Laurel Lance last night, for driving under the influence." The news came as a surprise. He knew Laurel was under stress, but never would have pegged her for a substance abuser. She had admitted that her father was a recovering alcoholic. Perhaps she shared more with him than Sebastian had thought.

"You didn't arrest her, did you?"

"No. I turned her over to Officer Lance instead."

"Good work, Brother Daily."

He arrived at Queen Consolidated to find Oliver standing at his desk, the mid-morning sun shining brightly through the windows.

"I guess it's true what they say," Sebastian commented. "One man *can* change the world."

"I'll leave changing the world to you, Alderman," Oliver countered.

"I'm only still *in* the world because of you, Mr. Queen. Thank you." He extended his hand.

"I was just acting on instinct," Oliver said, taking his hand.

"It wasn't instinct," Sebastian said. "It was strength."

Oliver smiled. "I see the signs and the graffiti. 'Blood for Mayor.'" The mention elicited a smile from Sebastian. "Now that your crooked counterpart is in jail," he added, "maybe you should run."

"There is more than one way to save a city," Sebastian replied, not yet ready to admit publically that he intended to run. But when that day arrived, having Oliver's support behind him would make the process all the easier. For now, however, there were other matters to which he needed to attend.

Later that night, deep beneath the Glades, the Church of Blood watched as the mirakuru ravaged Xavier Reed's body. Like the victims before him, he wailed to the heavens, straining against his restraints before falling silent, blood seeping from his eyes like tears. The men stood by, emotionless witnesses to the execution, the horror now old hat.

Brother Blood removed his skull mask as Dr. Langford and Clinton Hogue dragged away Reed's body, his heels scraping on the sewer's wet concrete. Blood then turned to Officer Daily.

"Bring me another."

"Yes, Brother Blood."

As Daily headed off to fetch another test subject and the Technician prepared another syringe with the mirakuru, Blood was left alone with Cyrus Gold. He approached.

"May I speak?"

"Of course, Brother Cyrus," Blood said. "You know I value your counsel."

"You said the serum was a test of strength."

"That's right."

"Then let me take the mirakuru."

"No," Blood said firmly. "You're my closest advisor, and my friend. I won't risk it."

"There is no risk," Cyrus said, his chest swelling with conviction. "The men we take are weak because they lack faith, both in our cause and in themselves. I do not."

"You've seen what the serum does, the damage that results. Their torture doesn't faze me, not any longer, but yours... I couldn't subject you to that."

"The earthquake took my congregation and my church," Cyrus insisted. "There's no torture I haven't already endured."

"You're asking me for death."

"No," Cyrus said. "I'm asking to be reborn."

Blood regarded his loyal acolyte, saw his passion and certitude.

"If none of our remaining crop of applicants survives, I will grant your request." As the rest of the cult returned with another unwilling victim—this one named Max Stanton—Cyrus nodded to his leader. Turning to depart, Blood nodded back, trying to share his brother's faith.

7

Slade drove Isabel backward with an onslaught of strikes, his training sword cutting the air in sharp diagonals and thrusts. The attack didn't harry her, however. She expertly parried his attack with her own sword, drawing his momentum right as she spun left, landing a glancing blow to the shoulder. Chest heaving, she paused for a second.

Slade was impressed. His pupil was improving.

But still, she was just a pupil.

Using her momentary hesitation to his advantage, he advanced, taking her by surprise, cutting swathes through the air left and right, rattling her sword as she just managed to block. Then he grabbed her weapon from her, holding it to her throat.

"Don't stop to bask in a victory you do not yet possess."

"Point taken," she said.

Slade stepped away, tossed her sword back to her,

and they continued their sparring, circling each other. Once again she was on guard.

"What can you tell me about Oliver's team?" he said, swinging his weapon down onto hers. She blocked it and backpedaled into open space.

"Still only two," she said. "Diggle is his protection, Smoak the brains, though it's clear she has feelings for him." She spun, dropping low, trying to swipe Slade's legs. He jumped, avoiding her attempt. "Nothing you didn't already know."

"Does Oliver return those feelings?"

"Doubtful." They circled each other again. "Didn't think you'd be so interested in his love life, to be honest."

He leapt forward, an overhead blow driving her backward.

"I'm interested in making him suffer."

Isabel hurled forth a flurry of strikes in response, all of which Slade parried. Then he disarmed her again, sending Isabel to her knees. She smacked the mat, frustrated.

"Good," he said. "Remember that anger." He tossed the sword back to her. "What else?"

"Oliver is trying to use the company jet to go to Russia, of all places," she said, still gasping. "I don't know his aim, but I'll keep him grounded."

"No. Don't stop it," Slade said, ignoring the surprise in her expression. "Go with him. Use the change of scenery to your advantage. Build his trust. It'll be all the harder for him to resist your guidance later."

Isabel nodded. She rose to standing, flexing a kink from her shoulder.

"What about the centrifuge?" he asked. "Does it seem capable?" The Applied Sciences Division had built a prototype, a state-of-the-art, high-capacity centrifuge intended for the mass production of vaccines. It would be perfect for replicating the mirakuru in quantities great enough to serve his plans.

"More than capable," she said, "but considering the company's precarious financial state, I can't run it on a lark. I need a reason."

"Not to worry," Slade said. "By the time you get back from Russia, that reason will be more than clear." He then motioned toward her sword. "Ready?"

She nodded, and they began to spar again.

The community center at Zandia Orphanage was a bustle of activity. The kids were happy and rambunctious, enjoying a bundle of new toys given to them by Sebastian Blood. He had made a surprise visit, one of the few stops he made these days that served no publicity purpose. There would be plenty of time for that later—for now, his time at the orphanage was his to enjoy.

He watched as they lost themselves in play, remembering when he had run these halls. Some of the children were working on crafts at a nearby table, and he drifted over. One of the kids, a little boy no older than seven, was busy at work with crayons. He had drawn a big black box, a crudely rendered building of sorts, with stick figures of people in it. There were scrawls of red and orange, representative of fire.

"What are you drawing there?" Sebastian asked.

"That's the school. It's on fire after the earthquake."

"Did that happen to you?" The little boy nodded as he picked up a green crayon and started to scribble. "I'm sorry, son. I'm trying to make sure that never happens to you again."

"It's okay, I'm not afraid," the boy said. "He'll save us."

"Who?"

"The Arrow."

Blood looked at the scribble, now a stick figure in green, bow and arrow in hand. He scowled.

"You think he's a hero?"

"My brother Lunar says he saved the hospital and stopped the guns."

"You shouldn't believe everything your brother tells you."

Sebastian rubbed the boy's head and walked over to a wall, staring at the photo of him and Father Trigon, celebrating his graduation from high school, both optimistic about the future. Trigon had told Sebastian that, of all his pupils, he was special. It was his destiny to change the Glades for the better, and then the city would follow. Though he was on the verge of running for mayor, it was hard not to be disappointed. He would have thought he'd accomplished more by now, but his influence came second to that of a man in a hood.

He hated that damn vigilante.

Then he heard a voice behind him, familiar in its menace.

"A lovely picture, Mr. Blood."

Sebastian turned to find Slade standing behind him, impeccably dressed in his suit. The sight immediately put him on edge. He scanned the room for witnesses and he moved closer, dropping his voice.

"I thought you were trying to keep a low profile."

"You fear the claims of children?"

"You'd be surprised what they're capable of," Sebastian said, thinking. "There's staff here, as well."

"All I am is a businessman," Slade said, "looking to make a sizable donation." He held his hands wide.

Sebastian led Slade to an empty corridor outside of the play area.

"I would have met you back at the penthouse," he said, still angry.

"And miss an opportunity to see your humble beginnings?" Slade's smile was cold, calculating, sending a shiver down Sebastian's spine. "And besides, I'm in need of your services." He handed the alderman a slip of paper—it had a name and an address on it. "He's a man of extravagance, but his style is one that will be useful."

Blood recognized the name.

"Isn't he locked away in Iron Heights?"

Slade shook his head. "In addition to ravaging your city, the earthquake also set loose a number of inmates from the prison. It's the gift that keeps giving."

"This man was responsible for flooding my district with drugs," Sebastian said, condemnation in his tone.

"Truly a pity," Slade replied, doing his best to affect a reasonable facsimile of sympathy. It wasn't working. "But I intend to direct his talents… elsewhere."

"Where?"

"Downtown Starling." Slade gave a slight smile. "I want the city's most affluent to feel the same fear the Glades experienced."

"What about the Arrow?"

"He is of no concern of yours."

"If you haven't noticed, he's becoming a hero to my constituents. His influence is growing, and could pose a direct threat to my candidacy."

"Unless you expect his name to appear on a ballot," Slade said with some amusement, "I highly doubt you have anything to worry about."

"Worry isn't a problem. Inaction is."

"Who says we're being inactive?" Slade peered at him. "As I promised you at the beginning, you *will* be mayor." With that he turned and walked down the hall, disappearing out a side door and into the fading afternoon sun. Sebastian didn't share Slade's confidence, however.

The vigilante was a problem, one that demanded a solution.

* * *

Brother Blood, his skull mask terrifying in the moonlight, found the dilapidated motel on the outskirts of the city. Degenerates—men and women both—wandered between rooms like zombies. They paid him no mind. Their eyes were fixated on things he could not see as they mumbled incoherently to themselves, the language of minds driven insane.

He found room 327, and pushed through the door. A man and woman were slumped on the stained carpet, each chained to a bedpost. Like the denizens outside, they were too wrapped up in their own hallucinations to notice him. All around the room, tacked to the walls, there were scrawled pictures similar in style to that of the boy at the orphanage. The Arrow, crudely rendered in pen and pencil, but in each of these drawings he was suffering a horrific death.

A man emerged through a side door, holding a syringe. His hair was close cropped, though wild at the top, and there was a tinge of madness in his eye. He was happy to see Blood.

"Such a wonderful face!" the man known as Count Vertigo exclaimed. "And just when I thought there was no real honesty in the world. Be still my heart. Please, make yourself at home." Then he walked over to the chained man and woman and plunged the syringe into their arms, one after the other.

Almost immediately their bodies tensed up and

their eyes grew wide, peering intently at visions apparent only to them. Moments passed, and then they foamed at the mouth, going into spasms. Finally they fell silent. The Count nudged them, but they were entirely unresponsive.

"What a shame," he said, shrugging and taking a seat on the bed. "I was so hoping for a double date. Oh well." He turned to Blood. "Now, what brings you here, to my humble abode?"

"Putting you back in business," Blood replied, his voice muffled by the mask, "and creating havoc in the streets."

"Ah, work," the Count said. "I'm not sure about that. You see, I'm quite happy with my life of unemployment. Time to do as I please, with whom I please. To give this up, I need incentive."

"You will have unlimited resources with which to build your lab and network."

The Count lay back on the bed, arms outstretched.

"Boring," he said with an exaggerated yawn.

"Once your Vertigo drug is ready," Blood continued, "everyone in the downtown area will receive a free sample—in particular, a… test case, shall we say, in the district attorney's office."

The Count propped himself up on an elbow.

"Better."

"I've saved the best for last, though." Blood walked over to the drawings pinned to the wall, and pulled one down. "Then I want you to kill the Arrow," he said, slowly ripping the picture in two.

"*Bingo!*" the Count exclaimed. "I knew you saw the real me."

"Hate is insufficient to describe what we both feel toward the vigilante," Blood continued. "He tortured you with your own concoction, locked you away, put an end to everything that gave your life meaning." He glanced around, fully aware of the irony in his words.

"Then why let me have all the fun?" Vertigo responded. "Revenge is a delicious drug in its own right—why not share it?"

"Alas, I'm forced to live vicariously through you," Blood replied. He had promised Slade not to engage the vigilante. Using the Count in this manner would prevent him from breaking that vow.

"A vicarious life is what my drug aims to deliver," the Count said in all seriousness. "When do we start?"

"Immediately," Blood said. "I want the drug ready for distribution in time for the Moira Queen trial."

"Splendid. And how would you like the Arrow dispatched?"

"Any way you see fit," Blood said. "I'll be in touch." He exited the dingy room, wearing an evil smile under his mask. Finally, he had found the solution to his vigilante problem.

Thousands of miles away from Starling City, Isabel ordered another vodka, and one for Oliver, as well.

After a purposely contentious trip, she had scheduled meetings with Queen Consolidated's Russian subsidiary—ones she knew he couldn't attend. Later she found a contrite Oliver at the bar and decided, after two months of placing nonstop pressure on him, that it was finally time to show him a more vulnerable side.

The about-face, especially over alcohol, would make the seduction all the easier. She had playfully pushed his buttons, insinuating that Oliver was having an affair with Felicity, though she was fairly certain this wasn't the case. Regardless, the accusation was enough to put him on the defensive.

"Does everyone really think that Felicity and I are…" he began.

"No," she replied. "Just everyone who works at Queen Consolidated."

They shared a laugh over that. Friendly, the ice thawing between them. Isabel relaxed, the vodka loosening her up, reminding her of nights spent so many years ago drinking with his father, Robert. She could see him in Oliver's eyes. In his jawline.

"She's just a friend," Oliver said.

"You don't seem like the kind of man who has female friends," she said, turning toward him, flirting.

"Can I ask you a personal question?"

"With some vodka in me, I just might answer," she said, a sly smile on her face.

"Why does saving my family's company mean so much to you?"

Isabel hesitated for a second, thinking how to answer. Such irony, such *naivety*, believing that she was trying to save his company, instead of take it from him. She decided to give him a version of the truth.

"Despite what Sheryl Sandberg might say, it still isn't that easy to make it as a woman in business. I've given up a lot," she said, thinking of his father. "Which means if I don't succeed at everything, then what was the point of trying?"

Oliver nodded, holding her gaze. He was playing right into her hands. She smiled again, the flirting made easy by the vodka, enjoying the company.

"May I ask you a personal question?" she said.

"Others have tried and failed."

"Why do you try so hard to make me think you're a lazy idiot?" she asked. "I know you're not." That elicited a grin from Oliver. It was an educated gamble—figuring that, as Robert's son, he would have sought approval. She would play into that, scratching his ego, knowing how much he was balancing as both CEO and the vigilante. "Underneath that swagger," she said, "I see you pretty clearly."

"Really?" Oliver replied. "And what do you see?"

She stared at him, scanning his face, her knowledge of his double life giving her unfair insight into his psyche.

"You're intelligent. Driven. And lonely."

"How do you see that?"

"Because it's what I see when I look in the mirror."

Though she was playing Oliver, there was truth behind her words. Maybe it was the alcohol, or the fact that she was staring into an echo of Robert's face, but she was lonely. Falling into this union was proving easier by the second.

A waiter approached. "May I get you anything else?" he asked in Russian.

"I don't think I should drink any more," Oliver replied, speaking the language perfectly.

"You speak Russian?" she said, genuinely surprised.

"Only with my friends," he said, again in the foreign tongue. "Why does that surprise you?"

"I was raised in Moscow until I was nine, and then adopted by a family that took me to America," she said, leaning closer, pressing into his space. "Took me years to get rid of my accent. It isn't easy making friends in grade school when you sound like Natasha Fatale. But I've kept the ability to speak the language."

"It sounds as if you've been dealing with loneliness a long time," he said, still in Russian. His eyes were hungry. It was a look she remembered well, from many late nights spent in Robert's office.

"Pay the check," she said, her Russian matching his.

She had Oliver Queen exactly where she wanted him.

8

Slade watched the news from his downtown penthouse, pleased that all was going according to plan. The Christmas season was approaching, and it seemed as if his gifts had arrived early.

The Count had revealed himself to the masses, using Slade's technology to interrupt the local broadcast with a closed-circuit broadcast of him and his kidnap victim, Assistant District Attorney Adam Donner. He informed his audience that the flu-like symptoms many in Starling City had begun to feel were in fact signs of withdrawal.

"And the only way to stop the pain?" the Count said gleefully. "Vertigo, of course." To illustrate his point, he made Donner beg for a hit, the injection of which immediately alleviated his agony.

Though Slade enjoyed the thought of creating a city full of addicts, that wasn't his ultimate goal. The Count's antics were intended to stretch Oliver Queen thin as the vigilante while, as a son, he was dealing with his mother's murder trial. Even so, Slade assumed the Arrow would stop the Count, and perhaps even synthesize a cure.

Thus the reemergence of the Vertigo drug would provide Isabel with the necessary justification to test the capabilities of the centrifuge prototype housed at Queen Consolidated Applied Sciences. The city would need to produce an antidote in mass, at which point, Queen Consolidated would step in. It would be a trial run—when the equipment was ready, it would be available to reproduce mirakuru.

Picking up the phone on his desk, he dialed Sebastian Blood. It was time to check in and see how the tests were going. There was one more gift he wanted—the big one.

He had expected to have his warrior by now.

"It's been over two months," Slade said. "Yet still no success?"

Blood heard his tone, could sense his impatience. He stood in his lair beneath the Glades, four limp bodies tied to chairs before him, tears of blood running from their eyes. Again, no survivors. Cyrus Gold stood nearby, listening in.

"Not yet, but I believe we're close," Blood said. "We just need more time."

"My patience wears thin, Mr. Blood. It's time to step it up." A click, and the line went dead.

Blood looked up to see Cyrus staring at him.

"My offer still stands, Brother Blood," he said. "Allow me to lead your army."

Blood stared off into the shadows, mulling over his decision. Then he faced his longtime friend.

"You believe yourself strong enough to survive the test?"

"For this brotherhood, my strength is endless."

"Then when the next round of subjects is brought in, you will join them."

Cyrus nodded, his expression filled with conviction and pride. Blood grasped his shoulder in thanks, trying to share his loyal advisor's faith. Then he turned and walked out the door, his next destination the Starling City D.A.'s office.

Sebastian fell into step with Laurel Lance in the City Hall courtyard, both on their way to meet with District Attorney Kate Spencer. The area was a flurry of activity, assistants and staff members sent into response mode after the kidnapping of Adam Donner.

"I much prefer running into you at galas," Sebastian said, sidling up to her. "There's better food." Despite the stress of the moment, Laurel smiled.

"As do I," she said with a sigh. "I heard Spencer summoned you."

Sebastian nodded. "The city's in crisis. Without a mayor, she needs someone to talk to the people. I guess I'm that someone."

"You guess?" Laurel said, amused. "Somehow I doubt you're someone who relies on guesswork."

Sebastian shrugged as they continued inside.

"I'm just here to help."

The television was on in Spencer's office. Her expression stony and unreadable, she stood with Laurel and Sebastian, watching as coverage of the hostage situation continued. The newscaster urged residents to stay calm in the face of the Count's threats.

Unable to contain his nervous energy, Sebastian paced the room.

"The Count has turned Starling City into a city of junkies," he said, turning to Spencer. "Do you have any leads on where he's holding A.D.A. Donner?"

"No," she answered. "The SCPD's shaking down Vertigo dealers as fast as they can round them up—they haven't exactly been inconspicuous—but none of them knows where the Count's hiding." A frown furrowed her brow, and she turned to Laurel. "We've got other concerns, as well. What have you got for me?"

Laurel rifled through a folder. "Adam's trial notes are very thorough," she said. "We should be able to move forward... without him." A pained look flitted across her face as she said it.

"They better be," Spencer said. "You're lead counsel now."

"Ms. Spencer, you're the District Attorney," Laurel

argued. She continued to leaf through the documents, and suddenly her face went ash gray.

"Yes, but you're the one that the jury knows." Then Spencer saw the look on her face, and added, "You'll do fine."

"I know," she said, staring up from Donner's notes. "That's not it. I just found Adam's trump card."

"What is it?"

"Moira Queen was having an affair with Malcolm Merlyn."

"Brother Cyrus, are you prepared to give your life for this brotherhood?"

Cyrus Gold sat in the chair. The screams of his predecessors—Max Stanton among them—had not shaken his resolve. His fellows were gathered to bear witness. Each of them bowed their heads in respect, wishing him strength to survive, trying not to waver in their belief that he would.

"Yes, Brother Blood," Cyrus said.

"Then let us both hope that now is not that time."

"I don't hope," he said. "I know."

The men locked eyes, nodding to each other, ready to go. Blood raised the syringe, the green fluid as incandescent as ever in the darkness, and plunged it deep into Cyrus's arm.

As with the men before him, he began to tense, his muscles beginning to spasm as the mirakuru worked its way through his body. Clenching his fists, he tried to fight off the pain, his vocal expression not so much a scream as a guttural growl. Blood began to seep from his eyes as his voice grew louder—and then he slumped, falling to silence.

No! Brother Blood moved forward. No one breathed as the technician checked the preacher's pulse. He shook his head. Brothers Daily, Hogue and Langford bowed their heads in reverence.

Blood, however, was angry. *I should never have let it come to this*, he thought furiously. *Not Cyrus.*

His mask hiding his grief and fury, he retreated to his office.

Slade and Isabel watched from the penthouse as breaking news emerged from the Moira Queen trial. Despite all predictions, she had been acquitted of all charges in her involvement with the Undertaking. Interviews from the street showed that the majority of Starling City was shocked by the verdict, an undercurrent of anger evident.

The verdict itself, however, was of very little consequence. Slade had accomplished his goal— removing Assistant District Attorney Donner from the picture so that Laurel Lance could ascend to lead counsel, thereby putting her in direct conflict with Oliver Queen. It had been revealed that Moira had maintained an affair with Malcolm Merlyn, yet the jury had failed to look beyond the immediate implications. Moira, despite her protestations, had been more closely involved with Merlyn's plans than she had been willing to confess.

Thanks to Isabel, though, Slade knew something that hadn't yet come to light, yet was potentially more damning—and thus of greater value. Malcolm Merlyn had fathered the younger Queen child, Thea. That revelation would fracture the heart of Oliver's family, and cause him no end of pain. With the revelation of the affair, it was only a matter of time.

Isabel paced the penthouse, furious at the verdict.

"Acquitted," she said in disbelief. "That woman should have been sent to the electric chair." Her tone indicated that she relished the thought.

"This changes nothing," Slade said.

"How can you say that?" Isabel demanded. "Moira Queen won't stand idly by while I take over her company. This is *terrible*."

"This is an *opportunity*."

"Don't give me that 'lemons into lemonade' bull, Slade."

"As I recall, you said you had young Mr. Queen exactly where you wanted him," Slade replied. "Am I correct?"

"We had a night together in Russia," she said. "You expect that to trump blood? She's smart, and she knows my history. She'll figure out my intentions and warn him."

"You let me worry about that. For now, use your

newfound connection with Oliver to create tension between him and his mother."

"I don't know how you can be so calm about this."

He leaned back in his chair, putting his hands behind his head. "Because I've been planning this from the beginning. Now, do you have an update on the centrifuge?"

"The prototype is fully functional and currently replicating the Vertigo cure in mass quantities," she said. "Enough for an army."

"Then we wait on Mr. Blood," he said. Abruptly he looked over at the television, and sat forward. Coverage of Moira Queen's acquittal was interrupted by more breaking news. The Arrow Kills Again. Footage from outside Queen Consolidated depicted the body of the Count, splayed out on the cratered roof of a car, three arrows embedded in his chest.

Slade chuckled at the image.

"You see, Ms. Rochev?" he said. "He has revealed his true stripes." He stroked his beard, pondering the news. If Oliver had rekindled his bloodlust, perhaps their fight would be a fair one after all.

Across the city in the Glades, Blood watched as his world crumbled.

The loss of Cyrus Gold was still fresh in his mind. The Count being dead meant his plan had been a failure. He didn't take his eyes off the screen when

Officer Daily entered the makeshift office, closing the door behind him.

"I arranged for the Count to take out the Arrow," Blood growled, "and all I accomplish is reigniting the vigilante's killing spree."

"Sir, there's been a development," Daily said, and he held the door opening, indicating that he wanted Blood to accompany him. Honoring ceremony, Blood turned to retrieve his skull mask, concealed in a wall behind his desk. Putting it on, he followed Daily out the office, into the subway below, and back to the lair.

Cyrus Gold still sat in the chair—his eyes open.

"Brother Cyrus," Blood said, barely able to get the words out. Cyrus lifted his head, his tears of blood dried dark on his skin, black in the glow of the halogen shop lights. He looked up at his leader.

"How do you feel?" Blood asked incredulously.

"Stronger," Cyrus said. As the meaning of his words sank in, Blood's heart leapt.

"Wonderful," he said. "Then you're ready." He stepped away from Cyrus and removed his mask. Struggling to maintain his composure, he pulled out his phone and speed-dialed a number.

Slade picked up on the second ring.

"Do you bring me good news, Mr. Blood?"

"Very," Blood said. "When can we meet?"

9

Now that Cyrus had been empowered by the mirakuru, they could move forward to the next phase of the plan—stealing the components necessary to mass produce the serum, based on Gold's blood samples.

As Isabel listened in, Slade laid out the details.

"You will direct Mr. Gold to acquire three targets. The first is an industrial-grade centrifuge located at Applied Sciences at Queen Consolidated. Ms. Rochev has ensured that security will be light."

"Try to keep the damage to a minimum," Isabel interjected.

"What, insurance doesn't cover theft by super soldier?" Blood responded with a wry glance.

"I'd rather not pay the premiums."

"Second," Slade continued, "is a large supply of blood. Thirty thousand cubic centimeters of type O-negative. I'm sure you'll know where to procure it."

"And the third part of this holy trinity?" Blood asked.

"Sedatives," Slade said. "I'm currently locating a source that will provide enough for our purposes. When I find it, I'll be in touch."

"And we'll be ready," Blood said.

"One last thing," Slade added. "Mr. Gold is to operate with the utmost discretion."

"He's brotherhood. Just as I have my mask, so does he. His identity will be concealed."

"That's not what I mean." Slade leaned forward in his chair, closing the space between them. "There is a high probability that his activity will draw the eye of the vigilante. If it does, just as I warned you, he is *not* to seek confrontation."

"But if Cyrus is as powerful as you say, why shy away from a fight?"

"I have my reasons." He gave Blood a hard look. "Understood?"

Blood clenched his jaw but nodded acceptance. "So when do we begin?"

"Tonight."

Eager to get started, Blood headed off to dispatch Cyrus Gold to steal the centrifuge. As he disappeared behind the closing elevator doors, Isabel turned to Slade.

"We're stealing from Queen Consolidated. I'd say there's more than a high probability that this will attract Oliver's attention. I won't be able to keep it from him."

"I don't expect you to."

"You're not concerned?"

Slade sank back into his chair, a slight shake of his

head indicating no. "The mirakuru represents a past Oliver has long thought buried. Seeing its power at work in Mr. Gold will haunt him, like a ghost come back from the grave."

"Let's hope you're right," Isabel said, rising to leave, "so I can focus on dealing with annoyances from my own past."

"Moira Queen."

"I have a morning meeting scheduled with the board tomorrow. It would be just like her to drop by unannounced."

"I trust you'll handle the situation accordingly."

Early the following morning, Isabel was notified that the industrial centrifuge had been stolen. The news had to appear unwelcome—though that wasn't as difficult as it might have been. In addition to taking the equipment, Cyrus Gold had torn through an incredibly expensive titanium security door and left two security guards dead.

As expected, the break-in and its financial ramifications were the first topics of conversation at the board meeting. Isabel did her best to appear surprised by the news and mournful for the lost employees, before diving into the bottom line.

"This is going to wreak havoc on our insurance premiums, and our security costs will shoot through the roof," she announced. "We need to drill down on these numbers before the earnings call."

Just as she was about to move on to her next agenda item, she heard the door open and close. She looked up to watch Oliver and Moira enter the conference room. This was the first time she had been face to face with Moira since their encounter outside Queen Mansion so many years before. Though Isabel had anticipated this moment, she was unprepared for the flood of emotion and memory the woman evoked. She did her best to hide its effects.

"Oliver," she said. "I didn't realize your mother was stopping by for a visit today."

"It's not a visit," he said, pulling out a chair for his mother before taking a seat of his own at the table. "This is her company, too."

"Of course," Isabel replied, certain her fake smile failed to conceal her displeasure. "How are you, Moira?"

"Back, Isabel," Moira answered, delivering a fake smile in return. "I'm back."

Isabel saw a look in the older woman's eyes, and recognized it from years ago. Hidden behind the polite sheen was a gaze that communicated, very clearly, how utterly *superior* she considered herself to be. A fiery rage boiled up, and Isabel wanted to rip her throat out. Instead, she remembered Slade's directive.

"Mr. Queen, may I speak to you for a minute," she said, getting up from the table. He followed suit and she led him out into the anteroom and back to his office.

"I'm not sure this is a good idea," she said, carefully

keeping her tone neutral. "What sort of message does it send to the investment committee, to the city, if we hand Queen Consolidated right back to your mother?"

"She was acquitted," Oliver replied flatly.

"By a jury," she countered, allowing herself to sound agitated, "but not by the city." Then she paused a moment, pretending to calm herself. "Oliver, stop thinking like a son and start thinking like a CEO." With that, she turned and exited, headed back to the conference room. On her way out, she saw John Diggle and Felicity Smoak headed his way, their expressions urgent. No doubt they were delivering news of the break-in, and the timing couldn't be more perfect.

Arriving back in the boardroom, Isabel locked eyes with Moira for a long moment, letting her know she would not be intimidated. Then she addressed the board members.

"An issue has come up with our Russian subsidiary overseas. I'm afraid we'll have to adjourn this meeting and meet at another time." There were nods and murmurs of assent, and as the board members rose to leave, she smiled at Moira, offering faux contrition. "So sorry you came all this way for nothing, Moira."

"Not to worry, Isabel," Moira said. "I've got nothing but time. I'm sure we'll be seeing each other again very soon." With a smirk, she exited the room.

Now alone, Isabel crumpled her meeting notes in her hand. How she hated that woman. One day, hopefully soon, Isabel would gain complete control over Queen Consolidated, and wield the power to kick Moira to the curb. For now, however, she'd be content with driving a wedge between her and her son.

A throng gathered in the orphanage's playroom that afternoon, watching as Sebastian doled out holiday gifts to the children. Channel 52 was there, as was the *Starling City Star*. Unlike his last visit to Zandia, this appearance was completely staged by his publicity team, every detailed planned, even down to his jeans and rolled-up sleeves. It was meant to paint him as a leader of the working class.

"So often on television, we're asked to help children from around the world, in countries less fortunate than ours," he told the reporters. "The thing is, there are plenty of children suffering right here in Starling City, particularly in the Glades." He looked up to find Laurel in the back of the crowd, watching his interview. They smiled at each other, the chemistry between them still very much in play.

"Thank you for coming," he concluded. "Let's get the word out. These kids need us." The crowd of onlookers applauded and the reporters dispersed, clearing a path between Laurel and Blood. He walked over, happy to see her. She looked somewhat puzzled.

"Hi," he said. "I'm glad you could come."

"I thought you were above conducting staged photo-ops."

"This isn't what you think."

"Then why did you call me down here?" she asked, her eyebrow raised.

"I want you to know a little more about me," he said, "and thought you might want to see where I came from." With a sweep of his hand he indicated the orphanage. He could tell Laurel was caught off guard, not quite sure what to make of the revelation.

"You were raised here?" she said.

"I lost my parents when I was six," he lied. "It's funny. I was an only child, and then I came here. Found an endless supply of brothers."

"Sebastian, I had no idea..." she said, reaching out with a kind touch to his forearm. Suddenly the moment was interrupted by his ringing cell phone. He glanced at the screen, seeing that it was Cyrus. With an apologetic shrug to Laurel, he moved out of earshot and took the call.

"What is it?" he said.

"I'm back," Cyrus replied, "but there's something we should discuss."

"I'll be right there." He hung up then turned. "Please accept my apology, Laurel. I'm sorry to do this, but I've got to go take care of some business."

"Is everything all right?"

"Yeah. Just... city planning." He gave her a kiss on the cheek. "I'll check in with you later."

* * *

Blood met his brotherhood in a forgotten warehouse located off Crescent Circle in the Glades. They had picked the location for the centrifuge, its white metal panels arranged in a circular shape around an exposed chrome center, where empty vials awaited the mirakuru. A medical refrigerator stood against the wall, its glass door revealing thirty thousand CCs of bagged blood. Cyrus was loading the last of the supply when Blood arrived.

"Your tone suggested complications," Blood said, "yet this looks like it all went according to plan."

"It did… mostly," Cyrus replied. "The vigilante tried to stop me."

Blood walked over to the fridge door, opening it to take out a bag of blood.

"It seems our hooded nuisance is on our scent," he muttered. "Did you leave anything behind that could be traced back here?"

Cyrus shook his head. "I was careful. He knows only of my power."

As Blood examined the red liquid under the fluorescents above, his phone rang. Glancing at the screen, he picked up.

"It's Daily," the officer said. "Someone's looking for Maxwell Stanton." Blood paused for a moment, trying to place the name. Max Stanton was one of their many serum test victims—part of the last batch of bodies sacrificed before Cyrus's success. Dr. Langford had identified the boy as being a loner.

"Then they should find him," Blood suggested.

"Yes, Brother Blood," Daily answered, and the connection went silent.

Satisfied the issue had been put to bed, he walked toward Cyrus Gold, the pouch of blood still in his hand.

"Blood provides life," he said. "Blood provides power—and with power, there's no limit to what I can do."

"What next, Brother Blood?"

"We wait for the location of the sedatives," he said. Then, with fire in his eyes, he looked at Cyrus. "And the next time you cross paths with the Arrow, I want you to kill him."

Slade's instructions be damned.

Isabel bristled when she received the invitation. Oliver was throwing a celebration to commemorate his mother's return—as if a party could wipe away the stink of the Undertaking. Yet Slade insisted she go.

She arrived to a disaster. Servants outnumbered guests two-to-one, and the string quartet played to an empty floor. The message being sent was clear—the Starling City elite wanted nothing to do with Moira Queen. And when the guest of honor made her entrance, Isabel had to hide a smirk. Yes, Moira's presence would make her task more difficult, but tonight she would have to revel in the elder Queen's embarrassment.

As Moira made the rounds, however few, Isabel

saw Oliver head over to the bar, shoulders slumped. She enjoyed the added benefit of knowing that his woe was amplified by his life as the vigilante. If Slade had surmised correctly, Oliver was weighed down by ghosts from his past—unearthed by the appearance of Cyrus Gold. This was a perfect opportunity to play the sympathetic, understanding partner, and build his trust.

Plus, Isabel could do so while his mother watched.

Making sure she passed through Moira's line of sight, Isabel headed over to join him at the bar. She sidled up to him as he ordered a couple of shots of vodka.

"I tried to warn you," she said. She grabbed the two shots from the bartender and offered him one with a sympathetic smile. Oliver regarded her with weary eyes, and she could tell he was surprised that she had showed. But also grateful.

"I tried to ignore you," Oliver admitted.

They locked eyes and clinked their glasses, quickly downing the vodka. She closed the distance between them slightly, the alcohol reminiscent of their time together in Russia. The residual sexual chemistry was still palpable. She could feel Moira's eyes on her from across the room.

How this must drive her insane, she thought.

"I *am* sorry, Oliver." Her fake sincerity came easily now. She could sense his vulnerability in that moment—that he was allowing her to penetrate his defenses, if only a bit. Regarding her, accepting her apology, the silence between them intimate.

"Yeah," he said, the word heavy, an admission of his failure. "Well, I'd best make the rounds." Then he headed off toward the few attending party guests, playing the role of dutiful host.

As Isabel turned back to the bar for another drink, she saw Moira beginning to head across the room in her direction. To the guests, Moira appeared to be procuring another glass of champagne, but Isabel knew better. Rather than wait for her opening salvo, Isabel decided to take the offense.

"Oliver threw you a lovely party," she said, her derision bubbling between the words.

"He's a good son, if not the best judge of character," Moira answered, turning to look at her. For a long, heavy moment they stood toe-to-toe, neither breaking the other's gaze. The standoff ended when Oliver returned, stepping between them.

"Is everything okay?" he asked.

I wonder if she'll tell him the truth, Isabel thought, and she prepared herself for the possibility. As Moira turned to regard her son, Isabel kept her eyes trained on the matriarch.

"Everything's fine, Oliver," Moira said. "I was just thanking Miss Rochev for coming this evening."

Isabel relaxed, the tension of the moment drifting away.

"Everything's going perfectly," she answered as she moved away, leaving Moira in her wake.

* * *

Back in the Glades, in the warehouse off Crescent Circle, Sebastian Blood and the Technician awaited Cyrus Gold's return. Earlier that night, Slade had called to provide the location of the sedatives they needed to begin production of the mirakuru. Blood had dispatched Cyrus, confident that the mission would go according to plan.

Officer Daily walked in, still in his SCPD uniform, back from stashing Maxwell Stanton's body.

"It's done," he said. "Made it look like an overdose."

"Let's hope that kills their curiosity," Blood said.

As Daily nodded, Cyrus Gold walked into the warehouse, the cache of sedatives in a crate held high overhead. Carrying it as if it was light as feather, he placed the heavy mass on the ground in front of the Technician, who attempted to pry the top off with a crowbar. Seeing this, Gold plunged his fingers through the wood and ripped the lid away with a flick of his wrist, giving his brother a small smile.

"Excellent work, Brother Cyrus," Blood enthused, clasping his loyal acolyte on the shoulder. The Technician began removing the containers of ketamine, preparing to begin production of the serum.

"How long until we're ready?" Blood asked.

"I need a few hours to get it under way," the Technician replied. "After that, the serum will require forty-eight hours to cook."

Blood nodded, pleased. Soon, he would have enough serum to begin building his army. He turned back to Cyrus.

"Any run-ins with our hooded friend tonight?"

"Yes," Cyrus said. "He tried to stop me again."

"And did you do as I asked?"

Cyrus nodded. "The vigilante won't be a problem anymore."

A broad smile spread across Blood's face. Finally, the Arrow was dead. This was very good news.

10

Slade paced behind his desk as Blood watched from the other side, Isabel seated to his right.

"How is the death of the Arrow a problem?" Blood asked. He glanced at Rochev, who maintained a stony silence. "You should be ecstatic about this."

This stopped Slade. He turned, glaring at Blood.

"Ecstatic," he gritted. "And what, pray tell, should I be ecstatic about?"

"I've alleviated a major thorn in our side."

"So you saw his body?" Slade answered. "Felt his blood warm on your hands?"

"I don't need to," Blood answered. "You know better than anyone the power Cyrus wields. If he said he killed the Arrow, that's good enough for me."

"Then you underestimate your enemy's resources," Slade growled, "and it is that arrogance that will be your undoing, Mr. Blood." He nodded to Isabel, who handed Blood a folder. "Because it leaves you blind."

Blood flipped through the folder, studying its contents. Pamphlets for the blood drive he sponsored, as well as an access log of files pulled from the city archives—including information on the Langford Institute.

"What is this?" he said, looking up.

"We asked you to get closer to Laurel Lance," Isabel commented dryly. "Yet it appears she's been getting closer to you."

"But why?"

"As a favor to Thea Queen—who happens to be dating Roy Harper," Isabel explained, "which, from your expression, I gather you didn't know."

"Lucky for you, Mr. Blood, you've proven competent in keeping your hands clean," Slade growled. "I suggest you take measures to ensure they stay that way."

Nodding, Blood left. Slade turned to Isabel.

"I'm afraid our mayoral candidate has gotten quite sloppy," he said.

"I'm monitoring things," Isabel answered. "If the heat's on him, I'll know about it."

"Good," said Slade. "We can't afford for our pet politician to become a liability."

Having been chastised by Slade and Isabel, Blood arrived back to the warehouse to find out more bad news. Cyrus Gold had found someone snooping around his motel room. He tried to apprehend him, but the African-American man had training, and was able to escape. Whoever he was, it seemed clear that someone had connected Cyrus to the thefts.

As if on cue, Blood's phone rang. It was Officer Daily.

"The police are on to Gold," Daily said, his voice low. "They're looking for him. I made sure I'm kept in the loop."

Blood glanced at the centrifuge, the vials spinning, the digital display counting down to completion.

"We're too close to let the police interfere," he said, a reminder to both himself and Daily. "Keep us posted on *anything* that occurs." Then he hung up and turned to Cyrus, and a thought struck him. If his cover had, indeed, been blown, what point was there in hiding?

"Brother Cyrus," he said. "The police are eager to meet you. Perhaps it would be best for you to introduce yourself."

Cyrus smiled, understanding implicitly.

"Where should this occur?" he asked.

"There's an old sawmill on the outskirts of the Glades," Blood suggested. "Let them track you there, then show them your power. Send them a message they won't forget."

"Yes, Brother Blood."

"Also, Officer Daily cannot emerge unscathed, lest we raise suspicion. He'll understand. Once you're done, I want you to meet Brother Langford at his psychiatric office."

"What for?"

"To burn it to the ground," Blood replied. "Leave no evidence behind."

Cyrus nodded. "If we need you, where will you be?"

"Out shopping with Laurel Lance." Blood grabbed his coat and headed off to the Starling City pier, to find out what exactly Laurel Lance knew about him.

Sebastian and Laurel walked the Starling City pier, department store bags in each hand, the night sky twinkling above them. The air was crisp, and they could see their breaths. Under normal circumstances, it would have been a picturesque romantic evening fit for a kiss, but Sebastian had other objectives tonight. Under his normally charming façade, he was on guard, scanning Laurel's face for any hint of her suspicions.

"Thank you for being my shopping guide," he said. "We weren't exactly showered with gifts this time of year when I grew up at the orphanage." Laurel didn't respond, and her look was distant. "Are you okay?"

"Yeah, it's just… can I ask you a question?" she said, giving him a look. "It's about the blood drive you sponsored."

"Of course," Sebastian said. He answered with breezy nonchalance. "It's a wonderful cause, especially given the underfunded hospitals we're dealing with. What about it?" He could tell Laurel was mustering up the resolve to press forward when her cell phone rang. She didn't recognize the number, and answered.

"Hello?" she said. Then her face paled. "What?!"

Sebastian knew instantly what the call was about.

"Okay," she said, still on the phone. "I'll be right over." She hung up, shock in her expression. Sebastian tried to feign ignorance.

"What happened?" he said.

"My father…" Laurel struggled for words. "He's in the ICU. I'm so sorry. I have to go." She tore away from him, tears beginning to well in her eyes. As he watched her go, he thought how lucky she was. Detective Lance might be badly injured, but at least he was still alive. Sebastian doubted that the rest of his squad—outside of Officer Daily, of course—had been as fortunate.

Blood looked at the night sky as he left the pier. Cyrus Gold had singlehandedly defeated both the Arrow and a squad of the SCPD's finest. If one man could do all that, what could an army of men like him do? Just like the stars overhead, the possibilities were endless.

Blood marveled at the vials of mirakuru hanging in the centrifuge's center, glowing green in the dimly lit warehouse. Soon, he would have his army, and be able to remake the city as he saw fit. No vigilante would stop him.

The Technician and Cyrus Gold returned from the

destruction of Dr. Langford's psychiatric office and all the evidence therein. Cyrus was carrying surprise cargo however—one of the kids from the Glades who Officer Daily had seen looking for Maxwell Stanton.

"I didn't know we were expecting a guest," Blood said.

"His name's Roy Harper," the Technician explained. "We caught him poking around the office, just before burning it down."

So this was the boy who had been seen patrolling the Glades in the Arrow's absence, who had attempted to stop the theft of the medical supplies. Blood recognized him now. He looked so diminutive in Cyrus's grasp. Like a bothersome flea.

"Perhaps he wants to join our brotherhood," Blood said thoughtfully. "And who am I to deny him? Strap him to a chair. Let's see how well he takes to the serum." As the Technician headed off toward the centrifuge, Cyrus deposited Roy in a chair, securing his arms in two leather restraints. Then they watched as he began to regain consciousness, and glanced around the room.

The Technician pulled a syringe of the mirakuru from the machine, holding it up and gazing at it in the light.

"It's ready," he said. Then he handed it to Brother Blood.

Taking it, Blood approached Roy, the visage of his skull mask bearing down. The boy struggled against his chair restraints, then peered angrily at his captors.

"Is this where you killed Max Stanton?" He saw the syringe and panic took hold. "What are you doing? If you stick that in me, I'll kill you."

"No, Brother Roy," Blood said, grabbing him viciously by the throat. "You'll kill *for* me." Then he plunged the syringe into Roy's shoulder, causing him to howl in pain.

Without warning, the ceiling above them gave way and the Arrow appeared, zip lining down into the warehouse. The Technician tried to pull his gun, but the vigilante beat him to the draw, taking him down with an arrow. He quickly nocked another, pointing it at Brother Blood.

Blood stared at him, marveling at the sight. Finally, he was face to face with his nemesis, the great hero his constituents so idolized. Apparently, he wasn't so easy to kill. Part of Blood was happy about that, relishing the opportunity to witness his death firsthand.

"Brother Cyrus told me he killed you."

"Guess he's not as strong as you'd hoped," the Arrow replied. "Where'd you get the mirakuru? Who gave you the formula?"

"It was a gift. A gift I would use to save this city from itself."

As Roy continued to bellow in pain, blood seeping from his eyes as the serum ripped through his body, Cyrus Gold charged at the Arrow, drawing his aim away from Blood. The vigilante fired an arrow, finding purchase in Gold's shoulder, but it failed to stop him. Gold continued charging.

The Arrow tried to spin into a kick, but Gold was too fast, catching him by the leg and throwing him across the room, sending him crashing into the wall. Pieces of drywall fell away from the impact. Still the vigilante struggled to get up and fight, but Cyrus Gold stalked him, a vicious kick sending him skidding across the floor. His momentum was halted with a sickening thud by a support column.

Roy fell silent, his face streaked with blood.

Blood checked his pulse, then shook his head.

"Another failure," he said.

The Arrow slumped to the ground at the sight, and Blood was doubly disappointed. He turned toward Cyrus Gold, his acolyte.

"Kill him," he said.

Charging his enemy's slumped body, Cyrus expected an easy kill. He was surprised when the vigilante suddenly leapt to his feet, his energy and determination renewed. Cyrus reared back and let loose a punch, but the Arrow avoided it, countering with a kick to his mid-section, followed by quick left-right, left-right punch combos to his throat.

Cyrus tried to counter with a punch of his own, but he was too slow. The Arrow ducked, avoiding the blow, and spun into a roundhouse kick that sent Cyrus stumbling back toward the centrifuge. As he regained his balance, the vigilante quickly nocked two arrows and fired them into the machine, causing it to explode, sending metal shrapnel and liquid mirakuru flying in all directions. Cyrus was caught point blank by the blast, the serum reacting with the flames like napalm, covering his face and burning him alive.

Taking cover in the shadows, Blood could only watch in horror as his loyal servant screamed in agony. Then chunks of concrete ceiling began to fall, damaged by the explosion, the debris crushing both Cyrus and the Technician under its weight. Two of his loyal brothers, gone in an instant.

The sight left Blood staggered.

Then he saw the Arrow watching him from across the room, and his survival instinct quickly snapped him out of his shock. He did the math—as much as he wanted to make the vigilante pay for these deaths, Blood knew challenging him one-on-one was a fool's errand. He couldn't risk being exposed. The mayorship was too close.

With a heavy heart he dashed off, leaving the bodies behind.

11

In the back seat of a black car, Sebastian sat in silence, his mind going over the prior night's events. The thoughts sent his adrenaline spiking, his heart pounding in response, racing in his chest. He knew he needed to accept the fact that his friend had died, but imagining a life without Cyrus was too hard to bear.

I am the reason he is dead, Sebastian thought to himself. *I allowed him to be injected with the serum. I used my friend as a weapon.*

He remembered days with his parents that he wished he had never been born… until Cyrus. He recalled the night that Cyrus found him on the street as a young, timid boy. Sebastian had been wandering around aimlessly for hours, feeling the despair. The man had saved him, and Sebastian had hoped that one day he could return the favor.

The black car slowly came to a stop.

Slade will deliver on his promise. Must pull it together—

the city is about to be yours, he told himself.

The driver opened Sebastian's door as cameras flashed, blinding him. Sebastian shielded his eyes the best he could as he entered City Hall, was led down a long corridor, and guided to a backstage area. He heard the hushed tones of an audience talking, and swallowed hard, feeling his nerves starting to boil over. Breathing deeply—once, twice, three times—he reconnected his mind and body to the task at hand.

"Mr. Blood, they're ready for you," an official said to him.

Sebastian felt a bead of sweat roll down his back. He panicked for a moment and wondered if he was sweating through his suit jacket. He closed his eyes and took the moment in...

...then stepped onto the stage and smiled to the audience before him. He waved his hands in the air, smiled, and they cheered as he made his way to the podium. It boasted a bright red-and-blue sign.

SEBASTIAN BLOOD FOR MAYOR

He straightened his tie, smiled again, and began.

"Good evening, Starling City and thank you for coming out tonight," he said, pausing to let the applause die down. "As many of you know, I am Sebastian Blood—Alderman for the Glades. What many of you *don't* know is that I am a child of this great city. It has been the only home I have ever known, and it has been my lifelong goal to make this city—my city—better.

"I want to take this time to officially announce my candidacy for the mayorship of Starling City." More applause, and he waited, buoyed by the response. "My devotion to the city runs deep, and being a product of its streets, I care about nothing more than the people who live here. The people who deserve to be heard, the people who need to exercise their voices. I can assure you, I am not going to make anyone any empty promises.

"My one goal is to serve the *people* of Starling City— not the men and the women who *think* they own it. Together, we can help rebuild our city into a place where there are no elites and no oppressed. A place where we are all brothers and sisters. A place that makes us a united front, a stronger city.

"We are in this together!" Sebastian finished.

The crowd erupted in applause and rose to their feet. Sebastian waved his hand, feeling alive. The support for him seemed unshakable—he was the man for the job. He waved to them, feeding off their excitement as he made his way off the stage and out of City Hall.

Perhaps Brother Cyrus's sacrifice was not in vain.

Sebastian's high continued as he arrived at Slade's office, yet as he entered the elevator, he was suddenly unsure about how the man was going to react about the events of the night before. The centrifuge had been destroyed, and Sebastian couldn't help but feel a sense of dread in his gut, as if he had let Slade down.

He told himself to remain strong, as Cyrus had taught him.

The elevator rang as Sebastian exited cautiously and saw Slade watching the news coverage of his announcement.

"Your campaign begins, Mr. Blood."

"This city needs a leader, and sending the copycat Hoods to assassinate the mayor was just the beginning." He approached Slade. *Take a deep breath.* "The vigilante is alive—he destroyed the centrifuge, and the serum along with it."

Slade turned, and Sebastian saw the anger.

"I will arrange for you to receive another sample of my blood, and you can begin to mass produce the serum again. But when I ask you... *tell* you not to confront the vigilante... you will *listen*," Slade said. "Remember that your mask can be worn by another."

"Any mask can," Sebastian replied. "Do you know who wears the Arrow's hood?"

"He is my friend," Slade explained, "and killing him would be a release from this life, yet his sentence has yet to be carried out. I am going to tear away everything he cares about, destroy those who choose to follow him, corrupt those he loves. Once he has lost everyone and everything he values, I will send an arrow through his eye."

Sebastian swallowed hard.

"I don't care how this gets accomplished. The lives that will be taken will be just the beginning," Slade added dryly. A sudden ping of pain shot through Sebastian's heart as he realized that Cyrus had been disposable to Slade.

But not to him. Against all odds, Cyrus had taken his serum and survived. Deep down he had been a good man, and it hurt to know that no one would ever know about all the great things he had accomplished. The media would only reveal that Cyrus Gold had been a thief—tarnishing his legacy forever.

I need to turn this around, Sebastian thought.

"The good news is that I still remain the favored candidate for the mayoral race," he said with a small smile. "Last night was a minor setback, but we still seem to be moving in a good direction. Tonight with my announcement—the crowd, the city, they are ready for this change."

Slade ran his fingers through his salt and pepper hair and swiveled his chair around to gaze out over the rooftops. His single eye sparkled in the outside light.

"They have no idea how much change their city will see."

12

While most people were out on their lunch break, Isabel sat behind her desk at Queen Consolidated. With most of her staff and her assistant, Theodore, on break, she took the time to do a little research on Sebastian Blood. She couldn't shake the feeling she'd had about him since day one. Something remained *off* about him, and she was determined to dig into his past—specifically with regard to Zandia.

Who are you really, *Sebastian Blood?* she wondered.

She hit several dead ends with zero results, and started looking into the murders in the Glades around the time Sebastian arrived at Zandia. Scanning website after website, she located reports of many shootings in the city, specifically in the Glades, but none of them indicated domestic fight, which was how Sebastian told them he ended up at the orphanage.

There's something there, she mused. *Something we don't know, and we dare not allow for loose ends.* Yet before Slade would believe her, she would need to have evidence—

incontrovertible proof. So as her staff returned from their breaks, she got up from her desk and donned her impeccable charcoal jacket. Her assistant settled back at his desk as Isabel headed for the door.

"I won't be back—I have business to attend to."

"He's hiding something," she said firmly. "I know he is."

"Of course he is, Miss Rochev. Aren't we all?"

"I didn't work this hard and get this far to have us go down on his account," she pressed. "He's lying, it has something to do with his father's murder, and that means he may have baggage we can't afford."

"Given the position he has attained, Alderman Blood has many friends, and probably twice as many enemies," Slade said, taking a sip of water from his crystal glass. He set it down, and looked thoughtful. "It is curious, though, that the details are not lining up." He sat back in his chair and reached for the newspaper on his desk. He scanned it, landing on a photo of Sebastian. In it, he was shaking the hands of the members of a homeless shelter, smiling wide and proud. Slade squinted at the image.

"Being a woman of power," he said, "you must have connections within the city government—persons who could help you obtain files on government officials— say, persons like Sebastian Blood."

"Perhaps..." Isabel said with a smile.

"Make sure you're not seen or recorded on camera," Slade continued. "Let's find out what the man behind the mask is actually hiding."

Isabel nodded. "I'll be in touch," she said as she picked up her bag and headed for the elevator.

Days later, Sebastian sat in the back of his black town car, reviewing the updates from the week. The polls were strong, and despite the fact that Moira Queen had thrown her hat into the ring—with surprising success—he imagined what life was going to be like when the city was his. In his mind's eye, he saw everyone cheering; he couldn't help but itch for the day to come.

His reverie was interrupted by the buzzing of his cell phone.

"Alderman Blood here."

"Brother Blood," the person on the other line said. There was too much background noise for him to tell who was speaking. He pulled back his phone to see a restricted number on the screen.

"Brother Blood," the voice repeated. "It's Brother Daily."

"Yes," Sebastian said, breathing a sigh of relief. "What's up?"

"Laurel Lance has been asking questions about you, especially around the precinct," Daily told him. "It looks as if she suspects something is up."

"I know, my friend," Sebastian replied. "She paid

me a visit a few days ago, in my office. She wanted to know how I knew Cyrus Gold, and asked about my parents. But I can assure you that she was convinced by the answers she received. We have nothing to fear."

"I don't know, brother. She came in this morning and I could overhear her telling someone how she went to Saint Walker's yesterday." He paused, and continued, "While her father is recovering, she's likely to receive a lot of support from the cops on the force. Saint Walker's has been a safe haven for us, and to expose it now would be catastrophic."

As Brother Daily's words sunk in, a tightness gripped Sebastian's chest. This was far worse than he had suspected. While he had been playing the part of the supportive friend, concerned for Quentin Lance's health, she had come fishing for answers about Cyrus. If Brother Daily's report was accurate, it was entirely possible that Laurel Lance was close to discovering who was behind the skull mask.

"Thank you, brother, for bringing this to my attention," he said calmly. "I've been a neglectful nephew the past few years. It is time I paid my aunt a visit, to see how everything is holding up at Saint Walker's." He cut the connection as the driver pulled up to a valet stand.

Sebastian got out of the car and buttoned his suit coat as some of the local paparazzi snapped his photo. He smiled and waved his hand to them, when suddenly the camera lenses were turned in the opposite direction—toward the doorway of a restaurant. He frowned as he saw Oliver Queen exiting the establishment, yet he approached Oliver as the paparazzi continued to snap photos.

"Mr. Queen, good to see you!" he said effusively.

"Alderman," Oliver responded. "What brings you here?"

"A campaign luncheon," Sebastian said.

"How is the campaign treating you?" Oliver asked.

"I can't complain," he replied. "Now that your mother has decided to enter the race, as well, I'm sure you see firsthand how difficult it can be." He was careful not to show how incensed he was about the competition, and remembered the poll numbers.

Oliver smiled. "Well, it's good to see you, Sebastian—you take care," Oliver said as he climbed into his car, which sped away.

Sebastian returned home after a late night visit to Saint Walker's. His eyes were heavy as he reached his bedroom, pulled a briefcase from underneath his bed, and placed it on his dresser. He reached into his coat, pulling out the skull mask and a syringe—the one he had just used to inject Maya with an undetectable serum that would cause her heart to stop slowly, killing her discreetly.

Feeling no sense of remorse for what he had done, he placed the items in the briefcase and locked them up as he got ready to turn in. Tonight, for the first time in a long while, he would sleep easy.

As the sun started to rise in Starling City, Sebastian wrapped himself in the sheets and slowly opened his eyes to see how much longer he would be able to remain in his cozy bed. He sat bolt upright when he saw Slade Wilson hovering nearby.

"Slade... Slade! What are you doing here?" he croaked, trying to wake up.

"Sloppy," Slade said, holding up a file. "Sloppy work."

"What are you talking about? What is that?" Sebastian demanded as he rose to his feet.

"It's yours, Mr. Blood—the police file of your father's murder, the murder you said was done by your mother as self-defense, before turning the gun on herself." Slade let out a laugh, fake and unsettling. "We both know that is a lie. It was you." Slade smiled. "Sloppy work."

Sebastian struggled to process what Slade was saying.

"I have to admit I had my reservations about you," Slade continued. "As I did my research on you I thought I had been thorough. I thought you were a boy in love with the Glades through and through, doing what you believed to be your part for the city, safe behind that mask of yours.

"But this, this confirms that you are everything I

need you to be," he said. "A ruthless killer."

"I am *not* a killer," Sebastian fought back.

Without warning Slade dropped the file to the floor and punched Sebastian in the stomach. Sebastian fell to the ground, grasping his abdomen, gasping and coughing, sounding as if he wanted to retch. Slade grabbed his arm and twisted it behind his back. Sebastian cried out in agony.

"Regardless, your work is sloppy, Mr. Blood," Slade said as calmly as if he was chairing a board meeting. "I should have been made aware of your history— especially as it concerns my work. And you have been sloppy again when it comes to Laurel Lance." His voice grew louder, until he was practically shouting. "Now it's up to me to clean up yet another mess, all due to your incompetence."

Sebastian's eyes started to water from the pain. He knew that Slade would waste no time in killing Laurel, even though she was digging into *his* past. Her death would continue the city's spiral of violence.

"Please, no," he gritted through the pain. "I'm sorry. I can fix it, I promise, please!"

"Enlighten me, Mr. Blood," Slade said, releasing his grip.

Sebastian fell to the floor, gripping his shoulder, his mind racing.

"Laurel Lance is a drug addict," Sebastian said, slowly rising to his feet. "She has shown all the signs of one, and I know for a fact she is medicating herself. We can have her arrested. Her name will be discredited. No one will believe her wild accusations, once she is exposed."

Slade paused, considering the new information.

"You have till tomorrow morning to handle this situation, Mr. Blood," he said. "This is your one chance, then I will deal with Miss Lance as I see fit." With that, he left. Sebastian reached for his cell phone and jabbed a number.

"Brother Daily, meet me for coffee in an hour," he said, still grimacing through the pain. "We need to discuss Laurel Lance." He cut the connection, then lifted up his shirt, seeing a black bruise already forming on his ribs.

He rose slowly to his feet, knowing what he had to do to ensure that he never again received a house call from Slade Wilson.

Officer Daily took a sip of his steaming black coffee, followed by a bite of a pastry as Sebastian entered the coffee shop. Daily smiled as he joined him in the booth, but the smile quickly faded when he saw the expression on Brother Blood's face.

"Laurel Lance needs to be taken care of," Blood said. "She's getting too close, and it needs to end… tonight."

"What do you need from me, Brother?" Daily answered. "I'm here to serve you and the city—you know that."

"I need you to arrest her tonight in her apartment,

on the charge of drug possession and use," Sebastian replied, his voice low and harsh. "She has been using for some months now. It needs to be visible, but before she can be processed, we need to take her to the Starling City Cannery, drawing out the vigilante."

"How do you know the vigilante will come?"

"From what I've been able to piece together, he keeps an eye on Miss Lance," Blood replied. "When the vigilante comes to save Laurel, I need you to reveal yourself as the man behind the skull mask."

Officer Daily paused, took another sip of his coffee, then nodded.

"Anything you need, brother," he said, "I will do."

"This mission *has* to succeed," Blood continued. "When you reveal your identity to the vigilante and Lance, it will lead them away from me, and thus the brotherhood. After you are revealed, however, it will be in your best interest to leave the city as quickly as possible. Once Laurel Lance sees your face, she will stop at nothing to bring you down."

"We've been through a lot together through the years, Brother Blood," Officer Daily said. "My best memories of Zandia have you in them, and sharing in this journey with you for the city has been an honor. There isn't anything I wouldn't do for you." He smiled, taking another bite of his pastry.

"Thank you, my friend."

* * *

Glass shattered as Oliver was hit over the head, and fell heavily to the floor. Out of the shadows of Lance's apartment, Brother Daily appeared in the skull mask.

"Leave him, he isn't important," he said, looking contemptuously at Oliver as two men grabbed Laurel by the arms. "Hello, Laurel," he said, his voice muffled. "I hear you have been talking about me." He reached into his bag and grabbed a bottle of chloroform. The rank smell filled the room as he dampened a towel with the sedative. Laurel did her best to try and escape, but Daily managed to shove the towel in Laurel's face.

Her eyes rolled back into her head, she stopped struggling, and passed out.

"Put her in the back of the van," Daily said. "I need to leave a message." The two men dragged her through the door, leaving him alone with Oliver. He went into his bag again and pulled out some red paint, which he quickly used to smear instructions on Laurel's white brick wall.

Tell the Arrow
Starling Cannery

The red paint dripped down the white wall as Brother Daily smiled behind his mask, finally understanding the power and strength that the mask possessed. He darted out of the apartment to continue his mission for Brother Blood.

* * *

When Laurel regained consciousness, she peeled herself off the concrete floor where she had been deposited and walked slowly around, examining the pipes and debris, looking for the man whom she believed to be Sebastian Blood. Her breath grew short as suddenly a figure emerged out of the shadows in the dark, wearing the mask. He stayed in sight just long enough for her to spot him.

"If that mask is supposed to scare me, all it is doing is confirming what I've already known for a while now…" she cried out as he disappeared again. "You're one sick son of a bitch, Sebastian."

"Thirty thousand years ago, masks invested their wearer with authority," a voice said from the darkness. "Like a God."

"You're insane!" Laurel screamed.

"I'm not the one making drug-addled, unsubstantiated accusations against Starling's favorite son," the figure said as he leapt out again, putting her in a headlock.

Suddenly a green arrow blazed past, grazing his arm.

"Get away from her," a guttural voice said, "or I will put you down."

He tossed Laurel to the hard, wet concrete as he reached for something in his pocket. She struggled to get up as the man aimed a gun at the Arrow, but he didn't get a chance to shoot as the Arrow knocked the gun out of his hands. The Arrow pressed his advantage, punching and kicking him, then the masked figure leapt onto the Arrow's back, sending him down onto the concrete.

The vigilante struggled to break free, finally pulling an arrow from his quiver, and stabbed it deep into his assailant's leg. The man screamed as blood began to pour from his wound. The Arrow elbowed him in the face, knocking him off.

There was a moment's hesitation, and the masked man seized the opportunity, grabbed his gun, and aimed directly for the Arrow…

BANG!

A bullet entered the masked man's back, then another, and another, and another as Laurel charged him with a revolver. He went down, twisting in uncontrollable spasms, grunts of pain coming from behind the mask, blood appearing from his wounds. The Arrow recovered his equilibrium, bent down, and removed the mask.

Laurel gasped. It was Officer Daily, from her father's unit. He looked up at her, and *smiled*. Tears started to well up in her eyes. Then he started to gasp for air, and stopped breathing altogether.

Sebastian arrived at Slade's headquarters late at night, flanked by a pair of newly minted bodyguards. He was proud that he had succeeded in his aim of throwing Laurel Lance off the chase. He felt relieved that Slade wouldn't harm her. And he tried to bury the guilt he felt for sending Brother Daily on a mission that had cost his life.

Another life taken for the cause. He greatly admired Brother Daily for his devotion, and swore that his death wouldn't be in vain.

"It's done," Sebastian said to the figure in the shadows. After his run-in with Slade, he had decided that having round-the-clock bodyguards would help avoid situations like that. "The police think it was Daily," he announced. "He sacrificed himself for our cause."

"It's a good start," Slade growled, "but the magnitude of your negligence requires a greater sacrifice." He emerged from the shadows wearing black-and-orange armor. Before they could even twitch, he stabbed Sebastian's bodyguards and slit their throats as if carving a Thanksgiving turkey.

Sebastian froze, unable to move.

"Your incompetence has now cost four lives, Alderman," Slade said, holding his sword to his throat. "Fail me again, and yours will be the fifth." He put his sword back in his sheath and faded back into the darkness.

13

A few weeks later, Isabel Rochev's black Mercedes Benz roared to a stop at Slade's headquarters. She emerged, slamming the car door, her anger palpable. The walk to Slade's office did nothing to diminish it.

"It's been weeks, and nothing is happening," she raged.

"These things take time, Miss Rochev," Slade responded calmly. "We are still on target."

"You say that, yet the Queens are still out there, scot free," she countered. "I agreed to work with you, *train* with you, because you convinced me I would have my revenge, yet months have passed, and *nothing*." She slammed a fist on his desk, and he just peered at her in silence. As she began to speak again, he held up a hand, silencing her.

"You are a lucky woman, Miss Rochev—you will get your wish, tonight in fact," he said, and she frowned with confusion. "And you need wait no longer. Tonight will be the commencement of our plan," he continued as he rose to his feet. Slade walked to a cabinet, unlocked a drawer, and pulled out a silver briefcase. He placed it on his desk, twirled the numbers on the lock, and was rewarded with a satisfying *click*.

"Tonight we both will visit the Queen Mansion," Slade said as he held up a tiny spy camera, an acquisition from his time at A.S.I.S. Isabel approached the desk and saw several such cameras in the briefcase. "With these I will show my support for Moira Queen's mayoral campaign. I'm going to bug their palace so we can observe their every move. The cameras are so sophisticated that not even Oliver's dear Felicity can hack into them," he said as he placed the camera back in the briefcase. "I have waited five years for this night, and I cannot wait a moment longer for the gratification of seeing Oliver Queen suffer," Slade said.

"But what will I be doing while you're breaking and entering?" Isabel asked.

Without answering, Slade made his way to a nearby closet. He reappeared with a sealed garment bag.

"You have been most loyal, Miss Rochev," he began, "devoted to the cause, and you have successfully completed your training." He hung up the garment bag. "The word 'ravage' means to wreak havoc or destruction," Slade said as he unzipped the garment bag to reveal a suit of armor. A rare smile appeared on her face as she moved closer to admire her new attire.

"Tonight, you begin your career as the Ravager,"

Slade said. "I need you to stand guard at the Queen Mansion. Oliver will choose to keep his vigilante identity a secret from his family tonight, which means he will send John Diggle to stop me. I need you to fight off Diggle. There is no need to kill him, though—killing him will come later, but I have faith that you will be able to disarm him." He placed a hand on her shoulder.

Isabel touched the jumpsuit, which was made of high-quality leather. She ran her fingers over it, admiring the handiwork. Then she picked up her mask, an orange-and-black affair that echoed Slade's own, though it still showed her expression. She placed it over her head and grinned, eager for the night's events.

"Thank you, Mr. Wilson," she said from behind the mask.

Slade gave her a half smile. "Thank me when Queen Consolidated is yours."

"It's a pleasure to meet you, Mr. Queen," Slade said, grasping Oliver's hand as he stepped into the Queen Mansion living room. Oliver's face went white.

"What are you doing here?" he demanded.

"Mr. Wilson just made a sizable contribution to my campaign," Moira told him, glaring at her son for forgetting his manners.

Without letting the façade slip in the slightest, Slade explained to Oliver that he had been impressed with his mother's campaign efforts, and believed that she was the type of mayor the city needed, praising her budget proposals, plans for lowering unemployment rates, and closing wage gaps. He went on to sympathize with what she had experienced over the previous year.

"All I can say is that you and I have something in common," he concluded. "I know how difficult it is to pick yourself back up after others have written you off." He picked up a glass of rum, then handed one each to Oliver and his mother, offering a toast to their new relationship. Oliver hesitated, then took a small sip as Slade let his gaze fall on an antique model boat in the Queen living room. While Moira and Oliver sipped their drinks, he took the opportunity to place one of his spy cameras on the boat.

"Does your family get out on the water much?" Slade asked. Moira explained to Slade that after Robert's death, no one in the family went out on the water.

"Now that you mention it, I remember reading about that in the papers—I'm sorry," Slade said turning to Oliver. "You were a brave soul—being on that island must have been hell," he added. In his head, however, all he could see was Shado's face.

"Are you married, Mr. Wilson?" Moira asked. "Do you have any children?"

"I'm afraid not," he responded. For a moment, Slade felt his heart ache for how his life used to be—before the island, before meeting Oliver. "There was someone special once, but she died a few years ago," he continued, picturing Shado in the grass with a bullet in her brain—all because of Oliver. He took another sip of his rum and got up from the couch, stepping over to closely admire a painting hung above the mantel.

"My first husband had a love for nineteenth-century American landscapes," Moira said. The conversation continued as Slade said he would love to see their full collection, which was hung around the house. Oliver quickly dismissed the idea.

"We have some family business to attend to," he said curtly as Moira rolled her eyes. She left the room to locate a member of her staff who could show him around to see the paintings. As soon as she did Oliver snatched a letter opener from the desk and advanced, but Slade saw him coming and grasped Oliver's wrist tightly. Using his mirakuru strength, he forced Oliver to drop the makeshift weapon.

"Not yet, kid," Slade said, "I still have to meet the rest of your family." He released his grip as Oliver's sister came through the front door.

"Thea! What perfect timing!" Moira said, re-entering the room. "This is Slade Wilson. I was just about to show him our art collection, but you are far better suited." The girl looked pleased, and agreed to act as an impromptu tour guide.

Thea showed great pride as she led Slade around the mansion. He expressed amazement with how many pieces the Queen family possessed, studying several of them carefully, and told her he was impressed with how insightful she was about the art. The tour came to an end, and Slade thanked both mother and daughter for their hospitality. Then he started to make his way toward the foyer.

"Thea, are you home?" The shout came as the group approached the front door.

"Roy?" Thea said loudly. "I thought I was meeting you at Verdant."

Moira introduced Roy Harper to Slade. The two men shook hands, and Slade smiled, knowing that Roy had been one of the successful test subjects. Judging from the firm grip he received, Slade guessed that Team Arrow anticipated trouble, and that his enemies had made ready to attack.

His plan was going accordingly.

"Ollie!" Sara Lance called out, coming down the stairs, and he strove to maintain his composure at seeing her again so unexpectedly, the girl that Oliver had chosen over his beloved Shado. The two exchanged pleasantries as their time in Lian Yu burned behind their eyes.

"What would you like to do now, Mr. Wilson?" Oliver asked, and he no longer seemed off balance. Slade scanned the room, knowing they were chomping at the bit to make a move on him.

Fools, he thought to himself as he thanked Moira for having him in her home. Oliver offered to walk him out to his car.

* * *

John Diggle shifted slightly on his perch, arranging his sniper rifle, ready to take Slade out as soon as he left Queen Mansion. He spoke into his comm, then he waited.

As soon as he saw Oliver walk out with Slade, he peered through the sight, lining up the shot. Suddenly he was struck in the head, and instantly unconscious. He never heard his assailant approach.

Ravager beamed, pleased with herself, a rush of adrenaline running through her at combat that wasn't just training. She was surprised how good it felt, and was ready to do it again.

"Cyrus Gold," Oliver hissed angrily. "The man in the skull mask, his associates—they all work for you!" As calm as could be, Slade got into his car. "What do you want?" Oliver demanded.

"Five years ago I made you a promise, and I am here to fulfill it. Sara was only the first," Slade said. "See you around, kid." With that he slammed the car door, shutting down the conversation, and moments later he was racing off into the night as the moon glistened in his eye, and his heart filled with hate.

* * *

A few days later, shortly before dawn, Sebastian visited Slade's office. He was wary as he entered the room.

"I have news, Slade, and it's not good," he called out.

"What is it now, Mr. Blood?" Slade asked, turning in his chair. "Something more about your inability to follow simple instructions?"

"I'm afraid it's yours, sir," Sebastian replied, bracing himself.

"Go on," Slade said, a hint of humor in his tone.

"My eyes in the Glades have told me that the Russian mob has been looking into your business," Sebastian reported.

"What do you mean?" Slade asked.

"Someone is looking to label you as the vigilante," Sebastian said. "From what I've been told, they were asking about a man with an eye patch—someone who not long ago arrived in Starling. It could be nothing, but we're at a crucial moment, and we can't take chances now."

"I am impressed, Mr. Blood," Slade said. "Who do you know who might be involved with this?"

"Alexi Leonov is the head of a business that they run in the Glades," Sebastian answered. "I believe he would know more."

"Then I will have to visit Mr. Leonov tonight," Slade said.

* * *

Dressed in his Deathstroke armor, Slade approached the car shop in which Alexi Leonov worked. As soon as he arrived, he killed the first two men he saw in mechanic's jumpsuits. Then he powered on through the shop, found Alexi behind a desk, and whisked out his sword from its sheath.

"Who are you?" Alexi asked, his eyes going wide.

"Someone you and Oliver Queen are too curious about," Slade said.

Alexi tried to get up to defend himself, twisting to reach for a drawer. Slade stabbed him in the back, sending him sprawling to the ground in pain, blood spurting from his body. Then he reached back and pulled an orange arrow from his pack. He stared down at Alexi.

"What have your men found?" Slade demanded.

"I will tell you nothing," Alexi sneered dismissively. The threat of stabbing him in the leg did nothing to loosen his tongue, so Slade drove the arrow down, feeling the arrowhead puncturing the bone. It crunched again as he pulled the arrow back out. Alexi howled with pain, and when Slade motioned to repeat the process, the Russian motioned for him to wait.

"I gave him bank account number," he confessed, "that is all. Enough is enough."

"I couldn't agree more," Slade said as he stabbed his orange arrow through Alexi's eye, killing him instantly.

"Nice try, kid," Slade said.

* * *

Having thrown Alexi's body into the back of the car, Slade arrived back at his penthouse office knowing that it wouldn't take Oliver long to figure out where he was. Smoak would do that.

His mind seethed with anger as he dragged Alexi's body savagely out of the elevator and into his office, the shaft of the arrow protruding from the eye socket and scraping against the floor. He lifted the body with one swoop of his arm and slammed it into a desk chair, then peered at it in disgust as blood dripped from the wound, already slower than it had been. Slade's mind raced with memories of his past—his time on the island with Oliver and Shado, waking up in the ocean feeling lost and alone—but the familiar feeling of retribution soon returned.

He went to his filing cabinet, rummaged through a drawer, and returned with a film canister and projector reel. He carefully opened the canister and pulled out a roll of film, then placed it gently on the projector. He started the machine, shining the footage against the wall. He was mesmerized as he watched the footage of Shado—recordings he had stolen from A.S.I.S. She smiled at the camera playfully, her beauty and essence shining through. Her face was as beautiful as ever, her black hair blowing freely in the wind.

The anger dissipated as he watched, attempting to breathe her in, and remembering what it was like to have her alive and close. He imagined a life with Shado, back in Australia, coming home every day to her loving arms. He went to the wall, touched her face, wishing that he could feel her soft skin.

After a moment he stepped back, regained his focus.

Shado was gone.

Shado was dead because of Oliver.

Snapped back into reality, Slade reached into his pants pocket and pulled out his cell phone. He composed a text to Isabel and Sebastian, instructing them to meet him at a storage depot outside Starling City.

Then he placed his phone back in his pocket and grabbed his suit coat off of his desk, leaving Alexi's body for Oliver to find, hoping that the Arrow would understand the message. He gazed one last time at the footage of Shado, then he turned and left the office— knowing that the yearning in his heart would remain forever.

14

Slade pulled up at Tosca Cartage, a storage depot outside of Starling City. He got out of the car, buttoned up his suit jacket, and entered the warehouse. Blood and Isabel were waiting patiently for him in an office.

"Tomorrow marks the beginning of the final phase," he began, "for tomorrow the Queens will start to unravel."

Isabel smiled smugly. This was the moment for which she had been waiting. To her, it felt like an eternity since she had met Slade, that night in the parking garage. She had done her best to be patient, but every day that passed since becoming part of the team had made stronger her hate for the Queen family.

"Here's how it will go down," Slade said. "First we will take the adorable Thea, tomorrow night. She'll be working at her club in the Glades, and snatching her should be simple. Unlike her brother, she has no bodyguard—very sloppy.

"Mr. Blood—I will handle that, then meet you at the location we discussed. Once I've delivered her I trust you to keep an eye on her, and keep her safe until I return." Blood nodded. "Another kidnapping, and the possibility that she might be killed, will destroy Moira's confidence. She will drop out of the race, leaving you to reign in this city."

He turned to Isabel.

"As for her loving brother Oliver, well, it's time for you to do what is necessary to take control of Queen Consolidated, Miss Rochev."

"How can you be sure this will all work? How can we be certain Moira will just crumble?" Blood asked.

"You *will* be mayor, Mr. Blood, with or without Moira Queen in the picture," Slade replied, then he returned his attention to Isabel. "Miss Rochev, please rent a car in my name, to leave some bread crumbs for the vigilante. Make it a Porsche." She nodded, remembering that Sebastian was still in the dark as to who was behind the green hood.

"Isn't that giving the vigilante the whole loaf?" Blood asked.

"Exactly my point," Slade said as he turned on his heels. Finally he was ready—to destroy the Queens, and put an arrow into Oliver's eye.

* * *

"Your mascara is running," Slade said, handing Thea a tissue with which to dry her eyes in the back of his black sedan.

"Thank you for the ride, Mr. Wilson," she said, heaving a deep sigh. "It's just my boyfriend... ex-boyfriend now. He just ended things—out of nowhere." She stifled a sob.

"Heartbreak is something I know all too well," he responded, sounding entirely sympathetic. "It's not an easy thing to recover from, and sometimes you never do." The car came to a stop.

Thea looked out the window.

"This isn't my home."

"You're not going home, Thea," Slade said, and he turned. "*GET OUT!*" he bellowed.

Terrified, Thea bolted from the car. She looked around, frantically trying to get a sense of where she was. She ran, anxious to get away from Slade and the car, her heart pounding with fear. Stumbling through the shadows, she ran right into someone, bounding off of them and struggling for balance. Looking up, she saw a skull mask, and gasped.

"Hello, Thea," the man said. "It's a pleasure to meet you." He grabbed her arm firmly.

She tried to scream, but no sound came out.

Hours later the manhunt for Thea's abductor was well underway. The lobby at Queen Consolidated buzzed with reporters and paparazzi trying to get a statement from any member of the family or staff.

Floors above, Moira met with Detective Lance and members of the Starling City Police Department. She broached the idea that somehow Malcolm Merlyn was behind her daughter's capture. Oliver watched his mother, his own mind a chaotic jumble, knowing that somewhere, somehow, Slade had Thea.

This is my *responsibility*, he thought. *I should have had her followed.*

Suddenly Isabel Rochev knocked on the door, motioning to him. Before his mother could spot her, he excused himself and joined her in an empty conference room.

"I'm sorry to remind you of this now, but at today's meeting the board nominated new officers," she started. "Unfortunately, voting has to take place within twenty-four hours, and can't be suspended. It's a Securities and Exchange Commission mandate."

"I don't give a damn about the rules, Isabel," Oliver told her. "There are more important things I need to address right now."

"I'm sorry, but you have to give a damn," she answered back, an edge appearing in her voice. "You have responsibilities, to your company and your employees."

Oliver began to pace back and forth. "You have to cover for me," he said. "It's my sister's life we're talking about here."

"There's nothing I can do—I don't have the authority," she responded. "Unless…"

"Unless what?"

"No, it's not a good idea," she said. She paused, then continued, "You could appoint someone CEO *pro tempore*, but you would need to choose carefully—find someone who's qualified."

Oliver grabbed a notepad, and started scribbling.

"I appoint you," Oliver declared. He picked up the pad and showed Isabel.

I hereby transfer my authority
as CEO of Queen Consolidated
to Isabel Rochev.

Then he signed it.

"Congratulations," he said. "You are the new temporary CEO." There was gratitude in his eyes. "Thank you."

"You can have Thea thank me when she's back, safe at home," Isabel said. Before she could say anything more, Felicity Smoak appeared at the door to take Oliver out of the conference room.

As soon as Oliver left the room, all pretenses vanished. Isabel looked down at the notepad, hardly daring to breathe, astonished that she held exactly what she needed to destroy Oliver and his family. Her shock quickly diminished as her assistant approached her.

"Call together the board of directors," she told

Theodore. "There will be an emergency meeting." He nodded and rushed away to comply. She looked down at the piece of paper again, fire burning in her heart. The Queens would finally get what they deserved.

The hostage video of Thea elicited exactly the effect he wanted.

Across town, Slade got into his rental car, knowing that the Queens were spiraling out of control trying to find her. Everything was going exactly according to plan. He drove to a nearby factory, knowing that Team Arrow would have identified his rental car from surveillance video. They would put together the pieces, use GPS to trace the vehicle, and come to find him.

Entering the factory, Slade took a seat in a leather club chair as he waited for Oliver to arrive. While he sat, he reached into his coat pocket and pulled out a picture of Shado. It was torn and cracked from the years of wear, but her beauty still shone. He stroked the photo with his index finger, wishing that she were still alive. Though he knew better, he could almost feel her presence.

He closed his eyes and tried to forget the eternal regret.

Then the sound of a motorcycle appeared in the distance, and he sat bolt upright.

Oliver. It has to be him.

He put the photo back in his coat pocket.

* * *

"Where is she, Slade?" Oliver demanded as he stormed in with Roy and Sara. Slade stood, taking pleasure in seeing his hated enemy squirm.

Roy leapt forward and punched Slade in the face.

"Tell us now, or—"

"Or *what*?" Slade responded. "What are you going to do, kid? Kill me? Then you'll never know where your beloved Thea is."

Harper stepped back, and Oliver grabbed an arrow filled with some sort of liquid, shooting Slade in the chest. He fell back in the club chair, passing out almost instantly.

The cold marble glistened in the semidarkness of the conference room at Queen Consolidated. Isabel sat at the head of the table going over files. A single LED light shone overhead. She eagerly anticipated the events that were about to unfold.

Theodore pushed open the door and looked in.

"Board members are starting to arrive, Miss Rochev."

Isabel looked up from her work, rose to her feet, and straightened her coat.

"Please send them in," she said with a confident smile. She moved closer to the door. Theodore stood to the side, holding the door as each of the ten members filed into the room.

"It's good to see you, and thank you for coming at such short notice," Isabel said as she shook hands with each person as they entered, one by one. She remained polite and courteous, offering everyone water, taking their jackets and hanging them on hooks. As everyone settled in their seats, she moved back to the front of the table to gather her material.

"Again, thank you—I want to apologize for interrupting your evening," she began, "but I wanted to act accordingly, given the dramatic new events that have transpired." She paused and looked from face to face. "I think we can all agree that, over the past year, Oliver Queen's involvement with the company has been... well, sub par."

Murmurs rose, and some heads nodded in agreement.

"As acting CEO, Mr. Queen frequently has been unavailable for meetings or important decisions that have needed to be made. Under Mr. Queen's leadership, QC has suffered two major break-ins. As you recall, when I first arrived in Starling City, street thugs held us at gunpoint during our first meeting." She gave a shudder. "I have never feared for my life more.

"As well, a few weeks ago our Applied Sciences department suffered a break-in, also happening under his watch." More nods. "Now, it could be argued that he and I are partners, but as half of the partnership, I say that this ends now."

Isabel reached into her file folder, producing

the notepad with Oliver's scrawled message and signature, giving Isabel authority as temporary CEO of Queen Consolidated.

"As many of you are no doubt aware, Mr. Queen has other matters with which he is dealing, so he has appointed me as CEO for the duration. This is why I called everyone here tonight." She leaned forward, looking again from face to face. "I believe it would be in all of our best interests to take a vote, to see if this appointment should be made permanent."

She stood back, allowing the murmur of conversations to ripple through the room. Finally one of the board members spoke up.

"Let's take a vote to it," he said. "There's no sense in delaying any further. All in favor of electing Miss Rochev as a permanent CEO of Queen Consolidated—raise your hand."

As ten hands rose into the air, Isabel took a seat and unbuttoned her black blazer jacket. She sat back and ran her hands through her long brunette locks. Leaning back in her chair, she felt a flood of emotions—finally getting the resolution that had been years in the coming.

I finally did it, she thought to herself.

"Well, Miss Rochev," the board director said, smiling, "it looks like congratulations are in order." The men and women of the board rose from their chairs, clapping their hands together, saluting her.

"Thank you very much, that's too kind," Isabel said, struggling for breath. "But now we have a lot of work to do. Shall we get started?" She opened up her portfolio and pulled out her agenda. For a moment, however, she thought of the naive young woman who had looked at Robert Queen as if he could move mountains. Now, his company was hers.

In a dusty interrogation room at the Starling City Police Department, Slade sat handcuffed to the table. The room had just one other occupant, and the surveillance camera had been disabled.

"Why are you doing this?" Oliver asked.

"You know why," Slade said calmly, content that his plans had played out perfectly. "I tried to let go of the island, but it still has a hold on me. And if that hood you wear every night is any indication, it still has a hold on you, as well."

"She never did anything to you," Oliver protested. "Blame me—Thea is innocent. Do you want me to beg? I am begging you. You win!" he cried. "Please tell me where she is."

Slade just sat back silently, reveling in Oliver's pain. Without proof of his involvement, they would need to release him, and his alibi was perfect. All he had to do was wait.

The black car purred through the late-night city streets. It had been child's play to find the tracking device, and he had thrown them off by cloning the tracking symbol. He looked over his shoulder to make certain he wasn't still being followed, then made his winding way back to the warehouse.

"She's still inside," Blood told him.

"Very good, Alderman—that will be all," Slade said as he entered. He took a seat across from Thea, and told her that she was no longer a prisoner.

"I only needed you to make a point, and the point has been made."

"Those guys will shoot me the second I walk out," Thea said.

"My men's instructions were to keep you here until I returned. Now that I have, you are free to go."

Thea stood cautiously, and moved toward the door.

"*However*," he continued, "if you leave, you will never know your brother's secret." He looked her in the eye, enjoying the puzzled look on her face. "Would you like to know what it is?"

She turned around, and took a few steps toward him.

"What is it?" she asked.

"Your brother has known for some time now that Robert Queen is not your father," he said, suppressing the pleasure he was feeling. "Your father is Malcolm Merlyn." Her face filled with confusion, even horror. He began to walk away from her.

"No hard feelings, Thea," Slade said as he exited, slamming the warehouse door behind him.

* * *

Isabel sat at the head of the conference room table, finally feeling at home. For the first time in a long time she was happy—excited and eager to start her new job. The job she was once promised—the one she should always have had. The job she was born to do.

Suddenly, the door swung open and Oliver interrupted her reverie. As he stormed into the room and demanded to know what was happening, she was momentarily thrown off balance. Then she stood up from the chair—*her* chair—composing herself.

"You are the one that made this possible when you made me CEO," she said scornfully. "As of thirty minutes ago, your company belongs to me. The directors unanimously voted to make my appointment permanent. I'd say they had lost faith in your leadership, but that would imply that there was some in the first place." There was an icy calmness in her voice.

Oliver's head spun as he walked closer to her. His heart began to pound, and he felt as if the rug had been pulled from underneath his feet.

"Maybe you should have focused a little less on your... evening activities," Isabel said spitefully.

"Slade," he growled. "You're working for him." His eyes grew wide as he came to the horrible realization.

"I'm working *with* him," she replied. "He knew planting me in your family's business would draw you back to Starling City. Truth be told, I was skeptical."

Oliver rushed her and grabbed her by the throat. After a moment of knee-jerk panic, Isabel became calm and collected. She had won, and she wasn't going to let Oliver shake her in any way.

"*Where is Thea?*" he gritted furiously.

This is what you have trained for, Isabel thought to herself. She smiled, knowing that she wouldn't be giving up any information. She wouldn't give him the satisfaction of besting her—never again.

"Why are you doing this?"

"I think it's sad that you don't know," Isabel said, remembering the path that had brought her to this moment. "The sins of the father are the sins of the son," she continued, thinking of her former lover.

Suddenly, Isabel remembered herself, all those years ago with Robert. She remembered the happiness she had once felt, that was built on a foundation of lies and broken promises. Suddenly filled with volcanic rage, she kicked her leg up, hitting Oliver in the side of the head.

He deflected the next strike, but she used the opportunity to spring on top of him, sending them crashing to the floor. She rose first and jump-kicked, but he caught her leg, grabbing her arm, as well, slamming Isabel's body onto the conference table. Again he gripped Isabel's neck, the pressure cutting off her breathing.

"Where is she?" Oliver demanded like a man possessed.

He might do it, she realized, and panic welled up in her.

"He's holding her at a storage depot, just outside the city limits," she said, barely able to talk. "Tosca Cartage."

"How do I know you're not lying?"

That amused her. "It's cute how you think this isn't playing out exactly as he wants it to." She giggled as Oliver released his grip. "And he wants you to come alone. If he even *smells* your partners, he'll gut sweet little Thea like a trout."

He stepped away from her, staring at her as if he had never seen her before. Then he turned to leave.

"It was a pleasure doing business with you, Oliver," Isabel called out to him. She looked down at her disheveled clothes, and attempted to fix herself. She walked out of the conference room and into the executive office, tucking her blouse back in and straightening her jacket as she reached for the office phone. She punched in a number.

"The location has been given," she said.

"You have far exceeded all my expectations, Miss Rochev."

"Your office will be ready and waiting for you," Isabel responded, hanging up the phone.

* * *

Slade stood on a cold, dark, empty street, wearing his Deathstroke armor. Not a car went down the road. He took the moment to reflect. His plan had taken years to fashion and execute, and the moment of redemption was approaching. Suddenly, in the distance, he saw headlights.

Here we go.

The headlights grew closer, and revealed a bus. Slade stood his ground in the middle of the street as the vehicle came to a slow and cautious stop. Passengers were visible, though only as shadowy figures—prison inmates on their way to Iron Heights. They peered out through the windows, their orange jumpsuits all but indistinguishable. The scum of the city—men who would make fine soldiers.

An officer with a shotgun in tow stepped off the bus.

"Halloween was six months ago, ass hat," he said. "Now get off the road or get put down."

A moment later the man was staring at his chest, and the sword that protruded from it. The officer fell onto the cement road, crumbling to his death. Two others, still on the bus, reached for their guns—but Slade won the draw, downing them with just two bullets through the windshield. The inmates, unsure of what was happening, just stared. Slade motioned, and they slowly made their way out, one by one.

"I have a proposal for you men," he said. "Starling City has turned its back on you. You've been called the slime of the city, but you are not. You are exactly what the city needs, you are exactly what *I* need. Together, you will become an army. With my help you will become stronger than anyone in the world.

"Your one goal will be to destroy the city, and everyone in it. We will take no prisoners, we will stop at nothing, and after we're done, we will rule the city."

"What if we don't want to be a part of no army," one inmate called out. "What if we just want to make a run for it?"

Having no patience for anyone questioning him, Slade pulled his other sword and lodged it in the inmate's chest. The man coughed up blood as he slowly fell to the ground.

"Anyone else have questions?" Slade asked as the rest stared at him in silence. Then he glided past the inmates and entered the bus, placing himself behind the steering wheel. The inmates climbed back onto the bus, as well, taking their seats quietly.

He pressed his foot to the gas, and drove the bus into the dark of the night.

15

"How did the hijack go?" Isabel asked.

"Everything has been satisfactory so far," Slade said, taking a seat at his desk. "Do we have Thea's status?"

"According to my sources, she hasn't yet reported to the police, which makes it more likely that she's shared the news with Moira and Oliver, just as you said she would. It's just as likely that they'll want to keep the details to themselves."

"Wonderful," Slade said, and he smirked.

"Also, I wanted to talk to you about the boy—the one who follows Oliver around in the red hoodie," Isabel said.

"Roy Harper. I met him at Queen Mansion—he was a test subject months ago, and was a success. What about him?"

"Tensions appear to be high over there, and it may be in our best interests to keep an eye on Oliver's little protégé," Isabel said. "There may be a way to turn it to our advantage."

At that moment, Sebastian Blood barged into Slade's office, seething with anger.

"What is it this time, Mr. Blood?" Slade asked without rising.

"Turn on the news," Sebastian barked.

Slade turned to the desktop screen in front of him to stream the news. A surprisingly chipper Bethany Snow delivered the late-night reports, and he turned up the volume.

"It's been a wild few hours for the Queen family after Thea Queen, daughter of Moira Queen, was kidnapped and held hostage. At the mayoral debate tonight between Moira Queen and Sebastian Blood, a horrific video played to show Thea's captor. Then, hours later Thea Queen arrived at the Starling City Police Department, unharmed and claiming that a man named Slade Wilson was the person who kidnapped her.

"On the political front, in what can only be called a 'sympathy bump,' Moira Queen has pulled far ahead of Sebastian Blood in the latest poll, conducted over the last twenty-four hours," she continued, and Blood slammed his fist on the desk, causing the screen to shake.

"This whole thing just blew up in our face," Blood raged. "How the hell do I get elected now? You said I would be mayor, yet you just delivered the election for Moira Queen—and for what? What is this obsession you have with the Queen family?"

Isabel snickered, but held her tongue.

"You promised me," Blood gritted. "Where are your promises now?"

"I promised you this city," Slade said, rising suddenly and charging toward the alderman until they were only inches apart. "I promised you an army with which to take it." He turned to peer at Isabel. "What is our status?"

"Queen Consolidated Applied Sciences Division is now fully dedicated to replicating a serum based on your blood sample."

"You see," Slade said, calm again. "Everything is proceeding as planned." He grabbed his suit coat, putting it back on, and headed for the door.

"Where are you going now?" Blood demanded.

"To service my 'obsession'—Oliver Queen needs one more distraction," Slade said, the ghost of Shado lingering in his mind.

Sebastian turned to face Isabel.

"I *demand* that you tell me what is going on with the Queen family," he said, his voice echoing through the space.

"Excuse me?" Isabel snapped.

"The goal of the kidnapping was to push Moira Queen to drop out of the race and search for her daughter. Yet the entire focus seems to be on Oliver— the one member of the family who at least *seems* to try to do the right thing. The only one I might call my friend."

"Friend? God you are a fool, Sebastian," Isabel snapped back. "Open your eyes, and connect the dots."

"Just tell me—what is going to happen to Oliver?" Sebastian said.

"Don't be an idiot, Mr. Blood—it's going to get you killed," she replied, turning on her heel and heading for the elevator.

Slade knocked on the door to Laurel Lance's apartment. When she opened it, the look of surprise, tinged with fear, almost made him laugh. She immediately tried to slam it shut, but he easily blocked and pushed his way in, sending her back-pedaling into the living room.

"Don't worry," he said, pointing a black-gloved finger. "I'm not here to harm you."

"Go to hell," she replied.

"All in good time, I'm sure," he said. "But before then, I've come to Starling City to see Oliver Queen suffer."

"Oliver…?" she said. "What? *Why?*"

"Because he's not the man you think he is."

"And how would you know that?"

"Because I know Oliver Queen is the Arrow." Slade watched as the revelation landed on Laurel. She gasped, stunned by the information. It was the reaction of someone finally realizing a truth long suspected, but buried deep. Then Slade turned… and left.

He exited her apartment building feeling virtuous. He had dropped a bomb into Oliver's world, the result of which could only be catastrophic. Slade remembered his first year on the island, and how Oliver had boasted about the most beautiful woman, back in Starling waiting for him. He scoffed at the thought.

Laurel Lance, Shado, Sara… Slade thought fiercely. *He takes whatever he can get from anyone.* As he walked, he looked up, and froze in his footsteps.

Shado stood before him.

"He never had me," she confessed to Slade, "I was never his to take."

Slade squinted at the beautiful woman standing before him. He took a tentative step closer, then relaxed, seeing that his love was in fact real.

"I should have been stronger," he said. "I should have taken you away from him when I had the chance."

"You have already done so much for me, Slade," she answered. "Don't you see that? You have spent *years* seeking to get to this moment—and it's here. I am so proud of you."

"I have done all of this for you." Slade reached out to touch her. "It's always been you."

"I know, and now you need to finish what you started—what we should have done together back in Lian Yu," Shado said with a glint in her eye. "Kill him."

"I will," he promised. "For you, for us. There are a few more steps before that sweet moment can come." He took another step closer to Shado, then another, remembering the smell of lilac. He extended his hand, ready to take hers, and she smiled back at Slade—a look both beautiful and devious. Just when Slade was close enough to grab Shado's hand, take her in his arms, and finally kiss her—

His phone vibrated in his jacket pocket. Involuntarily Slade glanced down, pulled out the phone to check the caller I.D. It was Isabel on the other end.

When he looked up again, Shado had disappeared, a stealthy phantom in the night. He looked frantically over his shoulder, wondering where she went, and suddenly felt more alone than ever.

He jabbed his finger to answer the call.

"What is it, Miss Rochev?" Slade said crisply.

"Oliver's protégé, the boy in the red hood," she said. "As we suspected, he has left Oliver and his friends in the dust."

Slade's eyes widened at the news—a turn of events that not even Slade could have planned so well. He had to capitalize on it.

"Where are you now?" Slade asked.

"I'm trailing him. He just crossed over the Starling City border—my guess is that he is headed to Blüdhaven," Isabel said.

"Good. Keep me posted as to your location, and I will meet you." Then he hung up.

He stood in the street, frozen for a moment.

"Shado?" he called out, hoping she would reveal herself.

His heart ached, and the emptiness there left him feeling insignificant. He let the despair rush over his body as he called out her name again, then again, each time a little louder.

Suddenly Slade's despair dissipated as it turned into anger, mild at first, then became a boiling rage. He began to walk again, and reached his black Porsche.

Why are you always leaving me? Slade thought as he clicked on his seatbelt.

"Because of him," Shado replied from the back seat, and he could see her in his rearview mirror. "I have to leave you because of Oliver," Shado said as Slade pressed his foot to the pedal. The Porsche purred down the road leading to Blüdhaven, where Slade would take someone else away from Oliver Queen.

Slade exited his Porsche to find Isabel waiting patiently.

"Where are we?" Slade asked.

"A shelter, mostly for broken families that need help. Harper went in about thirty minutes ago."

"Very well," Slade said as he approached the building, "let's go get Mr. Harper to bring him home."

The two entered the shelter, passing through a lobby, and reached a makeshift living room. There was a mother sitting in a rocking chair, reading a book to her child. There were children playing checkers in the corner, and a group of men sat on the other side of the room playing chess. Slade's eye landed on a club chair, the occupant's back to them. He motioned to Isabel, the two approached the chair, and saw a red hoodie.

Slade put his hand on Roy's shoulder.

"Down on your luck, kid?" He felt muscles go tense, and he stepped around to face the chair's occupant.

"Oliver Queen is a foolish man," he said.

"Tell me something I don't know," Roy snapped back.

"You are special, Mr. Harper," Slade pressed. "He doesn't realize that."

"Special? Because I have your crazy serum in me?"

Isabel rolled her eyes. "Enough lip."

Roy stood up, coming face to face with Slade.

"You may scare Oliver, but you don't scare me," Roy said. But Slade just smirked, appreciating his boldness, knowing that this was far too easy.

"Well, then," he responded, his brow raised, "lead the way, Mr. Harper."

"You're not even going to fight?" Isabel asked as Roy turned on his heels.

"Why bother?"

16

"Coward.

"What else would you call someone who needlessly destroys Queen Consolidated Applied Sciences division, in which is housed scientific cutting-edge medical technologies with the sole purpose of making Starling City, and the world, a safer and better place?"

"That was the statement made this morning by the new CEO of Queen Consolidated, Isabel Rochev," Bethany Snow reported, "just hours after their Applied Sciences division was brutally destroyed in an explosion, late last night."

Slade continued to watch the broadcast, even as Isabel burst into the room, her attitude far less calm than she had exhibited in the news conference.

"I just lost a quarter of a billion dollar facility," she raged. "How can you just sit there so relaxed?"

"Change of strategy. A minor setback, Miss Rochev. Let them have their glory for a fleeting moment.

Because it will be just that—only for a moment. We need to reproduce the serum… again. However, this time we have something we didn't have before.

"Roy Harper," Slade said eagerly. "We use Mr. Harper's blood to replicate the serum—draining him of it in the process."

"But we still need a centrifuge large enough *and* precise enough for the process. How and where are we going to find another one in Starling City?" Isabel demanded.

"*We* aren't," Slade said. He opened the cabinet that housed his Deathstroke gear.

"What do you mean, Slade?"

"Nothing, Miss Rochev. You may keep doubting me, and Oliver Queen may think he is smarter, but I… always win."

Slade looked around the foundry, peering into shadows. He had retrieved the skeleton key he needed, so he could leave well before Team Arrow returned. Yet without hesitation, Slade decided to stay, eager to send a message. He stood in the middle of Oliver's underground lair, dressed in his Deathstroke body armor. Then he heard the click of a door on the level above.

"I know Slade." It was Oliver. "He's not going to stop until—"

"Welcome home."

Slade relished the look of shock on Oliver's face.

He was with Sara, Diggle, and Felicity. Slade pulled his Glock and opened fire, scattering the team. He had no intention of killing Oliver. The others, however… if they were lost in the crossfire, so be it.

Oliver grabbed Felicity and leapt over the railing. Diggle and Sara raced down the stairs and around the perimeter of the lair. Diggle was the only one holding a gun, so Slade continued chasing him with gunfire.

Diggle hit the breaker box, throwing the lair into darkness.

Almost instantly Sara charged from the shadows, grabbing the metal bar from Oliver's salmon ladder, then leaping over Felicity's workstation to attack. Before she could land, Slade caught her by the throat and held her suspended in the air above him.

"Hello, Sara," he said, then with one smooth motion he threw her into a supply table, her momentum taking her past it and into a support post.

One down.

Diggle, the bodyguard, sprinted out from the shadows, firing his Glock.

"Diggle!" Oliver shouted. "Stay back!"

Some of the bullets struck home, but Slade didn't flinch. They bounced harmlessly off his promethium-enhanced body armor, sparks flying, until the clip was empty.

"You're wasting your bullets," Slade remarked wryly.

Yet Diggle continued forward, using his gun like a

club, punching Slade several times in quick succession across the helmet. The blows had no effect, and once he became bored with the man's efforts, Slade snatched Diggle's arm and threw him into the glass case that held Oliver's Arrow suit.

Oliver entered the fray, sprinting over a table and snatching up Sara's bō staff, wielding it over the shoulder like a baseball bat. He let his momentum carry him, and Slade saw him coming. He evaded the swing, unsheathing one of his tactical swords in the process.

They exchanged a rapid flurry of blows, Oliver splitting the bō staff and wielding the halves like Eskrima sticks, just as they had sparred on Lian Yu. With his enhanced reflexes, though, Slade easily parried his opponent's assault. Their weapons locked, each pushing into the other, but Oliver was no match for enhanced strength. Slade shifted and pushed the blade into his arm, cutting it.

Oliver bellowed with pain.

Slade flipped him onto his back, then knocked him unconscious with a punch to the face.

"Don't forget who taught you how to fight, kid."

Scanning the room, he confirmed that there would be no more opposition. So he exited the lair, leaving Oliver and his team behind—broken, shaken, message received.

Nowhere was safe.

* * *

THWAT!

Slade's knife penetrated the spine of the S.T.A.R. Labs security guard, and the sound echoed down the hall. He continued on, firm in his resolve. The Arrow believed he had stymied Slade by destroying his centrifuge.

Not this time, kid, Slade thought to himself as he stalked the Starling City facility, decked out in his Deathstroke armor. Superior even to Queen Consolidated, S.T.A.R. housed the most cutting-edge technologies.

He turned a corner to find two startled employees, identified by their security tags as Caitlin Snow and Cisco Ramon. Slade unsheathed his sword and the two bolted, tearing down the hallway, their progress marked by the loud *clack clack clack* of their footsteps. He followed calmly.

"The longer the chase, the slower the kill," he called out.

Snow and Ramon ran into a restricted area that was the home to the weapon prototypes. The young woman frantically looked around for something they could use as a weapon, while Slade's own footsteps drew closer.

"Help me," she called to Ramon, sweat forming above her brow. She approached a wooden box, opened it, and stared down at the contents, recoiling slightly.

"Please tell me you can work this thing," she said as Ramon approached the box. He lifted out an energy rifle, hefting it with both hands, his eyes wide.

"I think so," he responded, "and anyway, it's our best shot. Get in front of me, so he won't see it coming."

Their voices were just murmurs as Slade approached the area, and his heart raced at the thought of killing. As he entered the room, Snow stood before him, unarmed and scared. The puissant Ramon was cowering behind her. Slade stared at her, whipping out his sword, ready to slit her throat.

"I take back what I said," Slade announced. "I'll make this quick." As he took a step toward her, Snow ducked out of the way.

"NOW!"

Ramon was holding some sort of rifle. He pulled the trigger, unleashing an energy blast that knocked Slade to the ground, stunning him. Their footsteps resumed their din as the two ran out of the storage facility, finding safety.

Damn me, that was an amateur thing to do!

As Slade tried to gather himself, the blast echoed in his head. Then he looked up and saw it… the bio-transfuser, a piece of equipment more advanced than the QE centrifuge. Pushing himself to his feet, he eagerly grabbed the machine.

The hell with those two, he mused, his excitement growing. *I've got what I want—come to Papa, baby.*

Oliver was due to arrive at any moment, and somehow Isabel didn't think he'd be late today. She sat behind her desk, preparing for the inevitable confrontation, when suddenly she heard a commotion coming from the elevator.

It was Oliver accompanied by Diggle.

She didn't care to look up, instead focusing on her paperwork.

"Whatever you came here to say, it takes Security about sixty seconds to reach this floor," she commented, "so if I were you, I'd start talking."

"Where's Slade?"

Did he honestly expect her to tell him? She smiled at the absurdity. Yet his response to her silence was... unexpected.

"I just wanted to give you the chance to do the right thing."

"I'm under 30, and I'm the CEO of a Fortune 500 company," Isabel observed. "I'd say I've already done the right thing."

"Do you even know who Slade Wilson is, or why he's doing this?"

"I don't care," she replied, still without looking up. "I got what I earned."

"What you earned? You think that sleeping with my father entitles you to my family's company?"

"You have no idea what you're talking about."

"Wow," Oliver breathed. "He fooled around with a lot of girls. More than you can imagine. I don't see any of them ordering hostile takeovers."

That got her. She looked up at him.

"Fooled around?"

"Yeah."

"Is that what your mother told you?" She gathered her papers. "Of course she would—she'd write me off as a meaningless affair." Then she stood, marching away from Oliver and into the conference room. "Slade Wilson put me through hell. His training nearly killed me. Would I put myself through all that just because I was a jilted lover?"

"Honestly, I don't know what you are!"

"I was your father's soul mate," she said. Oliver scoffed, and it infuriated her. "He was going to leave your mother, leave the company, leave *you*. Our bags were packed."

"Really."

"Your sister had to go and break her arm—doing something ridiculous, no doubt."

"She fell off her horse."

"We were at the airport when he got the call." She walked around the conference room table, arranging papers for the upcoming board meeting. "I begged him not to go, and reminded him that Thea wasn't even his."

"Are you saying that my father knew?"

"Of course he knew—he was a fool, not an idiot. And like a fool, he loved her anyway. He promised me that we would leave the next day. But instead, my internship was terminated, and he never spoke to me again."

"Oh, so that's what this is really about," Oliver said, his expression mixing understanding with incredulity. "He chose us over you."

Three security guards pushed through the door.

"Please escort Mr. Queen off the premises."

"Don't touch me."

"He's no longer welcome in this building," she said. "*My* building."

She watched Oliver exit the conference room, her brave face faltering. He was right. This was about Robert choosing his family over her.

It always had been.

17

They picked an abandoned warehouse near Collins and Main. A cavernous industrial space. Slade and Isabel surveyed their newly acquired bio-transfuser—a collection of canisters, gauges, and cables, fastened to a large open metal rig with a digital display. Above it, bolted to a platform, was a medical-grade chair built in the shape of a cross. It was encircled by a halo of metal scaffolding from which plastic tubing hung, draping down toward the floor like tentacles. The tubing led to a series of IVs attached to gurneys, fifteen of them, arranged in a semi-circle.

Slade turned to the assembled prisoners from Iron Heights—more than thirty in all. Some were strapped to the gurneys while others hung back, waiting for their chance to become reborn.

"Now is your moment," he said. "The people of Starling City have turned their backs on you, and this is your chance to show them you are not forgotten.

That you will not go easily—that this is *your* city." He paused for dramatic effect, then continued. "I am here to make you invincible—this is the moment where you all go from good to great." Slade approached Roy at the center of the platform, fastened, shirtless, to the chair—still sedated, his arms held in place by four metal rings.

"Together we rise."

At the end of each tube was one of the fifteen men. All were sedated, lying on metal gurneys, the IVs connected to their arms. The machine fired up with a loud hum. Blood—a dark, vivid red—flowed from Roy's body into the transfuser, where the mirakuru was extracted. Then it was pumped via the plastic tubing toward the sedated prisoners, the liquid flowing green and incandescent into their bodies.

Great care had to be taken not to remove too much, too fast, thus killing Roy prematurely and ending his effectiveness as a source for the drug. Their calibrations had to be precise.

As quickly as it began, the operation was complete.

"What next?" Isabel asked.

"Now we wait," Slade said.

When the Arrow arrived, nearly all of the inmates had been transformed. Thanks to the sedative, they were still unconscious. Slade, dressed in his suit and holding his sword, and Isabel, in her business attire, watched from the shadows. Slade was impressed by the vigilante's resourcefulness in finding the location.

Too bad it's too late.

When he discovered it was Roy hooked up to the machine, his body being sucked dry of blood, a look of horror swept across the Arrow's face. He began checking the connections, and was about to pull a wire when Slade decided to reveal himself.

"I wouldn't touch that if I were you."

The Arrow turned with a shaft nocked.

"Removing him in the middle of the cycle will surely end his life," Slade continued.

"If I don't stop it, he'll die anyhow," the Arrow said. "Slade, he's just a kid!"

"A kid who's here only because you pushed him away." Slade's voice rose. "You were the one person he looked up to, and for that, you crushed his soul."

"We found him in a shelter in Blüdhaven," Isabel said. "Pathetic. He didn't even put up a fight."

"Well, I will," the Arrow said. "Tell me how to shut it down."

"If you could feel the power that is surging through me," Slade said, his fury building, "you would know that I do not fear an arrow. I am stronger than you can even imagine, and soon, I won't be alone." He used his sword to indicate the many prisoners who were receiving the mirakuru.

The Arrow responded by firing his arrow, not at Slade, but at a warehouse fuse box, temporarily cutting power to the machine. It whirred down with a dying hum. Then he fired a volley of arrows at Slade, which he easily deflected with his sword. Isabel crouched to one side and returned fire with her pistol, causing Arrow to dive for cover—away from Roy.

Murder in her eyes, Isabel stormed after him, still firing. The Arrow disarmed her with a flechette, knocking the gun from her hand. Without hesitation she charged him, using a gurney to launch herself into a wheel kick, driving him back. She let loose all the frustration she had bottled up, cathartic payback for Robert's betrayal. She would kill what Robert held precious. The Arrow deflected her flurry of roundhouse kicks, and then delivered a punch to her face, knocking her to the ground.

Slade charged, knocking the Arrow violently backward into a pillar, breaking old concrete. Before the Arrow could recover, Slade grabbed him by an arm and a leg, then tossed him so that he landed with a sickening thud on the floor.

The arrow recovered quickly, rolling to his feet and nocking two arrows, pointing them at Slade, who just grinned.

"You can't hurt me, kid."

Ignoring him, the Arrow fired—but the two arrowheads were adhesive, rather than sharp. They stuck to Slade's chest, and he looked down at the glowing heads, confused, hearing them beep. A countdown... Before he could react, the arrows exploded in a blinding flash, sending him flying backward.

Instantly the Arrow turned his attention to Roy and the vials of mirakuru, not noticing Isabel stirring on the ground. She struggled up to her feet as he unshackled the young man from the machine. Then she found her gun, picking it up and leveling it at Oliver.

The motion drew his attention, but it was too late to react.

She started to squeeze the trigger.

BANG, BANG!

Two shots rang out, the bullets hitting her square in the chest. Stunned, she looked up to the rafters, seeing Diggle standing there, gun pointed and smoking.

Isabel fell in a heap.

Slade struggled to his feet, still staggered by the explosions, unable to prevent the Arrow from firing a grappling arrow into the ceiling, steadying his grip on Roy, and escaping into the night. He saw Isabel on the ground, lying in a pool of blood. Slade picked her up and carried her to an empty gurney, hooking her up to the IV. He restored power to the machine, bypassing the destroyed breaker box. It whirred up again.

Then he took Roy Harper's place in the chair, hooking himself up to the bio-transfuser, resuming the procedure, his blood now fueling his process. The unconscious Iron Heights convicts began to ooze blood from their eyes, looking like tears.

Then they began to wake.

It was the birth of his army.

But was there still enough time for Isabel? Had he started her on the procedure in time? Slade kept himself hooked to the machine, hoping to save her with his blood. Finally her eyes began to bleed—and then, she woke up.

Freeing himself, Slade stood over her, his fist trembling, the inmates surrounding him in various stages of wakefulness. Soon they would be his army.

He would be ready for war.

18

Sebastian Blood was on the phone at his campaign headquarters when Clinton Hogue, his old friend and bodyguard, opened the door. Moira Queen marched into his office.

"I'll have to call you right back." He hung up and stood from his desk, surprised to see her.

"Do you want me to stay, Mr. Blood?" Clinton asked.

"Uh, no, no thank you. I'll be fine." Hogue exited, leaving the two in privacy. Blood apologized. "My new bodyguard. He's a little over-protective." He pointed to his guest chair, offering it to Moira. "Please."

"No, thank you."

"I'd say this visit is unexpected, but I despise understatement."

Moira cut straight to the point. "I'm dropping out of the race," she said flatly. "I'm making a concession speech at my rally tonight." His eyes went wide.

"But you're ahead in the latest polls," he said. "Even the most skeptical of pundits are saying you could actually pull this off."

Moira waved the idea away. "I felt I owed you the courtesy of informing you in person," she said. "I don't, however, owe you an explanation as well."

"No you don't," Blood said as Moira turned to leave. "But I'd appreciate one." She paused, and he pressed. "What you're doing, Moira, as much as it benefits me, doesn't really make much sense."

She paused, then spoke over her shoulder.

"It's my daughter. At the moment she needs me more than Starling City does."

"Well, you're doing the right thing," he replied. "I'm going to change this city, Moira. A new day is coming. A better day—for all of us."

Moira nodded. "You really believe that, don't you?" she said. "We may not see eye to eye on all things, but I appreciate your sincerity, Mr. Blood. I know you care about this city." She began to walk again. "Good luck."

With that she exited the room, leaving behind a dumbfounded Sebastian Blood to bask in his sudden, unexpected victory. He had come so far, from the orphanage to the streets of the Glades, to the precipice of his ultimate destination—the office of the mayor.

Could he really be this close to victory?

It didn't seem real. Suddenly he was wary.

Moira seemed sincere, but she had made promises before, only to break them. Could a leopard like her—a predator by nature—really change her spots? He wanted so badly to believe her this time.

Did he dare?

His entire staff was there in the campaign office, watching the telecast of Moira Queen's rally at Verdant. Sebastian Blood gripped his pen, counting the seconds until he could finally declare himself mayor of Starling City, and begin to affect true change.

"As the weeks progressed, good people such as you raised your voices in support," Moira said from the podium, "and I began to think that I could make a difference. I could help save this city." Then she paused, and there was a haggard look to her. Sebastian could sense that this was the moment. The hairs on his arms stood up, and his heart began to race.

"But recent events have changed things, and…"

Why are you pausing again? he thought anxiously. *Just say it.* He saw something change in her eyes. Confidence blooming. A renewed sense of purpose.

His heart sank.

"…and now I *know* I can make a difference." The audience erupted in cheers.

It took all his discipline not to scream in that moment. He gripped the pen tighter, fighting the urge to crush it, staring daggers at the screen.

"Starling City is my home," she continued, "you are my family, and there is nothing more important to me than family. Thank you!"

The staff left, confused and disheartened, and Sebastian shut his door, still fighting off his anger. She had done it again. Changed her mind. *Always* changing her mind, typical of the one percent, doing whatever she pleased, whatever stood to benefit her most. Regardless of the cost to anyone else.

He sat behind his desk and placed a call.

Slade picked up.

"Mr. Blood, I presume."

"You said this was a done deal," Sebastian growled. "That Thea would be enough. Why did Moira change her mind?"

"I find your lack of faith disturbing."

"Faith isn't what brought me to the doorstep of City Hall!"

"No," Slade agreed. "*I am*." Something in his tone stopped Sebastian cold.

"Look, I appreciate what you've done," he said, changing his approach. "But she's more popular than ever. She's going to *win*."

"Dead women don't win elections."

"What are you going to do?" Sebastian asked, feeling the blood drain from his face.

"What's necessary," Slade replied. "Start writing your acceptance speech."

There was a click and the line went dead.

* * *

Slade pocketed his phone and kept watch from the shadows outside of Verdant, Moira's campaign headquarters. He saw the Queens exit the venue and enter a limousine. Moira, Thea, and Oliver had their defenses down.

"Are you ready, my love?"

Slade nodded, turning to see Shado. She stroked his face.

"Give him just a taste of the revenge to come," she said.

As the limo pulled away, Slade climbed into his SUV, following and waiting until they were passing through the desolate area of the Glades, untouched since the Undertaking. Isolated from any intervention. Then he revved his engine and blindsided them, crunching the side of their car.

Making certain they were unconscious, he pulled each Queen from the wreckage, driving them to a field he had scouted ahead of time. He chose it for its uncanny resemblance to the Lian Yu forest where he had found Shado's body. Where Oliver had made his fateful choice.

Slade would make him choose again.

He bound their hands behind their backs, arranging them as he imagined Ivo had done to Shado and Sara, when he forced Oliver to choose which life he held more dear.

"Is this like it was?"

"Perfect," Shado said.

Oliver was the last to wake, and Slade reveled in the look of horror that appeared on his face when he recognized the scenario. Moira and Thea whimpered nearby, nearly hysterical from the trauma, having no idea what was about to transpire.

"I was dead the last time you were offered this choice," Slade said.

"What's happening?" Thea cried as Oliver struggled to sit up, testing the rope. It held fast, as Slade knew it would.

"I often wondered how you looked when he pointed the gun at Shado," he said, kneeling down to Oliver's eye level, "and took her from me."

"You psychopath," Oliver gritted. "Shado wasn't yours."

"No, she was yours," Slade rasped. "Until you chose another woman over her."

"That's not what happened!"

"It *is* what happened. It is! She told me." He pointed to Shado.

"What do you mean, 'she'?" Oliver demanded. "There's nobody there!"

"Slade," Moira said. "You were on the island, with Oliver?"

"I thought I had known true despair, until I met your son," he responded, staring down to where she slumped at his feet. "I trusted him to make the right choice."

"Let me make the right choice now," Oliver said, his

voice pleading. "Kill me. Choose me… please!"

"I am killing you, Oliver." Slade pulled a gun from beneath his black overcoat. "Only more slowly than you would like." He pointed the gun at Moira.

"Choose."

Then at Thea.

"Choose."

The women gasped in fear.

Oliver strained at his bonds.

"I swear to God, I am going to kill you!"

"*CHOOSE!*"

"No," Moira said. Twisting her body, she stood to face Slade.

"Mom, what are you doing?" Oliver cried.

"There's only one way this night can end," she continued, facing her captor. "We both know that, don't we, Mr. Wilson?"

Oliver and Thea both pleaded with their mother, their words tumbling out, but she ignored their pleas, and stood firm. Slade met her gaze, then raised his gun.

"Thea, I love you," Moira said. "Close your eyes, baby."

"NO!" Oliver shouted, still struggling in vain.

"You posses true courage," Slade said, pocketing his gun. "I am truly sorry…"

"What?" Moira said.

"…you did not pass that on to your son."

Then he unsheathed his sword and drove the steel straight through her heart. Her body fell to the ground, lifeless eyes staring at Oliver. Thea cried inconsolably.

"There is still one person who has to die," Slade said, stalking toward Thea, "before this can end." Instead of killing her, he sliced the ropes that bound her hands. Then he walked away into the night.

One more life, then his revenge would be complete.

19

Slade returned to the abandoned warehouse near Collins and Main, just as the sun was getting ready to rise. He walked in to find Isabel sparring with one of the mirakuru soldiers. She was stronger than ever. She looked up and hesitated as he entered, dragging his sword behind him.

It still glistened with Moira Queen's blood.

"Don't let me interrupt," Slade instructed.

She nodded and continued, using a bō staff to land a solid blow against the side of the soldier's head. Astonishingly, she felt her power grow with each hit.

"This serum… it really is miraculous," she said between breaths. She landed another strike, harder than the last, and sent him to the ground. "Although the army… may need a little work."

"They are strong and ready," Slade said.

Isabel cocked her head to the side, noticing Slade's sword.

"You want to tell me something?" she asked with curiosity. "Did you decide to kill Oliver earlier than expected?" She suppressed a giggle at the thought.

"Moira, actually," Slade said coldly, turning his back to her and walking away.

"*What?*" she yelped. "That's it?! That's all I get?" She followed him. "I've been visualizing her death for *years*, and now you claim it's a done deal."

In the next room Slade stopped to view the video feed from the Queen Mansion. Everything was still. It reminded him of his surveillance of the Queen family from A.S.I.S. Yet soon everyone would arrive and he would have a front row seat. Diggle, Felicity, Laurel, Quentin, and Walter Steele—they would all be under the same roof—

—and suddenly an idea sprang into Slade's mind.

"You have to go attend the service, Miss Rochev," Slade said, staring at empty rooms.

"Over my dead body," Isabel said, then she cocked her head as she heard her own words. "I hated that woman—I'm not going to mourn her."

"You must make an appearance," he insisted. "Show them you are alive and well—intimidate them. I want them to be frozen in fear when they see you at the house."

She started to answer, then stopped, letting the concept settle in.

"I understand," she said at last.

"Have you heard from the next mayor of Starling

City?" Slade asked. With Moira out of the way, Blood would take office immediately.

"No, he hasn't called to check in," she responded. "Now that he has what he wants, how are you going to make sure he stays in line?"

"I have my ways of keeping our mayor... motivated," Slade said.

The mood was palpable when Sebastian entered Queen Mansion. This soon after his induction, he had to hide the elation he was feeling. He had done it— after months of endurance and struggle—but for now, he had to play the concerned leader of a city that had suffered a tragic loss.

The first person he encountered was Thea, her face white and emotionless.

"Ms. Queen," he said, "I wanted to offer my sincere condolences on your loss. Your mother was a good woman. She would have made a wonderful mayor."

"Thank you," Thea responded.

"I'd like to speak with Oliver," Sebastian said, "if I may."

"Well, if you see him, tell him he missed his own mother's funeral."

"No one's seen Oliver for days," Laurel said over Sebastian's shoulder. He turned and stared at her, burying his disdain, bordering on hatred. Felicity Smoak and John Diggle entered the room, as well.

"We all deal with grief in different ways," he said, "and the loss of a parent is…" His words trailed off as he remembered his mother. "Well, it changes you. When you realize that your ancestors now look to you—that your family's legacy, their continuing works, rest solely in your hands. If you see Oliver, please tell him I came by."

He turned away from Laurel, headed for the door.

Laurel stared at his back, smelling something wrong. She looked over to Felicity and Diggle, who stood across the room. Felicity was weeping, and Laurel thought it was as much for Oliver as it was for Moira. Diggle handed her a tissue.

"Where is he, Dig?" she asked, her eyes red behind her glasses. "How could he not be here?"

"I don't know…" Diggle said.

"If Oliver's smart," Isabel Rochev said, entering the room, "he ran back to his island to hide." They stared at her, shock preventing them from responding. "But maybe he'll attend your funerals," she said, turning and walking off.

Mayor Blood sat his desk, signing documents, surrounded by reporters. Reveling in the moment.

"This legislation is the first step toward making Starling City the jewel that it once was," he pronounced.

"The jewel that it can be again."

His assistant approached through the throng of reporters.

"Phone call for you, Mayor Blood."

"I'm still getting used to people calling me that, Alyssa," he said cheerfully. "Please take a message."

"The caller insisted," she replied. "He said he's your father."

"That's impossible…" he said, but he stopped himself before he could say any more. "Never mind. I'll take it." He picked up the receiver.

"Hello?"

"Hello, Sebastian," Slade said, his tone threatening. "Sorry to bother you. I just wanted to check in and see how your first day is going."

"Very well, thank you," Blood replied, wary of the fact that there were still reporters gathered round. "But I'm a little busy right now, so if you'll allow me to call you back, I'll do that as soon as I can."

"No need," Slade said. "I'm sure you have quite a lot of business to attend to. You are the mayor now, after all.

"So get to work." The line went dead, and he hung up, his mind racing. He finally was mayor, but he owed a debt to Slade that was yet unpaid.

What would be the cost?

He knew what the man was capable of doing.

* * *

Isabel burst into Verdant and found Thea Queen working at the bar, wiping it down.

Excellent work ethic, she mused, *especially for a Queen.* She extended her hand to shake. "Isabel Rochev."

"I know who you are," Thea replied brusquely, continuing her work. "What can I do for you, Ms. Rochev?"

"I'm sorry for your loss, Thea," Isabel said.

"Is that why you came here? To offer me your condolences?"

"My condolences… and to give you this." She set her briefcase on a barstool, opened it, pulled out some paperwork, and handed it to Thea. "It's a notice to vacate the premises. This club and the steel factory in which it's located are all assets of Queen Consolidated."

"No, you can't do this!" Thea said, instantly deflated.

"It's already done."

"How long do I have?"

"A couple days." Isabel turned to go, but paused. "Thea, I know I'm probably the last person in the world you want to hear this from, but I've stood where you're standing right now."

"You don't know anything about me," Thea replied with a sneer.

"Maybe. But I know what it feels like to be alone— to have everyone in your life, everyone you loved, betray you." Isabel could tell that her words struck a chord. "I thought my life was over, too. Until someone helped me see that I'd actually been given a gift—the chance to start over, to build a new life." She continued toward the door. "Think about it."

As she closed the door behind her, she remembered how young she had been when she had met Robert. Thea had been dealt a bad hand in a life she couldn't control. She looked somewhat like him, and for a second Isabel felt regret, knowing that she had just stripped away everything the girl had.

When she returned to her office at Queen Consolidated, Slade was waiting. He had used her computer to tune into his hidden camera feed from the Queen mansion.

"You shouldn't do that," she said. "It can be traced."

"You're just in time to watch some heartbreak, Ms. Rochev," he replied, ignoring her comment.

She sidled up to him, viewing the screen over his shoulder. Oliver and Thea were standing together in the empty sitting room, the furniture covered with tarps. Slade brought her up to speed. After Isabel had taken Verdant from her, Thea had decided to leave Starling City. Oliver supported her decision, and implored her to get as far from Starling City as possible.

"You have the purest heart," Oliver told Thea, "and I can't ever have you lose that. Okay? You promise me?"

"Okay," she said, and then Oliver hugged her. It was a desperate embrace, of the sort given by someone who was about to set forth on a journey from which they didn't expect to return.

"I know that I haven't always been the best brother," he said. Even on the grainy security cam footage, it was easy to see the tears pooling in his eyes. "Or friend, or whatever you've needed me to be—but there hasn't been a day since you were born where I didn't cherish having you as a sister."

"So touching, isn't it?" Slade said, as the screen showed Thea leaving the room. He switched to a different camera, and they watched her exit the mansion.

"I'm surprised you even let him say goodbye," Isabel commented. Secretly, there was a part of her that hoped Thea would make it out of the city before it was brought to rubble.

Switching back to the sitting room, they watched as Oliver pulled out his phone and tapped in a number. Then Isabel's phone began to ring. Glancing at it, she turned to Slade. "It's him."

"Then let us see what the rat has to say."

Isabel switched to speaker and answered.

"It's Oliver," he said.

"I was just thinking about you," she replied. "Your sister was very sad when I took her club away."

"This ends now," he said, getting straight to the point. His voice sounded hollow, as if all the fight was gone.

"The mighty Oliver Queen is surrendering?" she responded. "I find that hard to believe."

"I'll be at the pier. I'll be alone." Then he ended the call.

On screen, Oliver wandered over to the mantle over the fireplace, touching it as if to say goodbye. Then he exited the mansion, just as Thea had.

Isabel turned to Slade. "He's given up. Like a coward."

"No," Slade said. "Surrendering is too easy. He must suffer. If he's truly broken, then now is the perfect time to begin our siege.

"Get ready. We attack tonight."

20

In Starling City, the place to see and be seen was Rokkaku, a high-end restaurant located a few blocks from City Hall. Located on the top floor of the tallest skyscraper in downtown, it was both the literal and figurative mountaintop of the city's social scene—and Sebastian Blood was its newly crowned king. It was customary for every new mayor to dine there on his first day in office to meet and greet the social elite.

Blood had always hated this ritual. It was symbolic of the very evils he hoped to expunge from his city, yet as he stepped off the elevator, the fact that he found himself welcomed by these people was oddly validating. He also pitied them, for they had no inkling of the destruction that was about to commence.

For this evening, however, he would enjoy a meal on their dime. It was a moment he wanted to enjoy by himself. He turned to Clinton Hogue, still acting as his bodyguard.

"Clinton, you can wait in the car," he said.

"Are you sure that's a good idea?" Hogue said.

"Nothing's going to happen to me here."

Hogue nodded, and headed back toward the elevators. Sebastian entered the restaurant, glad-handing his way through the dining area, making the rounds. It was a strange feeling, being the center of attention after he had struggled his entire career just to get people to listen. It was a feeling he could get used to. But that reverie was shattered when he found Oliver Queen, seated at his table, staring at him with an intensity that was unnerving.

"Sebastian, may I join you for dinner?"

Blood tried to mask his surprise. He nodded as he slowly took his seat.

"I missed you at your mother's memorial service," Blood said. "I wanted to offer my condolences."

"You're the mayor," Oliver replied. "Congratulations. You've always wanted that."

"Believe me, Oliver, I wish it had happened a different way. Your mother and I, we didn't agree on much, but we both wanted what was best for Starling City. I will help this city find its heart again, I promise you that."

Oliver leaned across the table, dropping his voice low under the din.

"Do you really think that *he* will let that happen?"

Blood felt his defenses rise. He tried to play it off, tilting his head slightly in question, and feigning nonchalance.

"Do I think *who* will let it happen?" he responded.

"Slade Wilson."

Blood swallowed. "How do you..." The words caught in his throat. "How do you know I've been working with Wilson?"

"Because I'm the Arrow."

Blood sat back, his mouth open but saying nothing. Then he scoffed at his own ineptitude, shaking his head.

How could I have been so dense? he wondered. "Of course," he said, lowering his voice to match Oliver's. "It all makes sense now. It was right in front of me." He leaned forward, hoping to convince his friend that they were still allies. "You came to my office and you shook my hand. You said that together we can save this city."

Oliver was incredulous. "You think there will be a city to be saved, after you unleash Slade's mirakuru army?"

"It's under control," Blood replied. "They'll only cause enough damage to make the city ready."

"Ready for your leadership?"

"For my vision of what this city can be. A better place to live—and after the storm they're about to suffer, the people will support me, and follow me to that city."

"Whatever Slade promised you, he won't deliver," Oliver said. "He wants to hurt me. You're just a pawn in a much larger game."

Blood felt his anger rise, and with it came conviction.

"Slade promised me City Hall, and he delivered. He makes good on his promises." Then he brought his cup of tea slowly to his mouth, his eyes gleaming. "I understand he made you a promise, too."

Anger took hold of Oliver. On instinct, he reached for a dinner knife. Blood noticed, and leaned back.

"What are you going to do?" he asked grimly. "Are you going to stab the mayor in a restaurant full of people?" Knowing he had the upper hand, he relaxed with a smirk. Oliver couldn't touch him—nor could the Arrow. Then he rose from the table, buttoning his coat. "It's a new day in Starling City, Oliver, and there's nothing you can do to stop it."

Blood exited the restaurant, feeling Oliver's eyes burning a hole through his back. Yet once out of sight, his confidence began to falter.

Was Oliver right about Slade Wilson?

Why had he withheld Oliver's secret identity?

He arrived back at the car to find it empty. It was unlike Hogue to just up and disappear without giving word. There had to be a reason, and that worried Blood. He tried to call the man, but his attempts went unanswered, and he began to suspect the worst.

Hogue knew the details of the plan. If the Arrow had allies, they might extracting that info from him.

Blood quickly stepped into the car and peeled out, headed toward Queen Consolidated.

* * *

Sitting in Oliver Queen's office, Slade and Isabel looked out over the city, preparing for the destruction to come. They relished the prospect of sweet revenge.

Dressed in his sharp suit, Slade walked out the office and entered the conference room. There, he found a group of twenty men waiting—the convicts he had freed and given the mirakuru. Isabel wore her Ravager armor, and handed each of them a mask designed to echo hers and Slade's. Split into orange and black halves and made of fiberglass, each one sported deep recessed eyeholes and breathing slits that lent them a demonic appearance, intended to intimidate.

Slade marched up and down the line of men, his movements slow and sure, giving them their marching orders.

"The people of this city viewed you as nothing more than rabid animals, in need of a cage," he said. "Tonight, I want you to show them, *they were right.*"

The men grinned, filled with spite. He instructed them to meet Blood beneath the sewers.

"Spread yourself among the masses," he continued. "Infiltrate the places they feel most safe—shopping malls, train stations, police precincts. Then, when the clock strikes nine, put on your masks and bring this city to its knees." He stopped and looked down the line.

"Go."

As the faction of men exited the conference room and headed down the hall toward the elevators, they passed Sebastian Blood. He stared, frowning, and made a beeline for Slade and Isabel.

"We may have been compromised," Blood said breathlessly. "Brother Hogue has disappeared, and the Arrow may be responsible." He peered directly at Slade. "Or should I say, Oliver Queen?"

Slade and Isabel gave each other a look. He could imagine what they were thinking. *The idiot finally put two and two together.*

"You didn't feel that information was important enough to share with me?"

"What difference would it have made?" Slade answered. "Are you not mayor?"

"Well, for one thing, I wouldn't have left my men so exposed," Blood said. "Hogue wouldn't be missing."

"It doesn't matter," Slade countered. "The Arrow can't stop what's coming. Now, calm down and continue as planned. Go lead your army out onto this night, and take back your city."

Blood just stood there.

"Is there a problem, Mr. Blood?"

"No problem."

"Good."

Without another word, Blood turned his back on them. He would meet the fifteen soldiers in the sewers beneath downtown, commencing their assault at 9 p.m.

As he left, Slade turned toward Isabel.

"I want you to patrol the streets above our launch point. Also, assign some of our men to keep watch in the surrounding tunnels. If any of them find Oliver, they are not to kill him. Not yet."

"What about his companions? Mr. Diggle and Felicity Smoak."

"They're yours to do as you wish."

Down in the sewers, Blood arrived to find his mirakuru soldiers ready and waiting. Taking his mask from its case, he held it in his hands, staring deep into the skull's sightless eyes. He paused before putting it on, reflecting on the cusp before waging war on the city. He would do so to honor the brothers he had lost. He would do so to fulfill his promise to Father Trigon.

He would save this city.

His resolve fortified, his strength summoned, he fastened the mask for what he hoped would be the last time. After tonight, after the siege, he would be able to affect change in broad daylight as mayor, not from the shadows as Brother Blood.

He turned to address his soldiers.

"Tonight we forge history," he said. "Tonight we rise up as one, and take back this city. Because Starling doesn't belong to the rich, the powerful, the corrupt. Not anymore. Starting tonight, it belongs to us."

The group of men all roared in approval, their orange and black masks menacing in the low light of the sewer. Blood visualized the terror they were about to inflict on the controlling elite. Finally, they would feel what he had felt on the day the Glades shook.

"We will lead this city out of the darkness, and each one of you will help me. Because you are not just men. You are the most powerful weapons this world has ever seen, and when you fight together, brother to brother, nothing will stop us."

The men roared again, their sheer physicality making their numbers seem twice as many. Then, with a wave of his arm, Blood unleashed them upon the city.

As Blood rallied the troops below, Isabel patrolled the streets above. Per Slade's instruction, she focused her search on the areas of greatest vulnerability—structural points where careful, targeted detonations would drop the streets to the sewers below, pancaking their army.

Sure enough, she found Diggle attaching explosives to one of the support pillars. He was so intently focused on the task, he didn't realize she was there. The din of traffic blocked out any sound she might make.

Launching herself silently, she kicked him to the ground. He grunted loudly and landed on his back, which pleased her. She wanted him to see her face, and know who it was that sliced his throat.

"You killed me," she said, unsheathing her dual swords. "Let me return the favor."

As she charged, Diggle scrambled to his feet, backpedaling and narrowly avoiding the arc of her blade. But she was relentless, charging him with swipe after swipe of her blades. Diggle reacted purely on instinct, narrowly evading her swords' edges—until he ducked under her assault, and delivered an overhand haymaker to her face.

Infuriated, Isabel countered with a vicious kick to his abdomen, sending him sprawling backward.

"You can't kill me," she said.

"You're not invincible," Diggle said. Then, in one quick, continuous motion, he pulled a fighting baton from his jacket, flicked his wrist to telescope it outward, and swung for her head. But Isabel was far too fast, too strong. She parried, then countered with a sharp elbow to his ribs, hearing them crack. Another kick sent him spinning to the gravel.

"Do you want to save me some time and energy?" Isabel asked, stalking forward. "Then tell me where I can find Felicity Smoak. I've been aching to put a bullet in her smug little face ever since the day—"

CRASH.

Unheard over the din of traffic, Diggle's van slammed into her, Felicity sitting behind the wheel. Smacked by the fender, Isabel was sent sprawling, her body rolling some twenty yards over the ground until it came to a sickening stop. It was a blow that would have killed a mortal woman five times over.

Yet Isabel wasn't mortal—not any longer. With the serum in her blood and the armor protecting her body, the impact had merely stunned her. Shaking off the impact, she rose to her feet and began stalking forward, a thin trickle of blood flowing from the side of her head. Seeing her, Diggle jumped into the passenger side of the van, and Felicity peeled out.

Running. Like cowards.

21

Blood arrived at City Hall just as the first wave of chaos descended upon the city. Already his office was a beehive of activity. Panicked staffers worked phone lines and laptops, trying to follow the unfolding crisis. Emergency lines were jammed and live footage of the assault played on televisions throughout the office suite. The destruction emerged in real time, growing in scale by the second.

"Terrorists" in masks had appeared at multiple locations around the urban center—train stations, the theater district, the midtown power plant—even the sports arena. In each instance they exhibited superhuman abilities, and when they lashed out, it seemed to be with the goal of causing as much damage as possible, regardless of the cost in human lives.

"Starling General Hospital is preparing for possible casualties," an aide called out.

"Power is out south of Harbor Boulevard," another said.

The sheer ferocity with which the inmates were attacking shocked even Blood. Each mirakuru-powered individual was an army unto himself, and their savagery was all part of the plan. He would be the calm eye of this storm, and the citizenry would look to him. Not a millionaire or a corporation, or even a rich brat with a bow. Him.

"What do we do?" another staffer asked frantically.

"We stay calm," Blood said, putting a reassuring hand on his shoulder. "Emergency personnel have been dispatched, and we're in contact with the police department. We'll have this under control... soon."

His secretary rushed over, holding up the phone.

"Mayor Blood, the Governor is on the line."

Blood strode through the bullpen into his office to take the call, giving his staffers reassuring looks on the way, trying to instill them with confidence. As soon as he answered, the Governor offered to send in the military—the last thing he and Slade wanted. His job was to keep reinforcements at bay.

But he was prepared for this.

"Governor... *Governor*," Blood said. "Sending in the National Guard will only cause mass hysteria. At the sight of armed soldiers, people will panic all the more. We need to keep this local—trust our own police force. The incidents seem to be relatively isolated, and we'll keep them that way. We have this situation under control."

No sooner had he hung up than the district

attorney stepped into his office.

"What is going on?" Spencer demanded. "There are men in masks, tearing through the city."

"Yes, I know," Blood said with measured calm, "and we're doing everything we can. The SCPD special units have already mobilized."

Spencer looked shocked. "You can't do that. These guys are targeting high-density locations, where the most civilians could be caught in a crossfire," she said. "Worse, these men in masks, they're enhanced— strong, fast, and ruthless. It's like they're not even human."

"Not human?" Blood shot her a look designed to make her feel like a child, afraid of the boogieman. "Kate, can you even hear yourself? Look, I know you're scared, but you need to pull yourself together. Starling City needs both of us to be thinking clearly."

"What are you talking about? Have you seen what's happening out there?" She stared at the live footage. "How are you so calm?"

Blood followed her gaze, doing his best to dispel his own creeping misgivings at the sight of the rising destruction. He turned back to her, stepping closer, trying to reassure her.

"Because I know we're going to get through this— and when we do, Starling City will be stronger and better for it. Can I count on you? I need you with me on this."

She stared at him for a moment, as if trying to find

the words. Her brow wrinkled in a frown, but finally she nodded.

"Good," Blood said. "Then let's save the city together." He then turned his attention to Channel 52, where the information was going from bad to worse. The newscaster, Bethany Snow, looked ashen as she read her report.

"We've lost contact with our reporter on the streets, but we've had more than two dozen confirmed sightings of masked men attacking numerous municipal locations."

Blood could feel D.A. Spencer's eyes on him. He focused tightly on the television screen, but his thoughts were a whirlwind. If the havoc continued to escalate at its current rate, he would be hard pressed to keep reinforcements at bay.

"Officials are asking that citizens stay indoors while they try to get—"

The television went to black as the power cut out, the lights overhead flickering out, plunging the office into darkness.

What the hell is this? Blood thought.

Outside his office door, he could hear screams from the bullpen.

No, he wouldn't—

Suddenly the body of one of his aides crashed through the double doors leading into his office. Spencer gasped as the body came to a rolling stop at her feet. One of the costumed soldiers followed the body through the doorway, lifted his gun, and targeted the district attorney.

"Wait!" Blood bellowed. "Stop!"

"No no *no*!" Spencer yelled, backpedaling, but the soldier snatched her up, putting her in a chokehold, increasing the pressure on her neck.

"Enough!" Blood shouted. "This isn't part of the plan!"

"Sebastian?" Spencer gritted, struggling to breathe. Blood ignored her, stepping closer to the soldier, commanding him as he had the others like him in the underground tunnels.

"I am mayor of Starling City," he said, "and I *order* you to let her go."

The soldier paused, as if considering the request. Then, with effortless brutality, he broke Spencer's neck.

Blood watched her body hit the floor.

"No." He stared down at her body in shock, horrified. *This wasn't supposed to happen.*

"I don't take orders from you," the soldier said. He stared down Blood, as if daring him to object. Blood cowered, knowing he lacked the sheer power to combat the man. The soldier then turned heel and exited the office. As Blood watched him go, one thought raced through his mind.

Oliver Queen was right about Slade Wilson.

22

From high above the city, in the penthouse office of Queen Consolidated, Slade watched Starling City burn. Multiple fires could be seen, scattered across the landscape, each representing a soldier with mirakuru flowing through his veins. He reveled in the chaos and destruction—at long last, his plan was nearing completion.

Isabel joined him for the view.

"You look like you've been run over," he said, half-joking.

"I was."

Slade raised an eyebrow. He was met with a look meant to cut him off. Then an electronic bleep from his computer drew his attention back toward his desk. Like the SIIRA program back in Australia, Slade had enacted a search for the voices of Oliver, Felicity, and Diggle, hoping to eavesdrop on their telecommunications.

His search had turned up gold.

Isabel stood at his shoulder as the call sparked to

life on his speakers. It had been initiated from Felicity's phone, made to an unknown number—though the area code placed it in Central City, home to S.T.A.R. Labs. If Oliver had successfully fashioned a cure from the sample of mirakuru he stole from the centrifuge, it had to have been with their expertise.

"Hello?" an unidentified man said, picking up the call.

"Hey, it's Felicity Smoak. Where are you?" It sounded as if she was using a speaker phone.

"Fourth Street, I think," the man said. "I don't know what happened. A guy in a hockey mask came out of nowhere and attacked my car. Please help me."

The next voice was Oliver's.

"Stay where you are," Oliver said.

Bingo! Slade thought. Judging from the urgency in their voices, the unknown man had to be a courier— they had synthesized a cure! And the courier had become caught up in the chaos on the streets. He told them he was pinned under an overturned car, his leg broken, unable to move.

Slade pinged the call, pinpointing his location on a bridge in the middle of the city. Under normal circumstances, it would be a race to reach his location. But Slade had men powered by the mirakuru.

He called through the door, summoning one of his soldiers.

"Find him," he said, and he gave the location. The man took off at a sprint, the serum giving him the speed he would need to reach the cure before Oliver and his team.

Slade smiled, feeling victory close at hand. Then he stood and walked over to the window again, gazing out over the fire and ash.

"They say Nero sang as he watched Rome burn," Slade said to Isabel. "Now I understand why." Then his voice became tinged with an unexpected melancholy. "If only Shado were here to witness this."

"Who's Shado?" she asked, and she looked confused.

Before Slade could answer, Blood tore into the office.

"What the hell is going on?" he said, his voice hot with anger. "One of your juiced-up jackboots just killed my entire office staff, and snapped the district attorney's neck!"

Slade barely turned his head to respond.

"And?"

"*And*," Blood gritted. "And I never agreed to this! You were supposed to call off your dogs."

"That was your plan, Mr. Blood, not mine."

"We had a deal."

Fed up with the man's insolence, Slade finally turned away from the window to face him. He stalked forward, closing the space between them until they were standing face to face.

"And do you feel that I've not lived up to my end of it?" he demanded. His proximity intimidated Blood, and he became desperate.

"Those are innocent people dying out there," he

said pleadingly. "You don't need to kill them."

"*Yes, I do*," Slade replied, the rage within him finally erupting. "I made a promise to someone once, and I will uphold it."

"So this really is all about you just trying to hurt Oliver Queen," Blood said, as if trying to convince himself.

"I vowed to him that I would take away everything and everyone he loves," Slade said. "And he loves this city."

"But this city…" Blood argued. "It's mine, too."

"Not anymore." Slade stepped even closer, and Blood retreated backward. "As of tomorrow night, it'll be nothing but rubble, ash and death. A land only good for one thing…" He turned away and moved back to the window, taking in the view of the destruction.

"Graves."

Sebastian paced behind Slade as news about the siege continued to pour in.

"The situation has intensified, as law enforcement officials struggle to contain this historic assault gripping our city," Bethany Snow reported over images of masked soldiers overwhelming badly outgunned cops. Sebastian swallowed, tasting bile.

He was directly responsible for the destruction of the city he had fought so hard to save. In a few short hours, he would be the mayor of a ruin. A failure to the

Glades, to his brotherhood, and to Father Trigon. He wasn't a man given to prayer, but in that moment, he found himself remembering the cross his mother wore. In order to save the city, he would need the type of miracle she believed in.

Then he scoffed at the thought—that in his darkest hour, he would try to find salvation in a memory. His city was truly doomed.

Abruptly the soldier Slade had dispatched to receive the mirakuru cure returned. He held a metal briefcase, the logo for S.T.A.R. Labs embossed on its side. He placed it on Slade's desk.

"Mr. Wilson, is this what you're looking for?" he asked.

Slade opened the case, revealing vials filled with an incandescent blue liquid. The cure.

"Yes it is," he said.

Sebastian peered over his shoulder.

A miracle to combat a miracle.

He looked out upon the city he loved, fires still burning, and knew he would need what was in that case. Behind him Slade dismissed the soldier, then closed the briefcase, putting it on the credenza behind him. He noticed Sebastian staring out at the night.

"You've been very quiet, Mr. Blood," he said. "Something on your mind?"

Sebastian thought quickly.

"Regret," he said. "That I ever trusted Oliver Queen."

Slade nodded. "So you finally see."

"I acted rashly before," Sebastian agreed. "But watching the city burn, I understand this is all his fault—and he has to pay."

"Soon," Slade murmured. "The last phase of my plan is in place."

"When does this end?"

"When I've taken the person Oliver Queen holds most dear."

Sebastian waited until Slade headed off to prepare himself for the final battle. Then, left to his own devices, he removed the S.T.A.R. Labs briefcase and headed down the hall toward the elevator. He pulled out his cell phone, dialing as he walked. It rang once, twice.

"Pick up, dammit, come on." Then, finally, Oliver Queen answered.

"What do you want?"

"Same thing you do, Oliver. To save this city before it's too late."

"It's already too late."

"You were right about Slade Wilson. I should have listened to you." Sebastian waited for the elevator. "But I'm here now and I can help you."

"Why should I trust you?"

"Because, Oliver," Sebastian replied, "I have the mirakuru cure." He entered the elevator. "Meet me at City Hall."

* * *

Entering City Hall, he had to step past the corpses of his office staff—all people who had trusted him. Reaching his office, he found Spencer's body, her neck at an impossible angle, her eyes staring. Gently he picked her up, took her through the door, and placed her on a desk.

Back in the office he paced, holding his skull mask, studying it. Then he stared through the slatted blinds of his window, gazing out on his broken city. Fires still burned, casting flickering light on columns of billowing smoke. Behind him Oliver and Diggle entered, and in the reflection he could see their weapons at the ready.

Expecting a double-cross, no doubt, he mused. Then he spoke. "As a young boy, I was plagued by nightmares. Every night, I would wake up in a cold sweat, frightened and alone. It was my father's face that haunted me, and this is how I saw him." He showed them the mask, holding it in the air. "The embodiment of desperation and despair. I made this mask to conquer my fears, and remind myself why I fight—every day—to give this city's most desperate a chance. All I ever wanted to do was help people, Oliver."

"Then help me believe," Oliver responded. "Where's the cure?"

"Slade Wilson will not rest until he honors the promise that he made you."

"I won't be so easy to kill, once we level the playing field."

"He's not interested in killing you," Sebastian said. "Not until he's taken away everything and everyone you love."

"After he murdered my mother, he said one more person had to die."

"Whoever you love the most."

Sebastian headed over to his desk, bending and reaching behind it, into the space underneath. He pulled out the briefcase, and when he straightened up, he wasn't surprised to see Diggle's gun trained on him.

"I hope you can beat him with this," he said, handing the case to Oliver. "For all our sakes. And when this is over, I promise you, I will do everything in my power to rebuild Starling City. I won't just make it what it was. I will make it better. Like I always planned."

Oliver looked at him as if he was insane. "You really think after everything that's happened, after what you've done, that they'll still let you be mayor?"

"Why not?" he said. "No one knows that I've done anything except try to save this city. And if you tell anyone about my mask, I will tell them about yours."

Oliver just stared, and set his jaw.

"Do what you have to, Sebastian."

He turned and they left, Diggle leading the way. Sebastian watched them go, the city's last hope held in a gray metal briefcase.

* * *

Later, he poured himself two-fingers' worth of thirty-year-old Scotch, retrieved from the decanter at his bar. A gift from his support staff—the ones whose bodies lay up and down the hall. Self-deception aside, he knew that his time as mayor was over. Not because of Oliver, but because of Slade. Sebastian wasn't an idiot. There was no way he'd be allowed to live.

As he took a sip of Scotch, Isabel arrived, sword drawn.

"You gave it to him, didn't you?"

"I did what I thought was necessary." He took another sip.

Isabel moved to his desk phone.

"Don't worry," Sebastian said. "I'll tell Slade."

She ignored him and hit speed dial. Slade picked up on the first ring, his voice coming over the speaker.

"Does he still have the cure?"

"No," Isabel said.

"Slade," Blood said, loudly enough to be heard. "You betrayed—"

"Goodbye, Mr. Blood."

The line went dead. Sebastian turned to face Isabel and was met with her two swords, driven through his chest. He stared her down, the blades buried up to the hilt.

"I loved this city."

Isabel ripped her blades free from his chest. He

stood wobbling in place, looking down in shock at the rapidly spreading blood, almost black in the gloom. Then she pushed him, sending him toppling to the desk, splayed out on his back, the last bit of life within him leaving.

The last thing he heard was his skull mask dropping to the floor with a thud.

23

Slade turned his attention back to the television. Aircraft were approaching the city, and the news reporter identified them as incoming military support—but Slade knew there was no military base close enough for that to be the case. Judging from their flanking formation, those troops hadn't arrived to save Starling City from his army. They were there to corral his men.

Keeping them within the city's borders.

His telecommunications tracker buzzed again, notifying him of another outgoing call. This time, it was Oliver on the line, calling a restricted number Slade could not trace. The woman's voice on the other end was harsh and abrasive, the telltale indicators of a commander. It reminded him of Wade DeForge.

"How did you get this number?" the voice demanded.

"Amanda, what are you doing?"

"Not sure what you mean, Oliver."

"The troops taking up position at the city's exits,

they're not Army. They're A.R.G.U.S. Those are your men. So you tell me what you're up to."

So they are *A.R.G.U.S.*, thought Slade. Still the woman didn't answer the question.

"Amanda!" Oliver shouted.

"Slade's followers are a clear and present danger," the woman, Amanda, replied hesitantly. "I cannot allow them to escape the city. They need to be contained—by any means necessary."

Slade knew exactly what that implied.

"You can't," Oliver said.

"There's a drone en route carrying six GBU-43/B bombs. Enough firepower to level the city."

Despite his protestations, the woman told Oliver that he had until dawn. If he couldn't neutralize Slade's soldiers by then, she would turn Starling City into a crater.

Perfect, thought Slade. Even if the cure proved successful, there was no way Oliver could neutralize his entire army by dawn. He simply lacked the numbers. Whether he stopped Slade or not, Oliver's precious city would still become a hole in the ground— rendered that way by the very same organization Slade had helped A.S.I.S. track.

Funny how the world works sometimes.

Slade used the computer to identify Oliver's location, tracing the call back to a clock tower in the Glades. He radioed his men, instructing them to raid both that location and the sublevel lair at Verdant, just in case. They were to destroy everything in their path, except for two people. The Arrow and the A.D.A. Laurel Lance.

Those two lives were Slade's to take.

He retreated to the inner anteroom to change out of his suit and into his Deathstroke armor. The final battle was rapidly approaching.

Isabel arrived to find Slade in his armor, helmet at his side. Fifteen soldiers—freshly returned from laying waste to the Arrow's lair—milled about, awaiting their next task. She walked past them to talk with Slade.

"Blood has been dispatched, as asked," she said, "but his is not the body I want at the end of my sword."

"Then you're in luck," Slade replied. "Because it's time we took the fight to the Arrow."

She smiled. Finally, she could issue payback to Felicity Smoak. She would kill her slowly, relishing every second of her pain.

They heard a commotion out in the hall, at the elevator banks. They both turned to watch the Arrow enter, followed by Sara Lance in the uniform of the Canary. Isabel was shocked that Oliver would make such a brazen offensive move, when he lacked the numbers to support it.

Slade was of the same mind.

"You must have quite a bit of faith in this cure, if you've come alone," he said.

"We didn't come alone," Oliver responded. As if on cue, the office windows shattered inward as members of the League of Assassins—led by Nyssa al Ghul—swung their way in. They landed, firing arrows into the nearest mirakuru soldiers, dropping them instantly. They shook on the ground, their bodies wracked with spasms as the cure took effect.

Oliver took aim, firing cure arrows at each of Slade's shoulders. With simple shifting in his torso, Slade allowed his armor to deflect them. Then when Oliver squared his aim and fired at his eyehole, Slade cut the arrow off mid-flight.

On the other side of the room, Isabel rushed Sara, her swords matched against Sara's bō staff. She swung her blades in an arc, a hurricane of deadly movement, the sharp edges of her blades bearing down. Sara spun away, her staff twirling in the air, deflecting those deadly swipes.

As they fought, the League of Assassins continued to dispatch Slade's men. Seeing their numbers dwindle, Slade knew they were quickly being overmatched. Giving no mind to Isabel, he dashed toward an open window and leapt out, grasping an outside cable and zip lining to safety on the building below, too fast for Oliver to follow.

Though she fought ferociously, Isabel's mirakuru-enhanced skill was no match for Sara *plus* the League of Assassins. Nyssa launched an attack from behind, plunging a cure arrow into her bicep. Instantly her strength sapped, and Sara and Nyssa easily subdued her, the assassin kicking out Isabel's leg, dropping her to her knees, and ripping off her helmet in quick succession.

On instinct, Sara raised her bō staff , ready to deliver a killing blow.

"Sara, don't!" Oliver shouted. Sara lowered her weapon.

Isabel just shot them a dirty look.

"Kill me, don't kill me," she said. "It doesn't matter. I beat you. I took away the one—"

Nyssa grabbed Isabel's head and bent it backward, using her knee as leverage. With a sickening snap, Isabel was dead. Her life ended in Robert Queen's old office.

24

Slade's escape took him to an abandoned industrial space located just outside of downtown, in the city's factory district. Formerly a steel mill, the hallways were a labyrinth of concrete and copper piping, valves and gauges. It was where he intended to accomplish the end of his plan.

He found one of his soldiers waiting there with Laurel Lance, having taken her from the police precinct. Though she tried to hide it, he could see the fear in her eyes—recognized it from their encounter in her apartment, when he told her Oliver was the Arrow.

"Hello, Laurel," he said. "I hope you don't mind me dispensing with formalities, but we've known each other far too long now not to call each other by our first names."

"You don't know me, Mr. Wilson," she said. "If you did, you'd know I'm poor bait."

"You are anything but," he said. "Did you know I

was with Oliver on that godforsaken island? I saw him look at your picture every day for a year. I know he loves you."

She looked startled at that revelation.

"Oh, yes, Laurel—deep in Oliver's heart, there is a very special place reserved just for you." He got close to her, smiling with menace. "Your death will bring him unimaginable pain."

Laurel looked him in the eye, defiant. "He'll stop you."

"But he's already failed."

There was a buzz from a tablet, lying on a concrete platform—he had prepared the location, should he need it. The security cameras he had hidden throughout Queen Mansion were reporting new movement. Stepping over and lifting the tablet, he saw two figures enter the foyer—Oliver Queen and Felicity Smoak. He listened in on their conversation.

"Oliver," she said. "What are we doing here? The whole city's falling apart."

"I know," he replied, and he led Felicity to the center of the room. "You need to stay here."

"What? Why? You can't just ask me to—"

"I'm not asking," he said. "I'll come and get you when this is all over."

"No!"

Such loyalty, thought Slade. *A pity its beneficiary is such a coward.*

"Felicity…" Oliver said, the utterance meant to

silence her. Then he started to exit.

"No," she said again, following him. "Not unless you tell me why."

He turned back to face her. "Because I need you to be safe."

"Well, I don't want to be safe. I want to be with you, and the others… unsafe."

"I can't let that happen."

"You're not making any sense."

Oliver pulled Felicity close. Slade recognized the look in his eyes, because it was the same way he had looked upon Shado.

"Slade took Laurel because he wants to kill the woman I love."

"I know, so?"

"So he took the wrong woman."

"Oh."

"I love you," he said. "Do you understand?" He reached out and touched her arm, holding her hand. It was tender and sweet…

"Yes."

…and it marked her for death.

Slade watched as Oliver exited. He nodded to his soldier.

"Go to Queen Mansion, and bring me Felicity Smoak."

Less than an hour later, the soldier returned, dragging Felicity along. Her hair was disheveled from a night spent on the run, and she had a gash on her forehead, the blood long having clotted. Still, he could see her unassuming beauty. Of all the women in Oliver's life, she was the most diminutive physically. Slade imagined that she could scarcely harm a fly, let alone wield a weapon.

He studied her, and took a Bluetooth headset she wore. It was incredibly disappointing, he mused, that this scared, frail twig was the love of Oliver's life. Killing her would almost be a waste of his blade.

"I must say, I'm surprised that a sniveling mess like you would win Oliver's heart."

The insult seemed to snap her out of her fear.

"One, it's dusty in here," she replied angrily. "And two, Oliver is *not* in love with me—"

"*Liar.*" He jerked in her direction, and yelled not from anger, but to provoke a reaction. As expected, she jumped and let out an involuntary yelp.

"And you're just about the level of scary crazy person I was expecting," she said, her words coming out rapid fire.

"And you certainly talk a lot for being terrified," Slade responded.

"What do you want with me?"

"Like I told Oliver, this cannot end until I take the one person he loves most in this world."

"Okay, fine, it's me," she said. "Little ol' snivelly me has Oliver's heart. So why not let Laurel go? She's worth nothing to you."

So this woman possesses strength after all.

"Perhaps," Slade said, "but maybe I just want to see him suffer twice."

He walked off a few yards away and keyed the Bluetooth headset. Oliver answered on the other end.

"Go."

"You've been busy, kid," Slade said.

"It's over, Slade!" Oliver cried. "Your army is broken."

"And I pity them, but once again, you miss the point." Slade flexed his hand, feeling the familiar tremor. He would relish this moment, one he had spent five years engineering. "I have the one you love. You're going to meet me where I say. Otherwise, I'm going to kill her."

"You do what you have to. I'm done playing your games."

"You're done when I say you're done!" The rage boiled again in Slade. "I was surprised. I thought you had a thing for stronger women. But now that I've met her, I can see the appeal. She is quite lovely, your Felicity."

"What do you want, Slade?"

"To see your face when I open her neck and stain her lovely skin with blood."

"Don't you touch her."

"Not until you get here. I promise."

Slade hung up and sent Oliver his coordinates. Then he prepared for his final confrontation with the spoiled rich kid from Starling City. After five long years, Slade would finally avenge his beloved.

25

Slade held Felicity firmly with one arm, while holding his blade against her neck with the other. He could hear Oliver's footsteps, and spoke to him through the din of the industrial plant.

"Twitch and I will open her throat," he said loudly, the sound echoing. "My first words to you. Do you remember? I do," he continued. "I remember the exact moment. My blade against your neck—just like my blade is against the neck of your beloved. If only I'd killed you then, everything would be different." Slade wasn't wearing his helmet, exposing his face. He wanted Oliver to see him clearly, in the moment he took her life.

Oliver emerged from behind a cluster of pipes that stretched from ceiling to floor.

"Drop the bow, kid." Oliver continued to advance with arrow nocked. Slade responded by pressing the blade against Felicity's neck. "Do it."

Oliver finally lowered his bow, placing it on the ground. From behind Slade, one of his soldiers brought out Laurel, clutching her with an arm around her throat.

"Yes," Slade said. "Countless nights dreaming of taking from you all that you took from me."

"By killing the woman I love?"

"Yes."

"Like you love Shado."

"Yes," Slade admitted with uncharacteristic vulnerability. Hearing her name, he stared off into the darkness, seeing her shape just a few yards away, looking on over the scene. Her face was beautiful and without expression.

"You see her, don't you?" Oliver suggested. His question sent Slade deep into his memory, causing him to release his grip on Felicity, dropping her to her knees in front of him. He kept his blade trained on her neck while he paced in tight, close steps, and Oliver continued.

"Well, what does she look like in your madness, Slade? What does she say to you? I remember her being beautiful. Young. Kind." He peered intently at his opponent. "She would be horrified by what you've done in her name."

"What I have done?" Slade responded, his intensity growing. "*What I have done…* is what you lacked the courage to do. To fight for her!" He brought his blade closer to Felicity before him. "So when her body lies at your feet, her blood wet against your skin, *then you will know how I feel!"*

"I already know how you feel," Oliver said. "I know what it's like to hate—to want revenge—and now I know how it feels to see my enemy so distracted he doesn't see the real danger is right in front of him."

As Slade paced, thinking the danger was Oliver, he didn't register Felicity slowly rising to her feet, withdrawing a syringe from her coat pocket. She gripped it in her hand, gathered herself, and plunged it deep into Slade's neck.

Then she ran.

Slade dropped to his knees, instantly feeling the cure work its way through his body, sapping his strength. As it began to neutralize the serum's power, Slade watched Shado begin to fade into the darkness. Then she was gone.

Furious, struggling against the cure's effects, he yelled to the soldier holding Laurel.

"Kill her!" he bellowed.

Before the solider could do anything, however, Sara emerged from the rear of the building, and hit the soldier with a cure dart. Then Laurel turned and punched him, first with a right, then a left. He dropped to the concrete floor with a *crack*.

"Get them out of here!" Oliver shouted. Sara gathered Laurel and Felicity and led them to safety, leaving him alone with Slade.

Oliver picked up his bow.

Mustering what was left of his strength, Slade charged him, bringing his sword down with an overhead chop that Oliver deflected with his bow. They danced back and forth, delivering strikes. Though weakened, Slade was enraged. Nevertheless, they were on even ground now, and as Slade lashed out, Oliver countered with a kick to the chest, sending his opponent backward through a glass door, shattering it.

Landing on the building's rooftop, still gripping his sword, Slade quickly recovered and sent Oliver down with a kick. He then raised the blade over his head, smashing it downward. Again Oliver blocked the strike with his bow, then he sprung up into the blow to deliver a kick to the mid-section.

They continued to fight across the rooftop, the Starling City skyline behind them on the horizon, pockets of flame still visible in the streets below.

"The mirakuru isn't what made me hate you." Slade swung his blade, forcing his enemy to duck, leaving him vulnerable for a strike. He took advantage, grabbing Oliver by the throat. As he squeezed tighter, choking him, the roar of a jet engine overhead drew his attention skyward. A drone sent by A.R.G.U.S. cut through the night, its course set for downtown.

"The end is near," Slade said, "but maybe I'll be merciful enough to let you live and see your city burn!"

Suddenly Oliver mustered enough energy to kick himself free. The two backed away, circling each other, trading kicks and blows, Oliver using his bow as a makeshift sword against Slade's blade, their weapons arcing around them. Oliver landed yet another kick to Slade's mid-section, and while the armor protected him, it sent him flying backward.

Shaking his head to clear it, Slade launched himself into another attack, hitting Oliver squarely in the face with a punch. They grappled, then threw each other backward, both spent and falling to the floor.

"We both know there's only one way that this can end," Slade said, struggling to rise. "To beat me, kid, you're going to have to kill me." He pushed himself to his feet through sheer force of will, as did Oliver. "But in the moment of my death, you'll prove one thing— that you *are* a murderer." Strength gathered, they rushed each other again, clashing at the roof's center, the impact carrying them over the edge and dropping them to a lower level.

Their fighting had become crude, fatigue transforming skill into primal desperation. Each reared back, throwing his full weight behind any attack, their blows slow and telegraphed. Oliver tried launching a haymaker against him, but he ducked the blow, allowing Oliver's momentum to take him toward a pillar. Pivoting, he landed a left hook to Oliver's face, followed slowly by another, each landing with a sickening thud. At this point, Slade's entire goal was to cause as much damage as possible.

Momentum on his side, he rushed forward, thrusting his blade toward Oliver's chest, intending to deliver a final death stroke. When it was inches from contact, Oliver summoned a last burst of energy, deflecting the blow with his bow, spinning away. He cracked Slade over the back with his bow, stunning him, then quickly nocked and fired two lasso arrows.

Slade was cinched tight to the column, bringing an abrupt end to the conflict.

All his energy spent, he slumped into the restraints, allowing them to take his weight.

"You can kill me or not," he said. "Either way, I win." Then he turned his attention toward the horizon, waiting for the drone to drop its payload, vaporizing him, Oliver, and the entire city. But Oliver ignored him. With barely enough strength left to stand, he tapped his communications earpiece, dialing into A.R.G.U.S.

"Amanda, it's over," he said. "Slade's down, his army's been taken out. Call back the drone." There was a heavy silence as he awaited her reply. Slade felt the seconds tick, counting them with his heartbeat, wondering if the kid's luck would save him again.

"Amanda, it's over!" he yelled again.

After a few more tense seconds, the roar of a jet engine cut through the silence. They looked overhead as the drone returned, retracing its path back to A.R.G.U.S.

The two enemies regarded each other for a long moment, their breathing heavy and visible in the cold. Five years had led to this moment. Their long battle had finally been brought to an end. Oliver, however, looked anything but victorious.

"So what now, kid?"

Slade watched as Oliver pulled an arrow from his quiver, nocked it, and fired.

Then, like many years ago, the world went black again.

26

Slade awoke with a gasp. "Where am I?"

His mouth was dry and his throat hoarse as he sat up. His body responded with a sluggishness that suggested he had been unconscious for a while. Disoriented, he found himself on a cot in the middle of what appeared to be a prison cell. Bars enclosed the area on three sides. However, the back wall was made of rock and the ceiling was low, like the inside of a cave. There were no windows, the only light emanating from harsh halogen lamps above.

Turning, Slade found Oliver Queen staring at him through the bars. He sat on a stool facing the cell, his face still showing signs from their battle.

"As far away from the world as I could get you," Oliver replied. "Where you can't hurt anyone ever again."

"That's your weakness, kid." Slade finally found his footing and rose to standing, staggering closer, leaning on the cell bars. "You don't have the guts to kill me."

"No, I have the strength to let you live."

"Oh, you're a killer," Slade said, pacing his cell, keeping his eye trained on Oliver. "I know. I created you. You've killed plenty."

"Yes, I have," Oliver said. There was an odd calm to his voice. "You helped turn me into a killer when I needed to be one, and I'm alive today because of you. I made it home because of you, and I got to see my family again. But over the past year, I've needed to be more. And I faltered.

"But then I stopped you. Without killing."

Oliver stood up and stepped closer to Slade's cell.

"You helped me become a hero, Slade." He regarded his prisoner, meeting his gaze with sincerity. "Thank you."

Slade came to a stop, taking him in. Feeling his rage burn bright again. Not from the mirakuru, but from the depths of his soul.

"You think I won't get out of here?" Slade said. "You think I won't kill those you care for?"

Oliver opened the door to exit, revealing the insignia of A.R.G.U.S. This was its supermax prison. Inescapable. Impenetrable. Classified. He turned to face Slade.

"No, I don't," he said. "Because you're in purgatory."

Slade watched as he pulled the door shut behind him, the sound reverberating throughout the spartan cell. As silence fell, he realized he knew exactly where

Oliver had doomed him to exile. He was back where his journey began. Stranded on Lian Yu. A prisoner of the island once again. It was a sentence far crueler than death.

Anger boiling over, Slade shook the bars of his cell…
"I keep my promises, kid."
His voice growing louder…
"I keep my promises."
Reminding Oliver of his vow…
"I KEEP MY PROMISES!"